THE MAN OF HER DREAMS . . .

Joachim moved closer and grasped her by the elbow. "Teddy . . ."

Teddy's heart, which had been agitated all evening due to his nearness, now took off racing. She was wound so tight, she figured that if he touched her anyplace other than her elbow, she'd explode all over him and they'd become one tangle of limbs groping one another, and wouldn't part until the sun interrupted the night.

". . . I'm very attracted to you."

Breathe, she told herself. She backed into the sink. Joachim allowed his hand to fall to his side. Teddy quickly grasped one of his hands in hers. She felt his grip tighten as they faced one another. "I feel the same way," she told him. "It's just that it's been a long time since I met someone who made me feel the way you do—and I guess I don't trust my emotions after . . ."

Joachim pulled her into his arms, his big hands on her back as he held her securely against him. He said softly in her ear, "You don't have to explain. I know about loss, Teddy. And I'm as confused as you are right now. I wasn't expecting you, either."

Teddy closed her eyes and simply let herself relax in his arms. He was so right. How could she have guessed that coming here would present her with such a pleasant conundrum. Joachim West, the man of her dreams . . .

A BITTERSWEET LOVE

Janice Sims

ARABESQUE
★BET
BOOKS

BET Publications, LLC
www.msbet.com
www.arabesquebooks.com

ARABESQUE BOOKS are published by

BET Publications, LLC
c/o BET BOOKS
One BET Plaza
1900 W Place NE
Washington, D.C. 20018-1211

First Printing: March, 2000
10 9 8 7 6 5 4 3 2 1

Printed in the United States of America

This book is dedicated to my siblings: James E. Jones, Sam Nattiel jr., Lillie Elaine Nattiel, Isaac Howard Hammond, and Charles Hammond. If you hadn't pestered me like crazy while we were growing up, causing me to retreat to my room with a good book, I might never have discovered writing. Thanks for being so darned irritating. You helped create a monster. Now you have to live with her!

ACKNOWLEDGMENTS

I'd like to thank my editor, Karen Thomas, for always making me feel confident about my work. You're wonderful to work with, Karen!

Also, I have to offer a big thanks to the readers who have shown me so much support over the years. Your words of encouragement mean so much to me.

Finally, I continue to count myself fortunate for having such a big, loving, supportive family. To all the Joneses, Nattiels, Simses, Simpsons, Jacksons, and Hammonds. Thanks, guys!

Give me juicy kisses, breathless sighs, strong
  hands massaging satiny thighs.
An inexhaustible number of passionate embraces
  that, when you're gone, leave traces of sweet
  memories that linger on.

All good . . . But more than that, I want
  something to believe in; something *real* . . .
A strength I can rely on, honesty so fierce it
  can kill; a soul-deep dependability I don't
  have to question.

These are the things I want to feel when you
  hold me, mold me to you.
Not just your body as it moves against
  mine, but your spirit, a beautiful thing, so
  fine . . .

Now that's something to believe in.

—The Book of Counted Joys

One

What am I doing here? Joachim West thought, shaking his head as he stood on the forward deck of a slow-moving ferry inching its way toward the town of Ballycastle in Northern Ireland. But a promise is a promise.

The sound of the rain on the hood of his oilskin macintosh reminded him of the times he'd lain awake in bed at his grandmother Eva's house in Selma, listening to the rain hit the tin roof. He smiled, the corners of his generous mouth turning up. This was a long way from Alabama.

In all the travel guides he'd leafed through of Ireland, the Enchanted Isle, there'd been scenes of rolling green hills and valleys, the sky invariably blue and cloudless. He'd been here for three days, and it had rained every day.

A fellow passenger, a young woman, standing a few feet away from Joachim, peered out at the expanse of the North Channel. She was tall, willowy, and dressed in a black slicker with matching knee boots. A wisp of dark brown hair protruded from her hood.

Joachim had noticed that for the past few minutes she'd been taking furtive glances in his direction. He was definitely not going to be the first to make a move. He was a visitor in this land and wasn't aware of how the Irish people looked upon strange men approaching women in public places.

While he was contemplating this, the woman slowly turned and looked him squarely in the face. Joachim saw her large blue eyes widen in surprise, and then to his astonishment sparkle with keen interest as she smiled warmly at him.

In all the years Gillian McEwan had ridden the ferry between Rathlin Island and Ballycastle, she'd never seen a black person on board before. It was an even rarer occurrence to see such an attractive male, no matter what shade he came in.

Joachim smiled as well, inclined his head in her direction, then turned on his heel and strode to the rear of the ferry where there was an enclosed area with seats for the passengers. She was even younger than he'd thought. Nineteen. Twenty, tops. He wasn't to encourage conversation with potential jailbait.

He thought about tomorrow instead as he took a seat across from an old woman dressed entirely in black. Her white head was covered with a woolen scarf, and her black brogans had two-inch-thick soles. They weren't fashionable, but looked highly suitable for walking.

Tomorrow Joachim would stand up for Conal, as his longtime friend termed being best man in his wedding. Joachim had met Conal in 1989 in the lounge at the Ritz Carlton in Paris.

Joachim and his new wife, Suzanne, had been sitting at a table enjoying an after-dinner cordial, when their attention was drawn to two obviously intoxicated gentlemen arguing. Joachim's initial thought had been: *It doesn't matter where you go. Too much booze will turn the most well-mannered man into a buffoon.*

"You aren't a writer," one of the debaters, a stocky fellow of average height with curly light brown hair and a thick Irish brogue accused the other derisively. "At best you're a hack, and at worst, a pest, a gnat who feeds on the blood of popular trends, then regurgitates and calls your vomit art. You wouldn't know real art if it jumped up and bit you on the arse!"

"And I suppose *you're* an artiste," the other man, a Frenchman, said with a hateful guffaw. "Your last book had so much blood and gore in it, it should have come with a warning label: *Read at your own risk. Contents liable to make you sick to your stomach.*"

"That splendid novel won the Booker Prize," the Irishman spat, his face red. "And there was no gratuitous violence in it. I told the story of the Battle of the Boyne realistically. But you wouldn't know about research. You just make up your facts."

"Facts?" cried the Frenchman. "You said the French were a bunch of marauders—"

"No"—the Irishman corrected him with satisfaction—"I said the French stood aside and waited to see who the victor would be, then were prepared to swoop in and snatch the spoils for themselves. The battle was fought between Irish Catholics and English Protestants. Your Louis XIV was supposed to be a supporter of James II, leader of the Irish. But he failed in that support, and the Irish lost."

"You're rewriting history to suit your own purposes," the Frenchman concluded with a smirk. "You should be happy we allowed you Irish to seek refuge here. Otherwise your backward nation might not even exist today."

That was when the Irishman struck the Frenchman in the nose.

At Joachim's and Suzanne's table, Suzanne, seeing the blood pouring from the Frenchman's large proboscis, gasped.

And Joachim, angered at the fools for behaving so abominably in front of his bride, got up from his chair and entered the fracas.

Since he was younger and stronger than either of the two pugilists, he was able to pull them apart. The Frenchman, shocked by the copious amount of blood on his shirtfront, grew weak and fell to the floor. The Irishman, like a dog with the taste of blood in his mouth, tried to push Joachim off him in order to take another swipe at the Frenchman.

Joachim held on to him. "Calm down, buddy. The Irish won this one."

The Irishman gazed up at Joachim as if he'd just noticed the third person in the drama. "You're black." It came out sounding like "You're bleak." But Joachim had gotten the gist of it.

The bartender and another white-jacketed worker had

coaxed the Frenchman to his feet and was walking him out of the room.

Joachim led the Irishman back to the bar and sat him on a stool.

"Look, fellow," he said to him as he sat next to him at the bar. "My beautiful wife and I are trying to enjoy our honeymoon. If you're predisposed to fights, I wish you'd start them elsewhere."

The Irishman turned his bleary eyes on Joachim and laughed. "The name's Ryan. Conal Ryan."

Joachim, being a writer himself, had recognized the name at once. In his opinion Conal Ryan was the best writer to come out of Ireland since John McGahern.

Suzanne, no doubt concerned that the irate Irishman might get it into his head to attack Joachim, walked over to where the two men sat. "Joachim, is everything all right?"

At the sound of those dulcet tones, Conal looked up at Suzanne, an exquisitely formed brown goddess, in his estimation, and sat up straighter. "My God, man, you didn't lie. She's a vision."

Then he'd apologized profusely to Suzanne—he never did apologize to Joachim—for making a public spectacle of himself.

The next day a dozen red roses were delivered to Suzanne. The handwritten note read: *I hope this example of natural beauty helps to erase the memory of the ugliness you witnessed last night. Conal Ryan.*

And from that inauspicious beginning, Joachim, Suzanne, and Conal had become friends. So much so that whenever Conal visited the States, he spent at least a week with the Wests in their San Francisco apartment. When Suzanne had taken ill in 1995, Conal had practically moved into their guest room in order to lend moral support. And in June of 1996, when Suzanne had succumbed, her body wasted by bone cancer, Conal had sobbed openly at her memorial service.

Afterward, when he and Joachim had sat alone in the apartment, both of them imbibing whiskey, and Joachim had declared that he'd never love another woman as long as he lived,

Conal hadn't tried to disabuse him of the idea. He'd been so heartbroken himself, all he could do was shake his big, shaggy head in agreement.

Now four years later, Conal was marrying Erin Donagal, an Irish American whom Suzanne had introduced him to the year she'd spent more time in the hospital than at home. Erin was an English professor at California State, where Suzanne had been studying for her doctorate in English.

Conal had been amazed that he had to go all the way to America to fall in love with a woman whose name was synonymous with Ireland. But love her he did. And no longer claiming to be the world's oldest living confirmed bachelor, he asked her to marry him. When she said yes, he was the happiest formerly confirmed bachelor alive.

He deserves his happiness, Joachim thought now as he settled onto the bench seat, resigned to another twenty minutes or so of the seemingly interminable trip on the ferry.

He'd left the eighteenth-century Georgian manor Conal called home early that morning, hoping to discover the Rathlin Island of Michael McLaverty's *Call My Brother Back,* a book in which the author reminisces about his life on the island.

Conal had warned Joachim that Rathlin Island wasn't exactly scenic, but Joachim was the type of person who had to see for himself. In this case Conal had been right. There wasn't much to see. However, the people had been friendly and talkative when engaged in conversation—often asking him more questions than he asked them—and until it started raining, it had been a lovely day.

So he'd come away with something positive from his day trip.

"You're after visiting Rathlin Island, then?" a feminine voice inquired softly. Joachim looked up into a pair of large blue eyes.

The young woman who'd smiled at him on deck had followed him inside. "May I?" she asked before joining him on the bench.

"Please do," Joachim said. She continued to meet his gaze

a moment longer, then shyly observed her hands. "I'm sorry to disturb you."

"You aren't disturbing me," Joachim assured her with a smile. "In answer to your question—yes, I spent the morning on Rathlin Island."

The girl laughed nervously. "Of course you did. I don't know why I asked such a silly question. Everyone on the ferry is returning from Rathlin Island. How did you find it?" She was less uncomfortable now that he hadn't been offended by her curiosity. She was around twenty, had clear healthy skin, a full mouth, pert nose, and wide-set eyes.

"I found it very hospitable," Joachim replied equitably.

The girl laughed again. "As opposed to habitable?" She regarded him through narrowed eyelids. "You're American, aren't you?" She didn't wait for his answer. "Of course you are. I can hear that sort of cowboy affectation in your speech. What part of America do you come from?"

Joachim pressed his back against the wooden slats of the bench, observing how, with every question she asked, she'd move a bit closer to him. He hoped the old woman sitting across from them was truly sleeping as her closed eyes and bowed head denoted. At any rate he would stay alert with this one.

"I'm from California," he said at last. "It's on the—"

"West Coast," his seatmate effortlessly supplied. Grinning, she reached into her voluminous bag and produced a dog-eared copy of a North American movie magazine. On the cover, smiling broadly, was Brad Pitt. She showed it to Joachim as if it were a prized possession. "Hollywood, Disneyland, earthquakes, and Brad Pitt. His accent was atrocious in *The Devil's Own,* but how can you be disappointed when he has a face like that?" She gazed rapturously at the photograph.

"How indeed?" Joachim replied amiably.

She looked up at him suddenly, her eyes stretching with excitement. "Is that what you are, an actor?"

Joachim couldn't help it, he guffawed. "Me? No, definitely not. I'm a writer."

She inched a little closer. "Oh, then you must be in town for Conal Ryan's wedding," she accurately deduced.

Joachim smiled slowly. Ballycastle was a small town, he wasn't surprised that she knew about the event. Conal had told him that after the ceremony, it was customary for the whole of Ballycastle to drop by the manor and wish the couple a long and happy life together.

"It's true, then? You're here for the wedding?"

"Yes."

"I knew it!" she exclaimed happily. "So you're a writer. I love books. Tell me your name. I'm Gillian McEwan, by the way; no relation to the famous writer unfortunately. Come on . . . I've read all of Conal's books. That's what we call him around here. He wasn't born here, you know. He was born in Baile Átha Cliath, that's Dublin to you. But all that success made him restless—so seeking peace and quiet, he searched out a small town to live in. He chose Ballycastle because it's close to the sea and so far from a big city, it's like being in another era, or so that's what the *Star*, our daily tabloid, quoted him as saying." She took a breath. "Go on, who are you?"

"Joachim West," Joachim told her, fully expecting her never to have heard of him.

He was mistaken, however, for Miss Gillian McEwan fairly burst with joy. "Oh my," she sputtered, her hands going to her cheeks, which had colored. "You just won the National Book Award for *The God Gene*." Staring at him with admiration, she continued. "That book kept me up nights. What with scientists already able to clone animals, I wondered, Is it possible that one day, they will clone humans? And because they are humans themselves, will they leave out the all-important God gene that makes us all what we are? Oh, it was terrifying, the thought of someone creating a human being without a soul." She paused, catching her breath. "You wrote the modern-day *Frankenstein*." She smiled at him. "I'm honored to have met you, Joachim West."

Her eyes raked over his medium brown, square-chinned face. He had large warm brown sexy eyes that held her gaze like a magnet. Gillian had an impulse to touch his short, black natural hair to see if it was as soft as it looked, and if it would spring back to its original shape when she removed her hand.

But he was Joachim West, a famous writer, and he'd think her totally daft if she tried something like that. Anyway he was wearing a wedding band. Even when faced with the opportunity of a lifetime, and the temptation of a man as talented and gorgeous as Joachim West, Gillian McEwan was a good Catholic girl. She was adept at resisting temptation.

The ferry came to a halt, and a voice came over the loudspeaker. "Ballycastle. Watch your step when disembarking."

Joachim and Gillian got to their feet, allowing the elderly woman across from them to precede them as they waited their turn to walk down the gangplank and onto the dock.

"Good day to you, Joachim West. It's been the thrill of my life meeting you!" Gillian called out to Joachim as she departed, not caring if others heard her resounding endorsement.

"It was nice meeting you, too," Joachim returned, laughing softly. What an exuberant spirit the girl possessed.

With a wave, Gillian turned and began walking west, toward the pub where she worked as a barmaid, while Joachim continued east, being mindful of the puddles in the cobblestone streets.

All in all, it had been an interesting morning.

"You should have invited her to the wedding," Conal told him later that evening as they stood in the library of the manor, sipping glasses of good Irish whiskey following a fortifying meal.

Conal hadn't changed much in the eleven years the two had been friends. He was still stocky. No amount of jogging seemed to make those ten extra pounds disappear. His hair, while thick and curly and brown with blond highlights, was too long by far. He kept promising his mother he'd cut it. Maeve Ryan had grown accustomed to his shaggy appearance by now.

He wasn't handsome, but possessed a rugged, masculine charm that won most females' hearts and didn't foster envy

in males, which served him well because he still derived pleasure from having a drink or two with the boys down at the
pub. But he hadn't gotten into a fistfight since that night in
Paris, a feat which he credited Suzanne with accomplishing.
She always told him he was much more becoming when he
wasn't in the process of making someone bleed.

At forty-five, he was a kinder, gentler Conal Ryan.

He eyed his thirty-seven-year-old friend with concern.

Joachim swirled the whiskey around in his glass, looking
intently at the golden liquid, his thoughts more than ten years
in the past. It had been raining then, too. Otherwise everything
else on that June day had been perfection itself.

Bethal A.M.E. Church in Selma had been beautifully be-
decked in white roses. Suzanne's parents were both deceased,
so the young couple were footing the bill for the lavish ceremony themselves. Joachim's grandmother, Eva, who had
raised him when his parents, both teens when he was born,
had reneged on the responsibility, had wisely counseled them
to use carnations to decorate the pews and the stage of the
church.

Joachim, though, had just received the advance, his first
huge advance, for a book he'd written that his publisher was
predicting would be on the best-seller lists within a week of
its debut. So he'd ordered roses. Dozens of white roses for his
Suzanne.

The sight of Suzanne, walking down the aisle, had been
worth every penny.

Suzanne had skin that was a satiny, unmarred chestnut-
brown, so rich of tone and vibrancy that Joachim found himself just wanting to touch her continually. She'd glowed that
day. Love radiated, full and pure, from within her. It had
made him realize, once and for all, that someone besides
his grandmother truly loved him for who he was. Her big
cognac-colored eyes, those windows of the soul which he
could gaze into for hours on end, saw only him. And he,
well . . . there was a permanent photograph of Suzanne in
her wedding gown, etched in his memory forever: how her
auburn hair, like a dark halo, had framed her lovely heart-

shaped face. And the way the dress, a frothy, lace creation with an eight-foot train, in all its splendor, had been but a vessel containing the true star of the moment, Suzanne.

"I should have phoned Celia and asked her to come. At least you would have had someone on your arm," Conal was saying, bringing Joachim, inwardly kicking and screaming, back to the present. "You are going to love her. She's an actress on the London stage. Five four, a hundred and twenty pounds. Beautiful complexion . . . her mother's Nigerian, her father's Scottish. She's truly exquisite."

Conal, at five eleven, was three-inches shorter than Joachim. He looked up into his friend's face now and frowned. "Have you heard a word I've said in the past fifteen minutes?"

Joachim smiled, making crinkles appear at the corners of his eyes. "Something about a woman. Between you and Erin, I'm continually having strange women foisted upon me."

"If you'd put forth more of an effort, we wouldn't feel obliged to round them up for you," Conal returned in their defense. A chilling wind had risen. He strode over to the French doors that led to the garden and closed them against the cold. "April in Ireland . . . I miss San Francisco's sunny days. I'll be happy to get back there day after tomorrow."

He and Erin were spending the next six months in the States while she finished the semester at California State and tied up loose ends concerning her professorship. After that she was to become a permanent citizen of Ballycastle along with her husband. Or as permanent as a globe-trotting author could be. Conal had convinced her to pull those manuscripts out of her desk drawer and try to become a published author. She had talent, and Conal hated to see anyone waste what God had so graciously given them.

As for Joachim, he was planning to remain in Ireland for a few weeks in order to see if he could be moved by the land and the people, to get started on his next book. Lately he hadn't had a desire to write, which was surprising to him and everyone who knew him. Since childhood he'd wanted to do little else.

Each year since Suzanne's death, whenever the month of

June bore down on him, he fell into a funk. The previous three years he'd gone on drinking binges. Last year he'd tipped the bottle so often from April to the end of June, that he couldn't recall what he'd done on June sixteenth, the anniversary of Suzanne's death.

This year he'd taken control of his imbibing—and aside from the occasional drink he took with Conal, had sworn off alcohol. He had started jogging again, too, which had helped to fine-tune his musculature and make his mind clearer. Mental alertness had its down side though. Now he was ever mindful of the fact that he had not written a word in more than eleven months. Not a word since completing *The God Gene*. Any serious writer knew that one couldn't rest on one's laurels. You were only as good as your next book.

Besides that, the very process of writing tended to make one anxious. Sure the critics loved your previous books, but did you have another good book in you? Perhaps you'd already exhausted your inspirational supply and when you went back looking for more, you'd find the larder empty.

Such was the mental anguish of being an acclaimed author. He almost wished for the days when he was just a struggling unknown, collecting pitifully small royalty checks every six months. Almost.

"When was the last time you held a woman in your arms?" Conal asked, walking toward Joachim and reaching for his glass. "Give me that, you aren't going to finish it. I believe you've lost the taste for it."

Joachim handed Conal the glass and watched as Conal drank the remaining whiskey in one gulp. "Perhaps you could use a holiday from it as well."

Conal laughed. "My liver's just fine, thank you. Back to my question: When was it?"

Joachim's dark eyes narrowed as he rubbed a big hand across the day's growth on his chin. He was about to say something when Conal interrupted him with "You took too much time to reply, which can only mean it's been so long, you don't recall." Giving a sympathetic sigh, he turned away to go to his desk and consult his phone file. "I'm giving Celia a call right now. I don't want to hear any protestations. If she can't come for the wedding, I'm issuing an open invitation. She can come as soon as her schedule allows. Besides, I think the play she's in is about to run its course." He looked up at Joachim, an expectant glimmer in his gray eyes. "You're going to love her, really."

The muscles worked in Joachim's strong jaw. He hadn't come to Ireland to meet women. He'd come to stand up for Conal and perhaps be inspired by the surroundings. But he held his tongue. He knew Conal was experiencing a sense of guilt where he was concerned. There Conal was in the happiest state he'd ever been in, and he was still actively mourning Suzanne after four years. It tended to put a damper on the festivities. So if getting Celia—he didn't even know her last name—to come to Ballycastle for a visit gave Conal some pleasure, then so be it.

Two

"If you tilt the whole country sideways, Los Angeles is the place where everything loose will fall," Melodie Morrison said as she pursed her famous lips in a sexy pout for the benefit of the camera. "At least that's what Frank Lloyd Wright thought of the city."

A supermodel quoting an architect, Theodora, Teddy, Riley thought cynically as she focused the Nikon and took several shots of Melodie in quick succession. *We are living in the last days.*

"Are you saying Los Angeles is full of kooks?" Teddy inquired, her brown eyes meeting Melodie's blue ones.

Melodie playfully spun around in her ankle-length sleek white Poleci dress. "L.A. is fast. Compared to the people I knew back home in the Midwest, I'd have to say yes. This town is populated with some strange birds. But I'm diggin' it." She grinned, revealing large yet perfect teeth in her beautiful suntanned face. It was her signature smile.

Teddy snapped the remaining exposures on the roll of film and straightened up. Slinging the camera onto her shoulder by its strap, she looked up at Melodie and said, "That should do it."

They were standing on the beach in Malibu, the beachside community near L.A. where glitterati paid exorbitant prices for the privilege of living among their own kind.

The day was sunny, and a breeze from the Pacific kept the eighty-degree temperature comfortable.

Earlier, just after she'd arrived at Melodie Morrison's beach house, Teddy, a freelance photojournalist on assignment for *Contemporary Lives,* an entertainment news magazine, had asked Melodie where she'd most like to be photographed. It always paid to put your subject at ease. Melodie had chosen the beach, using her new house as a backdrop.

Teddy had also taken photos of the interior of Melodie's home, a three-thousand-square-foot open-style bungalow on stilts. Stairs curved from the back of the house down to the beach.

They ascended those stairs now, with Melodie preceding Teddy.

"Why don't we talk over lunch," Melodie suggested, glancing down at Teddy with a smile on her lips. "I asked Ana to make us a lobster salad. You do like lobster, don't you?"

Her eyes hidden behind sunglasses, and her curls underneath a nifty boater made of pale-colored straw, Teddy returned Melodie's smile. "I'm a native Californian. I've eaten every imaginable type of seafood. Yes, I love lobster."

Melodie's face had a content expression on it as she continued up the stairs. She liked Teddy. Since moving West to pursue a modeling/acting career, she hadn't met many people who made her feel like a regular person. The agents, the clients, the photographers all made her feel like a product. Which, she supposed, she was. She sold herself to the highest bidder. The only reason *Contemporary Lives* was doing a piece on her was because she'd recently been awarded the largest cosmetics contract in the history of the industry: twenty million dollars a year to exclusively represent Celestial Cosmetics. She was their new Heavenly Body girl.

Ana, a petite Mexican woman in her middle forties with a pleasant round face and a cheery disposition, had been at the kitchen window watching Melodie and Teddy climb the back stairs.

She turned from the window now and went to the refrigerator and began removing the various dishes she'd prepared for Melodie and her guest. They were going to have lunch on the deck, and she'd already set the table out there. Now all she needed to do was arrange the food on the plates and fill their wineglasses. Melodie and Teddy were standing on the deck chatting when Ana got there. Teddy had deposited her camera equipment on a chair in the shade, along with her hat and sunglasses.

"Ana," Melodie called, "come let me introduce you to Teddy Riley, who's with *Contemporary Lives* magazine."

Ana, shorter and stouter than either Melodie or Teddy, gave the jeans-clad reporter a warm smile. "Hello, Ms. Riley. I hope you enjoy the lobster salad."

Teddy met Ana's eyes with genuine warmth reflected in her own. "It's Teddy. And, thank you, I'm sure I will."

Ana regarded Melodie. "Will the chardonnay be all right?"

"Teddy?" Melodie inquired, wondering if Teddy partook.

"That would be perfect," Teddy replied, a bit self-consciously. She wasn't used to being treated so well by subjects while on assignment. Many of the celebrities she did stories on were brusque and businesslike. Ready to get the publicity out of the way so they could return to their self-important lives.

Melodie Morrison had been open and friendly from their first hello. Which made Teddy feel a bit guilty because her own behavior throughout the shoot, had been more than a little reserved and perhaps even a bit condescending. One more supermodel with air in her head where her brain should be? In her career she'd shot dozens of models, and it was the rare one that had shown any interest whatsoever in her as a person. What was Melodie up to?

Sometimes Teddy wished she could be less cynical, but life had made her that way. Especially after her divorce from Adrian.

To tell the truth, Adrian was the cause of her not-so-cheery mood today . . .

"Teddy?" Melodie said, leaning closer to Teddy as they stood side by side at the railing.

Meeting Melodie's gaze, Teddy sighed heavily. "I'm sorry, Melodie. I've been preoccupied all day."

"Let's sit," Melodie suggested, gesturing to the umbrella-topped table. After they were seated, Melodie turned to Teddy and said, "You've got a problem, haven't you?"

Teddy slouched in her chair and ran a hand through her chin-length, sooty-black waves. Looking up at Melodie, she said, "You don't want to hear them, believe me."

Melodie laughed shortly, continuing to regard Teddy with warmth and kindness. "I'm dying to dish with someone, Teddy. I mean really dish, none of that superficial stuff the people in the business talk about, like bigger percentages and the right plastic surgeon, or where to go to discreetly cop some illegal substance or other. No, I mean real meaty human issues. May I be frank with you?"

Teddy had sat up straighter on her chair, Melodie's confession had certainly gotten her attention. "Please do," she encouraged her.

"You know how, when you meet someone, you get an instant impression of them? You either like them instinctively, or there's something about them that turns you off? Well, when you introduced yourself to me two hours ago, I liked you right away. I don't know, maybe it was that sporty hat you were wearing; and when you removed your sunglasses and looked straight into my eyes, I thought, this is a gal who would probably tell you the truth, even if it hurts." Melodie paused, her brows arched in an askance expression. "You know what I mean?"

"I feel terrible," Teddy began, "because all I was thinking when we met was—"

"Let me guess," Melodie interrupted her. "You were prepared to meet another narcissistic Barbie doll with oatmeal for brains."

"You nailed it," Teddy admitted, but was quick to add, "although when you quoted Frank Lloyd Wright, I knew I wasn't dealing with the average supermodel."

Laughing, Melodie tossed back her heavy mass of auburn hair and said, "We all have to deal with stereotypes, don't we?"

"I'm sorry," Teddy said sincerely.

"Forget about it," Melodie said, alluding that she already had. Her eyes were more solemn as she met Teddy's gaze now. "What I'm trying to say is, I'd like to be your friend, Teddy

Riley. I'd like you to be mine. Admittedly this isn't the normal route one would take in order to establish a friendship, but we live in a world that is spinning ever faster. And I always trust my gut reactions—about women—I'm not too good at choosing men. Boy, have I chosen some rotten apples!"

"You?" Teddy said, leaning forward and grasping Melodie's arm. "I *married* one!"

"I'm all ears," Melodie said, placing a hand atop Teddy's.

"You might know him," Teddy began, her voice low with a bitter edge to it. "Adrian Riley."

Melodie's mouth fell open. "You were married to *him?*"

"It isn't something one soon forgets," Teddy replied, eyes narrowed. She blew air between full lips and continued. "We were married five years ago. We were your average pair of go-getters. I was determined to win the Pulitzer, and he was aiming for Dan Rather's spot on CBS News."

"Well, he's almost there," Melodie put in. "He's on another network, but I hear he has major pull. Lead anchor on the evening news. A one-hour prime-time news magazine."

"You sound like a fan," Teddy noted with laughter evident in her tone.

"Nah," Melodie denied. "I just like to keep up with what's going on in the entertainment world. Adrian Riley is hot right now. You did know he's dating Victoria Rollins?"

"No," Teddy said truthfully. "I try to avoid any news tidbits associated with him."

"Oh, sorry," Melodie intoned.

"It's okay, I probably should keep up with what's going on in his life. I may need that kind of information one of these days."

"What do you mean?"

"A little over three years ago, Adrian divorced me because, well, the reason he gave was, I got pregnant."

"You're kidding!" Melodie cried, aghast.

"Fool that I was, I assumed our marriage was rock-solid. I knew he had what he called 'the ten-year-plan,' whereby he'd charted our lives. No children for seven years. We'd been married for three. I didn't take his plan seriously. That isn't to say I got pregnant on purpose, because I didn't. But the upshot was, he accused me of trying to manipulate him. He knew I wanted children. I hadn't made that a secret. So he told me to abort the child, or he'd divorce me. I chose the child."

Teddy could state the facts coldly now, but she had been nearly devastated when Adrian had put the ultimatum to her more than three years ago.

After a leisurely Sunday evening together, she'd lain in bed attired in a sleeveless, low-cut black silk gown with spaghetti straps. It had been a gift from Adrian. She'd wanted to look especially good for him because she'd chosen that time to tell Adrian they were expecting a baby. In the deep recesses of her mind, she must have known what Adrian's reaction would be. She'd been extremely tense.

Adrian had come out of the shower with a towel draped around his waist. Teddy had watched him cross the room to the closet, admiring the play of muscles across his broad back and the way the towel, riding low on his hips, helped to showcase his washboard abdomen. Adrian worked out religiously and it was evident in the muscular perfection of his six-foot-tall body.

"Sweetheart," Adrian had called from the closet, "where is my gray pinstripe?" He always liked to choose his wardrobe for the next day the night before.

"The Armani?" Teddy asked, sliding to the edge of the bed and rising. They both worked full-time, but Adrian, spoiled momma's boy that he was, naturally assumed that it was her duty to keep track of their clothes. She had to have a talk with him about that.

Standing at the closet's entrance, Teddy had smiled at him. "It's at the cleaner's."

"Ah well," Adrian said regrettably, his dark eyes on her face. "Help me choose something else."

Teddy followed him into the walk-in closet, which was spacious enough to accommodate a full-size bed. On the right were Adrian's clothes, on the left, hers.

As she walked past Adrian, he reached out and sultrily drew

a finger along her arm. "You smell like a flower garden in spring."

Teddy, basking in the warmth of his compliment, went to his row of suits and withdrew his other gray pinstripe, the Hugo Boss. She held the suit up for his approval. "This one looks good on you."

Adrian sidled up to her and planted a moist kiss on the side of her neck. "Baby," he said huskily, "I want you right here."

Teddy had never denied him his proclivities, which ran toward seeking out unusual places in which to make love to her. Tonight, though, she wanted to talk first.

She hung the suit back on the rack, and turned into his arms. "Adrian, there's something important I have to tell you."

He lowered his head then and kissed her hungrily. Teddy let out a longing filled sigh and weakened. Her announcement could wait.

Afterward they lay on the plush carpeting of the closet floor, looking into each other's faces, smiling contentedly.

Adrian, a layer of perspiration on his brow, reached over and smoothed the hair out of her eyes. "I think you get more beautiful with each passing year," he murmured, his voice caressingly tender. His eyes raked lovingly over her face. Teddy had never been happier. It was the perfect time to tell him her news.

"Adrian, I went to the doctor today."

His face a mass of concern, Adrian sat up, regarding her closely. "Are you all right? Is something the matter? What?!"

Sitting up and facing him, Teddy laughed. "No, sweetie. I'm fine, really. I went because I've missed my period the last two months. I wasn't concerned at first because I'm a runner, and Dr. Prescott says sometimes athletes can be irregular. But when I started feeling a bit of nausea . . ."

It was the expression in Adrian's eyes that made her stop. He sat there shaking his head, his eyes riveted on her, and taking on the countenance of the sky just before a storm. Anger was building up within him. She knew that look well. But for the life of her, she didn't know why he was getting upset.

"You got pregnant." He said this coldly, his tone accusatory.

Teddy drew back from him. "I had a little help from you."

Adrian sighed heavily, picked up his towel and got to his feet. "I'm going to shower again," he announced.

Still sitting, Teddy reached for her gown and rose unsteadily to her feet. His attitude had taken the excitement she'd been feeling and had reduced it to an enervating malaise. She felt so alone at that point, all she wanted to do was put some distance between them.

However, she thought, there was no hiding from the fact that she was pregnant and she had to know why Adrian was being such a killjoy. They'd often discussed having children. Adrian thought putting it off for seven years was a good idea. He didn't want the responsibility of being a father until he was satisfied with the direction his career was heading.

For the last four years, he'd been the lead anchor at WSFX, the largest television station in San Francisco. He earned a six-figure salary. Teddy brought home around forty thousand a year with her freelance work. He drove an expensive sports utility vehicle. Teddy tooled around in her white 1967 Mustang convertible. Adrian wanted her to trade it in on something more to his tastes, but the Mustang was in cherry condition and Teddy, who'd owned the car long before she'd met Adrian, refused to give it up.

They lived in Pacific Heights in a refurbished Victorian home. How much more successful must they be before they could afford a child, Teddy had wondered.

Leaving the closet, Teddy slipped into the gown and strode across the master suite to the bathroom. She pulled back the sliding glass door of the shower stall. Adrian had his eyes closed, allowing the hot water to wash over him. He pretended as if he hadn't heard her come in.

"You're being childish," Teddy said peevishly. "I'm pregnant. You're supposed to be happy about it!"

Adrian reached down and turned the water off. He cut his eyes at her. "You've ruined all of my plans for us, and I'm supposed to celebrate?" He stepped around her and snatched a towel from the towel rack next to the shower stall. Turning to glare down at her, he added, "What was it? Was your biological clock ticking so loudly, you couldn't hear my telling you, for the last five years, that I didn't want to be a father?"

Teddy was five six to his six feet, so she had to crane her neck in order to meet his eyes. "It isn't as if I got pregnant to trap you. I'm your wife, for God's sake!" She felt perilously close to collapsing in tears, but she wasn't about to give him the satisfaction of reducing her to that pitiful state. There was a slight quaver to her voice when she continued, however. "I didn't plan this. It just happened!"

"Exactly!" Adrian shouted as if he'd proved his point. Pulling on his robe, he stormed past Teddy, out of the bathroom.

Teddy followed. "What are you getting at, Adrian? Are you trying to tell me that your ten-year plan is more important to you than I am?" she cried incredulously. "More important than this life growing inside of me?!"

Ignoring her ranting, Adrian calmly went to the bureau and began pulling a change of clothing from the drawers. "I explained everything to you before we got married, Teddy. I told you I wanted to be with one of the major networks by the time I was thirty-five. That's two years from now. I'm still stuck doing the evening news."

"In one of the best markets in the country," Teddy reminded him. "Some people would love to be in your shoes."

"I'm not some people," Adrian said through clenched teeth. He sighed as though he were weary of having to explain his position to her. As if she were a not-too-bright child. "I'm Adrian Riley. I have an image to uphold. I have goals, and I mean to reach them with or without you."

Teddy hadn't missed the implied threat in his tone and in his choice of words. She simply didn't want to believe she was hearing what she was hearing. Her husband would actually consider leaving her if she delivered their baby? Their baby, whose impending birth would, in his opinion, muck up his entire life?

She felt like she was stuck in a bad soap opera. The episode in which the trusting wife discovers she's married to a total stranger.

She could hear her father's words echoing in her brain.

"Please don't marry Adrian Riley, Theodora. There's something missing from that man's makeup. I can't put my finger on it, but somewhere down the road, he'll show his true colors."

Of course, Teddy had defended Adrian to Alexander Tate, her photojournalist father. Her mother had died when Teddy was three, so Alex had reared her alone, choosing never to remarry. He'd taken Teddy with him on assignments all over the planet, exposing her to different cultures, diverse races. They'd formed a special bond, one that made Teddy feel safe and secure. Then when she was twenty-four, and on an assignment in San Francisco, she'd met Adrian, then an on-the-street reporter for a San Francisco television station. Teddy fell in love for the first time. And her loyalties were divided. Teddy figured her father's dislike for Adrian stemmed from the fact that he was no longer the only man in her life.

Now she wondered if her father's opinion of Adrian had been on the mark.

"You can't mean that," she said, her tone soft, questioning. Going to Adrian, she gently touched his arm.

He recoiled from her touch. Then he looked down at her with a cold expression in his dark eyes. "Get rid of it."

Time seemed to freeze. Teddy thought her heart had momentarily stopped beating. She tried to inhale and found the act painful. Then she filled her lungs and the anger spilled out of her in a torrent. "What?!!!"

Adrian turned his back on her as he continued pulling on clothing. With one leg in a pair of jeans and hobbling on the other, he shouted, "You heard me. Abort it. I don't want it."

Teddy didn't know what got into her, but she rushed him, pushing him roughly onto the floor. Then she pounced on him—no, she literally threw her body on top of his, and began beating him in the chest, the face, anywhere!, with fists of fury. Her vision was blurred by tears, but she was so incensed, so totally consumed by anger, that she wouldn't have been able to see straight anyway. "You're a monster! I don't know you anymore!"

Being much larger and stronger than she was, Adrian easily

subdued her. Muscles flexing, he caught her, turned her over onto her back and straddled her. Firmly holding her down, he said, "No histrionics, please. You knew the score, babe. Now either go along with the script, or I'll walk. Those are your choices. Make a wise decision, because I'm deadly serious about this. I don't need a little brat running around here demanding my time and attention. And I have no use for a woman who won't support my decisions. Have I made myself clear?"

Clear? He was coming through loud and clear to Teddy. Still her mind was taking her places where she didn't particularly want to go at that juncture, like: What about love? What about your promise to love me in sickness and in health? In good times and in bad? What about the vows we made to one another?

"Get off me," Teddy demanded, her voice low and menacing.

Adrian cautiously released her and got to his feet. Their eyes remained locked. Teddy could have sworn she saw fear in his. *Good,* she thought. *You'd better fear me, because I'm not finished with you yet.*

She rose, smoothing her gown as she regained her composure. Taking a deep breath, she said, "Just to verify what I thought you said: You're actually ordering me to kill our child?"

"It isn't a child yet, it's an embryo," Adrian told her, sounding, for all the world, like the anchorman whose persona he adopted six nights a week. Totally unbiased. Ever so reasonable. An automaton. The mechanical man. He still looked like Adrian. The same smooth dark brown skin. Wide-spaced dark brown eyes. Square-chinned face with prominent cheekbones. Chiseled good looks.

Teddy stared at him. "Explain something to me. At what point did you become the type of man who would divorce a woman whom you have claimed to love for more than three years, because she wants to give you a child? I must have missed that transformation, *dear.* I must have been totally absent in mind and body when your heart turned to stone."

Fully dressed now Adrian saw no reason to linger. He stood for a moment, his eyes boring into hers. Then he lowered his, turned and walked toward the door. "I did love you, Teddy."

"Did?" Teddy jumped on that opening. "As in past tense, Adrian? What's going on in your head? You don't love me anymore? Is that why you're being so cruel, so detached?"

He paused at the doorway. "Don't put words in my mouth."

"Then talk to me. Why, Adrian? What's the real reason you don't want me to have this child?"

He was done talking though. He walked swiftly through the doorway, down the hall, traversed the landing and was at the stairs. He fairly ran down the stairs, with Teddy at his heels.

"I'm going out for a while . . . until you calm down."

"It's after midnight. Where are you going at this hour?"

"I'll spend the night at Jack's place."

"Jack isn't even in town . . ."

"I have a spare key."

"Why did Jack give you a key to his apartment?"

"He's my best friend, Teddy . . ."

"Joie's mine. But I don't have a key to her place."

"I'll be back in the morning."

"I won't be here in the morning."

"Oh yes, you have that interview in Chicago. Then I'll see you when you get back. You should have had time to make up your mind by then."

"When I got back from Chicago, he'd moved all his things out of the house," Teddy told Melodie now.

Melodie sighed and pushed her plate aside to grasp one of Teddy's hands in hers. The lobster salad had been delicious, the chardonnay crisp and refreshing, just as she liked it. But the conversation had been exactly what she'd needed. "And now?" she prompted Teddy, eager for more. "Earlier you said you'd been preoccupied all day. Is it Adrian again?"

"Yesterday," Teddy began, her voice low as she raised her eyes to Melodie's, "without warning, he showed up at my door." Her large brown eyes glistened with unshed tears. "Seeing him there shocked me so deeply that I shut the door in his face before I knew what I was doing. From the other side of the door, he swore all he wanted to do was talk. Do I look like a fool to you?"

Frowning, Melodie said, "Let me get this straight. He divorced you when you got pregnant. Didn't have anything to do with you throughout the pregnancy. Your son is how old?"

"Two and a half," Teddy supplied, a smile working its way from the corners of her generous mouth. Thoughts of Alex invariably elicited a smile. "His birthday's September eighteenth."

"I bet he's a sweetie," Melodie said with a wistful sigh. She was beginning to crave babies, a sure sign her heart wasn't in remaining a top model for much longer. "All right," she said, getting back to the topic. "Adrian hadn't made an effort to see Alex until yesterday. What about child support? Is he up on his payments?"

"Oh yeah, he's always paid child support like clockwork. No problem there. He knew I'd take him to court if he didn't. There's absolutely no question that Alex is his son; he looks just like him. Adrian simply didn't want any responsibility for rearing Alex, aside from a monetary one, that is. But what is fifteen hundred dollars a month to him? He's loaded."

"No alimony?" Melodie asked, hoping she wasn't being nosy, but risking it anyway.

"I don't want his money," Teddy said coldly. "I take care of myself. I got the house in the divorce, which I promptly sold and bought a condo. I insisted on child support because he had to assume responsibility for Alex. Alex does know who his father is. Adrian may not be in his life, but no son of mine is going to go through life not knowing who his father is. Right now Alex knows him only as that man on TV, who lives far away."

"You're tough, girlfriend," Melodie sincerely complimented Teddy, shaking her head. "I don't know, I probably would've been so angry with my ex, that I would've told the child he was dead or something." She laughed. "Heck, I might have even hired a hit man to ice him. That way I wouldn't have had to lie to the kid."

Laughing, too, Teddy said, "It crossed my mind. But I had great support throughout the pregnancy and after from my dad and my best friend, Joie. They brought me back to my senses. By the time I gave birth, I'd resolved that if I was going to be a single mother, I could handle it. Women become single mothers all the time, either through death, divorce, or desertion. I began to look at it this way: Both Alex and I were lucky to have gotten from under the tyrannical rule of that egomaniac, Adrian Riley. We were safe. And then he walked back into our lives yesterday."

Three

Later that day as Teddy fought L.A. traffic along the Pacific Coast Highway, several thousand miles away, in Ballycastle Joachim was in the garden of Conal's home at the wedding reception, trying his best to lose a hanger-on, the local constable, Liam Murdoch.

The day had been pleasantly unsullied by rain. Three hours after the ceremony, the large garden whose vegetation had grown lush and verdant due to the abundant steady diet of Ireland's rainfall, was packed with guests.

Joachim, dressed in a gray morning suit replete with cummerbund and striped ascot, could barely move an inch without rubbing elbows with someone.

The other guests also were adorned in their spring finery. The ladies in various pastel shades. The gentlemen in suits. Joachim supposed there weren't many occasions on which they got the opportunity to dress up.

A four-member band was playing Irish love songs. A young woman with dark hair that fell to her waist was singing Sarah McLachlan's "I Will Remember You" in a rich and full-bodied alto.

Joachim blamed Conal for Liam's vigilance. Earlier when Conal had introduced him to Liam Murdoch, Conal had told Liam, "I want you to keep an eye out for Joachim while I'm away. He's staying on here after Erin and I go back to the States. Don't let the local hooligans make trouble for him, aye?"

Conal had just been showing respect for Liam's position in

the community as constable. But Liam had taken his admonition to heart. He'd latched on to Joachim like a leech to a camper's leg.

Liam was prattling on now about the situation among the youth of Ballycastle. "The problem, as I see it, is lack of activities to keep them occupied. I have told the city council, more than once, that we need more youth-oriented organizations. But they won't listen to me. Petty crime is up. Purse-snatching, breaking into cars. The young ones are crying out for attention."

The one good thing about Liam's presence was the fact that Liam had been able to extricate him from the clutches of a tall redhead. Susan Mc . . . something. He couldn't recall her last name.

Liam was five eight, had dark brown hair and light brown eyes. His left eye twitched when he became upset. It was twitching now as he went on. "Last week a boy on a motor bike ran down an old woman out walking. Knocked her to the pavement, grabbed her pocketbook and kept going. We still haven't caught him. But we will."

Joachim noticed that Liam's accent also thickened considerably when his temper flared. "I'm sure it's only a matter of time," Joachim assured him politely. Then, "Excuse me, Constable."

"Oh, call me Liam, everyone does."

"Liam . . . I believe the bride and groom are preparing to leave soon, and I'd like a word with Conal before he goes."

Joachim sighed with relief as he strode in the direction of the French doors that led to the manor's kitchen. Inside he spotted one of the maids, Mary, preparing a tray of canapes to take out to the guests.

"Mary, do you know where Conal and Erin have gotten to?"

Mary, a stout brunette in her late forties, smiled at him. "I do believe they're upstairs getting into their traveling clothes, Mr. West."

"Thanks, Mary."

"You're welcome, sir," Mary said with a pleasant smile.

She turned again to her task and Joachim moved farther into the house. He decided not to bother Conal and Erin, but he didn't want to return to the garden, so he took the stairs, intending to retreat to the privacy of his suite of rooms.

Conal met him on the landing, looking particularly jovial. He'd changed out of his morning suit and was now casually attired in dark gray slacks and a long-sleeved tunic in light blue.

Conal was in a boisterous mood. The day had gone splendidly. Erin had made a beautiful bride, and, thank God, hadn't made a mad dash from the church before saying, "I do." And nary a drop of rain had fallen so far.

"Joachim, my friend," he said now, his smile wide, "leaving the party so soon? I'm sorry Celia couldn't make it for the wedding. But she tells me she will be along later in the week. I told her to come right ahead. The invitation stands." He eyed Joachim, no doubt hoping to get an approval of his actions.

Joachim, however, had been having second thoughts about the whole Celia affair. What if she was coming with the expectation of a physical relationship? He wasn't the type who could make love to just anyone. He had to feel an emotional connection, not just the physical pull of lust that so often manifested itself when two attractive people first laid eyes on each other.

His reticence, though, had put a look of sadness in Conal's eyes, and he couldn't have that.

So instead of telling Conal he'd changed his mind about inviting Celia for the weekend, he smiled ruefully and said, "Okay. I hope you didn't build me up to her. Making me sound like some kind of stud."

"The best since Casanova." Conal laughed heartily, slapping Joachim on the back. "And don't you go and make me out a liar."

At two forty-two London time, Celia O'Connell awakened, stretched languidly and sighed. Turning over in bed and resting her head on a thick, fluffy pillow, she contentedly gazed down into Trevor's sleeping face. He was even handsomer in repose. Imagine her good luck when after the second curtain call last night, and following a barrage of congratulations on a show well done, she'd returned to her dressing room and found Trevor Gordon waiting for her.

Trevor Gordon was one of the most sought-after actors on the British stage. And no wonder. Not only was he supremely talented, his physical presence took your breath away. Six feet six. Skin so black, it had a purple sheen to it. Delectable. A body that, when in motion, reminded one of a sleek jungle cat. Conversely when he was still, as he was now, and you could reach out and touch him, it was quite impossible to resist doing so.

Trevor was sleeping on his back, his breathing barely perceptible, he was in such wonderful physical condition. Celia placed her warm hand on his bare chest. A quiver of delight shot through her as images of their lovemaking last night rewound in her mind's eye.

Trevor opened his eyes and smiled at her, dimples forming in both cheeks. "Is it morning already?"

"Not even close," Celia told him, her voice husky.

Trevor reached up and caught Celia behind the neck, gently pulling her toward him. "That nap did me a world of good. Shall we have another go?"

"I'll certainly give it my best effort," Celia replied as Trevor's mouth found hers, and all talking ceased.

Two hours later after Trevor, truly exhausted this time, had succumbed to Morpheus's spell, Celia lay awake, satiated and believing herself on the brink of falling in love.

Then she remembered she was supposed to be taking the train into Ireland tomorrow morning to meet Joachim West, the American author her friend Conal Ryan had chatted up to her. Admittedly she'd found his photograph on the back of his book intriguing. But really what would they have in common? She wasn't very literate. All she ever read were plays and scripts for television or films. Besides, Trevor was here, warm and inviting, in her bed. A bird in the hand was better than one in the bush.

She'd write Joachim West a nice note, explaining that she'd been unavoidably detained. Better yet, she'd e-mail him. Then he wouldn't be expecting her, poor chap. Dumped via e-mail. What was this world coming to?

When Teddy arrived home Monday evening, shortly after nine, the first thing she did was phone her father in Carmel.

She stood in the foyer next to the cherry-wood hall table and reached for the cordless phone. Placing her big shoulder bag and the even larger leather satchel that contained her camera equipment on the hardwood floor at her feet, she leaned against the wall and closed her eyes, awaiting the reassuring sound of Alexander Tate's deep baritone.

When at last he did answer the phone, she didn't wait for him to say anything. "Daddy? How are my two favorite men in the whole world?"

Laughing, Alexander said, "Just fine, baby. Alex is sleeping in my arms as we speak."

"But, Daddy, it's after nine . . ." Teddy began. Her father enjoyed his grandson's company so much, he chose not to observe his daughter's stringent bedtime rules. The way Alexander looked at it, at the tender age of two, Alex had no responsibilities to speak of. So what if he stayed up thirty extra minutes? He didn't have a job to get up early for.

Teddy, however, from a mother's point of view, knew that if Alex didn't get sufficient sleep the night before, he'd be grumpy and whiny the next day. Sure he didn't have a job to get to, yet, but one day he would. He needed to learn that life had certain rules that you lived by. Structure had to be observed. Her father had always been a free spirit—a trait she sometimes envied. It was Alexander Tate's obligation as Alex's grandfather to pass on his zest for living to the next generation. Teddy felt it was hers to convey the other side of the coin, the levelheaded side.

"Well, when Dr. Seuss didn't put him to sleep, I thought a little NBA action might. The Magic and the Bulls are in the

third quarter, and he's out like a light," Alexander quickly said
in his defense, a note of laughter in his voice.

Smiling, Teddy shook her head. "All right, Daddy. I'll let
you slide this time."

"Thank you, warden," Alexander Tate returned, contrite.
"I promise, after our trip to the mission tomorrow and an
afternoon on the beach, by the time you get here in the evening, he'll be nicely worn out. Don't worry so much, Theodora. Your old dad knows what he's doing. You turned out all
right, didn't you?"

"The jury's still out on that one," Teddy joked with a laugh.
To which her father countered with, "You were just fine until
you hooked up with you know who . . ."

"Speaking of Adrian, Daddy, you haven't seen any suspicious characters hanging around, have you?"

"Besides the neighbors? No," her father replied. "If Adrian
knows what's good for him, he won't come within one hundred feet of me. When I was younger, it was two hundred, but
I'm slowing down in my old age."

"I can't fathom why he wants to see Alex all of a sudden,"
Teddy said, ruminating out loud.

"You could have asked him while he was there," her father
said, ever the devil's advocate. "At the very least, you wouldn't
be agonizing over his intentions, which, at this point haven't
been set forth. You know how to contact him. Call him and
demand an explanation. You aren't going to rest until you do."

Sighing, Teddy shifted the receiver to her other ear and
tilted her head back against the wall. Phone Adrian? Such a
simple suggestion. Seeing him yesterday had been quite
enough punishment to last her a while, however.

She could still feel the sick, roiling pain in the pit of her
stomach. It had been more than two years since she'd been
face-to-face with him. He sent the child support checks
through his attorney. His parents—Dr. Winston Mallory Riley,
a prominent plastic surgeon, and Margaret Elizabeth, boon to
the charitable circuit in San Francisco—were doting grandparents to Alex. They saw him on a fairly regular basis and
never forgot holidays or birthdays. Teddy assumed Adrian re-

ceived news of Alex through his folks. He had never, though, made any effort to see Alex himself—that is, not until yesterday morning when he'd shown up at her door.

"I don't want to know why he's changed his mind," Teddy petulantly cried now. "He gave up his rights when he tried to get me to abort our child, then divorced me when I refused."

"Old hurts, Theodora. Get over them. You can't continue to worry that sore spot. You're only harming yourself. It's done with. He turned out to be a nightmare instead of a dream. Move on, daughter," Alexander said emphatically. "Concentrate on what's going on now. He could sue you for joint custody, you know. Get to the bottom of this, Theodora. Don't wait idly by while he plots."

"You're right, Daddy," Teddy admitted after a long pause. "It is better to be prepared. Even though, with every fiber of my being, I dread having to converse with that snake."

"Too bad Eve didn't share your sentiments, we'd all be a lot better off," Alexander quipped.

Teddy chuckled deep in her throat. "Thanks, Pops. I needed a good laugh."

"Uh-oh," Alexander said, lowering his voice. "Little man stirred in his sleep. I'd better put him to bed, sweetheart. See you tomorrow night?"

"You know it! I'll bring the makings for dinner."

"Thank God. I'm getting tired of my own cooking," her father said with a short laugh. "Good night, then."

"Good night, Daddy."

Teddy replaced the receiver and bent to pick up her shoulder bag and the valise with her camera equipment in it. She then trudged upstairs.

Aside from having the black cloud of Adrian's unexpected visit hanging over her head, the day had been a rather pleasant one. Melodie Morrison had proven herself to be a down-to-earth, eminently cool person. She felt the two of them had forged a solid friendship in the few hours they'd spent dishing.

She had a 1 P.M. appointment with Irina Pasternak, senior editor of *Contemporary Lives* tomorrow. Tonight she had to whip the profile she was writing about Melodie into shape.

Opening the door and switching on the light in her bedroom, which doubled as an office, Teddy was overcome with loneliness. She hated admitting it, but lately she'd come to depend on Alex's presence to stave off certain tender longings. With Alex to care for, she was able to ignore the romantic notions that occasionally popped into her head. Thoughts of having a man hold her. A real man. A man whose devotion to her she didn't have to guess at. Someone honest and dependable, with the face of Denzel and the body of Adonis. She wasn't asking for too much, was she?

As she moved farther into her sparingly furnished bedroom, she came out of her leather clogs, bent, picked them up and carried them into the closet. The coolness of the hardwood floor felt wonderful on her warm feet.

Unbuttoning the fly of her jeans, her hand momentarily rested on her flat stomach. A delicious sensual sensation fluttered to life within her. Adrian had been the last man to touch her there. Since their divorce she'd dated a couple of guys, neither of whom ignited her interest or passions to the extent that she'd welcomed an intimate encounter with either of them.

She'd folded the jeans and placed them on the top shelf of the closet when the phone rang. Going back out into the bedroom, she answered the extension on her nightstand.

"Teddy Riley . . ."

"Whew!"—her best friend Joie exhaled—"am I glad I got you. You've got to make that Melodie Morrison profile the best thing you've ever written. I overheard Irina talking to Babs this afternoon. She's looking for someone to interview Joachim West. She hasn't chosen anyone else, so I thought—"

"Who's Joachim West?" Teddy interrupted, puzzled. She sat on the edge of the double bed. She had to hold the receiver away from her ear when Joie screamed, "Theodora Riley, you're a writer, you should know who Joachim West is. He's the hottest black writer since Toni Morrison, that's all. He won the National Book Award for fiction a few weeks ago. What planet have you been on?"

"Oh, is that how you pronounce his name? I might have

read an article in *Time* about him. I thought it was *Joe-ah-keem.*" Teddy laughed. She pulled her legs up onto the bed and sat back against the plumped-up pillows, getting comfortable. "So it's *Hakeem* with an African flavor, huh?"

Sighing, Joie came back with, "Girl, I'm glad we're having this little chat because if you'd gone in there tomorrow and called him *Joe-ah-keem,* Irina would've known you know absolutely nothing about our Mr. West."

"All right, all right," Teddy conceded, her voice rife with laughter. "I'll remember to call him Hakeem. Thanks for the tip, I owe you one. Now listen up, do you have a minute? I have something heavy to lay on you."

"You ain't heavy, girl, you're my sister," Joie encouraged her. "Lay on."

"Adrian came by here yesterday."

"The spook put in an appearance? I can't believe it. What did he want, your blood?"

Teddy smiled. The spook was their nickname for Adrian. In their opinions, he wasn't a living, breathing human being. He was cold, heartless and still walking this earth—therefore he was a ghost, an apparition . . . a spook.

"I didn't wait to see what he wanted. The moment my eyes focused on his face, I slammed the door in it. When he rang the bell again, I told him I'd call the police if he didn't go away. So he left."

"Curious!" Joie returned. Teddy could imagine the look of consternation on her friend's pretty dark brown face. "He didn't demand to be let inside? He didn't threaten to knock the door down? Are you sure it was Adrian Riley?"

"It certainly looked like him," Teddy replied with a short guffaw.

Indeed, yesterday morning when Adrian had rung the bell, Teddy had stood, momentarily dumbfounded, staring at him. Her trance had lasted but a few seconds; however, it was enough time to take in the chiseled jawline, dark wide-spaced eyes, high cheekbones, broad forehead, and determined chin. All features so familiar to her, she could probably identify him by touch when blindfolded.

He'd been impeccably dressed in designer duds of a sky-blue polo shirt and khaki slacks, his feet encased in brown leather Italian loafers. The fragrance wafting off him was Armani's signature cologne for men. His favorite. And hers.

She, on the other hand, was dressed in gray sweats and barefoot, her hair drawn back in a ponytail. Only God knew how her face had looked. Before hearing the bell, she'd been trying to coax Alex into eating his oatmeal. They'd gotten into a playful food fight and they'd both wound up with oatmeal all over them.

Upon seeing Adrian on the other side of the door, Teddy's hand had gone to her face in surprise, and she could have sworn she'd felt some of the goop on her right cheek.

Adrian had smiled at her and the moment he went to open his mouth to say something to her, Teddy had reflexively shut the door in his face. She'd stood with her back pressed against the door, breathing hard, with sweat breaking out on her forehead.

Adrian rang the bell again.

"Come on, Teddy, let's be adults here." His voice had sounded so calm, self-assured. "I'm not here to cause trouble. I just want to talk to you."

"Talk to my lawyer," Teddy managed.

"Please, Teddy," he'd softly said. Not in a pleading manner. No, Adrian had never begged for anything in his entire life. He definitely wasn't going to get on his knees to a woman whom he'd deemed unfit to be his wife. Of course, when that thought went through Teddy's mind, she became even more incensed.

"Go away. Go away now, or I'll call the police and have you taken away. You wouldn't like to see that on the six o'clock news, would you?"

She heard him sigh. It'd been the only sign that he might have been upset by the reception he'd gotten. Teddy waited five minutes before looking through the peephole. The hallway was empty.

* * *

"Well, ain't that a blip!" Joie said now after hearing Teddy's description of yesterday's events. "That doesn't bode well, my dear. Adrian Riley going away without another word? Something is definitely brewing in that diseased brain of his."

"You said it!" Teddy agreed, rising from the bed and walking over to her desk where she'd left her shoulder bag. She bent and rummaged inside until she'd found the pad she'd taken notes on during the interview with Melodie. "He hasn't shown his face since he came by the hospital after Alex was born. And then all he wanted to know was if I was going to claim he was the father."

"I know, girl," Joie said sympathetically. "I wish I'd been there to see his face when you told him off. I hear the staff at Memorial still talk about it."

"He shouldn't have upset me. There I was, in pain, worn out, less than two hours after giving birth to a nearly nine-pound baby and he came in there with his selfish concerns. He's lucky I didn't slug him."

Teddy could hear Joie's two-year-old, Bridgette, crying in the background. "I've got to run, Teddy. Bridgette just fell and scraped her knee. See you tomorrow . . . remember, you've got to dazzle Irina. This could be a huge chance for you!"

"All right, Joie. Love you, girl. Give Bridgette a kiss for me."

They rang off and Teddy went over to her desk, sat down in front of the computer, switched on the gooseneck lamp and began going over her notes. *Joachim West,* she thought pensively, *didn't I read somewhere that he became a recluse a few years ago after his wife died?*

Joachim was alone in the great brick Georgian manor except for the live-in couple whom Conal had hired six months ago, when the McNeils, the elderly caretakers who'd been with him nearly twenty years, had retired. The new couple, William Collins and his wife, Kathleen, were in their late forties. William had been a fisherman, but after an accident in which he'd injured his leg so severely, he now walked with a limp, he'd had to give up his boat. Kathleen, a longtime domestic worker, had convinced him to give the field a try. He was handy around the house, and was a whiz in the garden.

They'd heard Conal Ryan, who traveled a great deal, needed someone to watch his home while he was away, from Mrs. McNeil herself. She and Kathleen belonged to the same sewing circle.

They met each Wednesday night in the basement of Saint Bartholomew's Catholic Church in Ballycastle. Kathleen had eavesdropped on a conversation Mary McNeil had been having with another member and when the meeting was over, she'd pulled Mary aside and formally asked after the post. The following week she and William were living in the comfortable caretaker's cottage behind the manor. They earned a respectable wage and their food and board were taken care of. As an added bonus William was no longer risking life and limb on a fishing boat.

By the time Joachim got downstairs Tuesday morning, Kathleen, a petite woman of forty-seven with graying brown hair she wore in a boyish cut, and brown eyes that usually held a glimmer of disapproval in them whenever she turned them on Joachim, was putting his breakfast on the table.

"Good morning," Joachim said, trying to keep his voice light. He didn't know what Kathleen's problem was, but he was certain of one thing—he'd never done anything to personally insult her that he knew of. Therefore her sour demeanor had to do with something only she and God knew of. He didn't wrack his brain trying to figure her out. He was just grateful she didn't burn his toast and egg whites.

It was true what Conal had told him about Irish cuisine: meat and potatoes all the way. Joachim didn't like eating red meat. Okay occasionally he had a steak . . . maybe once a year, a throwback to the days when he was too poor to afford steak, he supposed. Eating it every now and then was affirmation that he wasn't the pauper he used to be.

The first few days he'd been here, Kathleen had piled the kitchen table—she'd wanted to serve him every meal in the dining room, but he'd assured her he liked the intimacy of the kitchen—high with platters of sausages, eggs, ham, and every imaginable Irish pastry. Joachim gently and kindly—he thought—thanked her for her generosity. Then he'd told her what he wanted for breakfast each morning: toast and soft-scrambled egg whites. Kathleen had stared at him as if he'd suddenly grown a second head. "How does a body exist on so little?" she'd asked, assessing his six-foot-two-inch frame. "You look like you could eat a horse."

Joachim had smiled at that remark, because truthfully some of those sausages she'd tried to feed him had looked like they could have indeed been made from horse meat.

Now Kathleen grunted, acknowledging Joachim's greeting. She placed the toast at his place setting, then walked over to the refrigerator to get the cream for his coffee.

Joachim pulled a chair out and sat down at the large table. Conal had furnished the manor with rustic country pieces in keeping with the pastoral surroundings. The table was made of a heavy pine.

"Do you still want to go fishing, then?" Kathleen asked as she set a cup of her strong coffee before him. She arched fine brows in expectation of a reply.

A few days ago Joachim had expressed interest in casting his line in one of the local rivers. William, who took every opportunity to return to his beloved occupation himself, had said he'd see about getting Joachim a pole.

Joachim met her eyes. "Yes, I'm still interested."

Kathleen wiped her hand on her apron and looked away. Joachim noticed that she became self-conscious whenever they were alone in a room together. "William was thinking that maybe you two could go down to the Tow River after you've had your breakfast. He's itching to get out there, as always. He said to tell you to meet him at the gardener's shed after you've had your fill. I told him that shouldn't take long."

Satisfied with her dig, she spun on her heel. "I'll fix you and William a lunch to take with you."

Joachim raised a cautionary finger, preparing to reiterate his dietary preferences, when Kathleen cut him off with, "I know. No red meats. I'm not dense. I made you a tuna salad, and I remembered to remove the yolk from the boiled egg before mixing it in."

"Thank you, Kathleen," Joachim said, smiling at her.

Kathleen's face softened a minuscule degree. "You're welcome, sir."

Sighing, Joachim said, "I've asked you to call me Joachim."

"It's unseemly," Kathleen reminded him. "It isn't done. In Mr. Ryan's absence, you're the master of the house. Of course, if your wife were here with you and you both insisted on my referring to you by your Christian names, I would abide by your rules. But as it stands, I can't. So sir you are, and sir you will be." With that Kathleen turned back to the sink and continued with her dish washing, so he supposed their conversation was at an end.

Joachim ate his breakfast thoughtfully. Until Kathleen had spoken of his wife a minute ago, as if she were still alive, it hadn't dawned on him that Conal hadn't given the Collinses any personal information on him. Because he was still wearing his wedding band, they'd assumed he had a wife, somewhere, wearing a matching ring. Only if . . . well, no use daydreaming about what might have been, Suzanne wasn't coming back to him.

Should he enlighten the Collinses about his marital status? He saw no immediate need to. If his writer's block refused to give up the ghost a week from now, he was going to abandon the idea of Ireland as a muse anyway, and head back to the States. No use going into detail about his life if his stay was to be of short duration.

"If you and William catch any fish, I'll prepare them for your supper," Kathleen announced, interrupting his thoughts. She was at the sink, washing dishes with the same brusque efficiency he'd seen her do everything else. "Of course, William hasn't caught anything in a month of Sundays, and I suspect you'll be just as fortunate."

Two digs in one morning, Joachim thought with a smile, *I think the old girl is loosening up.*

* * *

The offices of *Contemporary Lives* magazine were housed in a building on Geary Street in the Union Square area of San Francisco, known as the leading upscale shopping district. Among the luxury department stores found in the Union Square area were I Magnin, Neiman-Marcus, Sak's Fifth Avenue, and Macy's.

The atmosphere of *Contemporary Lives* was that of frenetic elegance. The furnishings, paintings on the walls, even the manner in which the staff dressed were stylishly posh. However, the energy of the place was chaotic.

As Teddy pushed through the double glass doors Tuesday morning, the first friendly face she saw was Sylvie Hernandez's. Sylvie was the receptionist. In her early twenties she had a mass of dark hair that fell to her tiny waist. Her mahogany eyes were of an Asian cast, her nose pert and her mouth, red and full.

"Hey, Teddy!" she said brightly. Sylvie rose from her seat behind the five-foot-high counter. With heels she was a head above the desk top. "Irina told me to send you right in. She's in a good mood today."

Smiling, Teddy leaned toward Sylvie. "Then everything must be going smoothly for her. I'd better get in there while she's between courses."

The office joke was that senior editor Irina Pasternak, no relation to the famous author, Boris, snapped off the heads of unwitting writers and ate them with abandon. On several occasions while Teddy sat in the waiting room, she'd witnessed writers leaving Irina's inner sanctum with faces thunderous with pent-up anger or eyes glassy with unshed tears.

She'd been lucky. For some reason unbeknownst to her, Irina liked her work.

"Oh, you don't have anything to worry about," Sylvie assured her as she checked out Teddy's royal-blue skirt suit. "I like that on you," she said admiringly. Sylvie was an inveterate clotheshorse. "You should wear skirts more often, you have super legs."

"Well, thank you, Sylvie. Since you possess a killer sense of style, I'm humbled."

"Aw, go on, girl," Sylvie cried, smiling and waving Teddy off.

Over the years Sylvie had bemoaned the fact that in her esteemed opinion, Teddy dressed like a boy: jeans, denim shirts, and an awesome collection of hats that she pulled down over her sooty locks on a nearly daily basis.

Teddy believed her wardrobe to be functional. One couldn't get on one's knees for the penultimate shot, the one you'd been waiting for all day, if one was attired in an expensive outfit one didn't want to get smudged.

Irina's office took up the entire west corner of the first floor. Outside the door Teddy smoothed her skirt, made sure her hat, a royal-blue bowler, was cocked at just the right angle before knocking.

"Enter, *s'il vous plait*," came Irina's high-pitched, French-accented voice.

Teddy turned the knob and strode in, her heels playing a staccato rhythm on the polished hardwood floor. She paused. Barbara Joseph—Babs to her friends—Irina's personal assistant, was there sitting on the corner of Irina's desk while Irina tossed off a letter to the owner of the magazine, media magnate, Wilbert Murphy.

Babs, an African American in her late twenties, with dark caramel skin, light brown eyes, and blue-black hair she wore in a pageboy cut, looked up at Teddy and smiled her greeting.

"Have a seat, Teddy," Irina ordered in her hurried way. "I just have to finish skewering Murphy, then we can have a look at your Melodie Morrison profile."

"If you aren't happy with my performance," Irina dictated, "then don't cash those fat checks you receive each month due to the diligence of my staff and myself."

Babs laughed. "You're really asking for it."

Irina's green eyes sparkled. "Darling, if he fires me, he'll have to buy my contract. And as we know, Murphy hangs on to a dollar bill until the eagle squawks. He rides me only because he likes to keep me on my toes. We've been parrying back and forth like this ever since I took control seven years ago. One of these days I'm going to thrust my sword into his heart and see if the rumors that he doesn't have one are true or not."

"End trans?" Babs asked intuitively. She rose.

"For now," Irina agreed, sighing. "Thank you, Babs."

"It was my pleasure," Babs said, walking past Teddy and winking at her. She closed the door behind her, and Irina turned her attention to Teddy, who rose and handed Irina a file folder with the Melodie Morrison piece in it.

"When can I see the photos?" Irina asked as she accepted the folder.

"This afternoon," Teddy told her.

"Sit, sit," Irina said, slipping on a pair of red-rimmed reading glasses. Silence reigned in the tastefully decorated office as Irina perused the material. After a few minutes during which Irina's facial expression had been unchanged and complacent, she broke into laughter. "She admitted that?" she inquired, glancing over her glasses at Teddy. Teddy assumed she was referring to Melodie's confession to being addicted to Fat Boy's burgers.

"Yeah, she says she has to work out double hard after one, but it's well worth it."

Irina smiled, her eyes meeting Teddy's. "I like her."

"So do I," Teddy replied, breathing a bit easier now that she was fairly certain Irina was going to buy the piece.

"I can tell," Irina said, peering at the article again. "It's not a puff piece, mind you. Good, solid writing. You've captured the human being behind the image. She's not just a pretty face. We'll run it as is." She placed the folder on her desktop, pushed a wisp of blond hair behind an ear, then regarded Teddy. "Now I have a proposal for you. Do you follow the highbrow literary world?"

"To an extent," Teddy said truthfully. She scooted forward on her chair, meeting Irina's gaze.

"I have it on good authority," Irina began, "that Joachim West is in an Irish hamlet called Ballycastle, working on his next book. No one, and I mean *no one,* has been able to get his reaction on winning the National Book Award. I want it, Teddy. Have you seen any photos of the hunky Mr. West? He's not only brilliant, he's way-cool looking. Our readers are mostly women. I have a feeling that, with him on the cover, we'll triple sales!"

She went into her desk drawer and came out with a large manila folder, a thick hardcover book, and a packet of plane tickets.

Spreading them before Teddy on the desktop, her jewellike eyes gleamed with the intensity of a slightly mad Svengali. "I had Babs collect all this information for you. Your tickets are open-ended in case you need more time locating him, or convincing him to talk to you. What do you say, are you game?"

Teddy sat eyeing the items on Irina's desk. She'd thought she was going to have to work up to asking Irina for the gig. But here was Irina offering it to her on a silver platter.

"Why not?" she said, smiling broadly at Irina. "I've never been to Ireland, and I've always wanted to go."

"Then it's settled," Irina said happily. She leaned back in her leather chair. "You'll leave tomorrow morning. Be sure to pack extra plastic bags to protect your camera equipment. I hear it rains continually over there. Oh, and pack warm clothing—it's chilly in Northern Ireland this time of year."

Teddy rose and collected the envelope, the book, which, when she got a closer look, proved to be a copy of *The God Gene,* the novel for which Joachim West had received the prestigious National Book Award, and the plane tickets.

"Get that interview!" Irina admonished enthusiastically. She walked Teddy to the door. "By hook or by crook. Use your considerable charm," she continued as they made their way across the room. "I don't care how you get it. Just get it."

Teddy laughed shortly. "I'm not exactly a femme fatale, Irina."

"Really, Teddy, you underestimate your attributes," Irina said as she grasped Teddy by the arm and faced her. "I was joking about the seduction, of course. We don't do things that way. Bribery isn't beyond me though. There's a staff position available. It's yours if you get this interview. You've been wanting to stay closer to home since having little Alexander. With this position you wouldn't have any assignments outside of San Francisco."

"It's a deal," Teddy said, more excited than ever. They shook on it. "Joachim West is mine!"

"That's the spirit!" Irina exclaimed as Teddy left the office.

Four

Teddy was so preoccupied with planning her trip in her head, that she nearly missed the messenger who'd just turned away from the door of her condo, a legal-size letter clipped to his board. Tall, thin, and tanned, the kid had dark hair which he'd pulled back and tied with a leather strap. Mirrored sunglasses hid his eyes. His teeth flashed white in the sunshine when he saw her.

"Hey," he said, "you wouldn't be Theodora Riley, would you?"

Looking up, Teddy noticed the insignia of a local messenger service stitched to the left pocket of the light gray, short-sleeved shirt he had on. Could Irina have forgotten some pertinent piece of information about Joachim West, and sent it to her via the messenger service?

"Yeah, that's me," she said lightly, her mouth turning up in a smile.

He grinned as he walked closer and presented the clipboard, a pen attached, for her signature on the dotted line.

Teddy hastily scrawled her name; the letter was in her hand, and the kid said, "Thanks, glad I didn't miss you."

"Thank you," Teddy returned absently. She continued up the steps to the portico, her thoughts on getting inside so she could begin packing her bags and throwing some extra things together for Alex's extended stay with his grandfather.

She'd phoned her dad and explained the situation to him on the the cellular while she was driving across town. Thank God for her father. Basically retired since 1998, he still accepted special assignments from magazines such as *Ebony* and *Life*, but only if he had a strong interest in the subject matter. Last year, he'd done an eight-page spread on Nelson Mandela for *Ebony*. He was currently working on a coffee-table book on the sights of the central coast of California. He'd chosen the central coast not only for the natural beauty that abounded there, but because he wouldn't have to travel too far afield. He'd resided in Carmel, or Carmel-by-the-Sea, as the locals referred to the village, for more than thirty years.

Carmel sat just below the point of the Monterey Peninsula, an exquisite jewel in the bosom of the myriad pine, cypress, and oak trees that grew there. Long a retreat for writers, painters, and celebrities such as actors, Carmel was little more than a mile across, but the charming, picturesque village drew thousands of visitors each year.

When Teddy wasn't traveling the globe with her father, Carmel was home.

As she turned the key in the lock with her right hand, her mind was on Carmel and how soon she could get there. She longed to hold Alex in her arms, feel his silky skin against her cheek, breathe in his sweet baby's breath. She smiled to herself, just imagining it. Then as her eyes drifted downward, afraid she wasn't putting the key in the lock correctly, she spied the return address on the envelope: THE LAW OFFICES OF DARTON, SUTHERLAND, AND EDWARDS. That's as far as she read before the envelope slipped from her fingers and glided down to land atop her foot. David Sutherland was Adrian's attorney. It wasn't as if she'd ever forget the name of the man who'd represented Adrian during their divorce proceedings.

Her line of sight remained targeted on the envelope, but as if guided by some superstitious taboo, she refused to bend down and pick it up. If she ignored it, maybe it wasn't really there. Maybe the impact of what was in that envelope would somehow be lessened. If she never read it, never touched it again, maybe everything associated with that off-white heavyweight business-size harbinger of doom would simply disappear, never to return to darken her door. Maybe . . .

Brushing the offending envelope from her foot, she hurried to the phone in the kitchen, totally forgetting the cellular phone in her bag on her shoulder.

Her father. Hearing his cool, soothing voice would stop this panic attack that was threatening to engulf her. He was always able to calm her, make her see the silver lining in every storm cloud, and, Lord, the wind was howling and the rain was coming down in sheets!

Tears blurred her vision as she tried to see the numbers on the keypad in order to dial. Her hands were trembling as she waited for Alexander Tate to pick up.

When he did, after the longest four rings she'd ever endured, she was so relieved, the first sound out of her was an anguished sob. Alexander knew his daughter's voice under any circumstances.

In Carmel his heart pounded with fear.

"Theodora!" he cried, "talk to me, child."

Teddy tried to speak, but as she opened her mouth, another wail came out. Her breathing passages were clogged up and she needed to blow her nose. She reached over and grabbed a paper towel from the rack above the sink. As she blew her nose, she could hear her father screaming into the receiver, "Theodora, Theodora Tate, you had better say something soon, otherwise I'm going to call the police and have them go over to your place and break the door down. Do you hear me?"

"A letter, Daddy. I got a letter from Adrian's lawyer today."

"What kind of letter, Theodora?" Alexander asked, attempting to make his voice as calm as possible. He was on the point of panic himself. His daughter had phoned him and was unable to speak for a full two minutes, and now she was talking about legal papers from the attorney of the slickest piece of work he'd ever had the displeasure of meeting. No, something wasn't right.

He heard a sharp sound and knew Teddy had put the phone down. He listened keenly for any background noises. He could hear nothing. His heart continued to hammer. He had put Alex down for a nap only ten minutes ago—he hoped the phone hadn't awakened him. They'd had a good time on the beach that morning. And visiting the San Carlos Borromeo de Carmelo Mission had been a treat for the both of them.

In the midst of those hallowed walls, Alexander Tate experienced true peace and serenity. Being there with his grandson, who, in the short space of his two years on this earth, had laid claim to a big chunk of his heart, was all the more satisfying.

Theodora had loved the mission, too. She had been no older than Alex when he'd first taken her there. The same rapt, awe-filled expression he'd witnessed on little Alex's face this afternoon had been so reminiscent of the way Theodora used to look upon entering the mission, that it had nearly made him cry. Him. A sixty-three-year-old man.

"I have it, Daddy," Teddy said a moment later. Her voice sounded calmer now. Alexander could hear her tearing open the envelope and unfolding the letter inside.

Another muffled sob.

"He's suing for custody. . . ." Her voice trailed off. It took her a minute or so to compose herself enough to continue. "Not visitation rights, custody. Sole custody, Daddy."

"He can't do that!" Alexander exploded. "No judge in the country would give custody to a father who wanted the child aborted."

Teddy sat down on a stool at the kitchen nook. She felt weak all of a sudden. Weak with fear. Remembering the way Adrian had smiled at her two days ago, she wanted to throw up. Why had he even shown up? To gloat? He apparently already had this in the works. Had he come to warn her about being served custody papers? To soften the blow? No, even that questionable kindness was too human a thing for Adrian to do.

"Read me the entire letter, Theodora," Alexander suggested. "I want to hear all of it."

Teddy began reading in a monotone. "Please be advised that my client, Adrian Xander Riley is suing for sole custody of the minor, Alexander Tate Riley . . ."

Five minutes later, finished reading, she sighed and said, her tone bitter and deadly, "I'll kill him first, Daddy."

For one millisecond Alexander had images of Teddy—à la *Beloved*—killing Alex in order to keep him from Adrian's clutches. But that gruesome specter quickly vanished.

"No, dearest," he told his daughter, "I'll kill him. You have your whole life ahead of you, and Alex needs his mother. I wouldn't mind languishing in prison if I'd have the satisfaction of knowing Adrian isn't walking this earth."

Teddy gave a strangled laugh, in spite of herself. "What now, Daddy?"

"First you need to phone Billie Roman and let her know what's going on. Then you've got to go to Ireland."

"I can't go to Ireland now, Daddy," Teddy said. "Not with all of this going on—"

"Theodora, as of this moment, you're at war. You need ammunition. Believe me, Adrian and his slime of a lawyer are going to do everything in their power to discredit you. To make you look like a neglectful mother. They could use your career against you. You're away on assignments at least six months of the year. I know you take Alex with you quite often, or you leave him with me when you can't. But it's still a man's world, and males still dominate the courts. You need to be able to say you have a steady income and a job that doesn't take you away from home. Irina has promised you that staff position if you get the interview with West. You need that job, Theodora."

Teddy knew her father was talking sense. But her instincts were saying she should stay close to her child when there were wolves at the door.

"I'm going to go pack and I'll think about what you've said on the drive to Carmel, Daddy," Teddy promised. She'd have to think long and hard before agreeing to leave Alex and go halfway around the world.

Joachim and William stood on the bank of the Tow River, cane fishing poles in their grasps. The briny smell of the river was carried on a light breeze. The sky was a rich azure with no clouds to speak of. Both men were mute in their silent appreciation of the moment.

Joachim shifted his weight, pulling up ever so slightly on the pole when he thought he felt a barely noticeable tug on the line. He paused, waiting for another indication that the bait had proven enticing to some unsuspecting fish.

No, nothing. He relaxed again, standing with his legs apart, his boots planted on the moist ground. Glancing in William's direction, he could have sworn the older man was asleep on his feet. William had his eyes closed, his face turned to the sun, a serene expression transforming his unremarkable features into an almost childlike visage. Joachim smiled. The man really got into his fishing.

Suddenly Joachim felt a strong jerk on the line. He had a taker. He knew it! Pulling upward and stepping back, he held on as the fish on the hook fought like mad to free itself.

William opened his eyes to see the writer moving backward, almost losing his balance, recovering, and grimacing as the line was pulled taut.

"Ease up on her!" William cried excitedly, going to stand close to Joachim and shout instructions in his ear. "You've got her now. Hold on, I'll go get the net!"

William turned away, going quickly, or as quickly as his bad leg would allow, to where they'd left the fishing tackle and supplies. Two hours without a bite—now the writer had one that had to be a whopper, judging from the fight it was putting up.

When he got back to where Joachim was standing, Joachim had successfully pulled the fish out of the water. It was a pike, a nearly two-pounder from the looks of it. The fish violently thrashed back and forth, still trying to get the hook out of its mouth.

"Hold her, hold her," William instructed, grinning so wide, the gap on the side where he'd lost a tooth years ago was visible. He went into the water, his feet and pants legs protected by the rubber waders both men wore.

Joachim wasn't about to let the pike escape. He could already taste it. And the look on Kathleen's face when they returned with this splendid catch would be priceless!

In a matter of seconds, William had the pike in the net and was walking back up onto the bank.

"She's a beauty, Mr. West," he said, offering congratulations.

Joachim accepted the net with the fish in it. It fought with such vigor, he almost felt regret at having captured it. But not so much so that he'd throw it back. No, broiled, baked, fried, or barbecued, they were going to dine on fish tonight!

"I'll go ahead and gut her and scale her if you don't mind, sir," William said, his hand out for the fish.

"No, I'll do it, William," Joachim replied, his brown eyes alight with humor. "You return to your fishing, maybe you'll get lucky, too."

"Wouldn't that make Kathleen's day," William said with a laugh, not needing to be told twice as he turned away and went and picked up his forgotten pole. He settled into his pose. "She had to make it a point of telling me that she'd made tuna sandwiches for our midday meal because it'd probably be the only fish we'd be tasting today!"

Joachim smiled to himself as he went about the messy task of scaling the fish, gutting it and placing it in the cooler of ice they'd brought along to keep their drinks cold.

He was remembering the fishing trips of his youth along the Mississippi with his grandmother, Eva.

The setting wasn't much different than the one he was in now. Except Alabama was probably populated with more blacks than anyplace he'd ever lived, and Ireland probably had only a handful of blacks on its soil as he breathed.

His grandmother was gone now. She'd died a year before Suzanne had left him. One cruel blow on top of another. The two women he'd loved more than his own life.

Could he ever begin to love someone else that much? He didn't believe he had it in him to risk getting hurt again, to give of himself in that fashion. It was much safer remaining distant, unreachable, his emotions under lock and key.

He would never let anyone near his heart again.

He'd finished cleaning the pike and placed the filleted fish atop the ice in the cooler, when his eyes rested on the gold band on his ring finger. He turned it around on his finger, testing its tightness. Nothing short of a miracle would get it off. The same could be said of the odds of anyone else replacing Suzanne in his heart. Highly unlikely. He'd welcomed the possibility of being alone the rest of his life.

"Something doesn't sound right about the wording," Billie Roman said when she returned Teddy's call. Teddy was driving southbound along State Highway 1, about thirty or so miles from Carmel.

"What do you mean it doesn't sound right?" Teddy asked.

"Not enough legalese?" Billie said. "Wait a minute. How was it delivered to you?"

"A kid from a messenger service walked up to me and had me sign for it."

"That's it? A kid just handed it to you after you signed?"

"Yeah . . ."

"Then it wasn't a court-appointed process server?"

"No . . . just a kid with a ponytail."

Billie laughed. "Those rats!"

"What?!" Teddy asked, puzzled.

"It's a scare tactic," Billie told her confidently. "You wouldn't talk to him, so he went to his attorney and asked him to send you that letter."

"But why would he do that?"

"You wouldn't talk to him. He had to get your attention. Listen, Teddy, I'll speak with Sutherland as soon as possible, see what's really going on. Don't worry. In the meanwhile I'd suggest you talk to Adrian. What his lawyer did was unethical in my book, but it wasn't illegal. They may be preparing to sue you for custody of Alex, and then again they may not be. You can't, however, get around talking to Adrian."

Teddy remained silent on her end.

"I know you don't want to," Billie continued, her voice sympathetic. "But the fact remains, he is Alex's father. If he wants to take a more active role in Alex's life, he has the legal right to do so."

"Maybe I shouldn't have named him as the father," Teddy said angrily, remembering the night Alex was born and Adrian had accosted her in her hospital bed with his asinine concerns about being put under public scrutiny for abandoning his wife and child.

"You don't have to worry!" she'd shouted at him then. "I don't want to be associated with you, Adrian. And I definitely don't want my son to be put under a microscope due to his father's celebrity. So rest assured. You're off the hook in that way. But, yes, Alex will have your name, if only because it's the truth. You are familiar with the truth, aren't you, Adrian? I don't know, you're a stranger to loyalty, faith, and true love—so, hey, you might not know what truth is either!"

It had taken two nurses and an orderly to get her calmed down. Security had escorted Adrian to the exit.

"All right," Teddy relented after a long pause. She heard her ever-patient attorney sigh on the other end.

"It's for the best," Billie Roman said frankly.

Teddy felt some of the tension slide off her as she pulled onto her father's street. By law there were no sidewalks, streetlights, or mailboxes to take away the pristine beauty of the residential areas.

The town of Carmel had originally been slated to become a resort for Catholics in the 1880s. However, that plan fell through and Frank Davendorf, from San Jose, bought up the land hoping to preserve its natural beauty and attract people of refined tastes. Then in 1905 poet George Sterling bought property in Carmel, liked the setting so much, he raved about it to friends and before long Carmel gained a reputation for being the home of the artistic crowd. Over the years it had been the home of such luminaries as photographer Ansel Adams, writer Lincoln Steffens, and poet Robinson Jeffers.

Alexander Tate had moved there over thirty years ago as a newlywed. He and Michelin, Teddy's late mother, effectively integrated the neighborhood. Three years after Teddy's birth, Michelin, an actress, was shooting a western on location in Mexico when she was one of five passengers on a private plane when it crashed. She died from her injuries in a Mexican hospital before Alexander could rush to her side.

Alexander had chosen to remain single, devoting his life to his daughter, the spitting image of his dear Michelin, and to his work, which was no substitute for his wife, but provided a great deal of satisfaction.

Teddy stopped the Mustang alongside her father's late-model SUV in the driveway and climbed out, her eyes on the screen door from which her father and son would spill out of any moment now.

She didn't bother retrieving her bags because she didn't want anything in the way of taking Alex into her arms.

She heard the creak of the hinges on the screen door before she saw Alex, running with breakneck speed onto the porch and down the steps, his little legs pumping.

"Mommy, Mommy!"

Teddy ran and scooped Alex into her arms, rising to her feet, hugging him to her breast, inhaling the little-boy scent of him, feeling his soft, fragrant skin against hers, marveling yet again at how perfectly beautiful he was.

Alex repeatedly kissed her cheeks, going from right to left, crying, "Mommy, I missed you!"

Teddy was laughing, while tears of joy moistened her face, making Alex's kisses that much more sweet. "I missed you, too, baby. I always miss you when I'm away. You're always on my mind, no matter where I am, no matter what I'm doing."

Alex giggled delightedly. "Even when you're sleeping, Mommy?"

His large dark brown eyes were so like his father's. A rich brown, like mahogany shined to a rich patina. His skin color was a cross between hers and Adrian's, not exactly her golden brown, but a darker chocolate brown with red undertones. And his hair, which was cut short now, since his grandfather had taken him for his first visit to a barber a week ago, was black and baby fine.

Teddy kissed his button nose. "So have you been a good boy for your decrepit old granddaddy?"

"I heard that!" Alexander said from behind her. He moved next to his daughter and planted a warm kiss on her cheek. Tall, dark, his skin nutbrown and vibrant, and handsome, Alexander was nowhere near being decrepit. He was a vital, energetic man at sixty-three as well his thirty-year-old daughter should know. She trusted him to care for Alex when she couldn't be there. She'd never left her son with anyone else.

Grinning, Teddy peered up into her father's dear face. "Seeing you two is like a poultice for my soul."

Alexander frowned. "Wasn't that on a Hallmark card?" Laughing, he placed a hand on the small of Teddy's back as they walked toward the house. "I'm glad to see you managed to calm down before getting here. Didn't want to see Alex upset, too."

Kissing the top of Alex's head, Teddy murmured, "Yeah, me, either. I spoke with Billie on the way here. She believes it's just Adrian's way of getting me to talk with him. Apparently that letter wasn't official. She called it a scare tactic."

"Mmm-huh," Alexander said, nodding sagely. "I wouldn't put it past him."

Alex wriggled in her arms, and Teddy reluctantly set him back on his feet. He was way past the age for her to be carrying him around. It was just that the thought of losing him had made her realize how precious he was to her. Alex was in his independent stage, though. Although he enjoyed the hugs and kisses she bestowed upon him, his attention span was short and there were other things an inquisitive two-year-old could be exploring.

A lizard, moving quickly beneath the frangipani bush near the front steps, caught his eye, and he was off and running after it; then he was on his hands and knees, reaching under the bush.

"Alex, don't you dare touch that snake-with-feet," Teddy warned, her voice rising in alarm.

"Oh, Theodora, let the boy be a boy," her father said, his brown eyes sparkling.

Teddy threw up her hands in resignation. Her father was right, she had to chill out. Adrian's sudden appearance in their lives had set her nerves on edge. That's all it was. Normally she would be on her hands and knees riffling the frangipani bush, searching out the lizard right alongside Alex.

Turning back toward the car, she said, "I'd just as well get Alex's things out of the car." Looking into her father's eyes, she added, "Sorry, Daddy, I completely forgot to stop by the market and get the makings for dinner."

"No problem," Alexander assured her, going with her to the Mustang to help if he could. "The state of mind you're in, you would have burned it anyway. We'll order Chinese."

Teddy tiptoed and kissed her father's cheek. "You're an angel. What would I do without you?"

She opened the driver's side door and reached into the back, getting the navy-blue duffel bag she'd packed extra clothes and toys in for Alex.

Rising, she was surprised to see a sleek black late-model Mercedes pulling into her father's drive.

"Who could that be?" Alexander said, walking toward the car.

Teddy dropped the duffel bag onto the cement driveway and stood watching as the person behind the wheel of the Mercedes parked, and the driver's side door opened.

A shiny pair of expensive men's dress shoes was the first thing she saw, followed by dark slacks. Adrian's well-shaped head came into view then, and he unfolded the rest of his tall, muscular form from within the confines of the luxury car.

He squinted in the bright sunshine. His smile was a little hesitant as his gaze settled first on Alexander, then Teddy. "I figured you'd be here," he directed to Teddy.

Teddy forced her legs to move forward. She was not going to freeze up like she had the day before yesterday. However, before she was within ten feet of Adrian, her father had moved around the Mustang and had Adrian backed against the Mercedes, both his big powerful hands around his ex-son-in-law's throat.

"You sadistic piece of slime," Alexander said, his voice low and menacing. "You treat my daughter the way you have, then come to my house expecting a warm reception?"

Adrian chuffed, his hands on Alexander's trying to loosen the older man's grip. Teddy had paused in her tracks because in the midst of the mayhem, her thoughts had gone to Alex. She didn't want Alex walking up and seeing his grandfather in the grips of insanity.

And just as the thought occurred to her, Alex shot by her like a rocket, running to his grandfather and wrapping his arms around one of Alexander's legs.

In anguished tones Teddy screamed, "Daddy, Daddy, let him go! Alex is right behind you."

Alexander abruptly released Adrian, who fell against the Mercedes, his hand going to his sore throat, rubbing it gingerly.

Alexander reached down and took Alex into his arms and slowly walked away with him, the little boy's arms wrapped tightly around his neck.

"There, there," he cooed softly. "Grandpa's all right now."

Adrian stood watching his son as the boy's big warm brown eyes stared back at him. They were accusing, those eyes. Eyes that didn't know who he was. Eyes that had labeled him a bad stranger. A stranger who'd come there and needlessly upset his grandpa.

Adrian started walking after them. He wanted to explain. He wasn't there to bring trouble. But before he could place his foot off the driveway onto the grass, Teddy was in his face.

"Just where do you think you're going?" she asked, her eyes narrowed. She thrust out her chest, ready to do battle. She only came up to his shoulder, but he took a step back nonetheless.

"Teddy, I didn't come here for a fight," he began, sounding a bit hoarse after being nearly asphyxiated. Their eyes met. His were contrite. Hers were seething with anger.

Teddy stood with her arms akimbo, ready to jump on him if he moved an inch toward her father's house. Adrian, at six feet tall and a hundred and eighty-five pounds of solid muscle could have lifted her, thrown her over his shoulder and walked off with her. But he instinctively knew she'd scratch his eyes out if he attempted that. He didn't want to risk it.

"You've got sixty seconds," Teddy told him firmly. "I'll listen to you for that long, and then you have to go. You've already upset my father and my son—"

"He's my son, too!"

"Forty-five seconds," Teddy counted down, glancing at her watch.

"Okay, okay," Adrian said, sighing. His eyes bored into hers. "I made a mistake, Teddy. I treated you like garbage. I abandoned you when you needed me most. I tried to get you to abort our child—"

"Tell me something I don't already know," Teddy interrupted, unmoved by his act. "Why're you really here, Adrian? The truth."

The truth was, Adrian Riley had come to the realization that Theodora Tate Riley had been the best thing to ever happen to him. But as he observed the fierce, barely reined-in level of animosity she was tossing at him with her eyes, he couldn't bring himself to admit that to her.

The truth was, more than three years ago when he had divorced Teddy, leaving her devastated and pregnant, he'd done it out of selfishness. She'd thrown a wrench in his ten-year plan for their lives together. His star was steadily rising in the network television galaxy. Already the top anchor at the biggest television station in San Francisco, he had his eyes on the Big Apple and a spot at the desk on a national affiliate.

He had everything he'd ever wanted now. Position and pres-tige. His present contract ensured that he'd earn over two mil-lion this year alone, plus stock options. Next year they'd have to renegotiate. He had a beautiful apartment in New York City, two luxury cars. He was buying a house in San Francisco so he'd be near Alex and his parents—and if only Teddy would . . .

"I want you back, Teddy," he blurted so suddenly, that it not only took Teddy by surprise, but the words shocked even him. That wasn't how he'd planned to tell her. He was going to play it cool. It was his intention to come and apologize for the letter from his lawyer first, explaining how angry he'd been when she'd slammed the door in his face. It was only a ruse to get her to finally talk to him, he'd been prepared to say. *I don't want to cause you any more pain than I already have, Teddy.*

But his regret had gotten the best of him. Regret for the foolish choices. Regret for his cruelty to a woman who'd never done anything except love him.

And it was the memory of the loving that struck him first when he saw her this afternoon. Teddy, still so lovely with her sun-kissed skin, all golden brown, smooth, made for tasting. Those big velvety-brown doe eyes that looked clear into your soul. Her pert little nose above that luscious, full mouth. God, he'd missed kissing her. Teddy's kisses could very nearly give a dying man reason to live.

His eyes rested on her face now. Neither of them had uttered a word since his declaration of longing. He was waiting for some reply from her. She was waiting for her tongue to come unstuck from the roof of her mouth. Shock had dried her mouth, thereby silencing her tongue.

Adrian wanted to pull her into his arms, remove that quirky sailor's hat from her head and ruffle her mass of curls the way he used to. He wanted to feel her jeans-clad body pressed against his Hugo Boss originals. They were poles apart in thinking, in style, in . . . everything! But he ached for what they once had. Because when all was said and done, what they'd shared had been real. He knew she'd loved him for who he was. He knew that every time he'd held her in his arms, every time they'd made love, it was him she wanted, not his bank account, not his clout, not what he could do for her in the long run. No, Teddy had loved him. Him! And he'd not realized the value of that love until now. Now when he should have been celebrating his stellar success. But here he was, trying to recover the halcyon days when love was fresh and love was kind. Love was in every word, every look, every touch. Teddy had done that for him. And he'd tossed her aside in favor of fame.

"I didn't hear you correctly, did I?" Teddy said, finally finding her voice. She smiled, shaking her head in disbelief. "Because I thought you said you wanted me back—"

Adrian went into action, grasping her by the shoulders, pulling her to him. He gazed into her upturned face. "I know it's hard to believe, but I'm different now, Teddy. My mother . . ." He laughed shortly, his deep baritone gravelly. "My mother recently told me that she was ashamed to call me her son. Ashamed! Of me! I'm the most successful of all her children, and I'm the one she wishes she'd never had. She told me that. She never thought she'd live to see the day, she said, when one of her children would behave as abominably as I have toward you and Alexander. It took a while to sink in, but I realized everything she'd said was true."

Teddy, half mesmerized by what he was telling her, still had the presence of mind to remove his hands from her body and put some distance between them. She'd learned never to take a word issuing from Adrian's mouth as gospel. Hadn't she trusted him completely the three years they'd been husband and wife? Her faith in him had been unshakable up until the moment he'd told her to get an abortion. That's how much she'd been under his spell. She wasn't going to fall back under now.

"Good for you!" she cried, hands on hips. "So you've been reborn. Adrian Riley has reinvented himself, improved upon the already perfect model. Well, whoop-de-do! And hallelujah, too! The world is a better place. But really it's all a bit too little and too late. You want to try again?"

She laughed harshly, throwing her head back and losing her hat in the process. She bent and picked it up, hitting it against her thigh to knock off any dirt clinging to it. Her eyes were on Adrian's unsmiling face. "You had to have known I'd never believe you, didn't you?"

"This wasn't exactly planned, Teddy. I just came by to apologize for the letter. I was angry when I had Sutherland send it. I don't want to sue you for custody of Alexander."

"We call him Alex," Teddy informed him quietly, the fight gone out of her. She was tired. She had a plane to catch in the morning. She didn't have time for his games. He wanted her back? She'd believe that when elephants flapped their ears and took to the sky.

"Alex . . ." He smiled. Their eyes met. "He looks just like I did at that age."

"That's what I'm told."

"I'm sorry, Teddy."

"Yes, you are."

"I know you're bitter," he said, his voice low. "I made you that way. I—"

"Now wait a minute," Teddy said, her eyes flashing fire. "Don't come here thinking that your behavior broke me, Adrian, because it didn't. I'm not some embittered, stepped-on ex-wife who lives on the hatred she feels for her ex. Oh no, I've done just fine without you. I'm happy. Don't think that I've been pining away for you the last three years, because you'd be deluded. Yes, I'm angry with you because you haven't been a father to Alex. But let's make this perfectly clear, Adrian. I do not harbor any warm—or lukewarm for that matter—feelings for you! I don't want you back. You're not getting anywhere near my heart again."

Adrian felt bereft of energy as he allowed her words to wash over him. He didn't know what he'd expected by coming here today. He'd been led by his passions. They'd gotten him in trouble on more than one occasion. It had been his hot-headed selfishness that had demanded she throw their child away, too. He'd reacted in an emotional manner, allowing all his hurt, scared feelings to surface, become words with which to wound her.

He wasn't going to make the same mistake twice.

He calmly turned on his heels and began walking back to his car. "You think about it," he tossed over his shoulder in her direction. "I'll be in touch, Teddy. I'm going to be in your and Alex's life from now on. We've got plenty of time!"

"The answer is no, Adrian," Teddy called, following him to the Mercedes where he climbed inside and she stood a couple feet away. "No!" In the car now, Adrian turned the key in the ignition and smiled at her. "You're as beautiful as ever, Teddy. Still the sexiest woman on the West Coast."

And you're still full of it, Teddy thought.

She hit the roof of the Mercedes with her rolled-up hat. "It'll never happen, Adrian!"

Adrian backed the car out of the driveway and waved at her as he sped away.

Teddy turned and walked back to where she'd left the duffel bag with Alex's things in it, bent and picked it up, then went into the house to answer what she knew would be a barrage of questions from her father.

Five

"I never saw that coming," Teddy said as she entered the kitchen a couple of minutes later.

Washing an apple at the sink, preparing to peel and core it for Alex, Alexander had regained his composure. Placing the knife he'd been using, along with the Granny Smith apple, on the cutting board, he turned and faced her. "I don't think either of us did. Look, Teddy, I'm sorry Alex witnessed that scene. But . . ."

Smiling, Teddy went to him and pulled him into her arms. "I'm the one who needs to apologize. I acted like a weakling when I got that letter. I broke down, when I should have been strong and confronted Adrian right away instead of putting it off because I didn't want to face him. That won't happen again."

She released him and looked up at him. "You were just being a protective father. Now it's my turn to step up to bat."

Alexander's formerly dour expression brightened when he heard the confident cadence to her voice. "Then you're okay, huh?"

"I'm better than okay, Daddy. Now that I know what Adrian is after, I can defend myself more effectively."

"And what exactly is he after?" His bushy brows shot up.

"He wants his life back," Teddy said with an incredulous note. "Can you believe it? He wants me to come back to him. He wants to play daddy. He wants to pretend the last three years never happened."

"Is he nuts, or what?" Alexander asked, his voice rising.

"He's definitely not hittin' on all cylinders," Teddy agreed with a laugh. "Not if he thinks I'd ever entertain the notion of going back to him."

Shaking his head in disbelief, Alexander regarded Teddy with a questioning expression on his face. "You ever give it any serious thought? What you'd do if he suddenly wanted you and Alex back?"

Teddy leaned against the counter, a pensive look fleetingly crossing her features. "I can't say that I haven't thought about it, Daddy." She met his eyes. "But in all these dream scenarios I imagined paying him back for everything he's put me through. He's the only man I've ever loved. He's also the only man who's ever hurt me that deeply. Go back to Adrian?" She pushed away from the counter, walking toward the door with the intention of going to check on Alex. "No, I'd never go back to him. And if it looked to you as if I were going to commit such a stupid act, you'd better have me committed, because I will have definitely lost my mind!"

Laughing, Alexander assured her, "Don't worry. I'd have you locked up and personally throw away the key before I'd let you do that."

Alexander watched his daughter's retreating back, his heart full. He wasn't sorry for trying to choke the life out of Adrian, but he regretted having his daughter and his grandson see him lose control in such a violent manner. By nature he was a peaceful man. He hadn't lost his temper with anyone in a very long time. Seeing the smug expression on Adrian's face, and then the glimmer of covetousness when he'd turned his gaze on Teddy, had made Alexander's blood pressure rise, and before he knew it, his hands were around Adrian's neck, squeezing.

Lord, don't let that man cause my daughter any more pain, he thought as he picked the apple up and started peeling it. *Otherwise I might have to finish what I started today.*

"I'll save you, R2-D2," Alex cried in imitation of C-3PO, the droid from *Star Wars* fame. He held an R2-D2 action figure in his right hand, and a C-3PO figure in his left.

Teddy stood in the doorway watching Alex as he acted out

yet again a scene he'd loved from *Star Wars: Episode I, The Phantom Menace.*

She had debated whether he was too young to enjoy the sci-fi epic, but she'd wanted to see it, and figured that if there were images in the film that she thought he shouldn't see, they could always leave. Alex had adored it. On the way home from the theater, he'd made noises reminiscent of the spaceships he'd seen on the screen—in his mind's eye, no doubt, the pilot of one of them.

In the last few months, Teddy had bought him every *Star Wars* action figure on the market, and he hadn't begun to tire of playing with them.

Alex's bedroom was small, with just a bed, a dresser, a nightstand, and a large toy box in the corner. His grandfather had painted Disney characters on one of the walls so Alex could enter dreamland with pleasant thoughts. His bedroom at home in San Francisco was larger, but looked much the same.

Teddy went and sat, crossed-legged, in front of Alex on the thick royal-blue carpeting. Alex smiled a greeting, and held the C-3PO figure up for his mother to see. "Mommy, C-PO"—he invariably left off the "3"—"broke his foot."

Teddy peered closely at the action figure. There was a small chip missing on its left heel. Squinting, she said, "A wound he sustained in the last skirmish probably. I'm sure Anakin Skywalker can fix him right up."

"Think so, Mommy?" He screwed up his face, thinking hard.

"Alex," Teddy said, pulling him into her lap, "I need to tell you something important."

Alex tilted his head up, his eyes studying her face.

Teddy paused, wondering how best to tell him the man he'd seen just moments ago was his father. *Father.* The man on TV. The man he saw in photographs whenever he visited Grandma and Grandpa Riley in their Nob Hill home. The man who must seem like a character in a story to him. He certainly couldn't have been real, this face he'd seen only in artificial images, never in the flesh.

Just this past year Alex, who sometimes noticed other small children in the arms of their daddies when his mother took him to the park, or to McDonald's, had begun to ask questions of his mother. Teddy had told him who his father was. She'd tried to explain the relationship between Adrian and Winston and Margaret Riley, telling him that, like he was her child, Adrian was theirs. She and Adrian had loved one another at one time, and produced him. Out of love. He was loved by them all. But how much of that could a two-year-old be expected to understand?

Teddy hugged Alex. She wouldn't tell him now. Not until she knew for certain that Adrian was sincere about being in Alex's life from now on. She didn't want to get Alex's hopes up, only to see them dashed.

"Mommy's going on a little trip, baby. She's going to a land far away called Ireland."

And then she told him everything she could remember about the country. How beautifully green it was due to the great amount of rain it received each year. She mimicked the accent for him, which drew a smile, and then she told him a fairy tale about a greedy leprechaun who, in his desire to guard his gold from others, became a lonely soul.

For some reason the leprechaun reminded her of herself. Could she be so busy trying to guard her heart that she wouldn't recognize true love when it presented itself to her? It had been three years since she'd made love to anyone—and she had to admit, she was beginning to wonder if she'd ever meet a man who would make her temperature rise and her libido-meter jump into the pleasure zone.

But, she thought as she looked down into the face of her son, *there are more important things in life than a man who sets your soul on fire.*

That night after putting Alex to bed and saying good night to her father, Teddy retired to the guest room.

After showering, she went back out to the bedroom, dressed in a short pink nighty. She'd placed all three of her bags—the shoulder bag with her personal effects in it, the valise which held her camera and related equipment, and the carry-on bag

with a couple changes of clothing in it—on the bed before
going to shower. Now she sat on the bed, opened the valise
and removed Joachim West's novel, *The God Gene.*

It was thick: 534 pages. The cover had a black background
and the picture of a nude, very well-built, black man with his
genitals concealed by a fig leaf. Were they trying to allude to
a comparison with the first man, Adam? A beautiful, eye-
catching cover. She'd probably pick it up if she saw it in a
bookstore.

Then she turned the book over, and on the back was a black-
and-white photograph of the author. Irina had been right, he
was way-cool looking. A square-jawed face with a broad forehead, chiseled features. He'd needed a shave. On some men
that might have looked unkempt, but it only made Joachim
West appear more masculine, rugged. He was smiling, and
there were deep dimples in both cheeks, his full, wide mouth
open, revealing straight, pearly teeth. A genuine smile. Teddy
had seen enough fake ones to tell the difference.

She drew her feet under her and scooted back on the bed,
reclining on several pillows. Opening the book to the dedica-
tion page, she read aloud, "For Suzanne." Then in a low voice,
asked, "Could Suzanne be his late wife?"

She turned the page and began reading then, and didn't
close the book until she'd reached page 107 and her eyes felt
too grainy to continue.

Yawning, she got up, set the bags on the floor and climbed
into bed. Tomorrow morning she'd be leaving at six, before
either her father or Alex awakened in order to have time to
drive back to San Francisco, and make the eleven o'clock
flight to London.

Joachim sat down at the computer in Conal's office, his
fingers flew over the keys and soon he was on-line. Not wild
about the Internet, even with the myriad forms of information
cyberspace offered, he checked his mail whenever he remembered, sometimes going days without logging on.

"You've got mail," the disembodied voice said.

After clicking on the open mailbox, six addresses and "in reference to" lines appeared. He didn't recognize the address of the first piece of mail, but he clicked on it anyway. It was a message from a computer software peddler. He deleted that one.

Next up was a message from Conal. *Erin and I are having a ball. Glad you're not here. Hope you're having one, too. Celia is really something, isn't she?*

Joachim laughed shortly. Celia. That's right, Celia O'Connell was supposed to be coming down from London some time this week. Maybe she wouldn't show up. Then again maybe she would and they'd have a good time together. She could be witty and lovely and an all-around wonderful woman. They could meet and immediately recognize in one another kindred spirits.

She could love books and long walks in the country. She could enjoy cooking on lazy Sunday afternoons. She probably loved old movies as much as he did. She . . .

He clicked on the next piece of mail and read. *Joachim, isn't it? I'm so sorry, but I've been unavoidably detained. I really can't say when I shall be free. Perhaps when you're in London, you can look me up. So sorry. Celia.*

"So much for that . . ." Joachim said aloud. He was relieved really. Now he could enjoy the rest of his stay in Ballycastle unencumbered by a female's presence. He ran a hand over the two days' growth of beard on his chin. If he wanted to, he could grow a full beard by the end of April. He'd return home looking like an entirely different man.

Teddy sat back in her seat in business class and flipped through the brochure she'd picked up on Northern Ireland and County Antrim, where the tiny village of Ballycastle was located.

So far she didn't have a seatmate and took advantage of the empty seat to her right by placing her shoulder bag in it.

She'd made it to the airport an hour before her flight. At the ticket desk, she'd presented the ticket Irina had provided and the woman behind the desk had looked at her, her green eyes a bit skeptical. "Ireland, huh?"

"It's business," Teddy had replied.

"Isn't it dangerous over there?" the ticket-taker had inquired, a frown creasing her brow.

"No more than over here, I suppose," Teddy said, accepting the ticket packet back.

Along with the tickets Babs had been kind enough to print out information on Ireland's present political status. It appeared that on May 22, 1998 a peace agreement for Northern Ireland had been ratified by voters in Ireland and Northern Ireland. They were in the process of forming a joint government, that hopefully would end the more than fifty-year-reign of violence between Protestants and Catholics. Of course, violence by groups opposed to the peace agreement remained a possibility.

The way Teddy looked at it, though, you had just as much chance of being mowed-down by gunfire on the streets of San Francisco as you did in Northern Ireland. She wasn't unduly concerned.

Now she got lost in the brochures, enjoying the photographs of the lush countryside. A photo of a farmer driving a cart being pulled by a Shetland pony, its shaggy mane a silky white. Thatch-roofed cottages. Thatched roofs! She hadn't seen a thatched roof since she was a child of ten and she and her father had spent nearly three months among the Masai in Kenya. Alexander had gotten an award-winning book out of the experience. Teddy had fallen in love with the people, especially the women, who did all the work in the village while the men concerned themselves with social and political matters. The women farmed, took care of their families. They were the backbone of the community. Teddy had learned how to grind corn, grow yams, shear sheep, build a hut, weave cloth, and dye it. She'd discerned at an early age that women were the foundation upon which the world was built.

"Hey, mind if I sit?" an Irish-accented, masculine voice said, breaking her reverie. Teddy peered up into a pair of smiling brown eyes. She removed her shoulder bag from the seat next to hers. "Sorry about that."

"No need to apologize," the man said as he sat. He grinned infectiously, revealing somewhat crooked, but white, teeth in a suntanned, angular face. His hair was long, falling to his shoulders, dark brown and extremely curly. Slender, almost to the point of thinness, he was wearing blue jeans and a long-sleeved Hunter's Run shirt in white. He wore a well-worn pair of brown hiker's boots. He placed his knapsack on the floor at his feet, then glanced at Teddy again and offered his hand. "Frankie Ahern of Dublin."

Smiling as they shook, Teddy said, "Teddy Riley of San Francisco. Good to meet you, Frankie."

"On your way to London, then?" Frankie asked, his eyes taking in the gentle slope of Teddy's lovely face. He liked her kind, trusting eyes which were the color of toasted almonds, he thought. And that mouth, so sensuous in its full-lipped perfection. He would love to sketch her.

"Ireland actually," Teddy said, momentarily holding the brochures up for him to see.

"You don't say! Dublin?"

"No, Ballycastle."

"Oh? That's in the boonies." He turned in his seat, his eyes more serious now. "I won't apologize for being nosy. Ballycastle is no place for a woman traveling alone. There may be one inn there, if that, and besides if you should get in trouble, it's nowhere near the Embassy. The Embassy's in Dublin."

"I'm not a tourist, I'm going on business. I wouldn't be going to Ballycastle at all if the person I need to speak with wasn't there."

Frankie regarded her with a touch of surprise in his depths. "Business?" His eyes raked over her casual attire of jeans, a denim shirt, and a pair of blue leather clogs. He smiled when he noted the multicolored knit hat sitting at a flirty angle on her head. He liked her style.

"You don't look much like a businesswoman."

"Well, here you are in business class and you look so laid

back, you're liable to fall asleep at the drop of a hat," Teddy accused lightly.

"Oh, these," Frankie said dismissively, a big hand waving away her comment. "I'm dressed like this because I've been on vacation. I'm a stockbroker by trade. Monday through Friday, I'm on the trading floor with a phone glued to my ear. Weekends, I pursue my one true love: the blues. I came to America on my two-week vacation to go to the places I've always dreamed of: Mississipi, for the Delta blues, New Orleans to visit Preservation Hall, St. Louis, where the blues were reputed to have been born. And last night I had the privilege of being in the front row at a Keb' Mo' concert. He's an up-and-coming blues man to be reckoned with."

"I love him!" Teddy exclaimed.

" 'Slow Down,' " Frankie said, giving the title of a favorite Keb' Mo' song.

" 'Tell Everybody I Know,' " Teddy countered, grinning and turning in her seat to face him.

" 'Angelina,' " Frankie challenged, smirking.

" 'Muddy Water,' " Teddy said confidently.

" 'Well, if I never get to heaven,' " Frankie sang in a passably bluesy voice, " 'I don't care . . .' "

" 'I've been down to the crossroads, and ain't no devil down there,' " Teddy sang in a clear, true alto.

Frankie laughed. "You've got a good voice."

Teddy smiled her thanks, liking this interesting Irishman even more. "It won't keep food on the table, but I love singing. It gives me—"

"Joy!" Frankie answered for her. He bent forward in his seat and rummaged in his bag for a moment, coming out with a Keb' Mo' CD. He handed it to her. "Here, it's his latest. I'd like you to have it."

"No, I can't take yours," Teddy protested.

"Go ahead," Frankie urged her. "I bought two."

Joachim awoke with a start. He sat up in bed, the darkened room foreign to him initially. Then he remembered, he wasn't in his familiar bedroom in San Francisco, but in one of the guest rooms in Conal's home. His heartbeat slowed to normal. He was glad he'd come out of that one. The dream had been mystic in its power to entrance him: he and Suzanne, spending a blissful afternoon in Golden Gate Park. They'd had a picnic, a stroll, shared a kiss in the midst of the Shinto gardens.

Then suddenly the park was a cemetery, and when he looked around him, he knew no one. Cloaked in black, hoods drawn over their faces. In shadows. The only thing that had color was the bronze coffin Suzanne lay in. Suzanne, looking healthy, vibrant unlike any dead person he'd ever seen. Any moment she would open her eyes and spring out of there into his arms.

But she didn't—and then two men, he knew they were men only because their arms were muscled and hairy like men's arms. Those arms, from within black shrouds, began shoveling inky, damp earth onto Suzanne. Soiling her white dress. Was that her wedding gown? Now in her face. He expected her to frown and brush the dirt off. She slumbered on.

"No!" he shouted, shoving one then the other shovel-wielding man aside. "Stop it! Stop it, she's not dead. Can't you see she's alive?"

Two more black-shrouded figures came forward and each grabbed him by an arm. The previous two men continued shoveling the dirt onto Suzanne, not bothering to close the lid of the coffin.

Joachim struggled to free himself, but they held him with a supernatural strength. Then the coffin began sinking. It sank six feet, then nine. It kept sinking until, when they allowed him to peek over the edge, he could see nothing except a patch of white that had to be Suzanne's dress.

A voice next to his ear said, "Let her go, son." He could have sworn it was his grandma Eva's.

Now as he sat in the dark, he wished letting Suzanne go were that easy. A word or two whispered in his ear, and he could release the grief, let it fall from his heart, allow the pain to seep from his bones and sinews. Be free of the what-ifs. What if we'd caught the cancer in time? What if the operation had been a success? What if we'd had children? At least a part of Suzanne would have survived.

He rose and went into the adjacent bathroom, turned the water on and doused the burning in his face. Looking at his reflection in the mirror, into his haunted eyes, he thought, *This isn't living.*

After dinner and more conversation, Teddy found herself deprived of her seatmate's company because Frankie, aided by two glasses of white wine, fell asleep, his head against the wall, snoring softly.

Teddy didn't drink while flying, she'd found it only made her jet lag worse; besides, alcohol rarely relaxed her, it stimulated her and made her hyper. She was already nervous about being able to convince Joachim West to give her an interview and allow her to photograph him there in his Irish retreat. Apparently Joachim West avoided the media circus like the plague. In the *Time* article she'd read, the reporter noted that he'd had to make do with a publicity shot provided by the author's publishing company, and a telephone interview, which, the reporter said, West had been coerced into doing by his publisher. And *Time* was one of the top news magazines in the nation. A serious periodical. Joachim West might look upon *Contemporary Lives,* although a reputable, perfectly legitimate entertainment magazine, as a tabloid.

Picking up his book, and beginning to read where she'd left off, Teddy couldn't help wondering what kind of man had written such powerful words. She'd become engrossed in the story from the first sentence, which was, *Dr. Simeon Temple wasn't the type of man to readily accept culpability.*

Teddy relaxed in her seat, her mind in the story, following Dr. Temple as he tried to stop the creature he has created from killing again. No, Dr. Temple didn't want to accept blame for cloning a murderer, but by the close of chapter eight, Teddy could see that the good doctor has no choice but to own up to his part in bringing Darien, the clone, into a world he is ill-equipped to function in. Dr. Temple wound up enlisting the

aid of police detective, Amanda Summers, in tracking down
Darien.

Teddy liked the character of Amanda Summers. Amanda
was smart, tough, and didn't take guff from anyone.

As Teddy eased on into chapter nine, she wondered if
Amanda and Dr. Simeon Temple would get romantically involved. She'd noticed the way Simeon looked at Amanda
when he thought the detective's attention was elsewhere.
Amanda, one intuitive cookie, always caught him watching.
But Amanda was all work and no play. She kept her focus on
the case. Teddy had no doubt Amanda would find Darien. But
what would happen when she did? Darien was extremely
cagey. The way he'd lured and killed the four victims, some
male, some female, had left few clues behind as to the nature
of the killer. If he hadn't left a message, scrawled on the wall
in the victims' blood, Dr. Temple wouldn't have known it was
his clone who'd been committing the atrocious murders in and
around Seattle, Washington. The words were, *A gift for my
father.*

Teddy read straight through the remainder of the flight,
devouring the pages swiftly in her eagerness to find out what
would happen next.

At one point Frankie awakened, smiled at her. She smiled
back but didn't say a word, hoping he'd go back to sleep so
she could finish the book. He did, for which she was grateful.
She read on.

Finally she finished the last page, and sat there exhausted
yet strangely exhilarated. What kind of book was it? A thriller?
Yes, definitely, but like no thriller she'd ever read. A suspense
novel? Sure it had kept her on the edge of her seat throughout,
but it was more than a suspense novel. A mystery? Undoubtedly. It had all the elements of a good mystery. A puzzle that
isn't solved until the very end. A villain so vile, you tend to
cringe whenever he's described in the pages of the book. West
had also posed questions that she wondered if anyone was
capable of answering, such as: Even though man has the ability to create himself, should he? Science and technology had
put man nearly on a par with God. There used to be only one

Creator. Now scientists were manufacturing living creatures in labs. Armed with this knowledge, how far would man go with it? And there would always be a scientist out there, like Dr. Simeon Temple, who in his arrogance would go that extra mile. It was a chilling thought.

Teddy turned the book over and studied Joachim's photograph. She was more intrigued than ever with the elusive author. Now she wanted to meet him, even if he didn't give her the interview.

Frankie awoke, stretched and smiled at Teddy. "Hey, when are they going to feed us, I'm starved."

"You've already eaten, then promptly went to sleep," Teddy told him, her brown eyes alight with humor.

"Well, that's gone now," Frankie said, his hand on his flat stomach. "I'm a growing boy."

He looked up and saw a flight attendant walking down the aisle in their direction. "Miss, what happened to those peanuts you all used to pass out to famished travelers?"

The flight attendant, a petite brunette with dark eyes and a ready grin, giggled. "Sir, I'd be happy to fetch you a packet." She stood in the aisle, addressing her next question to everyone within hearing. "Would anyone else like a bag of peanuts and a cold drink?"

About thirty hands immediately shot up.

On Thursday morning Joachim and William, having started out early, already had their makeshift camp set up by nine. Joachim, this time sitting on a folding chair on the bank, had the pole propped on his thigh, his grip relaxed. Fish sensed when you were tense. His Zen philosophy of angling.

The day was on the chilly side, but the sky was blue and the sun, bright. Joachim couldn't have asked for a more perfect day. Besides, it'd been his experience that fish bite better on brisk days rather than warm ones.

So far William, assuming his normal stance on the bank, feet set apart for maximum balance, face turned toward the sky, eyes closed, had caught three nice-size breams and a pike that had made the taciturn fisherman utter an expletive, it'd put up such a fight.

Joachim had added another couple of breams to their catch. Joachim glanced at his watch: eleven thirteen. They'd agreed to call it a day by noon, William had some gardening to get to and he wanted to venture out to Slemish Mountain after lunch. The seven-hundred-foot-high extinct volcano had been visited by pilgrims on Saint Patrick's Day for centuries. It was there that Saint Patrick was supposed to have spent several years of his youth, after being captured by Irish slave traders.

Since getting to the word processor and actually writing hadn't yet become a bona fide urge, a bit of sightseeing would help pass the time. After Slemish Mountain, he was thinking of going to have a look at the Giant's Causeway. It was only about sixteen kilometers from Ballycastle. It would be a shame to be that close to the geological wonder and not go see it. Legend had it that the Giant's Causeway was built by giants to enable them to step across the water from Ireland to Scotland. The basaltic, hexagonal columns actually did look like steps, and visitors to the site could walk on them, observe the sea while standing on them. But the thirty-eight thousand hexagonal columns were actually the result of molten lava being cooled about seventy million years ago.

Joachim felt a strong jerk on his line. He abruptly stood, his booted feet sinking a little in the mud as he moved closer to the edge of the river.

Yes, he had another bite. The line tightened as the fish tried to swim away with the hook and bait in its mouth. He let the line move away from him, and then he felt it, the exact moment when the fish realized it was caught. Joachim began moving backward, pulling up on the line as he did so.

When the fish came out of the water, he saw that it was young, barely six inches long. He planted the end of the pole in the soft earth and retrieved the net next to the cooler. Going to scoop the fish into the net, he reached in, firmly grasped the wriggling critter in his hand, gently removed the hook and tossed the fish back into the Tow River. "Maybe I'll see you next year, buddy."

It was dark out by the time the plane landed in Dublin. Frankie made a valiant effort to convince her to stay overnight in his hometown before venturing on to Ballycastle. After failing in the attempt, he insisted on accompanying her to the train station and making sure she got on the right train to Ballycastle.

When Teddy saw the traffic and heard the blaring horns of the cars, trucks, buses, and motorbikes on the congested road, she was grateful for his company.

They sat in the back of the taxi, Frankie pointing out interesting landmarks. Eighteenth-century canals ran straight through the heart of the city. Streets, more often than not, full of motorists, were built over them.

Teddy was captivated by the Georgian terraces of the houses they passed. "We have homes dating back to the seventeenth century," Frankie told her with a note of pride.

Teddy noticed he'd slipped his arm about her shoulders. The taxi was small, but there was plenty of room for the both of them.

She scooted closer to the window on her side, exclaiming, "What is that, a theater?" The well-illuminated building took up a city block, boasting baroque architecture and intricate decorative touches from several other eras.

"No," Frankie answered, a smile on his lips. "That's a part of Trinity College. The library, I believe."

"It's huge," Teddy said. She looked up into Frankie's eyes, her gaze more serious. "Frankie, don't you have anyone expecting you?"

Frankie sat back on the seat, sighing quietly. "There was someone, but we broke up about a year ago. She got a job offer in London and didn't see any point in continuing our relationship. It didn't matter to her that I saw plenty of reasons . . ."

Teddy placed a comforting hand atop his. "I'm sorry."

Frankie's brown eyes were smiling again. "It's her loss, right? Me? I'm a wonderful catch, as my mother keeps telling me. One day, she says, some girl is going to luck out when she gets me."

"Absolutely," Teddy agreed.

Frankie grasped the hand that she'd placed atop his, and held on to it. "I'm very attracted to you, Teddy Riley." His eyes searched hers. "It's not just the fact that you like the blues, it's the feeling I get when I'm near you, as if something wonderful is about to happen, and the expectation of that upcoming event hangs in the air, teasing me, enticing me."

"If you get any more poetic, I'm going to pull out me violin," the taxi driver said with a laugh.

They'd momentarily forgotten the driver.

"Ignore him," Frankie said, not in the least embarrassed. "What do you say, Teddy? Is there a chance that we'll, as the song says . . . meet again?"

Teddy considered his question. It wasn't that she didn't find Frankie attractive, because he was. And she liked his sense of humor, definitely liked his taste in music and his funky style of dressing. He'd kept her interest throughout the flight from San Francisco; not once had she wished she'd gotten another seatmate.

But as for that spark she looked for when meeting a man who awakened her romantic side, no, Frankie didn't do it for her. She saw no reason, however, to openly rebuff him. What were the chances of her coming back to Ireland after getting the interview with Joachim West? And on the average stockbroker's salary, Frankie wouldn't be visiting the States on a too-regular basis.

So she smiled at him and said, "I don't see why not."

Frankie quickly brought her hand up and kissed the palm. "I wish you'd stay over, at least one night. There's a club I think you'd enjoy, and restaurants . . . Dublin has some of the best restaurants in the British Isles."

"I really can't," Teddy said regretfully. She'd told him about Alex and how she didn't want to be away from him too long. She hadn't told him, however, about Adrian, and her fears that

If she didn't take him back—which she wasn't going to—he'd make trouble for her.

Sure he'd said he had no intention of suing her for custody of Alex, but there was no telling how he'd react when it finally sank in that she wasn't going to come back to him. Not after everything she'd gone through in the past three years.

At the train station Frankie pressed his business card in her palm. "It has my address, my phone number, fax, e-mail address, and my beeper number," he told her. "You will be able to get me . . . if you want to." He'd ended on a hopeful note, his whiskey-colored eyes looking deeply into hers.

Teddy had given him her card, too.

"And if you should get into trouble," Frankie shouted as he ran along the station platform, the train slowly pulling away, "don't hesitate to call me, I'll come."

Teddy stood looking down at him, wondering why some girl wasn't waiting at home for Frankie Ahern. "I will," she promised him, and waved one last time as the train picked up speed, leaving him behind.

She turned and walked down the aisle, looking for a seat. It seemed that all eyes were on her. But she knew she was simply feeling self-conscious because she was the only black person in the passenger car. She supposed it was normal for people to stare when faced with the strange and unusual. She was an alien in this land. She found two empty seats in the middle section and stowed her heavier bags in the overhead compartment and kept the shoulder bag on her lap. In front of her a toddler with rosy cheeks and big gray eyes grinned at her, two bottom teeth in its otherwise pink-gummed mouth. She smiled back and settled into the surprisingly comfortable seat. She hadn't realized how weary she was. The tiredness brought on morose thoughts. Why had Adrian chosen this time to reenter their lives? If it wasn't for him, she would be with Alex, probably frolicking on the beach, seashell hunting. Now here she was, in Ireland, in a desperate attempt to speak with a man who would probably take one look at her and give her a resounding no. No, he wouldn't give her an interview.

What difference did it make to him that she'd come halfway around the world just to see him?

Teddy yawned and closed her eyes, just for a moment.

The next thing she knew, the train was pulling into the station in Ballycastle. She rose, stretching her legs, then she reached up for her valise and carry-on bag that she'd stowed in the overhead compartment. They were there. She breathed a sigh of relief. She hadn't meant to fall asleep. And having no traveling companion who could watch her belongings while she snoozed, there had been the possibility that when she awakened, her bags could have been pilfered by some sneak thief.

Her bags firmly in hand and the shoulder bag's strap across her chest so she wouldn't have to worry about it slipping from her shoulder while she struggled with the heavier bags, she moved into the aisle behind the mother of the toddler, who was still watching her with wide-eyed innocence.

A few minutes later she walked out of the station into the night. When her plane had left San Francisco, it had been 11:10 A.M. In Ireland it had been 4:10 P.M. Now nine hours later it was a few minutes past 1 A.M.

One A.M., in a small village in Ireland. Would she even be able to get a taxi at this hour? Was it safe to walk the streets? Turning back around, she looked toward the small depot entrance. Would there be someone on duty at the ticket office?

There had been perhaps thirteen passengers getting off at Ballycastle. They'd all dispersed by now, either having been met by friends or loved ones, or in the case of a couple of late commuters, gotten into their cars and driven off.

As she was walking toward the ticket booth, she heard someone cough. Turning, she saw an elderly gentleman round the corner and walk purposefully in the direction of the ticket booth.

Assuming he worked there, Teddy said, "Excuse me, sir?"

He was short and stoop-shouldered, his gait slow and deliberate. Teddy met him halfway.

He squinted at her. "Traveling late, ain't ya?"

"Yes," Teddy agreed, smiling. "I was wondering if there was any possibility of my getting a taxi."

He laughed, a kind of cough really, but she detected glee in there somewhere. She'd obviously said something humorous.

With a rheumy-eyed stare, the old fellow said, "No taxis out this late. They stop running at eleven. Where ya going? Could be you're within walking distance."

"Susan's Inn," Teddy told him, remembering the name of the inn at which Babs had phoned ahead and reserved a room for her. There weren't many places in Ballycastle where tourists could spend the night.

"Oh, that ain't far," the fount of local knowledge told her as he wiped the matter out of the corner of his left eye. He looked at it on his finger. "Just go straight out the door yonder and turn right. Go a while until you see a three-story house, trimmed in green. You can't miss it. There's a sign out front."

"Thank you," Teddy said, inwardly sighing. Exactly how far would "go a while" take her? Two blocks? Six? A mile down the road? The old gentleman began his slow trek across the room to the ticket booth. "Uh . . . mmm, would that be a few blocks, or a bit farther?" Teddy asked.

"A bit farther," he replied, as though the notion of being more specific had never entered his mind.

Well, that's better, Teddy thought. *That clears it right up for me.* Convinced she wasn't going to get anything else out of him, she said, "Thank you," and headed for the exit.

"Oh," he said, as an afterthought, "watch out for stray dogs. They roam at night, ya know."

"I'll be sure to do that," Teddy murmured, now more apprehensive than ever about entering the darkness. She should have taken Frankie's suggestion and spent the night in a hotel in Dublin. At least there she would have had a warm bath, a bed, and maybe a bite to eat. At the rate things were going tonight, she might end up some ravenous beast's dinner. When Babs had made these travel arrangements, she apparently hadn't taken into consideration the different time zones. No use blaming Babs. She should have paid more attention. But she'd been preoccupied with personal matters. She could kick Adrian.

Coming off the last step from the railway depot platform, Teddy surveyed the night sky. Not even a quarter moon to help light her way.

Six

The smell of the sea was in the air. Having always loved the sea, Teddy took that as a positive sign. She'd gone three blocks along the darkened streets, passing shops with quaint names like Ye Olde Butcher Block, Kate's Bakery, and The Rose and The Thorn. The latter had a picture of an overflowing beer stein on its handpainted sign, so she guessed it was a tavern. Even the bars closed at a decent hour in Ballycastle.

She picked up her pace a bit, the wooden heels of her leather clogs playing a lively staccato on the cobblestone street. She listened for any noise. Except for the sound of her footfalls, she heard only the steady rhythm of her own breathing.

She was thankful she'd brought her down jacket, the one with the hood. The temperature was in the thirties, plus the air was damp, either from the sea mist or it had rained earlier in the evening.

Suddenly Teddy heard the sound of a flute. A thin, reedy song, played merrily; a reel, probably. She could imagine Irish dancers performing a jig to that jaunty tune.

Pausing in her steps, she looked around her. A streetlamp was burning every three blocks. She walked in the middle of the abandoned street, keeping away from the shadows of the alleys. Now she turned all around, checking out the shadows, wondering if some trickster were following her movements from a hiding place deep in the darkness.

The music continued, beautifully played by the lone flutist. Then the tempo changed. Where it had been lighthearted and joyous, it became somber and dark. A funeral dirge. Teddy had been about to speak out and challenge him to show himself, but this new tune seemed ominous. She wasn't foolish enough to antagonize anyone who enjoyed striking fear in the hearts of perfect strangers.

Then her thoughts took her back to the old fellow at the train depot. Could he have followed her to play a prank? When he'd admonished her to watch out for stray dogs, she'd seen a glimmer of mischief in his rheumy eyes. Blowing air between her lips, Teddy angrily turned and stared in the direction of the depot. She expected to see the man framed in the doorway, a flute in an arthritic hand. There was no one behind her.

Throwing caution to the wind, she called, "All right! Whoever you are, just knock it off. I'm not some superstitious yokel who just fell off the turnip truck! You've had your fun. Get going!"

She waited for a reply. Just in case some hulking figure appeared before her, she slowly placed her carry-on bag on the street next to her leg. If she had to sprint, she didn't want to leave behind the camera equipment and her shoulder bag with her passport and other important ID in it. The shoulder bag's strap was across her chest. She gripped the handle of the valise tightly in her right hand.

The flutist continued the dirge. The tune, so mournful and grief-filled that she felt chills run up her spine.

"You're wonderful, really. You should be in a band," Teddy said, talking to ease the tension. "Not out here playing to an audience of one."

No sound, save her breathing. She stood a moment longer, searching the area around her for movement. Nothing. "I'm leaving now. Thank you for the free concert. I enjoyed it. We must do it again sometime."

She reached down and collected the carry-on bag with her left hand. She walked swiftly now, not looking behind her, single-mindedly pushing on in spite of the weak-kneed sensation in her legs.

Six blocks later she'd broken into a sweat by the time she spied the lit sign at Susan's Inn. She ran up the steps, onto the porch and tried the doorknob. The door was locked. She shook the knob, then came to her senses. This was a small town. Susan—if that was the proprietor's name, maybe the Susan of Susan's Inn was a long-dead ancestor—probably rarely had a full house. Her guests certainly didn't arrive in the dead of night. Perspiring from having nearly run there; terrified out of their minds by an anonymous prankster with a talent for reed instruments.

Her hand shook as she pushed the doorbell.

She stood with her back to the door, watching the street.

Five agonizing minutes later, she thought she heard someone walking toward the door. A curtain was moved away from the window next to the door. A white face peered out at her.

"I'm sorry, but we're full up," a woman's voice, and none-too-friendly, either, called.

"I have a reservation," Teddy shouted, not caring if she woke the entire house. She knocked on the door. "The name's Teddy Riley. I'm an American. Let me in, I think some flute-playing crazy is following me."

"Oh, that's just George." Then "Teddy Riley? I've been expecting you." She hastily unlocked the door and flung it open. Teddy didn't have to be invited in. Her host was tall and thin, with short red hair stuffed under a sleeping cap. She was attired in a pale yellow chenille robe and her feet were bare. Glancing down at her feet, then back up at Teddy, she asked, "Whatever possessed you to travel at such an hour? Come in, come in!"

The woman switched on the light next to the door. Her dark blue eyes didn't register surprise when she focused on Teddy's face. "So you've met our George. You look none the worse for wear . . ."

She reached for Teddy's carry-on bag. "Let me help you."

Teddy gave her the bag, and the older woman turned toward the stairs. "This way." She paused on the third step, looking down at Teddy. "I'm Susan. We're informal around here. This is my home. It's been in the family for six generations. I'm the last of the MacLaretys. Never married, rich or otherwise. So I let rooms to help keep the house and myself going." With that said, she resumed climbing the stairs. "There are five rooms, all of them are taken. You'll meet the other guests tomorrow morning at breakfast. I serve three meals a day. Buffet style. And if you have a care to lend a hand in the kitchen, it's always appreciated. We don't stand on ceremony around here. Breakfast's at eight. Midday meal's at noon or thereabouts. Supper starts at six." She stopped again. Teddy almost ran into her. Her keen eyes studied Teddy's face. "Scared you, did he?"

Teddy tried to shrug it off. After all, she was safe and sound. So what if she'd been the victim of the town fool's sick sense of humor.

"I'm fine, really," she said. All she wanted now was a sandwich, a bath, and a warm bed. In that order. The perspiration had already begun to dry on her skin.

Susan chortled. "You're better than most," she genuinely complimented Teddy. "Most of the folks who've encountered George in the last seventy-odd years have been nervous wrecks for days afterward."

"Seventy years?" Teddy asked incredulously, her curiosity piqued. "You mean he's some old guy who's been pulling that prank on the townspeople since he was a kid? Hasn't anyone ever tried to have him arrested or something?"

Susan laughed harder, putting a hand over her mouth, mindful she had sleeping guests upstairs. "Dear, how are they going to lock up a ghost? I daresay he could walk right through the bars."

It was Teddy's turn to laugh. "Oh, now it's 'pull the leg of the gullible American' time, right? You don't expect me to believe that was a ghost?"

"Come on, Teddy Riley, nice Irish name you've got there. I'll show you to your room, then get you something to eat. You're hungry, aren't you? You look like you could use a thick roast beef sandwich."

Teddy's stomach rumbled. A roast beef sandwich sounded good about now.

The room was nicely decorated in rose chintz. It had an old-fashioned Victorian look to it. Teddy sat on the bed. The mattress was firm, which bode well for a good night's sleep.

"This is lovely." She smiled at Susan.

"Much better than one of those big, impersonal hotels," Susan said. "Of course, there are none of those around here." She moved about the room, her eyes lovingly resting on the antique furnishings. "My grandmother brought these pieces from Belfast when she married my grandfather in 1928." A faraway expression softened her angular features. "Those were the days, weren't they? When men and women stated their intentions clearly and there was no game-playing. My grandfather took one look at my grandmother, said, 'I want you for my wife.' And she said, 'It's a deal, let's make a life.' Now that's romantic!"

Susan snapped out of her daydreaming, "I promised you a sandwich, didn't I? You want to come downstairs, or would you rather put your things away, and I'll bring up a tray?"

"No, I'll come downstairs," Teddy offered, energized now that she'd found shelter and a friendly face.

She rose, following Susan out of the room.

On the landing Susan whispered, "I'm sorry your first experience in our town had to be with George. He's mischievous, but really quite harmless. Although he once made a fellow drive his car into a ditch one night a few years past. George materialized right in front of him. He swerved to miss him, and ran into a water-filled ditch. Thankfully he wasn't injured. When he got out to offer aid to the person he was sure he'd run over, there was no one there. Spooked the fellow so badly, he stopped drinking and took up the cloth."

Teddy enjoyed Susan's tale. Fanciful or not, it was an interesting anecdote. An alcoholic transformed by a mystical occurrence. It was the stuff that myths were made of. No wonder Ireland was known for hair-raising stories about banshees, leprechauns, and fairies.

"Then George did the fellow a world of good," Teddy said reasonably. "Getting him to quit the bottle like that and become a minister."

"I suppose you're right," Susan said, laughing softly. "Unfortunately for me, he was the last beau I had. Now he's devoted to the church and I'm left a shriveled-up old maid."

Unsure of what to say to that, Teddy followed Susan the rest of the way to the large eat-in kitchen in silence.

Once there Susan went to the refrigerator and removed sandwich makings. Placing them on the counter, she invited Teddy to wash up at the kitchen sink and join her.

A few moments later they were standing side by side constructing tall roast beef sandwiches made with lettuce, tomatoes, onions, and mustard.

They sat across from one another and began eating, washing the delicious sandwiches down with Diet Cokes.

"Mmm," Teddy said, "this hits the spot. Thank you."

Susan smiled at her and wiped a bit of mustard from her chin with her pinkie. "No need for that. I'm trying to put on a few pounds, so I take every opportunity I get to eat something."

She took another bite of her sandwich. Her gaze rested on Teddy's face. "Care to share why you're here? I can assure you, I take the privacy of my guests seriously. So if you don't want anyone else knowing, my lips are zipped." She moved her thumb and forefinger across her lips as though she were zipping them closed.

Teddy gave a short laugh. "I'm not a spy or anything so glamorous. I'm a photojournalist. Here on assignment hoping to interview writer Joachim West, who, I'm told, is here in Ballycastle somewhere."

Susan's eyes glittered with delight. "He's not somewhere here in Ballycastle, he's staying at his friend Conal Ryan's Georgian home about a mile east of here. It's close to the sea. A lovely spot, really. I was just there a few days ago when Conal married his American love, Erin Donagal. It was a wonderful celebration."

Teddy had sat up straighter in her chair, regarding Susan with respect. The woman was up on her gossip. She couldn't believe her luck—Joachim West falling in her lap like this.

Susan kept talking. "That wasn't you who phoned to make reservations, was it?"

"No," Teddy answered. "That was my boss's secretary."

"Very professional," Susan complained lightly. "I couldn't

get any information out of her aside from the credit card number, of course. You can stay for as long as you like. The bill's taken care of. I hope you'll stay a while. The porch could use a new coat of paint."

Teddy laughed. "There's no telling how long I'll be here. Mr. West could be a hard nut to crack. He isn't fond of newshounds."

Susan leaned forward and said with a conspiratorial note to her voice, "He'd be a delightful nut to crack, though. You married, Teddy?"

"Divorced."

"The reason I ask is, I was in his presence only for a few minutes—I met him at the reception—but I wanted to drag him off somewhere private, you know what I mean? Loads of sex appeal has our Mr. West. Charming, too. If our constable, Liam Murdoch, hadn't monopolized him the entire afternoon, I'm sure I could have had him over here for dinner or something by now," Susan finished regretfully.

Teddy sat digesting the sandwich and Susan's words, which were harder to stomach. And why should she be slightly irritated to hear an attractive woman go on and on about Joachim West's physical attributes? Had reading his book and spending more time than was necessary gazing at his photo on the back of it put ideas in her head? Romantic notions about the author? *No,* she told herself. *You just stop it now, Theodora. You have to be hard as nails where Joachim West is concerned. Don't go getting soft on me now, girl. Get that interview, by hook or by crook!*

"Well," she said to Susan, who was tearing into her sandwich with vigor. "I'm really looking forward to meeting Mr. West. I'll get on it first thing in the morning."

"Oh, take me with you!" Susan cried with her mouth full, managing to look, for all the world, like a teenaged groupie.

Adrian stood outside the home he'd just, for all intents and purposes, purchased for himself, Teddy, and Alex. All that needed doing now was for the both of them to sign the papers.

The house sat on a meticulously manicured lawn, surrounded by wooded pedestrian paths that he knew Teddy was going to love using. A stroll with Alex. Maybe it'd even become a Saturday morning tradition. A way to work off his homemade pancakes. He wasn't as familiar with the kitchen as he should be, but he could flip hotcakes with the best of them.

Adrian backed up farther, trying to encompass the entire house in his view. The two-story home was built four years ago by a local politician who'd recently been elected to Congress. Adrian had gotten a good deal on it. Six thousand square feet. Vaulted ceilings, oak moldings, Mexican tile on the kitchen floor. Teddy loved Mexican tile. A Jacuzzi in the master bath, and a sauna adjacent to the pool out back. He would spare no expense on redecorating their haven.

That's where Teddy came in. He couldn't very well decorate the house without her input. He'd already purchased it without consulting her first. He knew she'd always liked the Russian Hill area though, so that fact was on his side. Still if he knew Teddy, and he thought he did, she would let him have it for not discussing the purchase before adding her name to the deed. It was presumptuous of him, of course. But he was confident Teddy still loved him.

He walked around to the south side of the house, where the past gardener had planted portulaca. He avoided stepping on the low-growing plants. The gardener had put in several colors: purple, white, and yellow. The flowers were too small for Adrian's tastes. He liked roses, something with a fragrance. He made a mental note to have his gardener put in a rose garden.

Walking on, he came to the pool area. Pausing to squat and run his hand in the clear, blue water, he allowed it to strain through his fingers. Thinking of gardens had made him recall the last night he and Teddy had spent together. Just before they'd made love, he'd told her she smelled like a flower garden in springtime.

Frowning, he stood and turned his back to the pool. He had a lot to atone for. Moments before making love, she'd been

the sweetest thing on this earth to him. Then she'd confessed
to being pregnant and he'd felt his world crumble. After that
all he'd wanted to do was wash her scent off him. He'd been
cruel. He hadn't been able to be flexible enough to see Teddy's
viewpoint, to try to empathize with her. She'd been afraid, too.
He could see it in her big, brown eyes. And the hurt he'd
caused when he'd told her to get rid of their child. If he could,
he would take back that night. Wipe it from her memory forever.

Why couldn't he accept the baby two years ahead of schedule? Selfish. Selfish and cruel.

"Hello!" a feminine voice called from around the corner
of the house. Adrian looked up and saw Julia Greene, the real
estate agent who'd helped him find the house, walking toward
him, her shining blond hair floating after her in the breeze.

The sun reflected off the silver briefcase she held aloft for
him to see. "I've got those papers for you and your wife to
sign," she told him, smiling.

Wife? Adrian thought. That's right, he hadn't explained to
Julia that he and Teddy were divorced. It was just a technicality
in his estimation. He'd rectify the situation soon enough.

Julia, who prided herself on being able to read her clients,
took Adrian's long pause as an indication of a problem lurking
somewhere, just waiting to mess up her deal. "She likes the
house, doesn't she?" It wouldn't be the first time a deal had
fallen through because one of the partners decided the property wouldn't do for some aesthetic reason or other. Nothing
to do with function or style. She might not like the color on
the bathroom walls. Well, lady, that's what paint's for!

"No, no," Adrian said in conciliatory tones. "It's just that
my wife," there, he'd said it, "is a photojournalist and she's
presently on assignment in Ireland." He'd learned that much
from the spy on his payroll at *Contemporary Lives.* He had
to keep tabs on Teddy, didn't he? Winning her back would be
a delicate operation. He needed all the help he could get.

"No problem at all," he reiterated, moving closer to Julia
and placing his hand at the small of her back, directing her in
the direction of the patio door. "Why don't I buy you lunch

as thanks for taking the time out of your busy day to come all
the way out here? I'm famished. Do you have time?"

Julia brightened considerably. Their eyes met in the sunshine. Adrian smiled warmly, but he was weary of seeing that
expression in the eyes of lonely females. A kind of wistful
expectation that invariably put the man on guard. They put
their need out there for all the world to see. Maybe it was an
involuntary response to kindness from the male sex. Women
were so used to men lying to them, taking them for granted,
that at the first indication of kindness in a man, they allowed
their desires to be transmitted through their eyes, which, if
the proverb was correct, were the window of the soul.

He'd buy her lunch and treat her to a long, detailed description of Teddy, the only woman he wanted coming on to him.
Teddy however, was under the misapprehension that what they
had was best left in the past. He would help her to realize that
he was the only man for her. They'd be a real family, the three
of them. Living perfect lives in their perfect home. It was only
a matter of time. He'd learned to be patient. If it took Teddy
a while to get used to having him back in her life, that was
okay. He'd wait.

Teddy decided to take a walking tour of Ballycastle before
getting a taxi to take her to Conal Ryan's home on the outskirts
of town. She wanted to see what the tiny burg looked like in
daylight.

She started out soon after helping Susan with the breakfast
dishes, at which time Susan regaled her with the history of
Ballycastle and cautioned her to keep her eyes open—there
had been a rash of purse snatchings in the area recently. Teen
boys, from the description the victims gave the constable.

It was a sunny day, she'd dressed warmly in a pair of jeans,
a corduroy shirt, her clogs, and the down jacket. Although
with the warmth from the sun high overhead, she was debating
taking the jacket off. Carrying her shoulder bag and a camera,
on its strap around her neck, she looked every bit the tourist.

The locals gave her curious glances, but nothing hostile in

their demeanor. Some even smiled and said a cheery, "Mornin'," to which Teddy always replied, "Good morning, lovely day, isn't it?"

Outside the butcher shop, Ye Olde Butcher Block, a woman engaged her in conversation. Teddy was pleasantly surprised by how talkative the woman was. She was petite; her hair was short, brown with gray streaks, and her eyes were medium brown. A beige canvas shopping bag was in her right hand. She had on varying shades of brown: a knit sweater over a brown dress and tan flats.

"You're new in town, then?" she asked Teddy. Her eyes raked over Teddy's face. There was an excited aspect to them that made Teddy wonder why meeting a stranger on the street had delighted her so.

"Yes," Teddy said, meeting the woman's gaze. "My first day." Looking around them, she added, "Lovely eighteenth-century architecture you have here."

"Oh, some of it dates back to the seventeenth century," the woman informed her proudly. She pointed to the west. "Down that street, for example, you'll find St. Bartholomew's Catholic Church. It was built in 1689 by Baron Patrick Mulcahey. There are still a few Mulcaheys left hereabouts."

"I'll have to check that out," Teddy said, smiling.

"Yes, please do, someone is always on the property. I'm sure they'd love to have you take a look around." Her eyes lowered to the camera. "Are you a professional?"

"It's what I do for a living," Teddy told her.

Excitement glowed anew in the woman's eyes. "Will there be a pictorial of Ballycastle in some American magazine? You are American, aren't you?"

"That's right. I'm from San Francisco."

"Well," the woman said, all of a sudden in a rush to go. "I've kept you long enough." She held up her shopping bag. "Must not linger, this needs refrigeration." She looked into Teddy's face again, as if trying to commit her features to memory. "It was a pleasure meeting you. . . ." She glanced at Teddy's naked ring finger. "Miss . . . ?"

"That would take too long to explain," Teddy said jokingly. "And you've got to get your purchase into the refrigerator."

"Oh yes," the woman agreed. "Good day to you, then. Enjoy your stay."

"Thank you, I will," Teddy said, smiling. She watched as the woman hurried down the sidewalk, heading east. Then she walked across the street to a small café to get a cup of coffee.

In Carmel Alexander sat before the computer in his office. After getting on-line, he checked his mail. He was relieved to see a short missive from Teddy: *Hi, Daddy, the trip was uneventful for the most part, although the innkeeper, Susan MacLarety, insists that a bit of music I heard last night on my way from the train station was their local ghost, George, playing the flute. At any rate I'm just fine. Susan, whose computer I'm using, also gave me a line on Joachim West. I'm going to approach him tomorrow. Give Alex a hug and a kiss for me. Tell him I miss him and I'll be sure to bring him back something interesting. Love, Teddy.*

Alexander clicked on the Reply icon, and wrote: *Everything's fine here. Alex is asleep, I'm working late on the book. Adrian has phoned three times, the boob, wondering where you are. I told him to stop calling. No one here's interested in talking with him. Oh yes, he's also sent two bouquets of roses which I took down to the local nursing home for the nurses to give to patients who don't often get flowers. I didn't think you'd mind. Theodora, you must not have been forceful enough in your rejection of him. Next time you see him, you're going to have to go ballistic. But then Adrian has never heard anything he didn't want to. It may be difficult getting rid of him. Good luck on getting that interview.*

This done, Alexander went off-line and strode across the hall to check on Alex. Alex was sleeping soundly, his pudgy arms wrapped tightly around his favorite Teddy bear, a peaceful expression on his face.

* * *

Kathleen rounded the southern corner of the manor, her keen eyes searching for the familiar figure of William in his gardening apron. She spotted him, on his knees, pulling up wild mushrooms. In their rainy climate the fungi sprang up all over the yard. These were fortunately edible, so he pulled them and brought them inside for Kathleen to use in her cooking.

"William, William," Kathleen called, running now. "She's arrived. I just saw her on the street. As friendly as you please!"

William rose, wiping his hands on the apron front. He squinted at Kathleen as she came to a halt about two feet from him. Frowning, he inquired, "Calm down, woman. Who's arrived? You're not making sense."

Kathleen's cheeks were pink from exertion. Her brown eyes danced. "The missus, that's who!"

"You mean Joachim's missus?"

"Oh, it's Joachim now?" Kathleen asked, smiling, her hands on her hips. "Since when did you start calling him Joachim?"

"We get on right well since we've been going fishing." He looked serious again. "Where exactly did you see this woman?" He glanced in the direction of the manor. "Is she here?"

Kathleen pursed her lips. "You weren't listening to me, as usual. No, I saw her on the street this morning when I went to the butcher's to pick up a chicken. I was leaving the shop, and there she was, strolling along the walk, right in front of me."

"Well, did she tell you she was Joachim's missus?"

"Of course not!" Kathleen replied, sounding impatient. "We made general conversation: 'Nice day, new in town?' You know!"

"Then what makes you think she's Mrs. West?"

"I was getting to that," Kathleen said. She moistened her lips and cleared her throat. "She's black, for one thing. How often do we see black people in this part of Ireland?"

William nodded in agreement. She had him there. Joachim

West was the only black person he'd ever seen in Ballycastle, and he was forty-nine years old.

"All right, and . . ."

"She's a photographer," Kathleen went on excitedly. "And last but most certainly not least, she's from San Francisco." She ended with a superior note to her voice, as if to say, see William, your wife is smarter than you think.

They stood regarding one another, Kathleen smiling, William wearing a contemplative grimace. Kathleen hated it when he wore that expression. It meant he was turning something over in his mind. William was a great one for pondering a question. He could go days . . . Kathleen didn't have the patience for that today.

"William . . ." she warned, her eyes sharp.

"There's just one thing wrong with your reasoning," William said. "If she's Mrs. West, why didn't she come straight here, instead of going sightseeing?"

Kathleen smirked. Men, they never thought deeply enough. Surfaces, that's all they saw. Whereas women dug deeper, seeking out the underlying meaning behind each situation. In that respect women were like detectives.

"She wasn't wearing a ring. And when I asked if she was a miss, or not, she said rather cryptically, I might add, 'That would take too long to explain.' It's obvious they had a spat and he just took off without resolving their problems."

"But he and Mr. Ryan are the best of friends. It stands to reason that she would also be friends with Mr. Ryan. She would know where he lives," William protested weakly.

"This is Mr. West's first visit to Mr. Ryan's home," Kathleen pointed out. "When she and Mr. West argued, she probably wanted him to stay and discuss their problems, but he'd made a promise to stand up for Mr. Ryan and he didn't want to go back on his word. Now she's followed him halfway around the globe, hoping to mend their differences. It makes sense, William. She wouldn't know where Mr. Ryan lives. She'd have to inquire in town."

William turned and walked back to where he'd been pulling up mushrooms. "You're just being a woman, Kathleen. It would be romantic if it were Mrs. West, but there's no way of knowing for sure, except by waiting to see if she shows up here."

Kathleen left in a huff. Nothing excited her husband except holding a cold, slimy wriggling fish in his hand. Sometimes she wished he'd show more emotion, dream a little, live a little!

"Fáilte," the woman behind the counter called to Teddy as Teddy came through the diner's door. The small establishment was packed. Customers sat at booths lined along the wall and near the picture window. A row of stools traveled the long counter. There wasn't much difference in this diner, Teddy observed, than the ones she frequented in San Francisco. Except the faces were less diverse.

"What did you say?" Teddy queried, smiling at the woman. She hadn't understood the greeting.

"It's Gaelic," the woman, young and blond, her eyes a pale blue, explained. "It means 'welcome.' "

Teddy sat at the one empty space at the counter, between an elderly man and a younger one whose brown eyes swept over her with interest. "Thank you."

"Colleen," the blonde responded with a warm grin. "I'd venture to say you're new in town."

Laughing softly, Teddy nodded. "Teddy. Yes, and the subject of some curiosity," she said, meeting the younger man's eyes. He sheepishly lowered his.

"Oh, that's Ethan. He's always had an eye for a pretty face. Haven't you, Ethan?" Colleen said as she came to turn over the coffee mug in front of Teddy that she'd placed there when she'd opened up that morning. "Coffee?" she asked before pouring.

"Yes, please."

"So what brings you to Ballycastle?" Ethan asked. He was tall, rugged looking with dark hair and eyes. Powerfully built. His eyes were gentle though and Teddy, upon sitting down next to him, had noticed the smitten manner in which he was gazing at Colleen. He obviously came there for more than the coffee.

"I'm looking for a man," Teddy said jokingly, boldly meeting his eyes.

"Aren't we all!" Colleen cried, laughing. She poured Teddy a cup of coffee then stood there watching Ethan, who had colored.

Ethan rose and placed the money for his bill on the counter. Glancing at Colleen, he said, "I don't have to pay for the privilege of being the butt of women's jokes. I can get that at home for free." He then turned his gaze on Teddy. "Welcome, Teddy. I hope you have a pleasant visit to our town."

Teddy smiled. She was sorry she'd been a party to the ribbing, but sensed that Ethan was leaving for a reason other than her harmless comment. "Thank you, Ethan."

He left.

"What did he mean by that?" Teddy asked Colleen. "Does he have a wife at home who hassles him?"

Colleen rolled her eyes. "No, he's talking about his mother. You see, as an only child, Ethan feels it's his responsibility to care for her until her dying day. He's already thirty-five. I'm approaching thirty. If he thinks I'm going to wait much longer for him to pop the question, he has another think coming."

"Then you and he . . ."

"Are sweethearts, yes," Colleen said, lowering her voice somewhat. "If I didn't love him, I would've moved away to the city a long time ago." Teddy detected a sad note to her voice.

"I'm sorry," Teddy offered.

"Don't be," Colleen said, her smile restored. "We all make our choices. I chose to love him, even though it's bittersweet sometimes."

Before slipping beneath the covers last night, Teddy had set her watch to Ireland's time. It was nearing eleven and she'd promised Susan she'd help prepare the midday meal. Now she smiled at Colleen, who'd chatted amiably with her, between

filling other customers' mugs or delivering the occasional order that the cook had whipped up, and said regretfully, "I
should go. Thanks for the coffee and the conversation."

"I should be thanking you," Colleen told her. "It was a treat
talking to someone who's not from here for a change."

Teddy went to go into her bag for money to pay for the
coffee.

"It's on me," Colleen said.

"You never paid for my coffee," one of the regulars within
earshot protested, a twinkle in his eye.

"Oh, shut up and eat your eggs, Joe," Colleen said, her
smile directed at Teddy. "Bye, Teddy, don't be a stranger."

"I won't," Teddy assured her. "Thanks, and have a nice
day!"

In Teddy's absence Joe grinned at Colleen. "Have a nice
day, she said. Is that some kind of American colloquialism?"

"Joe!" Colleen said, astonished. "I didn't know you knew
that word, let alone how to pronounce it."

Teddy could see Susan's Inn, only about four blocks away,
up ahead. There was a spring in her step. She'd had an enjoy-
able morning what with meeting Colleen and Ethan, oh, and
the woman outside the butcher shop. She hadn't given her
name. After lunch, or whatever the locals referred to the meal
after breakfast, she was going to hire a taxi to take her out to
Conal Ryan's home. Susan had told her there was also a shop
where she could rent a motorbike. That might be fun, riding
along a country road with the wind blowing in her hair. Although she had that baseball cap, rolled into a ball in her
carry-on bag, that might be eminently more suitable than having bugs getting caught in her tresses.

She was imagining herself on a motorbike, putting along
at thirty miles an hour, when out of nowhere it seemed, a lad
on one of the infernal machines came straight for her. She
was on the sidewalk. He'd jumped the curb to get at her. Teddy
tried to get out of the way but he was on her before she could
react. The front wheel caught her on her left thigh. The pain

was excruciating. Burning, as if the wheel were eating through the denim of her jeans. She lost her balance and fell to the cobblestone street, hitting her head. She heard the *vroom-vroom* of the motor, smelled the acrid exhaust. The last thing she saw was the boy stopping the bike, laying it on its side, the back wheel still spinning.

An elderly woman returning from the grocer's saw what happened and began screaming at the top of her lungs, which wasn't very loud given the shrill racket the motorbike was making.

The boy, around sixteen, his face covered with acne, dressed all in black, went to Teddy and jerked the bag from her shoulder and the camera from around her neck. Then he mounted the bike and sped off. The elderly woman crossed the street, still screaming, "Help! Somebody call the constable. He's run her over with his bike!"

Several people peered out of shop windows, others spilled onto the street, hurrying toward Teddy's prone figure. The elderly woman knelt beside Teddy. "Dearie?"

Now the street was filled with twenty to thirty people. Colleen came out of the diner to see what all the fuss was about. When she got closer, she recognized the brown of Teddy's hand, the only part of Teddy that wasn't blocked from her view.

She ran the rest of the way. "Oh, my God." Kneeling beside Teddy, she felt for a pulse. It thumped against her fingertips. Looking up at the concerned faces surrounding her, she asked breathlessly, "Has anyone phoned for the doc? The constable?"

"Yes," Colm Mannix, proprietor of the butcher shop said. "I sent my assistant to phone the infirmary. Someone's on the way."

"Do you know who she is?" the elderly woman who'd witnessed the attack asked.

"Her name's Teddy, she's an American from California," Colleen replied. "She's a photojournalist, she said."

"Well, the boy took her camera," the woman told everyone indignantly. "He took that and her pocketbook!"

"Move back, move back!" Liam Murdoch bellowed. The crowd parted as he hurried forward to stand next to Colleen. "If you don't mind," he said to Colleen, asking for room to maneuver. Liam felt for a pulse on Teddy's carotid artery. "Strong pulse," he announced. Narrowing his eyes, he asked, "Did anyone see what happened?"

"I saw it all," the elderly woman said.

"Clara," Liam said, recognizing her as once. He took great pains to learn the names and faces of the citizens under his protection.

Liam listened patiently as Clara told him of the moment she'd noticed the pretty American on the street and how horrified she'd been when the boy purposely ran her down—then when she was knocked unconscious, he'd robbed her and taken off on his bike.

"Our streets aren't safe anymore," Colm Mannix said loudly, directing his complaint at Liam.

Liam ignored Colm's comment for the time being. He could hear the ambulance approaching. The most important thing was to get the stranger medical aid, and fast!

Sighing tiredly, he asked, looking from one face to another, "Can anyone here positively identify this woman?"

"I believe I can," William Collins said, stepping from behind two concerned onlookers.

Seven

In the place where Teddy was, she heard voices. Disembodied voices with Irish accents. Excited voices. One was deep and masculine, like the rumble of thunder. "Constable, I want you on that side; Mr. Collins, on the other. Now I'm going to wave a bit of ammonium alum beneath her nose and see if she likes it."

Suddenly Teddy's breathing passages were assaulted by the worst smell she'd ever experienced. She wanted to get away from the stink so badly, she awakened, coughing, abruptly sat up, hitting at the offending fumes with both hands as she did so.

Two men, one older than the other, but both dark-haired and of average height, stepped back from the table she'd been lying on. She glared at them, then she turned her head to direct her anger at a big, tall gentleman with a thick shock of white hair. He wore a white coat. "Are you trying to kill me?"

"It never fails," the big man murmured, coming to firmly push Teddy back down. "They either come out of it in a happy, drunklike state or ready to do battle." Assuming he was the doctor, Teddy relaxed on the table as he gingerly examined her forehead. He was so close to her, she could see the brown specks in his green eyes. "You took a pretty bad spill, young lady. The cut is going to require stitches, and you might have a scar to remind you of the incident for years to come."

"Some bedside manner you've got there. Care to introduce yourself before putting a needle to my skin?" Teddy returned.

That booming laugh again. "I do apologize. John

O'Shaunessy, at your service. And, yes, I'm the town doctor. Have been for the past thirty-odd years."

"How odd were they?"

John's ample belly shook with laughter. "Young lady . . ."

"Teddy."

"Teddy, will you be silent while I do this? My hands aren't as steady as they used to be."

"Oh, now you tell me. Perhaps I ought to get a second opinion before I wind up looking like the bride of Frankenstein."

There were tears in John's eyes now, and the other two men, who hadn't introduced themselves, were chuckling, too.

John, the suturing kit in his gloved hand, was in no condition to commence stitching, so Teddy sat up and regarded them. "Easy room. I should've charged admission."

At that point Joachim West burst into the examination room, followed by the woman she'd met on the street that morning.

One of the dark-haired men went to say something to the woman, but Joachim walked straight up to Teddy. His dark eyes narrowed as they scanned her face. Teddy's heart thumped in her chest. Her hand went self-consciously to her face. This wasn't how their first meeting was going to be. She was supposed to go to him as an intelligent photojournalist who would use her charm to finagle an interview out of him. Now here she was bedraggled and bloody. He had her at a distinct disadvantage.

John took Joachim's hand and pumped it. "Dr. O'Shaunessy. It's a pleasure to meet you, Mr. West."

Joachim reluctantly shifted his gaze to John.

"Don't worry, she'll be fine," John assured him. "I don't believe she has a concussion. Just a gash on her forehead, as you can see. She needs to be under observation for the next twenty-four hours, however. Take her home and put her to bed with a good hearty cup of broth."

To Teddy's utter amazement, Joachim West nodded in accord with everything the doctor suggested. Then looking at her again, he said, "May I have a moment alone with your patient, Doctor?"

"Of course, I can do the stitches later," John said. He ushered the other three people out of the room.

Alone now Teddy dangled her legs off the side of the table, smiling. "I thought we'd meet under different circumstances."

Joachim came close. He was wearing brown corduroy slacks, a blue denim shirt, and a beige jacket with a brown corduroy collar. Teddy glanced down at his brown suede hiking boots. With his size and musculature, he could have been a lumberjack in that outfit.

"What happened to your accent?"

"What accent?"

"Your British accent. Aren't you from London?"

"No, San Francisco. And I try my best not to sound like the proverbial Valley Girl. Were you expecting someone from London?"

"Sort of . . . no." He appeared puzzled. He bit his bottom lip, thinking. His eyes met hers. "If you're not Celia O'Connell, then who are you?"

Teddy thought fleetingly that if she were a devious tabloid reporter, and thought quickly enough on her feet, she could have pretended to be this Celia O'Connell and strolled right into the Ryan manse. But she wasn't a tabloid reporter, sleazy or otherwise. She never went after a story using underhanded methods.

"My name is Teddy Riley. I'm a photojournalist on assignment for *Contemporary Lives* magazine, and I was hoping to interview you."

There it was, the truth. She waited for his reaction. In the meanwhile she enjoyed the view. The photo on his book didn't do him justice. For one thing it was in black and white. It didn't capture the warm chestnut brown of his skin, nor his sheer physical presence. He looked like an athlete. His thigh muscles were clearly delineated beneath the corduroy slacks, as were the taut biceps straining to be unfettered from that jacket he had on.

It's warm in here, Teddy thought. *Why doesn't he take it off?*

"I don't give interviews," Joachim said after what seemed like a long time to Teddy.

"I know that you, as a rule, don't give interviews, but—"

His eyes were sharp, his tone even sharper. "But what?"

"Rules can be broken," Teddy said, undeterred. "I work for a leading entertainment magazine. We're not a rag. And I'm good at what I do." She slowed down. Her tone was becoming a bit desperate and she didn't want to go there yet. Not unless begging became her only option.

They sized one another up, Joachim standing there, immovable; Teddy, her mind going a hundred miles an hour, trying to come up with something that would get her in his good graces.

Joachim couldn't shake the feeling they'd met somewhere before. Earlier when he'd entered the room and saw her lovely cinnamon-brown face, he'd wanted her to be Celia. He'd thought he'd been relieved when Celia had e-mailed him with her regrets—but he supposed, he'd been starved for some feminine attention.

He'd not given her away simply because if she had been Celia, and he was prepared to take her back to Conal's home with him, which he had been, it would've been to their advantage to go along with the apparent misunderstanding—according to Kathleen—that she was his long-awaited wife from San Francisco.

But a reporter, no matter how attractive, was not someone he wanted under the same roof with him.

Suddenly, though, something his grandma Eva had taught him when he was growing up reared its ugly head. Always look after your people, she'd said. Meaning blacks had to support one another in every way they could. And if one of your people was in trouble, then you had to offer assistance. A good code to live by. But given Teddy Riley's occupation, fulfilling that edict would probably rankle a bit.

He had his reasons for not liking the press. They'd hounded him unmercifully after Suzanne's death. They hadn't even given him any respite on the day of the funeral. One photographer had climbed a tree at the cemetery in order to get the perfect shot of Suzanne in her coffin. That photo had appeared in several tabloids for weeks afterward. It was going to be a closed-casket service, but Suzanne's aunt Rachel had gotten emotional and insisted on one last look at Suzanne. That was when the photographer snapped the picture, using a telephoto lens, that gave him a close-up view of Suzanne's emaciated face.

The photojournalist was absently twirling ringlets of her coal-black hair around her finger. A nervous habit? Joachim hoped so. She should be uncertain of her next move. He wanted her to sweat.

He was remembering what Kathleen had told him on the drive there as she sat up front with him. She chirped away in his left ear as he drove Conal's Jaguar on the left side of the road. The steering wheel was on the right for some confounded reason Joachim couldn't fathom.

"I met her in front of the butcher shop minutes before it happened. She was so friendly, charming. A delightful girl. Now William says some hooligan on a motorbike ran her down, stole her purse and the camera she was carrying. Lord, what is this world coming to?" Then she'd looked over at him, and said sincerely, "I'm sorry I didn't just bring her back to the manor with me, sir."

"Well," Teddy said, interrupting his thoughts. She smiled at him. "Staring at each other isn't going to get us anywhere. I can understand your reticence about speaking to a reporter. Why don't we discuss it over coffee? I know this really nice diner here in Ballycastle . . ."

Joachim came forward and firmly grasped her by the shoulders. They locked eyes, and Teddy held her breath, or had his nearness momentarily cut it off? She felt a painful stirring in the pit of her stomach as the faint smell of his woodsy cologne drifted over her. And that five o'clock shadow was extremely sexy.

Joachim felt it, too. Her skin smelled like honeysuckle and it, upon closer inspection, was more of a burnished-copper shade than cinnamon. She opened her mouth to say something, and those heart-shaped rose-colored, full lips parted revealing small, straight white teeth. He couldn't hear what she was saying for the beating of his heart.

"What?" he asked foolishly.

"I was saying, all our readers want is your reaction to winning the National Book Award. And a photo or two of you here in Ireland," she said reasonably.

Joachim allowed his hands to fall from her shoulders. "Look, Ms. Riley, here's the deal. These kind people think you're my wife, come to join me while I work on my next book. You're in a bind . . ."

"I'm fine, just a bump on the head," Teddy begged to differ.

"The kid who assaulted you took your purse and your camera, I'm told. Did you have your passport and other ID in your purse?"

Teddy then realized the severity of her predicament. There was no visa required to enter or leave Ireland. But she needed her passport in order to return to the States. Standard procedure was, she'd have to go to the U.S. Embassy in Dublin and apply for a temporary passport. Without her bag, which had her passport, her credit cards, and other ID in it, she was stranded. She couldn't even afford train fare to Dublin.

"I *am* in a fix," she admitted, her voice soft. "But the bill at the inn where I'm staying is taken care of. And"—she met his eyes—"I can always e-mail my father and ask him to send me some money."

Joachim wondered why he'd been pleased to note she hadn't mentioned a husband or a boyfriend. He tossed that fleeting, aberrant thought from his mind and regarded her with sober eyes. "You can do that. But as for today you're coming home with me. Dr. O'Shaunessy says you need to be watched for the next twenty-four hours. Is there anyone at the inn who'd be willing to do that?"

"No," Teddy immediately answered. Susan definitely had her hands full. Susan! She'd promised to help Susan prepare the midday meal. But she expected someone had already told

Susan what had happened by now. News traveled fast in small towns.

"Can we stop by the inn on the way out of town?" Teddy asked, taking him up on his offer. "I'll need my things."

Joachim took a step backward. "Of course. I'll go get Dr. O'Shaunessy so he can finish patching you up."

"All right, sweetie," Teddy answered, a mischievous glint in her sparkling eyes.

Joachim's brows furrowed in a steely-eyed frown.

"Just getting into character," Teddy promised, with a grin.

Joachim turned his back to her, his lips curved in a smile. He was going to have to be on guard with this one.

Susan could barely contain her excitement when Teddy strode into the lobby of the inn on Whitepark Road a while later. The tall redhead had been conversing with another guest, but quickly excused herself and was at Teddy's side before Teddy could place a foot on the bottom step of the staircase.

"Lucy Mannix phoned to tell me what happened," Susan said, coming to solicitously take Teddy by the arm as they both climbed the stairs.

"I'm all right," Teddy said, smiling up at Susan. "I just hit my head when I fell to the street. Doc says I'll live."

"How did you get back?" Susan asked, under the assumption Teddy was just going up to her room to rest a while.

"Uh . . . Mr. West brought me so that I could pick up my things," Teddy said with a note of regret. "Dr. O'Shaunessy says someone has to keep an eye on me for several hours. I couldn't impose upon you. Luckily Mr. West volunteered."

Susan's mouth fell open in surprise. "You certainly do work fast, Teddy Riley. Here less than a day, and you not only get your interview, but he comes to your rescue. I'm in awe of your talents," she cried.

"It's nothing like that," Teddy said, pausing on the stairs to look Susan in the eye. She hadn't missed the accusing note in the innkeeper's voice. "For some reason the woman who cares for Conal Ryan's home in his absence—"

"That would be Kathleen Collins," Susan informed her, her voice stiff.

"Well, Kathleen has got the notion that . . ." Teddy stopped, thinking that their conversation should be continued in private. "Let's go to my room, Susan."

In the room Teddy began placing her clothing and toiletries back in the carry-on bag while she explained what was going on to a rapt Susan, who sat on the bed.

Folding a pair of jeans, Teddy went on. "I met Kathleen on the street this morning. We chatted. She asked a few questions. After I told her where I was from, she got in an all-fired rush to leave. I thought that was peculiar, but soon put it out of my mind. But Kathleen had put two and two together in her mind and came up with my so-called identity: Joachim West's wife. Close your mouth, Susan."

Susan clamped her mouth shut.

"After I was mugged, he was unceremoniously dragged to the infirmary by Kathleen. He obviously came because he'd been expecting some woman named Celia—because once we were alone, he told me about this Celia, who's a Brit."

"You fit her description," Susan deduced, enjoying the tale.

"Apparently we're both young and black. I don't know if our other characteristics jive or not."

"Go on," Susan prompted her, eager for more.

"So then Mr. West takes a good look at me. I must have been awfully pitiful, what with a gash on my head and dried blood on my clothes."

"You still look pretty terrible, so I get the gist," Susan told her, her lips curled in a grin.

Teddy laughed. "Well, anyway, to make a long story short—he doesn't give interviews, but he's a gentleman and offered me his home and his time until I'm able to go off on my own."

Susan sighed and crossed her long, thin legs. Throwing her head back languidly, she said, "Oh, why couldn't he rescue me!"

"Now don't be jealous, Susan," Teddy implored. She'd finished packing and stood with the carry-on bag in her right hand. "I have to ask you not to mention to anyone what you and I have discussed. I told you the truth because I feel like we're friends now, after bonding over a ghost. Let everyone think I'm his wife. It's a harmless ruse. And I'll be gone in a day or two anyway. He was really adamant about not giving me that interview. I don't know why he doesn't like talking to reporters, but he seems as hard as stone on the subject."

"You have my word," Susan promised, getting to her feet and bestowing a warm hug on Teddy. "No one will find out from me. I wish you the best, Teddy. And use the time you have with him wisely. You never know, he might change his mind about the interview."

She released Teddy and smiled. "It's been a pleasure."

"Same here," Teddy told her sincerely. "Thanks for everything."

They turned to leave the room.

"I'm sorry I couldn't stay long enough to contribute to the paint-the-porch fund."

Susan humphed. "You're paid up for the week, young lady. You don't think I'm going to refund the magazine's money, do you?"

Teddy enjoyed the drive in the country, even though her benefactor was not the most talkative of traveling companions. She watched his profile out the corner of her eye, wondering what he was thinking when he'd offered to help her and if he regretted it now.

She'd decided not to press him for the interview. Perhaps he had a very good reason for not wanting his photo plastered over millions—*Contemporary Lives*' circulation was 3.5 million—of magazines.

But, Teddy smiled, what a nice face it was.

"I enjoyed your book," she said, weary of the silence. Flattery hadn't been ruled out yet.

Joachim kept his eyes on the road. He'd more than once nearly killed himself by running into a herd of sheep, or frightening a skittish horse. The area had more horses than automobiles, he'd concluded. He'd certainly seen more equestrians on the roads than drivers.

"Which one would that be?" he asked, skeptical.

"The God Gene," Teddy replied. "I read it on the plane."

Joachim was suspicious of people who were needlessly honest. First she blurted out that she was there to coerce an interview out of him. Now she admitted she'd read his book only because he was her assignment.

"My editor gave it to me," she said, adding further credence to his theory. "I was prepared to hate it. You should hear how some people describe you: the hottest black writer since Toni Morrison—that's my best friend, Joie. He's not only brilliant, he's way-cool looking—that's my editor, Irina Pasternak."

"Why were you prepared to hate it?" Joachim found himself asking.

"Because I read everything, especially fiction, with the need to be convinced. Convince me that the characters are real, not just words on a page. Convince me that I should care about them, or, in the case of your character, Dr. Temple, have any sympathy whatsoever for them."

"So you're saying Simeon Temple got what he deserved?" He actually turned to look at her for a moment, then directed his attention back to his driving.

Teddy gave an imperceptible smile. "I didn't like him at all in the beginning. But I believe you didn't want your readers to like him. You wanted us to slowly develop an understanding of his psyche. What made Simeon Temple so ambitious that he'd secretly go ahead with an experiment both the government and his superiors had deemed dangerous?"

"Must there always be a reason?" Joachim asked, his grip on the steering wheel relaxing somewhat. He'd been a little nervous in her presence. It'd been a long time since he'd been around an attractive woman. And he wasn't a suave player on his best day. Shy as a child. Still shy as an adult. He was loath to share his thoughts with close friends and relations, let alone a stranger. What had possessed him to ask her to stay at Conal's home anyway?

Teddy considered Joachim's question, turning in her seat

to smile at him. "Yes," she stated emphatically, "there should always be a reason behind anyone's behavior."

Joachim had her then. Squinting he asked, "All right, then. Tell me why you came all the way to Ireland to interview a writer who is sought after for the moment, but will undoubtedly be relegated to obscurity next week?"

"Is that really how you feel about yourself?"

"It's how I feel about celebrity, not about myself," Joachim said, his voice low. "In this media-mad world, we're continually being bombarded with information. We're incapable of sorting, collating, filing these items in our brains. Today's news is hot; yesterday's, forgotten. It doesn't mean we care any less, but that we simply have no room to store all that information. And in the great scheme of things, how important is a writer, or his book about man's inhumanity to man? We hear about that every day on the evening news."

Teddy wholeheartedly agreed with him. What did another interview matter? She'd done over a hundred in her relatively short career. No, the interview didn't matter. It was simply a means to an end. Sure there were other jobs out there, and if she hustled, she could get on at another magazine in the Bay Area. But Irina had promised her this position if she got Joachim West to consent to an interview and she wanted to work for *Contemporary Lives*. She liked the purpose behind the magazine: to give the reader a window into the lives of people they can only dream of meeting, revealing them to be as human as the next person. She also liked working with the staff. Two excellent recommendations for wanting to snag the position.

All good reasons. But when it came down to the nitty-gritty, Teddy had come to Ireland because she was afraid Adrian was going to act the fool and sue her for sole custody of Alex once it sank in she wasn't coming back to him. Like her father had said, a permanent staff position on a well-known magazine would go a long way in proving that she could provide for Alex without Adrian's help.

So she sighed and said to Joachim West, "I need this interview because the editor promised me a staff position if I get it. And I need the job she promised because I'm afraid my ex-husband, who until recently wanted nothing to do with our son, is getting ready to sue me for sole custody."

Joachim was sorry he'd asked. He'd crossed the barrier of detached indifference, however, so he jumped another hurdle. "Would you care to explain?" he asked. And so she did.

Parked on the manor's paved, circular driveway at the front entrance, Joachim listened as Teddy told him of Adrian's bid to reenter her life. "So there you have it," she concluded. They sat facing one another. Joachim's eyes hadn't left her face the whole while she was speaking.

"I knew I'd seen you somewhere before," he said suddenly, his voice and eyes both animated. "You accompanied your ex to a charity function to benefit juvenile AIDS research at the Fairmont Hotel more than five years ago. Suzanne and I were there when they announced your arrival."

Teddy assumed Suzanne was his late wife.

"I heard you lost her. I'm sorry," Teddy said softly.

Joachim lowered his eyes. "She fought as hard as she could," he said resignedly. Raising his eyes to hers, he smiled, and breaking the awkward silence, suggested, "Let's get you inside. You must be tired and hungry."

"And in need of a good tidying up," Teddy said. "I must look a sight!"

"No, you look quite . . . well, actually," Joachim told her.

He quickly got out and trotted around to her side of the car and opened the door for her. Teddy alighted, pulling her bag after her. She felt uncomfortably shy around him all of a sudden. She'd already told him everything there was to tell. He knew how desperate she was for the chance to interview him. They'd already established a kind of connection. He'd remembered seeing her in San Francisco. She couldn't recall ever seeing him before today. She wished she had seen him and Suzanne together back then. She wondered what kind of woman Suzanne West had been.

They were met at the door by Kathleen, who took Teddy's bag from her and announced, "Welcome, Mrs. West." Joachim noticed her eyes held a warmth in them that had never been there for him. He smiled. Perhaps Kathleen had missed having another woman around.

"Please," Teddy said, her smile like a ray of sunshine, "call me Teddy."

"All right, Teddy," Kathleen returned as she closed the door and turned to regard the both of them. She took in Teddy's smudged jeans, ripped shirt, and bandaged face. "Shall I run you a bath, Teddy? You look like you could use a relaxing soak."

"Oh, I can do that myself, Kathleen," Teddy told her. She stepped down into the foyer, onto the hardwood floor and surveyed the beautiful surroundings. Modern furnishings in rich, warm earth tones. A riot of reds in the antique Persian runner that muted their footsteps. Truly elegant.

"This is a beautiful old house," she said, her voice soft and awe filled.

Kathleen took as much pride in the manor as if she owned it herself. "Isn't it though? Follow me, dear."

Teddy eagerly trailed Kathleen from the foyer through the grand sitting room, to the dining room where Kathleen pointed out an original Hepplewhite sideboard. Joachim shook his head at the women's obvious instant rapport with one another.

He went upstairs to his room to freshen up a bit, leaving Teddy and Kathleen to their tour. The beard he'd been thinking of growing was suddenly itchy and bothersome. It had to go.

When he got back downstairs, Teddy and Kathleen were in the kitchen where Kathleen was serving Teddy a second helping of her lamb stew. Teddy was ravenous after her ordeal and was enjoying the savory goodness of the stew, dipping big chunks of Kathleen's homemade bread in it to sop up the gravy.

Kathleen had a content expression on her face as she hovered. She looked up when Joachim entered the room. "Teddy was explaining why you don't eat red meat anymore," Kathleen said.

Teddy paused to frown at Joachim. "You shaved," she said before thinking. Joachim thought he'd detected a note of disappointment in her voice. He sat down across from her, his attention on her face which, he knew, would be red now if that were physically possible. Why had his shaving disturbed her?

"Yeah, sweetie," Teddy said, recovering. Why did he have to shave? Unless . . . She smiled at him. "I was telling Kathleen that after you had a problem with ulcers"—her gaze switched to Kathleen—"too much stress"—now back to Joachim—"the doctor told you to cut out all fatty meats. I don't know why you didn't simply tell Kathleen of your preferences when you first got here. That would've saved the poor woman the trouble of guessing what to feed you."

"Men!" Kathleen said, turning away to go to the refrigerator and get Joachim's garden salad. He liked it with boiled egg whites, sliced turkey, low-fat salad dressing, and hot peppers if they were available. He ate it with her homemade bread which, judging by the amount he put away, he had no aversion to.

Kathleen set the salad before him.

"Should I go upstairs and make room for Teddy's things in your closet?"

"No!" Teddy and Joachim immediately cried in unison.

"Dr. O'Shaunessy says Teddy needs her rest," Joachim said after clearing his throat. "She can stay in the room next door to mine. I'll sit with her until she falls asleep and then I'll sleep in my room."

"He snores," Teddy offered with a mischievous gander thrown Joachim's way. "And he has an irritating habit of getting up in the middle of the night to do pushups. One and two and three . . . it drives me nuts."

"You talk in your sleep," Joachim accused, getting into the game. "And you hog the covers."

"I'm just defending my territory," Teddy said lightly. "You toss and turn so much, you end up wrapped in the covers and I'm left without any. I've learned to get mine while I can."

Kathleen, apparently delighted by their exchange, went about her duties while they chatted. It was a pleasure to see Mr. West looking so happy. She never thought she'd ever see such a silly grin on his face. It was obvious they were very much in love.

Shortly after serving Joachim, Kathleen excused herself, saying she had to go to the garden to get fresh onions to use in the preparation of the evening meal.

Alone, Teddy and Joachim finished their meals in silence, stealing glances every now and then.

Joachim pushed his plate aside and took a sip of iced tea. "So I have an ulcer, huh?"

Having started before him, Teddy had completed her stew a few minutes earlier and was drinking her tea while she waited for him to finish his salad. She smiled at him. "You worry too much."

"About what?"

Teddy felt her face grow hot. It'd been a long time since a man she was attracted to had sat across from her at an intimate table for two and engaged her in conversation. Plus there was something entirely too familiar in the way he was watching her.

"About everything. You're a regular worrywart."

Joachim changed course on her in midconversation. "Where did we meet?" he asked, his keen eyes on her mouth.

Teddy moistened her lips. "Pardon?"

"People always want to know where a couple met," he explained, raising his sights to her eyes again. "Where did we meet, Teddy?"

Teddy thought for a second or two. If she could dream up the perfect scenario for meeting the man of her dreams, what would be the setting? What would they be wearing? What would have been the first words they spoke to one another? Here she was, being given the opportunity to construct her very own fantasy.

She sat, looking deeply into his eyes a few moments longer. She had wanted to run her fingers over that beard he'd worn on his handsome face earlier. Now it was gone, and she'd probably not be there long enough for him to grow another.

"We met at USC. I was a freshman, you were a senior," she began.

"How old are you?" Joachim asked.

"Thirty. How old are you?"

Joachim laughed. "You're a woman without guile. My grandma Eva used to say a woman who would tell her age, would tell the truth about anything. Are you always so truthful, Teddy?"

"None of us are without guile," she corrected him lightly. "But, yes, I try to be as truthful as possible. It saves a lot of energy. I don't have to keep track of everything I say, just in case something comes back to bite me in the can. By the way you didn't answer my question."

"I'm thirty-seven," Joachim told her. Then, "We couldn't have met at USC when you were a freshman and I was a senior, unless I started school later than the usual student does. The age difference is too great."

Teddy yawned.

"You're tired," Joachim declared, getting to his feet. "Come on, I'll show you to your room."

Teddy didn't want to end their conversation. Her body was feeling the aftereffects of the attack though. She had a headache, and her arm, the one she'd fallen on when the boy had pushed her, was throbbing painfully. Maybe a soak in a tub of warm water would help banish the soreness from her aching muscles.

She rose. "I don't know what Kathleen did with my bag," she told Joachim, remembering she'd given the bag to Kathleen upon entering the manor.

They looked around the kitchen. No bag.

"I'll ask Kathleen about it while you're bathing, and have her bring it up to you later," Joachim suggested.

This settled, Joachim showed her the back stairs and they went up them in silence. He then stopped at the third door on the right. Opening it, he allowed her to precede him. He stood at the door, with his hand on the knob. "The bathroom has everything you'll need to get started."

"All right," Teddy said softly. "Thanks."

Joachim closed the door behind him and Teddy walked farther into what could only be referred to as "the green room." Plush pale green carpeting covered the floor. The wall-paper consisted of miniature ivy leaves growing against a white background. The king-size bed boasted an avocado-green comforter and the pillow shams were white lace. Irish lace? Teddy moved over to the bed to examine it more closely. She sat on the bed, a pillow in her lap. The workmanship was exquisite. Someone had made those tiny stitches by hand. Probably a grandmother who'd learned the craft from her grandmother, as it had been passed down for generations. Much like the quilting sessions her own grandmother had invited her to sit in on whenever she visited her in Biloxi for the summer. Seven little old ladies, sitting in a circle in straight-backed chairs with cushions in them for maximum comfort, because quilting bees were notoriously drawn-out affairs.

She was thirteen the last time she'd sat among the mavens of stitchery. How out of place she'd felt, a young girl among women in their seventies and eighties, all with fingers still nimble due to years of putting needle to cloth. And their attitudes had remained vibrant, too. They talked about everything as they worked, these ladies. No part of life was left unexplored by them or left without commentary. They paid no never-mind to the fact that there was a virgin among them, going into detail about what a man was good for—for how long and how often. Listening to her grandma Phoebe and her cronies talk about that place where men went inside a woman, stayed a while, making her want to get up and fry him a hoecake in appreciation of his skills, was her first encounter with things of a sexual nature. Her father had never broached the subject. When she went back home and asked him where that place was that Grandma Phoebe and the other ladies had raved about, Alexander, though he dreaded it, knew it was time to sit her down and have "the talk."

Now as Teddy placed the pillow against her face, relishing the softness of the lace against her skin and the fresh lavender fragrance, she wondered if she remembered the recipe for hoecakes, and if Joachim liked them.

* * *

Teddy had been soaking twenty minutes when there came a knock on the bathroom door.

She sat up in the tub, causing bubbles to escape over the side. Quickly grabbing a towel and placing it in front of her, she called, "Come in!"

Kathleen stuck her head in the door. "I wanted you to know I put your things away, and left your nightgown on the bed."

"That was kind of you, Kathleen, thank you," Teddy said, smiling.

"Oh, and tonight is my and William's night off, so we're going into town. I'll leave supper on the stove for you and Mr. West. William and I will be staying in town with his mother tonight, she's a little under the weather, poor dear, and wants her son nearby."

Kathleen's words momentarily threw Teddy into a panic. She and Joachim were going to be alone in the house? She hadn't expected this turn of events. And she thought, eyeing Kathleen suspiciously, she wouldn't put it past Kathleen to have arranged it so that the long-separated couple could have some private time together.

What could she do? Short of coming clean and confessing she wasn't Mrs. Joachim West, that is? Nothing. She slid back down in the tub. "All right, Kathleen. You and William have a good time in town, and I hope his mother's better soon."

"Thank you, Teddy. You'll find Mr. West in the library when you're done."

Kathleen left and Teddy leaned her head back in the soapy water, wetting her scalp. She then reached for the shampoo sitting on the edge of the tub, poured a bit in her hand and rubbed it into her hair, creating a thick, white lather. There was no showerhead, and she didn't feel like bending over the sink, so she improvised. After rinsing well, she rose and stepped on the towel she'd placed on the floor prior to getting in the tub. Wrapping a towel around her head and securing it, she dried off and stepped in front of the mirror. The bandage had fallen off in the tub. She peered at the inch-long line the cut had left on her forehead. It would leave a scar, Dr. O'Shaunessy had said.

It would be worth it if, by some miracle, Joachim would change his mind and give her the interview. Then she could return home with some assurance that when Adrian launched his attack, she'd have something to fight back with. His past disinterest had made her complacent. She'd thought that she'd never have to worry about sharing Alex with anyone. He was all hers. Hers to love. Hers to fret over, too, when he was sick. Her responsibility. Adrian was just a bad dream. Someone she used to love. She could safely catalog him deep in the back of her mind under *Open Only When You Want to Wallow in Misery*. And more and more she hadn't wanted to open the Adrian file. She was getting on with her life. Now he'd come along to disrupt her peace, throw her in turmoil and generally muck up what she'd so carefully constructed over the last three years: a world in which Alex was the center. He was the sun and she was the mother planet, orbiting around him. No man had been able to break her concentration on her task. A few had tried, but none had been able to find the code that would automatically lower her defenses. It wasn't all that difficult to figure out really. If a man wanted the chance to love her, he had to be good father material.

Apparently Adrian thought he qualified simply because his sperm had helped create Alex. He was mistaken. Any healthy male could become a donor. All he needed was a sterile receptacle, a bit of privacy, and a copy of *Playboy*. It took a great deal more to be a father.

Eight

Adrian sat in the makeup artist's chair before a lighted mirror in his dressing room. Jocelyn Mendoza applied a thin layer of bronze powder to his face to minimize shine once he was on camera. Then she brushed his hair and turned him around in the swivel chair to admire her handiwork. "Perfect, as always, Mr. R."

"Thank you, Jocelyn," Adrian said with a small smile.

Jocelyn grinned, quickly collected her makeup kit and turned to leave. She wasn't comfortable around Adrian Riley. Jocelyn was African American, in her early forties, married with three school-age children. Adrian was a commanding taskmaster, the smallest slip up could very well land you in the unemployment line. Jocelyn had worked for the network nearly seventeen years. It wasn't fair that she, a seasoned veteran, should be at the mercy of Adrian, who'd been there only two. But he was the lead anchor on the evening news, and that position carried clout. Another example of the inequities to be found in the entertainment industry today. Jocelyn barely brought home thirty-five thousand annually, and Adrian, two million, just because America liked the sound of his voice and his square-jawed, masculine face, which was easy on the eyes. As for his credentials, she knew many in his field who had far better educations and more extensive experience. It's dumb luck, Jocelyn thought derisively as she smiled at the big lug once more before pulling the door closed behind her.

Adrian sat admiring himself for a moment or two before getting up, going to his desk and picking up the receiver to dial the number that would allow him to listen to his personal messages.

He had ten minutes before air time. The last five were spent in the anchor's chair having his microphone adjusted by tech personnel and sitting while the cameramen got him in their sights. He always got a thrill as the last few seconds were counted down and then the green light appeared and he knew millions of people were tuning in to hear the latest news issuing from his mouth.

Now, though, he was wondering how Teddy's assignment was going in Ireland, and how soon she'd be back home. His spy at *Contemporary Lives* was to phone him with any updates.

He smiled smugly when Victoria Rollins's voice, emotion filled as always, said, "Why won't you return my calls? I need to see you, Adrian. What did the note you sent with the flowers mean? *So long?* Are you dumping me, Adrian Riley? Because no one dumps Victoria Rollins. If anyone's dumped, it's you, you two-bit media-king wannabe! I'm going places. You? You're not fit to be seen in public with me." She laughed. "And you're not that good in the sack, either!"

"Baby, I was the best you've ever had," Adrian said with a satisfied laugh.

The funny thing was, though, Victoria could have had him. If she hadn't been so quick to say, "Marriage? Darling, why do you want to get married? Let's wait and see what next year brings, okay?"

They had shared a delightful evening together the night he'd proposed. Dinner at Tavern on the Green. Dancing at a jazz club in Harlem. Then they'd gone back to his place and made love.

After nearly a year of seeing one another, Adrian felt it was the normal progression of a serious relationship to go to the next level: marriage. He had nothing against the institution; as institutions go marriage offered many benefits—among them a sense of emotional security. You could stop playing games, get out of the meat market. Devote his attentions to one woman. He'd had that with Teddy. Sure he could have had a roving eye. Men of power, status, and looks often fooled themselves into believing fidelity was for lesser mortals. But he wasn't of that mind-set. He knew his limitations. He was a one-woman man. As long as she went along with the program, that is.

So when he'd asked Victoria to marry him, the two of them snuggled beneath the comforter, naked as the day they were born, and she'd given him that lackluster reply, something went cold inside of him. Then for no apparent reason, Teddy's lovely face had appeared in his mind's eye.

He instinctively knew what Victoria was talking about when she'd suggested they should wait and see what next year brings. She meant his star was rising now, but what if it plummeted to earth unexpectedly? She didn't want to chance being saddled with a has-been. She had to hold her cards close to her chest, and protect her ace. Victoria was an actor who'd appeared in three blockbusters. She commanded a cool five million per picture, and she saw even more dollar signs parading across her line of sight in the very near future. She might've been in love with Adrian, but she wasn't willing to commit to him until he had the potential of earning as much as she did, or more.

For the first time in his adult life, Adrian Riley had his heart broken by a female. He finally knew how Teddy must have felt when he'd left her. Fate had finally paid him back in full.

The very next day his mother, Margaret, got him on the phone and blessed him out for missing his father's sixty-fifth birthday party. And while she was at it, she took the opportunity yet again to harp on how shoddily he'd treated Teddy. Ending off with a litany of his faults—among them his being the world's worst excuse for a father.

Well, that got him to thinking. If he could convince Teddy to come back to him, he'd have everything he needed: a devoted wife, he could be a father to Alexander, his mother would get off his back, and he'd have a stable home life, something that would contribute greatly to his peace of mind and therefore to his career. Any fool could see his life hadn't been working. And Adrian Riley was nobody's fool.

Finally his patience was rewarded when a feminine voice he recognized as his mole at *Contemporary Lives* said, "Mr. Riley, good news. She's arrived in Ballycastle and contacted Joachim West. She doesn't know if she'll get the interview yet, though. I'll phone again as soon as I know more."

"For what I'm paying you, you'd better," Adrian said as he put the receiver back on its base.

"Five minutes," his assistant called over the intercom.

Adrian smiled and left the dressing room. Duty called.

Teddy found that her hair dryer wouldn't work in either the outlet in the bathroom or any of the ones she'd located in the bedroom. She wound up drying her hair with a towel, applying hair dressing and pinning it up off her neck in a halfhearted French roll. This done, she frowned at her reflection in the bureau mirror. What little makeup she'd brought with her, a lipstick, blush, and eyeliner, were in her purloined shoulder bag. So until she was able to buy more, she'd have to do without.

Walking into the closet, she saw that Kathleen had hung up all her outer clothing. Two pairs of jeans, long-sleeved shirts, one rust-colored ankle-length scoop-necked dress that was amazingly wrinkle proof that she'd thrown into the bag, just in case. But who would she need to impress with her one entirely feminine item of clothing?

Yawning, she decided a nap would be in order before debating whether or not Joachim West would change his mind about the interview once he saw her in the rust number.

Pulling the covers back, wearing only her bra and panties, she climbed between the lavender-scented sheets. In record time she was snoring softly.

In the library Joachim sat typing on the computer keyboard. He told himself they were just notes. Thoughts he wished to record in case he should be able to use them for some future project. But the next thing he knew, he was painting a picture of a character—a woman. A woman who'd been abandoned by her lover after learning she was carrying his child. Coincidental? No. Hearing Teddy's story had struck a chord within him. He wanted to write her story. Every single mother's story. His own mother's. But how could he begin to understand what these women had gone through when they were faced with futures without the support of the men who supposedly loved them up until the moment they were presented with real responsibility?

Did he have what it took to write such a story? No, not without intensive research. In order to know how his character thought he would have to go to the source.

Glancing at his watch, he saw that it was after five. Teddy had been upstairs more than three hours. Kathleen and William had recently left for town, saying William's mother was ill. So that left only him to see after his house guest.

She could be sleeping, but he had to make certain nothing was the matter, the girl had just taken a hit to the noggin. Something could be wrong.

Teddy was dreaming of playing with Alex in her father's backyard. Alexander had painstakingly re-created a Japanese garden complete with a redwood footbridge over a pond full of goldfish. Alex liked nothing better than to stand on the bridge with his mother and throw bread pieces into the water, watching expectantly as the giant carp, their mouths forming perfect O's in pursued the morsels.

In the dream it was a sunny day and Teddy and Alex were standing on the bridge. Alex was tossing bread crumbs into the pond and jumping up and down in excitement whenever a fish came to the surface to gobble up his offerings. In the dream the bridge was wobbly. "Alex," Teddy cautioned. "Don't jump up and down like that."

Alex behaved as if he hadn't heard her. He continued to jump up and down. Then the bridge collapsed, sending the both of them into the pond—which had become a raging sea. Teddy's dream persona reached out to grasp Alex, but he fell away from her, deeper and deeper into the ocean's black depths.

Teddy awakened to the sound of someone knocking on the bedroom door. She sat up in bed, her heart pounding. A nightmare. It had been only a nightmare. She was grateful to be out of that one.

"Teddy!" Joachim called from the other side of the door. "Are you all right?"

Teddy hurried to the door. "I'm fine. I fell asleep. I'm going to dress and come downstairs. Where will you be?"

"Meet me in the kitchen," Joachim told her. "I'll get supper on the table."

"All right, thank you." She wondered if she'd cried out in her sleep and if he'd heard her. "I'm sorry if I startled you. I don't usually talk in my sleep, you know."

Joachim laughed. "You didn't talk in your sleep. I was just concerned and came up to see if you were okay, that's all."

"Oh," Teddy said wonderingly. He was concerned about her. She looked down at her half-naked body and felt self-conscious, as though he could see her through the door. It wasn't an altogether unpleasant sensation.

"Well, I'm going," Joachim said, sounding a little reluctant to do so.

"All right," Teddy called, stretching out his departure. She smiled. They were being silly, two adults behaving like shy teens. However, that's exactly how he made her feel, like she'd just been handed a slip of paper by another seven-year-old with the badly scribbled line, *I like you, do you like me? Check yes or no,* written on it.

"Yes!" she said aloud as she hurried into the closet to get dressed.

Joachim had the roast chicken, baked potatoes, and garden salad on the table by the time Teddy entered the kitchen dressed in a pair of jeans, a long-sleeved crushed velvet top in royal blue, and her trusty clogs. Her hair had pretty much dried while she slept, so she'd finger-combed it, and now it was in its usual carefree curly style.

Joachim had been pouring iced tea in glasses, but paused to smile at her. He was also casually attired in a pair of jeans and a denim shirt in chocolate, which contrasted nicely with the cocoa color of his skin. He held up the iced tea pitcher. "If you'd like something stronger, there's wine."

"Not unless you're having some," Teddy said, moving forward and coming around the table to take the pitcher from him. "I'm not much of a drinker. Tea is perfect."

Their fingers touched briefly when she reached for the pitcher. Joachim, at six two, looked down into her upturned face. "I don't drink alcohol."

Teddy finished pouring the tea. "Serious runner?"

His eyes held a surprised expression. "How did you know I'm a runner?"

They sat down across from one another.

"You look like a runner. You've long, sinewy muscles, your skin tone is super healthy and I can't hear you breathing unless I'm very close."

"There was a California cadence to your voice when you said that," Joachim told her.

"What is a California cadence?" Teddy asked, amused.

"It's a sensuous, laid-back intonation. As if it would be perfectly fine with you if saying what you had to say took all day."

"You're not a native," Teddy stated, picking up her fork and piercing a piece of tomato with it. "You have a slightly southern accent."

"Alabama."

Teddy swallowed. "You don't say. . . . My father's from Mississippi. I used to spend summers in Biloxi with my grandmother."

"Is she still in Biloxi?"

"No, she died when I was fourteen."

"I'm sorry."

"She was eighty-four. My father was a late child. She had him when she was in her early forties. She already had six children, and thought she was done, and then she got pregnant with him. She named him Alexander, after Alexander the Great because she said he had conquered her heart."

"She sounds like she was quite a woman," Joachim said,

shaking his head. Hearing Teddy talk about her grandmother made him miss his all the more.

They ate in silence for a few minutes, then Joachim said, "I suppose you could borrow a camera from Conal's collection to take photos for the profile you're doing on me."

It took a second or two for what he was saying to sink in, but when it did, Teddy dropped her fork, swallowed hard and sprang from her chair to run to his side of the table and hug him.

Their faces were pressed together before Teddy realized how impertinent her actions had been. But it was too late then. Joachim's arms were firmly around her torso, holding her against his hard chest. The smell of his aftershave, the warmth of his skin, the feel of his strong hands massaging her back relaxed her better than an hour-long rubdown by a professional masseuse.

Embarrassed, she pushed out of his embrace. Joachim released her, even though she felt so right in his arms. He knew she'd just been excited, and the move hadn't been calculated. If she'd wanted to seduce him into giving her the interview, she would've tried something before now.

He didn't want her thinking he thought any less of her because she couldn't contain her excitement.

"What's a hug between friends, Teddy?" he asked with a shrug, smiling up at her.

She visibly relaxed, painting that gorgeous smile back on her face and went and sat down across from him again.

"What made you change your mind?"

"It was a combination of things, really. Your devotion to your son. How you talk about your father, Alexander. Your roots. I figure anyone who spent summers in the heat of Biloxi just to be with her elderly grandmother couldn't be all bad. Besides, if you make me look like a modern-day Edgar Allan Poe in the article, all dark and sinister, I'll create a character suspiciously similar to you and have Darien do terrible things to you."

Teddy shuddered. "Stop, you're frightening me." Then, "Oh my God, are you thinking of writing a sequel to *The God*

Gene? Because you could, you know. Darien wasn't killed by the end of the story. And there's the possibility that Amanda could be pregnant with Simeon's child . . ."

They lingered over supper for more than an hour, with Teddy trying to convince him to write a sequel to *The God Gene.* Joachim was adamant about not doing so. "Once I'm done with a book, I'm truly done with it. It's never occurred to me to write a follow-up to any of my books."

"Well," Teddy said, running out of steam, "if that's how you feel about it. I suppose the mark of a good writer is his characters leave a lasting impression on the reader. We think of them as real people and wonder what's going on in their lives long after the book's finished. Ah well, no sequel." There was a forlorn quality to her voice.

Laughing, Joachim said, "I could have used you when I was negotiating my last book deal. You would've had them eating out of your hands."

They'd both completed their meals and moved their plates aside.

"Is it true you're working on your next book?"

"That was the idea when I stayed on after Conal and Erin's wedding," he said truthfully. "But I haven't gotten much done."

Teddy was surprised by his admission, but was pleased he'd been so honest with her. She leaned forward, her elbows on the table in a breach of etiquette. "I don't suppose I could do anything to help?" She was immediately remorseful after making such a statement. Help him? What could she possibly do to help a man like Joachim West?

Joachim gave her an enigmatic smile, his eyes on her face. For one tense moment Teddy thought he would throw back his head and laugh. Then his smile faded, and he said, "Your presence is help enough."

Teddy released a relieved sigh, got to her feet and began removing their plates from the table. "You're very kind."

Joachim rose, too, and helped her with the dishes. They

moved around one another, clearing the table. Then Teddy
went over to the sink and began running hot water into it,
holding a capful of dishwashing detergent under the spigot.

Joachim joined her at the sink and they worked in a comfortable silence that was so perfectly familiar that, if there had
been a third party present, he would have sworn they washed
dishes together every night of their lives.

Toward the end as Teddy was transferring a glass to the
draining rack, it slipped from her fingers—but Joachim
quickly caught it and placed it in the rack.

Teddy gave him a sideways glance. "Sorry."

Joachim was looking at the lush lashes framing her almond-
shaped eyes. The curve of her pink mouth, that lovely chin.
He was imagining how her lips must taste when she was emotional as she was now. He knew he made her nervous. She
made him nervous, too. But it was a sweet kind of anticipatory
nervousness.

Teddy dried her hands on a dish towel.

She raised her eyes to his.

Joachim moved closer and grasped her by the elbow.
"Teddy . . ."

Teddy's heart, which had been agitated all evening due to
his nearness, now took off racing. She was wound so tight,
she figured that if he touched her anyplace other than her
elbow, she'd explode all over him and they'd become one tangle of limbs groping one another, and wouldn't part until the
sun interrupted the night.

". . . I'm very attracted to you."

Breathe, she told herself. She backed into the sink. Joachim
allowed his hand to fall to his side. There must have been a
panicked expression on Teddy's face, because he turned away,
saying, "I'm sorry."

Teddy quickly grasped one of his hands in hers. She felt
his grip tighten as they faced one another. "I feel the same
way," she told him. "It's just that it's been a long time since I
met someone who made me feel the way you do—and I guess
I don't trust my emotions after . . ."

Joachim pulled her into his arms, his big hands on her back

as he held her securely against him. He said softly in her ear,
"You don't have to explain. I know about loss, Teddy. And
I'm as confused as you are right now. I wasn't expecting you,
either."

Teddy closed her eyes and simply let herself relax in his
arms. He was so right. How could she have guessed that coming here would present her with such a pleasant conundrum.
Joachim West, the man of her dreams? She peered up into his
eyes.

He lowered his head and their mouths touched, his breath
mingled with hers, then she sighed and he moaned and their
mouths fused in a passionate kiss. His tongue entered her
mouth, taking possession of it as though he knew his way
around. She tiptoed, her height making it a necessity; if she
could have, she would have climbed him in order to get closer.

Joachim bent forward and grabbing her bottom, hoisted
her up. Teddy's feet were no longer touching the floor, and
her head was in the clouds as the kiss deepened.

They ended the kiss, but remained in one another's arms,
smiling happily. Their cheeks touched. "I don't know if that
was very wise," Teddy said, her voice husky.

Joachim turned his head to kiss the spot right next to her
mouth. "Oh? Why not?"

"With the Collinses out of the house all night . . ."

"They just went to visit William's mother."

"No. Kathleen told me they were spending the night in
town."

They parted to gaze into each other's faces; both of them
seemed to radiate with sexual energy.

"She didn't tell me that," Joachim said. He couldn't seem
to muster up any semblance of disappointment upon learning
the news.

Teddy smiled, felt the coolness on the bottom of her feet,
and realized she'd come out of her clogs while she'd been
kissing Joachim. She looked down. One was by the sink, the
other under the kitchen table.

"Oh, yes, I'm certain that's what she told me when she

brought my bag up. She and William are spending the night
in town at his mother's house."

"I don't doubt you," Joachim said, turning away and running a hand over his short, curly hair. He looked back at her.
"This doesn't have to pose a problem. We're both adults here.
Simply because we're alone, it doesn't mean we'll end up in
bed together. Unless, that is, you want to . . ."

"No!" Teddy was quick to reply, going to step in one shoe,
then the other. Their eyes met. "I mean, yes . . . *no!*"

Laughing softly, his head cocked to the side, Joachim regarded her with a bemused expression. "Which is it, yes or
no?"

Teddy decided to tell it like it was and let the chips fall
where they may. Standing in front of him, her hands planted
on her hips, she said, exasperated, "Okay! Yeah, I would *love*
to get naked with you, Joachim. The moment we met, I wondered what your lips would feel like on mine. I wanted to run
my hands over that beard you had—but you shaved it off—so
that's beside the point." Eyes narrowed, she continued. "My
body reacts crazily to yours, there's no denying that. But if I
acted on impulse, what would you think of me afterward?"

Joachim inched closer to her. "Is this some woman thing?
You believe I'm going to think less of you if we make love
the first night we meet? Is that it?"

He was watching her with such warmth and understanding
that Teddy was sure that at that moment, if he told her the
moon was made of cheese, she'd believe him.

"What would you think of me, Teddy? That I'm a lonely
reclusive author, too strange to go out and find dates in the
normal way? That I invited you here only because I wanted
to bed you?" He smiled. "Don't say that never occurred to
you. You're a beautiful woman. It never crossed your mind to
offer yourself to me in exchange for that interview?"

Teddy laughed. "I didn't think you'd be that desperate."

"A man doesn't have to be desperate to want you, Teddy.
He just has to be breathing."

Teddy's hand went to her face. She was only thirty, she
couldn't be having a hot flash. Was this some biological device

God had programmed into the human gene? When in sexual excitement, the body grows warm—then the next thing you know, you're coming out of your clothing in order to cool off, and you know what happens when the clothing comes off. What a way to ensure man would be fruitful and multiply.

Joachim decided to take another tack. He hadn't rapped this hard since he was a teenager. They could both use some space to think this thing through.

"I'll tell you what," he suggested. "You need to contact your father and let him know what's going on . . ."

Teddy hoped the relief didn't show on her face. "I should phone him," she agreed. "I'd like to hear Alex's voice."

Joachim smiled. "You do that. In the meanwhile I'm going for a short walk."

In the library he quickly showed her where the phone was and left her alone.

Teddy sat down at the desk and dialed out to get a Telecom Éireann operator. When the woman answered, Teddy told her she needed to place an international call.

A minute or so later, her father picked up.

"Hello?"

"Daddy, how are my two favorite men?"

Alexander laughed. "Theodora. When you didn't answer my e-mail, I was afraid something was the matter."

"Something has happened, Daddy . . ." Teddy began.

"I'll be looking for that e-mail, daughter. If your passport and ID aren't found soon, you make sure you tell me where to wire the money," Alexander admonished a few minutes later.

"I will, Daddy, don't worry about me."

"How can I not worry? You be careful . . ."

"I will be, Daddy. Put Alex on, please."

"Mommy!"

"Yes, it's Mommy, sweetheart. I just wanted to hear your voice, baby. I miss you!"

She could hear her father coaching Alex in the background. Giggling, Alex shouted, "I love you this . . . much, Mommy!"

Teddy envisioned her son stretching his arms out as wide as they could go.

"And I love you this . . . much, baby," she returned, her eyes misty. "Mommy has to go now." She made a kissing sound.

Her father came back on the line. "All right, Theodora. I'll expect to hear from you soon."

"Bye, Daddy. I love you."

"I love you, too, daughter."

Teddy hung up and got to her feet. Tears were rolling down her cheeks. She wiped them away, collecting herself. She didn't want Joachim returning and finding her in this state.

She walked over to a bookshelf upon which several framed photographs sat in groups. In most of them was a broad-chested man with a mischievous, exuberant light in his eyes. That must be Conal Ryan, she decided. Joachim was in many of them, along with a young, very pretty black woman. Suzanne. Teddy could see the happiness coming off of them in waves in those photos. So that was the type of woman Suzanne was. The type of woman who made him believe in himself and in life. It was obvious he adored her.

"Did you get your father?" Joachim asked from the doorway.

Startled, Teddy spun around and nearly knocked one of the photographs off the shelf. She righted it, her hand trembling a little. Their eyes met across the room. What could he possibly see in me? Teddy wondered. When he's had that beautiful woman in his life? How could I ever compare?

Joachim moved into the room, his eyes never leaving her face. He could see she'd been crying. "What's the matter, Teddy? Is something wrong at home?"

"Nothing's wrong," Teddy denied. She forced a smile. "I'm not used to being away from Alex for more than a day. Hearing his voice just made me miss him more."

Joachim stopped in front of her. "You'll be back with him soon." He grasped her by the upper arms, turning her around to face him. "If Liam Murdoch doesn't turn up something tomorrow, I'll take you to the U.S. Embassy myself."

"I couldn't put you to the trouble," Teddy protested.

"It's no trouble," Joachim assured her with a grin. "I could stand to get out of this house. The only thing I've done since I've been here is go fishing. It would be a welcome diversion."

As I must be to you, Teddy thought, her insecurities putting in an appearance. She'd fought to hang on to her self-esteem after Adrian left her. She supposed she hadn't done such a magnificent job after all.

But, she chided herself, *why am I thinking like this anyway? After I leave Ireland, I'll probably never see him again. So what if we decided to spend one night of passion together? Who would be the wiser? A secret two consenting adults would never divulge to another soul.*

However, she wasn't quite ready to throw herself upon the altar of adult free expression just yet.

"I was looking at those photographs," she said, glancing in the direction of the bookshelf.

They walked over to the photographs and Joachim picked up a five-by-seven of him and Suzanne standing in front of the Ritz Hotel. "Conal took this of Suzanne and me at the hotel where we stayed in Paris. We were on our honeymoon. That's where we met Conal. He got into a drunken altercation in the bar and I broke it up."

Smiling, Teddy glanced down at the photograph. "You look so young, the both of you. And so vibrant . . ."

"That was eleven years ago. We *were* young and vibrant, and very much in love."

"I could see that in all of them," Teddy told him softly, referring to the photographs. "She was lovely."

"In more ways than one," Joachim said wistfully, replacing the photograph and turning to Teddy. "She was amazingly resilient. She lost her parents at a young age, seventeen; but she went on to put herself through college—she never let anything stand in her way. And people! She had a way of making everyone feel special. She literally had Conal Ryan, a hard-drinking bear of a man, wrapped around her finger in the space of two minutes after they met."

"She sounds like someone I would've liked to have met."

Tears glistened in her eyes.

How she ached for what he'd had. To have a man love her with as much unadulterated affection. It broke her heart to witness it. To think that when she'd married Adrian, she'd believed they would grow old and doddering together. Their future lives had been clearly etched in her mind. Adrian hadn't been the only one guilty of mapping out their lives—only she had done it out of love, not with potential monetary success in mind.

"Are you going to cry again?" Joachim asked softly, his brows raised questioningly.

Teddy shook her head in the affirmative. They were silent tears though. She wasn't about to let him see her blubber. As the tears rolled into her mouth, she said, "I would give anything to have what you had with Suzanne. You should hear your voice when you talk about her. It has a sort of hushed, reverent quality. She was the only woman you ever loved, wasn't she?"

Full himself, Joachim swallowed hard. "Yes."

"I'm so sorry," Teddy said, going to pull him into her arms.

Joachim allowed her to hold him. He never thought he could have a conversation about Suzanne with another woman and not feel awkward, or, indeed, slightly irritated to hear another woman speak of her. But there was something infinitely compassionate about Teddy Riley that spoke to him.

"When I married Adrian, I truly believed he loved me," she said against his chest. "In a lot of ways, I was naive. It never dawned on me, the whole while we were married, that he looked upon me as he did everything else he owned. As long as it was to his advantage to own it, he kept it—and when it no longer pleased him, he bought something else he liked better."

She smiled up at him through her tears. "You're a nice guy, Joachim West. Are you sure you want to take a basket case like me to bed?"

"I'm sure," he told her, his dimples showing. "I just want you to be sure. So I'll tell you what: I'll leave my door un-

locked. If you decide you'd like to spend the night in my arms,
I'll be waiting . . . and hoping."

He smoothed her brow then and placed a kiss on her forehead.

Teddy stood looking out into the night, wondering if
George was out there somewhere playing his heart out.
George was probably suffering from unrequited love, poor
fellow. That's why he wandered the abandoned streets of Ballycastle late at night, scaring everyone. No lady ghost to go
home to.

She'd flossed and brushed, washed her face. Put on her
white nighty. Now all she had to do was walk next door and
push open Joachim's door and climb into bed with him. What
was she waiting on? She wanted him. Her body was ripe for
him. The tips of her breasts were alert, her limbs were tingling,
her feminine center, throbbing. Oh yes, the signs were there.

She went and lay on the bed, turning on her side, her eyes
on the door. Maybe he'd come to her. She hadn't locked it.
But that wasn't the plan. Joachim was a gentleman through
and through. Just as he'd promised, he would leave it entirely
up to her. She picked up her watch from the nightstand. It was
ten fifteen. Still early really.

She got to her feet and began pacing.

Next door Joachim had just come out of the bathroom after
a refreshing soak in the tub. He'd brushed and flossed. Now
he was dressed only in his pajama bottoms. He placed a hand
on his flat stomach. Would she come to him? God, he hoped
so. But if she decided not to, he would definitely understand.
They were strangers. Strangers who were physically drawn to
one another, for certain, but strangers nonetheless.

He wanted to get to know her better. He knew that. There
was no way he was going to let her slip through his fingers.

He struck his forehead with the palm of his hand. He hadn't
told her that. She probably thought all he wanted was a one-
night stand.

He went to head for the door with the intention of going

next door and telling her, but stopped. He'd tell her if she put in an appearance—and if she didn't, he'd tell her how he felt about her tomorrow morning.

He sat atop the comforter, his back against the headboard. And exactly how did he feel about her?

At this point he knew only that she intrigued him. She was gorgeous and smart and she brought out his humanity. Why else would he bring her here, not withstanding his grandmother's admonition? And when it came down to it, wasn't it always how someone made you feel that determined whether or not you liked them?

He liked Teddy Riley.

Nine

"If you yawn one more time, I'm going to suspect you didn't get a lick of sleep," Kathleen said to Teddy the next morning as the two of them sat at the kitchen table eating breakfast. Joachim, an early riser, had already—according to Kathleen—run several miles. "I can't imagine why a body would want to do all that running."

"Then he came back and had a whopper of a breakfast. The whole egg—two of them. Sausages and fried potatoes. I daresay your presence has increased his appetite." She said this with a certain twinkle in her eyes.

Teddy only smiled and ate a forkful of soft scrambled eggs.

If she had a mind to, she could tell Kathleen that her tiredness was due to sleeplessness. But not because she and Joachim had been up most of the night engaged in activities conducive to connubial bliss. No, she'd tossed and turned all night because she'd chickened out, and had regretted her decision so much, she hadn't been able to sleep because even though she'd mentally and intellectually made her choice, her body still craved Joachim's touch. It had been nearly three in the morning before she'd been exhausted enough to fall asleep.

"I'm glad you're here," Kathleen said.

Teddy perked up. Was Kathleen just making conversation, as she was truly adept at, or was there something more?

"I'm glad to be here," Teddy said pleasantly.

Lowering her voice, Kathleen meet Teddy's eyes and said,

"No, I mean I'm happy to see you with Mr. West. I think he missed you."

At this point Teddy was beginning to feel uncomfortable continuing the ruse of she and Joachim being husband and wife. She hated lying under any circumstances. She especially disliked misleading decent folks like Kathleen and William. But until Joachim informed her enough was enough, she'd go along with it.

How was she to reply to Kathleen's assertion that Joachim had been pining away for his wife? She was sure he missed Suzanne with all his heart. She felt like a fraud.

"I missed him, too. I hate it when we're apart."

Shaking her head in commiseration, Kathleen said, "It's not good for a marriage. William and I have been wed nigh on thirty years. We've never been blessed with wee ones. It's just made us closer. He isn't the type of man who is demonstrative, but I've never doubted his love, nor have I ever been separated from him for more than a night." She gave Teddy a sympathetic look. "So you've patched things up, then? That's wonderful."

Teddy had finished eating. She took a sip of strong, hot tea before smiling and asking, "Patched things up?"

"I figured you and Mr. West had had a row, and that's why he came to the wedding alone." She pointedly glanced down at Teddy's naked ring finger. "And you're not wearing your wedding ring."

Teddy laughed. "Oh, that. I've always had a hard time keeping up with jewelry. I left it on the sink at home." Holding her hand up for Kathleen to see, she added, "I take it off so often, I don't even have a tan line." She grinned. "You don't suppose that's a symptom of something, do you? My forgetfulness?"

Kathleen rolled her eyes. "Heavens no!" She laughed. "If my William didn't have his name sewn into his knickers, he'd not remember who he is from day to day."

Kathleen rose and began clearing the table.

"Let me help," Teddy offered.

"No, you don't," Kathleen said. "You go say hello to your

husband. I bet he's wondering where his good-morning kiss is."

Teddy smiled at Kathleen and turned away, pulling a face once her back was to Kathleen. Lord, the woman loved to talk. If she stayed around here much longer, she'd wind up creating an entire history for her and Joachim.

She ran her hands through her locks as she rounded the corner, heading to the library. Her clogs made crisp taps on the hardwood floor. She paused in the hallway and scrutinized the paintings on the wall. Originals by modern artists from the looks of them. She didn't recognize any of the signatures.

She wasn't interested in the paintings. She was stalling. What would she say to Joachim to explain her absence last night? Had he lain awake like she had? That would account for his burst of energy this morning, and hearty appetite. He'd run to expend sexual energy and had eaten well to satisfy another type of hunger? She wiped moist palms on her jeans. How could she possibly think of getting involved with anyone now anyway? When she returned home, she could be smack in the middle of a custody battle. Then all her energies would have to be concentrated on keeping Alex out of Adrian's hands.

Besides, she didn't believe she'd be capable of making love to Joachim and not wanting more. Knowing him twenty-four hours had awakened "the dream" in her again. All women had "the dream" somewhere in the backs of their minds. It involved love, commitment, and marriage. In that order. We might try to convince ourselves we'd be happy with Mr. Right Now. But actually we were always hoping for Mr. Forever and a Day.

"Looking for me?"

Joachim had come out of the library and was walking toward her.

Teddy raised her eyes to his and smiled slowly. He looked well rested. In fact, he looked darn good in his jeans, white short-sleeved athletic shirt, and Reeboks.

"I was just coming to find you."

Joachim stopped in front of her and pulled her into his arms.

"Is that any way to say hello to your husband?"

Teddy saw the gleam in his eyes and knew what it meant, and she tried to brace herself for the feel of his mouth on hers, but she wasn't able to lessen the impact in any discernible way.

Her body yearned to be held by his. Her mouth was as eager as his, and when their lower halves touched, she still wanted to press even closer to his male hardness.

Joachim thought he would put Teddy at ease by playing the role of a loving husband, even in the absence of an audience. She liked to joke around, testing him to see if she could make him blush. He thought two could play that game. But when he pulled her in his arms and her mouth met his, he knew he was no longer acting. He needed to taste her lips, feel her soft, pliant female form against his. He wanted to smell her hair and breathe in her breath, like vanilla ice cream. Sweet. He'd gone to sleep last night with the memory of her kisses playing over and over in his mind. And for the first time in a long while, he hadn't had the nightmares.

"Nobody's watching," Teddy whispered against his mouth.

Joachim turned his head a little and her lashes tickled his cheek. "Kathleen could show up at any moment. We should stay in character."

Teddy laughed softly. "I thought you'd be a little hurt because I didn't come to your room last night."

"No . . . I understood." He tenderly massaged her back. He straightened. Her nose was now buried in his chest as they held one another. "I don't usually behave that way. I'm sorry. Maybe I am a lonely recluse of an author," he joked.

Teddy peered up at him. Her big brown eyes were slightly dreamy. Her lips curved in a sensuous smile. "It was very hard to resist knocking on your door, Joachim. I tossed and turned all night." She blew air between her lips. "But I knew that if I came to you, that wouldn't have been the end of it for me. I would've wanted more."

Joachim groaned. "I'm such a jerk." He smiled down into

her eyes. "Teddy, I don't just want to make love to you. I want to get to know you . . . slowly. I'd like to court you, Teddy Riley."

Teddy laughed.

"I want to pick you up at your place and meet your son and let your father look me over with that stern look reserved for fathers of daughters," he told her with relish. "I want to take you out for seafood and watch you attack snow crabs with both hands and then I want to go dancing with you until we both drop."

Teddy squeezed him tighter. "That sounds good." Sighing, she added in a more serious tone, "But you've got a book to write. And I've got a profile to do . . . on you!"

Joachim laughed. "All right," he said, his dark eyes caressing her face. "When would you like to get started?"

"Whenever you have a free moment from your work."

They parted, just in time to see Kathleen coming down the hallway with a feather duster in her hand. "Don't let me interrupt," she said with a smile.

She went into the library.

Joachim marveled at how much warmer Kathleen had been toward him since Teddy's arrival.

"What do you say to a day trip?" Joachim suggested. "We could borrow one of Conal's cameras and head out to the Giant's Causeway. It's only about sixteen kilometers from here. I've been wanting to see it. We could talk, you could ask your questions and the Causeway would probably be a great backdrop for photographs."

"Okay," Teddy said at once. She'd heard about the Giant's Causeway and the legend attached to it. "When would you like to leave?"

"Why not right now? I'll go tell Kathleen we're leaving while you go upstairs and get your jacket. No telling how the weather will change between now and tonight."

Teddy slowly backed away from him. She loved the way he looked at her, a cross between a lustful craving tempered by compassion.

"It's a plan," she called as she quickly turned and hurried upstairs.

Joachim watched her go, his heartbeat beginning to slow down a bit. The last time a woman had excited him this much, he'd fallen in love with her. That woman had been Suzanne.

The thought unnerved him. A look of consternation marred his features. Did he want to love another woman as much as he'd loved Suzanne and risk losing her, too? Could his heart take it?

Buoyed by the turn of events, Teddy wore a grin as she reached the landing. She figured Joachim would be showing her the door at this time of the day, after doing what he perceived to be his duty and watching her overnight. But things had changed last night. In fact, the attraction they felt for one another had been present from the moment they laid eyes on each other. She'd known it. And apparently so had he. Who could explain it? Was there something the human spirit recognized in another spirit? Capable of stripping away the outer facade and getting to the bone? Sure he was physically appealing. She'd met many men who were just as handsome. Just as well built. However they hadn't commanded her undivided attention the way he had. Was it in the way he looked at her? Or was it because of the way he made her feel? *Like everything is possible . . .*

Liam Murdoch stood in the middle of the street, looking from one end to the other. He had been through every trash can in every alley in the vicinity. Nine times out of ten, pursesnatchers took the first opportunity to remove whatever cash or valuables from the bag and ditched the bag in the nearest trash can, or just threw it to the street. They didn't want to get caught with the physical evidence on them. Oftentimes cash couldn't be traced, because most people paid no attention to the serial numbers on the bills in their wallets. And, if there was anything of value in the bag, like jewelry, the pursesnatcher usually beat a hasty path to the nearest dishonest pawnbroker.

Liam strode onto the sidewalk and turned to head back to his office. Maybe the kid was an amateur, he reasoned. He could be stupid enough to keep the purses he took as trophies. Clara had said he was tall, pale-skinned, had dirty blond hair and bad skin and was dressed entirely in black. That described practically every teen from here to Belfast.

"Morning, Liam," Colm Mannix called as Liam approached his butcher shop. "Any luck in finding Mrs. West's attacker?"

Liam couldn't help noticing the note of skepticism in Colm's voice. He paused, his eyes narrowing. Colm was a burly six-foot-tall ex-footballer. He had Liam by at least thirty pounds. But he'd gone to seed in the last ten years, and Liam, though leaner and five years older, worked out regularly in order to stay in fighting form.

"No," Liam answered, looking at Colm through slits. "But I will. You mark my words, Colm Mannix."

"Oh, I know the criminal element in this town is all atremble at the prospect of being collared by you!" Colm said, his belly shaking with laughter.

Colm's wife, Lucy, came to the doorway. "Colm Mannix, you're always slacking off. You've plenty of work to do around here. You don't have time to be jawing with the constable."

Colm muttered some unintelligible expletive under his breath, tossed Liam an angry look and obeyed his wife.

Lucy winked at Liam and followed her recalcitrant husband. You couldn't let them get away with too much, they forgot who was the boss.

Liam smiled, shaking his head. Imagine Lucy Jenkins marrying a lout like Colm Mannix. He'd been in love with Lucy when they were teens. But he joined the army when he turned seventeen, and upon his return, five years later, learned his Lucy had hedged her bets and married Colm, who inherited the butcher shop from his father. He couldn't blame her. Although he often wondered if he'd had sense enough to correspond with her in his absence, if things would have turned out differently in the end.

She still made his heart race. Perhaps Colm knew that, and

that was why he took every opportunity to antagonize him. Out of jealousy. A bull protecting his territory.

Liam was a bachelor. He'd dated several of the unattached ladies in the area. Lately he'd noticed Susan MacLarety giving him the once-over. Susan was nice looking, if a bit bony. He liked his women with a little more meat on their bones. Like Lucy. Maybe Colm would have an accident. . . . No, he couldn't think that way. It hurt to think that Lucy might not be completely happy though. And sometimes he thought her lovely gray eyes appeared sad and wistful.

He was taken aback when he opened the door to his one-room office and found Kathleen Collins and Jimmy O'Neil sitting there.

It wasn't the fact that they were there that had surprised him. He left the office unlocked during the day in case someone needed to use the shortwave radio. It was the only one the village had, and in the case of an emergency, and the phone lines were down, the only means of communication with the outside world.

No, he was frankly shocked by the fact that Jimmy O'Neil was trussed up like a turkey: his wrists tied together. His mouth was covered and his legs bound tightly together as well. And Kathleen Collins had a vaguely smug smile on her face.

While Liam had been combing the streets in search of evidence, at Ryan Manor Teddy and Joachim were loading the Jaguar in anticipation of their trip to the Giant's Causeway. Kathleen, having the whole day to do with as she pleased, was thinking it might be just the time to visit her ailing friend, Irene. William had the garden to weed, so he begged off when she asked him to join her.

After a brief morning shower, the sky had cleared considerably and was a pale blue, and the sun shed its golden light upon the green earth. It was an ideal day for driving. Kathleen hated driving in the rain.

She packed a picnic basket with roast lamb, a loaf of her homemade bread, a jar of peach preserves—a treat for Irene, they were her favorites—and some fresh vegetables from the garden.

Irene was a widow with one young son, Jimmy, named for his father, who was shot and killed in an altercation on the streets of Belfast in 1988. Irene had been heavy with child then. She'd never agreed with Jimmy's politics, but she'd married him for better or for worse.

After Jimmy's death, Irene's aunt Martha, a widow herself, invited her to come to Ballycastle and live with her. Irene gave birth to Jimmy there. Dr. O'Shaunessy delivered the tow-headed boy two months after his mother arrived. Before she became ill, Irene was a waitress at The Rose and The Thorn, a popular pub in town. She'd kept her job until she started losing strength in her limbs and her face became drawn and pallid. Her weight dropped drastically. She couldn't do her job any longer.

Ireland had a national health program, so her doctor bills were paid. However, living from day to day became ever more difficult. She'd had to sell off pieces of her aunt's cherished antique furniture. The house was nearly empty except for her bedroom furniture and Jimmy's.

As the old Fiat Kathleen was driving pulled into the yard, Jimmy, who'd had his motorbike turned upside down, repairing one of the wheels, put down his wrench and grimaced at the familiar battered vehicle. It was that busybody again. Why wouldn't she leave them in peace?

Kathleen painted a smile on her face as she approached the house. Lately Jimmy did nothing but scowl. But she supposed it must be hard on the boy. His mother had been ill a long time and he had to be frightened.

"Good day to you, Jimmy!"

"Mrs. Collins," Jimmy said, acknowledging her, but not changing his facial expression one iota. She was his mother's friend, not his.

"Is your mother up and about?"

The boy's lips were sealed. He pursed them and showed her his back. "Why don't you go on in and see?"

"I beg your pardon?" Kathleen asked sharply. She'd heard

him well enough. But she didn't brook insolence from a boy she'd diapered, not even if he was upset over his mother's condition.

Sighing, Jimmy faced her. "Yes, Mrs. Collins. She's up."

"Thank you, James O'Neil. That's better."

Kathleen stepped under the ivy-covered awning over the front door and gave a quick knock. "Irene! It's Kathleen, I'm coming in."

Kathleen could barely make out a thing in the darkened house. And the smell was awful. Stale human sweat and urine. Irene usually kept a clean house.

She walked through the tiny front room, amazed she hadn't bumped into any furniture. Going to a window, she drew back a curtain and light spilled into the room.

What used to be a cluttered but cozy room was now nearly devoid of possessions. She walked back to the kitchen. Irene wasn't in there, either. Placing the picnic basket on the table, she went in search of Irene in the back bedrooms.

"Irene!"

"I'm in the bathroom, Kathleen. I'll be out in minute or two," came Irene's voice from the west end of the house.

Kathleen went into Irene's bedroom, to wait for her friend. This room was dark, too. She went to the nightstand and switched on the lamp. The room smelled as if it hadn't been aired in a long while. She looked down. Irene's sheets were soiled with urine and feces.

Tears welled in her eyes at the sight of that. She should have been out here before now, checking up on her. Irene didn't have many friends. Many of the other women considered her beneath them because she was a single woman who had worked in a pub. For some reason they thought they should keep their distance in order to protect their marriages.

Irene was a pretty woman. And she was outgoing. But if they had ever taken the time to get to know her, they would have learned she was also a very decent woman. Their husbands were safe.

Wiping her tears away, Kathleen went to the linen closet in the hallway and got clean sheets and pillowcases. By the time

Irene got out of the bathroom, her bed had fresh linen on it and Kathleen had gone to the kitchen and washed the dirty dishes in the sink and made a pot of tea.

Kathleen entered the bedroom with a tray filled with the teapot and mugs, plates and silverware, cream and sugar, warmed slices of bread, butter, and the jar of peach preserves.

Irene was lying in bed. She'd been in the bathroom trying to clean herself up. She had on a crisp gown now, and though she was painfully thin and extremely pale, her love for her friend shone in her eyes when she saw Kathleen coming through the door.

Kathleen placed the tray on the nightstand and hugged Irene.

"Hello, love, how are you today?"

She released Irene and set about filling mugs with the piping hot tea. She added sugar and cream to Irene's. She took hers black.

"Thank you, Kathleen," Irene said, accepting a cup. Her right hand smoothed the clean sheets. "And thank you for this."

"That was nothing, dear," Kathleen said, her keen eyes on Irene's face. For months she'd come by hoping that the next time she visited, Irene would be better. Some minute change in her color, or an added pound or two. Something. But now she knew that what the doctors had told Irene was true. Her dear friend was terminally ill. And no amount of wishing otherwise was going to change things.

She pulled a chair up. For a few minutes they didn't speak as they enjoyed the tea. Kathleen smoothed butter on a slice of the bread and added a generous amount of preserves.

She placed her offering on a plate and waved it under Irene's nose. "How about a taste? I made them just for you."

Irene smiled, and there were unshed tears in her eyes. "I wish I could. But nothing stays down anymore."

Kathleen put the plate back on the tray. "Well, we'll just have to try later." She smiled and rose. "You drink your tea while I see to the laundry, all right?"

Irene reached out and grasped Kathleen by the arm. "Kathleen, I need to talk with you about something first. Please."

Kathleen sat back down.

A few minutes later she burst out of the front door and walked purposefully toward Jimmy, who was still tinkering with his bike.

Jimmy happened to glance up before she reached him and the white-hot anger he saw in her eyes made his blood freeze in his veins. Had she gone around the bend? His first impulse was to take off, but he'd hesitated too long. Kathleen, at five two and a hundred and thirty pounds to his five six, one hundred twenty, shouldn't have been able to overpower him since he was decades younger and male, besides. However, when she grabbed him by the back of the neck, her grip was like a steel vise. "You're coming with me, you little bugger."

She literally dragged him back into the house and to his bedroom where she'd tossed his room and found his hidden booty. On the bed were several ladies' purses, along with other pilfered items like watches, rings, necklaces . . . and Teddy's Nikon.

Jimmy tried to wriggle free. "Let go of me, you ugly old witch!"

Kathleen ignored his remarks as she busily bound his hands behind him with duct tape that she'd found under the kitchen sink. Then she shoved him into a nearby chair. He kicked at her, but she quickly moved out of range. She was behind him before he knew it, had pushed him onto the floor and sat on him, facing his flailing legs. She grabbed them and wrapped the tape around them. Jimmy flopped on the floor like a fish out of water as Kathleen calmly got a pillowcase and began putting his ill-gotten gain into it.

"Did you think you could hide what you've been doing from your mother? She's sick, not blind. She told me she'd already told you she isn't going to get any better, James O'Neil. We won't go into your reasons for doing what you've done. You did it. You're guilty, and you're going to be punished for it."

"You don't know what we've been going through. How

sometimes Ma didn't have money for food. What was I supposed to do, get a job? I had to help her any way I could!"

"By stealing from your friends and neighbors?"

"That black woman wasn't no friend or neighbor . . ."

"That black woman, as you say, is my friend," Kathleen cried.

She peered down at him, her eyes fierce. "Your mother asked me to take you to the constable. She doesn't want to go to her grave ashamed of you. You are to confess your crimes, James O'Neil and take your punishment like a man, and maybe one day you will be worthy of being called her son."

The boy was so angry, he was red in the face. He appeared as if he were about to burst from the burning rage inside of him. Kathleen didn't let up though. "Do you think your mother worked her fingers to the bone all these years to raise up a boy who would end up dead on the street like his father, before he reaches the age of consent? Do you?!"

He screamed out of frustration. He bellowed until his throat was raw. Kathleen let him. He needed to get it out. She wanted him spent and limp as a dishrag by the time she led him to the car for the trip to the constable's.

After an hour, he quieted down.

He was drenched in sweat.

Kathleen thought she'd been in the presence of someone demon possessed. She'd crossed herself constantly while he'd ranted.

"Jimmy," a low voice said from the doorway.

Jimmy blinked to clear his vision. His mother toddled into the room and knelt before him. "Jimmy, I want you to go with Mrs. Collins. Return what you've taken to the rightful owners. I know some of the money has been spent, but you'll have to work to repay it."

Jimmy couldn't look into his mother's decimated face. He looked at the walls. At Kathleen. At anything other than his mother.

But his mother took his face between her hands and made him look at her. "I love you, Jimmy. I'll always love you. But I will have been a bad mother if I didn't teach you this one last lesson. No problem is solved by taking from others. And violence only begets violence. Haven't we seen that over and over again? Be a better man than your father was, Jimmy."

Teddy was glad she'd opted for her athletic shoes this morning. Walking on the Causeway—which was eleven miles of prismatic pillars that formed some seventy million years ago when lava burst through the earth's crust and cooled rapidly—was perilous. The Causeway stretched between Ireland and Scotland. Legend had it that the Causeway was built by giants who wanted a convenient way to get back and forth between Ireland and Scotland. The pillars, indeed, looked like stepping stones. In some spots they appeared to be stacked on top of one another. In others they were flat, much like the stones one would place in one's garden.

She and Joachim held hands as they walked nearly to the water's edge. The breakers were high, so they didn't want to get too close. "It is awesome," Teddy said, looking all around them.

"It nearly rivals the Grand Canyon," was Joachim's opinion.

"I've never been there."

The wind whipped about them, and with this gust, a spout of seawater doused them. They'd gotten sprinkled once or twice, but this time they were splashed quite thoroughly.

"I think the sea's trying to tell us something, don't you?" Joachim joked, wiping water from his face.

"Yeah," Teddy agreed with a chuckle, squeezing water from her hair. "Like it's time to leave."

Joachim held her hand more firmly as they turned and headed back to where they'd left the car. Joachim led the way, stepping confidently as they traversed the rocky terrain.

On the way there Teddy had interviewed him for the piece she was writing on him. Joachim had answered her questions openly and honestly. But there was still something she was dying to ask him. She wanted to know if he was still in mourning for Suzanne. She knew instinctively that when you lost a partner to death, you never forgot them. There was a part of you that would always love them. That was perfectly understandable. He'd already told her he wanted to continue seeing her. And perhaps his stating his intentions should be enough. However, she'd seen the bitter pain and longing in him when he'd mentioned Suzanne. Letting go of that kind of love was never easy.

"You're awfully quiet," Joachim said. "You're not getting chilled, are you? I don't know what I was thinking, bringing you out here after your injury yesterday."

His concern warmed her. It was cold out though, and the wind felt like ice on her skin. "I'm a little cold, but I'm fine really. And I wanted to come, remember?"

Joachim let go of her hand and came out of his coat, which was waterproof and hadn't gotten soaked through. "Here," he said, holding the coat open for her to slip her arms inside. "Take off your coat and put this on."

Teddy did as she was told. She was immediately enveloped by the residue of his body heat and the aroma of his aftershave.

Joachim took her wet coat in one hand and her right hand in the other and they continued their trek.

"You think the constable has come up with anything by now?" Teddy wondered aloud.

"He seems a competent fellow, if a bit talkative," Joachim said with a smile, recalling the reception. "It's a small town. Someone will undoubtedly be able to identify the kid from the description the old woman gave Liam."

"I hope so," Teddy said, not sounding too confident.

"Even if he doesn't turn up anything, you'll be fine, Teddy," Joachim promised with a reassuring squeeze of her hand. "I'll get you back to your son safely."

Teddy didn't comment. She knew he meant it.

They walked on in silence.

Fifteen minutes later as they were approaching the end of the formation, suddenly the sky opened and rain came down in torrents. They sprinted the rest of the way to the car.

Joachim fumbled with the key in her door, but got it open. Teddy pranced in place until he did. Once she was inside the relative warmth of the Jaguar, she reached over and unlocked his door. Joachim climbed in and shut the door. Grinning ruefully, he looked down into her face and joked, "Well, they say if you don't like the weather in Ireland, just wait a minute."

He turned the key in the ignition and switched on the heater. "It'll be warm in here soon."

Their eyes met, and he momentarily forgot what he was going to say next. Drenched, her hair plastered to her head, she was still so lovely she took his breath away.

Teddy thought steam should be rising off her body as when water met fire, because she was smoldering inside.

Her hand, of its own volition, went to his square jaw. She wanted to commit his face to memory, should something happen to interrupt or prevent his promise of courting her from coming to pass. What if this was just a transient case of infatuation on his part? What if he really was just lonely for female company?

Joachim grasped the hand she'd touched him with, turned it palm up and kissed it—then, still holding it, he ran her hand down his throat, to his chest and over his heart.

Outside, the rain fell in sheets, the wind howled. Others parked nearby were anxious to leave. Their vehicles formed a slow line exiting the parking area.

The Jaguar, however, remained motionless. Although the windows began to show signs of condensation.

The beat of his heart against her palm reverberated throughout Teddy's already heightened nervous system. She let out a strangled sigh, closed her eyes, and Joachim's mouth claimed hers. Up on her knees now, her hands had gone under his shirt and were stroking his bare chest which, she happily learned, was hairy and as hard as she imagined it would be.

Joachim had pulled his jacket off her and flung it across the seat. Now his two big hands held her warm, fragrant flesh in them. Teddy's shirt came off. He cupped her breasts through her bra, gently but firmly. Teddy moaned deep in her throat.

She turned her head a moment to say, "Did you bring anything?" Meaning condoms.

"No . . ." A wretched admission of omission.

She turned into the kiss again and Joachim's tongue parted her lips with slow deliberate intensity. Teddy was lost in sensory overload. Joachim pulled his mouth away to rain kisses along the curve of her coppery neck. Teddy arched her back to allow him full access. His right hand moved down to caress her bottom, a sensitive spot to Teddy. "Joachim . . ." She fell back on the seat, Joachim on top of her. Her hands went to his belt buckle.

It was then that Joachim came to his senses, and broke off the embrace. "Not here."

"What?" She was drunk with passion.

Joachim straightened up and pulled her to a sitting position. He tilted her chin up and looked into her eyes. If he were a libertine he'd take her right now, because he wanted her so badly, he was in pain. But he wasn't. He cared about her. And like he'd told her earlier, he wanted more from her than just a roll in the hay.

"Not here, not now."

With that said, he switched on the windshield wipers, the headlights, put the car in Drive and pulled out of the parking area.

Teddy adjusted her bra and pulled her shirt back on. Slightly shocked by her behavior, partly thrilled, she looked over at his profile. Joachim had his bottom lip between his teeth as though he were deep in thought. There was a contented gleam in his eyes though, and as he found a spot in line behind the other cars, he reached over and warmly clasped her hand in his.

"When it does happen, I hope you don't kill me."

"Buckle up, sweetie," Teddy said with a grateful smile.

And the both of them fastened their seat belts.

A black sedan was parked in front of the manor when they drove up. Joachim drove on around to the back to the garage and he and Teddy came into the house through the kitchen door. Kathleen saw them first. She was serving coffee to William and in her excitement, she moved the spout too far to the right and poured coffee on William's hand.

"Ow . . ." William cried, pulling the scalded hand back and quickly rising. Kathleen placed the pot on the table, and grabbing William by the cuff of his work shirt, led him over to the sink where she ran cold water on the burn. "Stay there," she ordered. "I'll get the ice."

Teddy and Joachim moved farther into the room, where Liam was sitting enjoying his cup of coffee and a big piece of Kathleen's homemade bread spread with peach preserves. He raised his cup to them, acquiring the role of host as Kathleen ministered to William.

"I've got good news for you," he said, his light brown eyes focused on Teddy. "Your belongings have been found."

Teddy's eyes sparkled at the news. "That's wonderful!"

"Oh no, you don't!" Kathleen cried, her head stuck in the freezer as she dug out a few ice cubes and wrapped them in a dish towel. This done, she handed the makeshift ice pack to William and made him sit back down at the table. "It's my story to tell, Liam Murdoch!"

Teddy and Joachim gave one another askance looks, shrugged and then sat down at the table. Kathleen picked up the coffee carafe. "Coffee?"

Knowing Kathleen and her penchant for long tales, Teddy answered for them both, "Yes, please."

Kathleen poured them mugs of the strong aromatic blend, then reclaimed her spot beside William.

For the next few minutes, Kathleen told them the tale of how she was paying a visit to her good friend, Irene, when . . .

"I don't care about the money," Teddy told Kathleen and Liam when they said a round of community service had been planned for Jimmy O'Neil and that he would send her the money he'd stolen from her in a matter of months.

She reached over to place a hand over Kathleen's. "I'm sorry about your friend, Kathleen. No one should have to suffer like that."

Kathleen sighed sadly. "Indeed." She ruminated for a moment. "But at least she has the satisfaction of knowing her boy has been put on the right path. William, Liam, and I will keep an eye on him."

She'd revealed that upon Irene's death, she and William would be Jimmy O'Neil's legal guardians. And Liam had been enlisted as a sort of big brother.

Shortly after that, Teddy and Joachim went upstairs to examine her returned belongings. Kathleen had placed everything on the dresser in Teddy's bedroom.

Joachim watched as Teddy went through her things. A sadness claimed him. He was pleased she'd gotten back what was hers—but he knew now there was nothing to keep her here any longer. He didn't want her to go.

Teddy gave him a tremulous smile after confirming that everything was there, except for seventy dollars in cash. "It's all there: my passport, credit cards, most of the cash, driver's license. The Nikon. All safe." Another smile. "That Kathleen's something else, isn't she? Wrestling the kid to the floor like that. She's a regular dynamo."

Joachim laughed shortly and came to stand close to her. "I'm glad for you, Teddy." He traced the outline of her jaw with his index finger as he gazed down into her eyes. "Now you can stop worrying about getting home to Alex."

Teddy's hand went self-consciously to her hair. It was still damp.

Joachim bit his bottom lip. "You'd better get into a warm tub. Don't want you catching cold." He backed away, worrying his lip more than ever. "See you downstairs in a few."

He quickly left the room, and Teddy stood staring at the closed door. She'd sensed a subtle change in him. As if he were building a protective barrier around himself. Effectively shutting her out.

She began peeling off her wet clothing. Maybe it was her imagination. Or maybe, she thought cynically, he figures it's time to cut his losses. They'd had a bit of fun. She was going home. She had her story. Mission accomplished. Maybe he figured that's all she was after.

Eyes narrowed in irritation, she decided the only way to find out was to ask.

Ten

Teddy borrowed Kathleen's blow dryer. She was not going downstairs with wet hair tonight. Her last evening with Joachim would be as close to perfect as she could make it.

She put on the rust-colored, body-hugging dress. Standing in front of the bureau mirror, she turned this way and that way, trying to decide if it would have the right effect. Would Joachim like the way it accentuated her female curves, or would it appear as if she were gilding the lily in order to bolster her waning confidence? She'd sensed a change in him earlier. Was that why she wanted his eyes to bug out the next time he saw her? Maybe.

Why am I overanalyzing everything? She ran her hands slowly along her sides, smoothing the dress. It felt like satin against her skin. The color highlighted the golden brown of her skin. It looked good on her. That's all that mattered. Let him think whatever he wished.

The only shoes she had that complemented the dress were a pair of sling-back clogs in brown suede with a three-inch heel. They went nicely with the ultramodern ankle-length dress.

She ran her fingers through her curly hair and shook it out. Scrutinizing her reflection, she frowned. Makeup, she'd forgotten to put on her makeup. She went and rummaged in her bag a moment and came out with the eyeliner and mascara. Digging deeper, she discovered the plastic tube of Red Riot lipstick had been broken. Probably when Jimmy O'Neil had yanked it off her shoulder, he'd inadvertently hit it on the cobblestone street, breaking the tube. She dropped the broken pieces in the trash basket next to the bureau and twisted the lipstick up. It had bits of clear plastic sprinkled on the red matte product. She tossed it in the trash, too.

Closing her bag, she looked into the mirror with a determined expression in her brown eyes. Forget the makeup. Joachim had borne her presence for the last two days without it. And where were these insecurities coming from anyway? She'd never cared what a man thought of her appearance. Her father had drummed into her that looks took a backseat to brains.

She left the room before another round of self-doubts could pounce on her.

To her surprise, Joachim met her in the hallway. Her efforts to look good for him were rewarded when she saw the appreciative, expressly covetous gleam in his dark depths as he scanned her from top to bottom.

"I was just coming to collect you. Kathleen has supper on the table. I asked her to serve it in the dining room."

He couldn't pull his gaze away. He'd known she was lovely and shapely. But the jeans and denim shirts simply hadn't done her justice. That dress was hitting on every softly feminine line and angle she possessed, from her full breasts, flat stomach, small waist, shapely thighs, and flaring hips.

He wanted to pull her into his arms and kiss her soundly. But that would betray the desperation he was feeling.

"You look wonderful," he said softly, his voice cracking a bit. Clearing his throat, he added more calmly, "But then you always do."

Teddy studied his muscular form. He was attired in black slacks, dress shoes, and a gray long-sleeved silk shirt that showed the outline of his pectorals and biceps. She could even make out the muscles in his washboard stomach. He looked so good to her, she almost forgave him his last comment. His tempering a heartfelt compliment with, "But then you always do" had felt as if he were taking it back somehow.

She wanted to test her theory, and stepped forward, a seductive smile on her lips. "Is that silk?" The entire length of her body pressed against his. Her hand went to his chest. She lifted her chin, meeting his eyes. His breath caught in his throat as he clasped the offending hand and gently brought it down.

"Kathleen went to a lot of trouble. I told her tonight was special . . ."

"Kathleen is a woman after my own heart. And she would understand if we were a bit tardy." She raised her lips to his and closed her eyes, her sooty lashes lying against her brown cheeks.

Joachim swallowed hard and said, "Oh God, woman, can't you see I'm trying my damnedest to resist you?"

Teddy's eyes shot open. "Trying to resist me? Why?"

Joachim sighed and put his arms around her. "You're uncertain of what you'll be returning to, Teddy. Will you have to face your ex in court? Do you run the risk of losing Alex to his father if you continue to reject him? You have a lot of tough decisions to make."

Teddy pushed out of his arms to stare up at him. "What has that got to do with you? With us?" she asked plaintively. He was confusing her. Hadn't they almost made love in the Jaguar less than two hours ago? Now he wished to protect her from bad decisions? No. He was protecting his own feelings.

She started to accuse him of being afraid of his feelings for her, but thought better of it. He was right. She did have difficult decisions to make over the next few months. Was it possible that Adrian would be able to get her back up against a wall, and the only way she could remain in Alex's life was by surrendering to his stipulations? Women had done that, and more, to hang on to their children. Could she be that desperate in the end?

She would never go back to Adrian. Joachim didn't know that though, so she couldn't very well fault him for being cautious.

"You think there's a possibility I'll go back to Adrian, don't you?" she cried incredulously.

"Have you had any lovers since your divorce?" Joachim asked evenly.

Teddy wasn't expecting that query. "What has that got to do with anything!"

"It's just an indication of whether you've gotten over him, or not," Joachim said, his eyes narrowing. "And by your reaction, I would guess not many, if any."

"Could we step into my room?" Teddy asked, her voice tightly reined. She reached for the doorknob and backed inside the bedroom, her eyes on Joachim as he followed her.

Closing the door, she stood with her back to it. Her chest heaved. "You think you're so perceptive, don't you? You believe you have me all figured out. It's true, I haven't had any lovers since my divorce. But there's something else you need to know about me: I didn't have any lovers before my marriage, either."

She heard Joachim's sharp intake of breath. But he didn't interrupt her. "I'm just made that way, I guess."

Teddy turned away, going over to the window and peering out at the night beyond. "We should slow down." She looked at him again. "I don't understand what's happening between us. Maybe I am going through so many changes that I'm looking for solace in your arms. That's a distinct possibility."

Joachim went to her and placed his hand on her cheek, allowing his finger to slide down her jaw. "I recognize the same thing in myself. I just want to lose myself in you, Teddy. You're sweet, kind, funny. I was hoping for someone like you. When you suddenly appeared, the cynic in me said, 'Stand back and analyze the situation.' But every time I looked at you, all I wanted to do was kiss your mouth, smell your hair"—he pulled her against him and buried his nose in her hair, inhaling the fresh, flowery scent—"and just hold you. You disarmed me, Teddy Riley. Me! The world's worst cynic."

"No, you're not," Teddy denied, her big brown eyes on his face. "You're one of the most hopeful people I know. How can you not be? You took a perfect stranger . . . a journalist! . . . into your home simply because she needed help. You're truly, deeply kindhearted."

Joachim laughed. "Don't be so quick to heap praise on me." His eyes bore into hers. "I was in full lust the moment our eyes met, Teddy. If you hadn't agreed to come with me, I might have thrown you over my shoulder like some caveman, and carried you out of the infirmary kicking and screaming."

"So where do we go from here?" Teddy asked, slipping her arms around his waist. Her full, rosy mouth was begging for his kiss.

Joachim had grown tumescent, and loosened his hold on her. But Teddy had already felt him on her thigh, and she was equally aroused. His hands fell to his sides. Teddy removed her arms from around his waist. They stepped away from one another, their eyes still locked, their breath agitated, bordering on panting.

"Kathleen's probably wondering where we are," Teddy reminded him, grasping at anything that would get them out of the bedroom. They'd obviously come to the conclusion that making love wasn't a good idea for them right now. Being alone in a room with a bed in it wasn't conducive to sticking to that decision.

"Right," Joachim said dazedly. He went to the door, opened it and allowed Teddy to precede him. Bad idea, he thought when he got a gander at her from behind. The back was stacked!

Alexander stood several yards away from the San Carlos Borromeo de Carmelo Mission, his camera focused on the two asymmetrical, Moorish-style bell towers. In the center of the bell towers was an intricate star window directly above the main entrance to the mission. The large flagstone courtyard was broken up by beautifully manicured flower gardens. In one section were roses, another, wildflowers; and the property was dotted all over by native trees like pine, oak, juniper, and cypress. For those who were spiritually minded, it was a place to find strength and rejuvenation. For others it was simply a serene, pleasing to the eye, bit of architecture. Alexander was in the former group. After Michelin's death, he'd visited the mission, oftentimes with Teddy in tow, so often that it had become synonymous with worship to him. He felt close to God here. He felt close to Michelin.

He snapped several photos. A book about the central coast wasn't complete without the addition of the Carmel mission.

Alexander felt a tug on his pants leg and looked down. Alex had hold of him. Alexander had Alex in a harness, and the end was attached to his own wrist with Velcro. He got censorious looks from passersby, but better safe than sorry. Alex was the average energetic two-year-old. And Alexander didn't have the energy to be chasing all over the place after him.

"What is it, son?"

Alex squinted up at his grandfather in the afternoon sun. "Bathroom, Grandpa."

Lately Alex had been making his wishes known with a minimum of words. Formerly quite loquacious, Alexander was beginning to worry that something was on the child's mind.

Alexander placed the camera in its case and swung the strap onto his shoulder. Reaching down for Alex's hand, he smiled and said, "Why didn't you go at home, son?"

"Didn't hafta, Grandpa."

Alexander nodded. That was perfectly reasonable. But then children Alex's age were usually quite logical, he'd found.

They began walking toward the public facilities. Alexander's attention was drawn to an Asian man standing nearby, his nose in a map of the area. Alexander had seen the same man at Carmel City Beach less than an hour ago. What were the odds they'd encounter the fellow at two tourist attractions on the same day? Pretty good, probably. However, it appeared suspicious to Alexander. Especially since Teddy had started asking him if he'd noticed any strange people hanging around lately.

Alexander tried to shrug it off. He had a dancing two-year-old to see to. He took the end of the thin leather strap attached to Alex's harness and flicked it as the driver of a team of horses might. "Giddyap, boy," he cried. To which Alex giggled delightedly and trotted off in the direction of the rest rooms, good horse that he was.

* * *

"I'm stuffed, I could use a walk," Teddy commented, pushing her plate aside. Kathleen was entering the dining room at that moment with the coffee. She regarded Teddy. "Why don't you and Mr. West"—she still couldn't bring herself to call Joachim by his Christian name—"go down to The Rose and The Thorn? They have good crack on Saturday nights."

Teddy shot Joachim a bemused look.

He smiled at her. "That means you'll be sure to have a good time there."

Kathleen laughed. "What did you think I meant?" she asked, her fine brows arched in curiosity.

"In the States," Joachim explained, "crack is an illegal, highly addictive drug that has ruined many people's lives."

Frowning as she poured coffee into their cups, Kathleen said, "Lord. You learn something new every day." Finished with her task, she smiled at Teddy. "Well, I'll be saying good night. William and I are going to play cards at the Kellys' tonight. They won last time and William and I have a little payback in mind."

"Thanks for a wonderful meal, Kathleen," Teddy said sincerely.

"Yes, it was delicious," Joachim agreed.

Blushing now, Kathleen backed toward the exit. "Oh, go on with ya!"

In her absence Joachim reached across the table and clasped Teddy's hand. "I believe she was pleased."

Teddy squeezed his hand. Another night alone together in the manor. Joachim got to his feet, pulling Teddy up with him. Their bodies automatically pressed closer.

"The Rose and The Thorn?" Teddy asked softly, her mouth on his chin. Joachim groaned. "We'll close the place." He reluctantly let go of her warm, soft, way too enticing body. "Let's go before I forget I'm a gentleman."

"It's your curse," Teddy joked.

* * *

The four-member band featured at The Rose and The Thorn consisted of an acoustical guitar player, a piano player, a flutist, and a violinist. They performed traditional and contemporary Irish tunes. Melancholy songs that evoked bittersweet memories. Jaunty jigs that went straight to your feet, making you tap them uncontrollably, or get up on them and hit the dance floor.

Teddy and Joachim danced to every song. Sometimes they'd be the only couple out there, swaying to the music, lost in each other's eyes. Or jumping around like whirling dervishes to the faster tunes, laughing at the fact that the moves they'd learned in blues clubs back home didn't cut the mustard there in Ballycastle. So . . . when in Ireland. They cracked each other up with their ineptness. The place was packed. Couples out for the evening at cozy tables for two. Groups of boisterous singles at booths along the sides, laughing and putting away pints of ale like it was water. A pool game going on in the corner, and several patrons engaged in a dart tournament in the back, loudly wagering on who would get the most points. While Teddy and Joachim danced.

In the middle of one fast-paced tune, a large fellow with dark hair tapped Joachim on the shoulder, denoting he wanted to dance with Teddy.

Joachim frowned at the guy, who was a couple inches taller than he was, and about forty pounds heavier. "I don't think so, buddy," he told him, smiling to keep things cool.

The room was dim, otherwise Teddy would have recognized the broad-shouldered figure as that belonging to Colleen's sweetie, Ethan. But Joachim, in a protective move, stood between her and Ethan, so she couldn't see him clearly.

"All's I'm asking for is a dance, fella," Ethan said in his thick brogue. It was then that Ethan peered around Joachim and into Teddy's face. "Let the lady decide."

"Ethan!" Teddy cried.

Joachim gave Teddy a quizzical frown. "You know him?"

Ethan was smiling broadly. Teddy could tell he had a buzz

on. What she was concerned about was what kind of drunk he was: friendly or belligerent?

"Yeah, we met a couple days ago, at the diner. His girlfriend, Colleen, works there." Teddy glanced behind Ethan, hoping Colleen was somewhere in the pub. "Ethan, I'd like you to meet my"—she hesitated—"husband, Joachim West."

Ethan held out his hand. Joachim took it and the two men shook. "A pleasure, Mr. West," Ethan said, his eyes moving to Teddy. "What do you say, is it all right if your beautiful wife and I have one dance? I promise to return her to you safely."

Joachim's eyes shot Teddy an askance look. Teddy nodded her acquiescence. What harm would one dance do?

Joachim's brows arched in disapproval, but he left the dance floor. The band began playing a slow waltz, and Ethan pulled her into his powerful arms. Teddy tried to encourage a suitable distance between them by holding herself stiffly, but Ethan wasn't having that, and firmly held her against him. Aside from perspiration, he smelled of stale beer and cigarettes. And he insisted on singing along with the sad song. He sounded like a wounded bull moose.

Sensing something had happened to depress him, Teddy said, "So, Ethan, where is Colleen tonight?"

"I don't know and I don't care," he said loudly.

"You might not know, but you certainly care," Teddy told him, her face turned to the side, away from his body, so that she could breathe the moderately fresh air of the pub. "What happened?"

"I'm a farmer," Ethan began, his voice filled with anguish. "A big dumb bohunk. Colleen's smart, pretty . . . lovely. What does she need with a man like me? And my ma . . . with Da gone, who's going to take care of her in her old age? I'm all she has."

Teddy didn't know what to say to comfort him. Caught between two women, one he felt beholden to and the other he loved but had resigned himself to never having. No wonder he'd decided to tie one on.

"Did Colleen break off with you?" That might account for

his exclamation of disinterest in Colleen's whereabouts a moment ago.

"No, she gave me until next week to propose to her. Then she says if I don't, she's selling the diner and moving to America where she's sure there are men who would be interested in marrying her and giving her a child or two."

Teddy's brows knitted together, thinking. Colleen owned the diner, she didn't just work there. That meant she was a businesswoman, someone with her head on straight. Then she must truly love Ethan to remain in Ballycastle. She could be a success anywhere. Then what was the problem? Could it be that Ethan was a bit of a chauvinist? And his pride was preventing him from asking Colleen to marry him?

She'd test her assumption. "Then why don't you ask her to marry you? Surely with her income and yours, you could manage to care for your mother and build a decent life together—"

"I'll not have a woman support me!" Ethan bellowed.

His voice was audible over the music, and out of the corner of her eye, Teddy saw Joachim coming to her rescue.

"You're stupid if you let that stand in your way of having the woman you love!" Teddy shouted back at him.

When Joachim got within earshot, she called, "I'm fine, Joachim. We're just talking."

Joachim shook his head. No, that wasn't good enough for him. He went over to them and firmly pulled them apart. "The dance is over," he told Ethan, who held up his mitts in resignation.

Ethan met Teddy's eyes. "You really think so?"

Teddy held Joachim by the arm. She had one last thing to say before getting off the dance floor. "I know this, Ethan: Colleen told me, a stranger, that she loves you. But she's getting to the point where she thinks she'll be old and gray before you do right by her. Don't lose her over pride, Ethan. It won't keep you warm at night."

She allowed Joachim to lead her away then. Ethan stood in the middle of the floor, deflated and conflicted. Give up his pride for love? His father would roll over in his grave. He turned and slowly walked from the dance floor. Colleen was probably curled up with a good book by now. When they didn't go out together on a Saturday night, she would take a bath and crack open a book she'd been meaning to get to. He would surprise her. But first he needed to make a detour by the men's room to wash the stink off him.

Outside the pub Teddy breathed in the crisp night air. Joachim was shaking his head, a smile on his lips. "What was that all about?"

Teddy, feeling pretty confident that she'd gotten through to Ethan, told Joachim about the couple as they walked toward the parking lot, three blocks away, where they'd left the Jaguar.

"Advice for the lovelorn, huh?" Joachim said with a laugh when she'd finished. "What is it about you that makes people want to spill their guts, Teddy?"

Laughing, too, Teddy replied, "I don't know, but ever since I can remember, people have taken one look at my face and wanted to tell me their life stories."

"It must come in handy in your present occupation," Joachim joked. He was thinking of Suzanne. She'd also been a people magnet. Peering down at Teddy, who was fairly floating along the cobblestone street, her body moving with sensuous fluidity, he knew he'd chanced upon another free spirit.

"Know what I want to do now?" Teddy asked suddenly, pausing in her tracks to gaze up at him.

"What?"

"I want to dance in the streets."

As if on cue, a flutist began playing a merry melody.

Teddy's mouth fell open in delight. "It's George!"

Joachim laughed. "Not the ghost?" he said skeptically.

"Ghost, prankster, whatever . . . let's dance," Teddy suggested, slinging her shoulder bag's strap across her chest so she didn't have to worry about it slipping off her shoulder.

Joachim gladly assumed the position, pulling her into his arms, just so, and leading her down the street toward the parked car in an energetic do-si-do.

The street was almost abandoned at midnight, but they did

come upon a young couple, making their way home, who stood for a moment, applauding their shenanigans.

By the time they reached the car, they were breathless. Teddy leaned against Joachim as he unlocked the door. He turned to face her and she naturally fell into his embrace. "It was good of George to give me a nice send-off."

Neither of them had drunk any potent potables, so it wasn't alcohol that had them high. Joachim felt his euphoria vanishing when she mentioned leaving him, though. "I wish you didn't have to go," he said without thinking. They'd been over that. They had made their choices. So why was he bringing it up again? Teddy had responsibilities at home and he had no right wanting to keep her from them. He didn't say anything else on the subject.

Teddy closed her eyes, listening to the rhythmic beating of Joachim's heart. She had the satisfying sensation of being on the brink of something truly special. *God, let it be so,* she thought.

"You're sure you've got enough cash on you?" Joachim asked, worry lines creasing his brow. "What if you have an emergency . . ."

The tiny train depot wasn't exactly bustling on Sunday morning, but the same oldster who'd given her directions the night she'd arrived assured them the trains ran on time.

"God forbid," Teddy said with a short laugh. "I've already had my share of mishaps, thank you!"

Hearing the train approaching, she tiptoed and put her arms around him. "Happy writing, Joachim. I hope I haven't been too much of a distraction."

Joachim held her at arm's length. His dark eyes crinkled in a warm smile. "You've been a very sweet distraction, Teddy. And considering the fact that I hadn't written a word before you got here, and I've now gotten through the first chapter, I believe you've become my muse."

Teddy flashed her pearly whites. "I've never been anyone's muse before." The train screeched to a stop, the air jets on the brakes sounding like a loud asthmatic wheeze. Their eyes met. "E me," Teddy said, reminding him to e-mail her. She tiptoed to meet his mouth. Her bags were on the floor, alongside her. Joachim's strong arms enveloped her, as hers went around his waist seeking a way to hold on to him as he tipped her backward, the kiss deepening. Teddy gave as good as she got. She reveled in the hard, snug safe harbor his body made. The taste of his clean, sweet mouth. The sensuous circuits his hands were making along her body. The feel of their tongues touching, exploring, causing pleasure points all over her to awaken with sweet expectation. If only . . .

When they came up for air, Teddy sighed happily, smiling up at him. "I'll be dreaming about that one for quite a while."

"You're not the only one," Joachim told her, his dark eyes devouring her face.

Teddy reached up and ran her hand over his beard. "Another couple of days, and it would've been just right."

Joachim grasped her hand and kissed the palm. "I'll let it grow. Next time I see you, it'll be ready for you to play in."

A male voice reeled off all the destinations between there and Dublin over a loudspeaker.

"That's me," Teddy said regretfully. She bent and picked up her carry-on bag. Joachim took the heavier valise.

They went outside to the platform, where several passengers were already boarding. Teddy got in line, Joachim standing beside her. The line moved swiftly. Joachim gave her one more quick buss to the lips as she placed the ticket in the conductor's hand, then he gave her the valise. He helped her up the steep steps. She turned to peer down into his face, but the woman behind her was in a hurry, so she had to move along.

She hurried along the aisle of the passenger compartment, looking for a seat near a window. She found a couple of empty seats and quickly deposited her bags in them, rushing to the window to stick her head out. Joachim saw her immediately and jogged alongside the train which was making hissing sounds, denoting it was preparing to leave the station. "Thank you!" Teddy cried.

"For what?" Joachim asked, puzzled. Straight white teeth showed in his face.

"Just . . . everything!"

For restoring my faith in "the dream," Teddy thought. The train began pulling away from the station. Teddy waved; Joachim held up his hand in a wave and slowly closed it as the train picked up speed and disappeared in the distance.

Joachim turned away and slowly started walking back to the car. He had the fatalistic notion that he'd never see Teddy again. But then life had taught him that everything he loved was eventually snatched from his grasp.

Why should this time be any different?

Teddy's train arrived at Connolly Station without incident. She took a city bus, called Airlink, which left for the airport every fifteen minutes, to Dublin International Airport. While she waited for her flight, she thought she'd try Frankie's home-number. The answering machine kicked in. She hung up then dialed his work number, not expecting him to be there on a Sunday afternoon.

Frankie answered his office phone on the third ring. "Franklyn Ahern."

"What are you doing in the office on Sunday?" Teddy asked, laughing. She was standing at a public phone a few feet from the desk of her carrier. She wanted to be nearby if the carrier's personnel announced any changes in her flight's schedule.

"Catching up on paperwork. Teddy, it's great to hear from you!"

"How did you recognize my voice?"

"There aren't that many American females who phone me, especially ones with your deep, sexy voice," Frankie told her. His voice had a lazy quality, like he'd leaned back in his chair and gotten comfortable. Too comfortable for Teddy.

"I'm at the airport, waiting for my flight, and I just wanted to say so long—"

"At the airport!" Frankie said excitedly. Teddy heard a loud squeak, as if he'd gotten up out of his chair in a hurry. "When does your plane leave? I could be there in half an hour."

Teddy glanced down at her watch. "Two forty-five. Can you just leave work like that?"

"Well, I sorta own the company."

Shaking her head in disbelief, Teddy chuckled softly. "You said you were a stockbroker. All right. I wasn't exactly honest with you, either. Frankie, how do you feel about tall women with auburn hair?"

Frankie laughed. "It's come to this, huh? You're letting me down easy by trying to fix me up with a friend? I'll have you know, Teddy Riley, that I can find my own dates."

"She's a supermodel . . ."

"Give her my number."

"I'll do that. And, Frankie, it's been real."

"She's gotta be something else to take my mind off you," Frankie warned lightly about Teddy's offer. "She has to be bright and interesting and she'd better like the blues."

"Oh she is, and she does," Teddy promised.

They rang off shortly afterward and Teddy laughed to herself. There he was listing requirements for his perfect woman. And once he met Melodie face-to-face, he'd forget he had a tongue or a brain to dictate to it what to say, let alone that he had certain requirements a woman had to meet in order to please him. She couldn't wait to tell Melodie about him. Melodie had bemoaned the fact that men who asked her out were interested in only one thing: being the envy of other males because he had her on his arm. She wanted a man of substance. Well, once Frankie stopped staring, Teddy thought he might just fit the bill. He and Melodie could play phone tag, or e-mail each other until they got tired of electronic romance, and then maybe they'd bite the bullet and meet in the flesh.

"She got the story!" Babs cried as she strode into Joie Jackson's office. Joie, who was fashion editor for the magazine, got up from her desk to high-five Babs.

"I knew my girl could do it," she said, her dark brown face breaking into a wide grin. She was five seven, physically fit. Her short black hair was styled in a pixie cut which framed her heart-shaped face to perfection. She was attired in a purple designer pantsuit, Ferragamo pumps in the same shade, and her nails, done in French tips, could be classified as lethal weapons.

Babs, also stylish in a taupe skirt suit and bronze Italian pumps, sat her size forty-two hips on the corner of Joie's desk. "Miss Thang not only got the story, but girlfriend was, and I quote, 'invited to stay at the home of Mr. West's friend, Conal Ryan, while I recuperated from a minor injury I sustained when I was assaulted and robbed by a misguided teen on a motorbike.' That's right"—Babs chortled—"she went all the way to Ireland to get mugged."

Joie frowned. "She's all right, isn't she?" She didn't find the situation comical.

"Oh sure," Babs returned, waving her hand dismissively. "She's on the way back home as we speak. Irina's thrilled of course. She scooped the competitors—she'll be grinning like the Cheshire cat from *Alice in Wonderland* for days."

Babs rose. "Well, gotta get back. Just wanted you to know Teddy's about to join the staff. Though why she'd want a permanent position, I don't know. Traveling all over the world on assignment sounds exciting to me."

"That's because your butt's stuck to a chair all day," Joie joked.

"Yeah, girl, and it's getting so wide, it's starting to look like my aunt Delia's."

"Babs, you're always complaining about gaining weight, but you never do anything about it. Why don't you go jogging with me and Teddy Saturday mornings?" Both she and Teddy tried to jog at least three times a week, but on Saturdays they invariably met in Golden Gate Park and ran together.

"And sweat on purpose?" Babs exclaimed, tossing Joie a disbelieving glance. "There are only three occasions upon which I don't mind sweating: when I'm walking through the mall, when I'm in the hot tub, and when—"

"You're making love to Hank," Joie answered for her. Hank was Babs's husband of seven years.

"You said it, girl." Babs grinned, walking toward the exit. At the door she spun back around as though she'd forgotten something. "Do you think she did it?"

Joie was momentarily perplexed, then it dawned on her to what Babs was referring. Had Teddy slept with Joachim West? As Teddy's loyal friend, she wasn't going to gossip about her behind her back. "That's none of our business, now is it, Babs?"

Babs rolled her eyes. "Oh please, I'm just making conversation and you get all serious on me."

"I just don't talk about my friends like that."

Sighing, Babs placed her hands on her hips and grimaced at Joie. "Well, I don't, either. I just hope she got some, that's all. The child has been experiencing a severe dry spell."

Laughing in spite of her irritation, Joie tossed a balled-up piece of paper at Babs. Babs loved to gossip, but she had the type of disposition that made it difficult to stay angry with her for any length of time.

"You know you're bombing when they start throwing things at you." Babs laughed, turning to leave. But not before saying, "Even if she didn't give it up, I bet he gave it his best shot. A widower and a divorcée under the same roof, both of them extremely attractive. Girl, you know sparks flew!"

She really left then, her hips undulating like two bowling balls underneath her tight skirt.

Joie smiled. Girlfriend needed to get out there and exercise.

Teddy's plane landed in San Francisco late Monday night. She'd slept en route and driven straight through to Carmel, wanting to be there when Alex and her father awakened Tuesday morning.

Arriving at her father's cottage a little after 4 A.M., she quietly unlocked the door and went back to Alex's room. Her dad had night-lights placed strategically around the house in case Alex awakened in the middle of the night in search of him.

Teddy had dropped her bags on the couch in the living room, her mind on her son. Now she inched his door open and eased inside his bedroom. The *Winnie the Pooh* night-light in the socket gave off enough illumination for her to see her son's cherubic face. She leaned in, breathing in his little boy scent, a mixture of sweat, new skin, chocolate chip cookies, and milk. She had to warn her father about that. He and Alex both enjoyed their nightly snack of cookies and milk. She hoped her father remembered to make Alex brush after every indulgence.

She longed to kiss his chubby cheek, but resisted. Alex was a relatively light sleeper. Low noises didn't rouse him, but the least little touch instantly awakened him.

Remembering the stuffed toy leprechaun she'd purchased for him at the Dublin airport gift shop, she went back out to the living room, got it, returned with it and placed it on the bed next to him. When he opened his eyes in the morning, it would be the first thing he saw.

She left the room, leaving the door ajar, as they always did.

Outside the door she bent to retrieve the bags she'd brought with her from the living room on her second trip and went next door to the guest room. Too tired to properly undress and change into her nighty, she pulled off her outerwear down to her bra and panties, tossing everything onto a nearby arm-chair, pulled back the covers and climbed between the cool, inviting sheets.

She was sleeping soundly ten minutes later when Alexander, returning from one of his nightly trips to the bathroom, opened her door and reassured himself that that was indeed the sound of her breathing he'd heard from the hallway.

He resisted the impulse to go plant a kiss on her forehead.

At that exact moment in Ballycastle where it was 9:30 A.M., Joachim was returning from a seven-mile jog. Drenched in sweat, his clothes clinging to him, he encountered Kathleen on the landing on the way to his bedroom. Apparently wanting to say something to him, she blocked his path. Pursing her lips and shaking her head disapprovingly, she said, "So we're back to running ourselves to death, are we?"

Joachim was interested in only one thing: getting into a tub of lukewarm water. He was hot, tired; he thought he'd pulled a muscle in the back of his right thigh. What did he think he was anyway, a teenaged boy? And on top of that, he missed Teddy.

His dark eyes narrowed. "Kathleen, I don't want a lecture. I want a bath." He began removing his fleece jacket. "Now unless you don't mind seeing a grown man naked as a jaybird, I'd suggest you mind your own business and leave mine alone."

Kathleen humphed. "You haven't got anything I haven't already seen," she said, calling his bluff. "A little testy, aren't we? It wouldn't have anything to do with Teddy leaving, would it?"

Joachim snorted. "And if I said it didn't?"

"I'd say you were a liar."

"Kathleen . . ." Joachim warned through clenched teeth.

"What is it with you artists? You're so temperamental. Why can't you write in San Francisco? It isn't good being separated from the one you love for long periods of time. What if something happened? Didn't her getting attacked make you think? Your place is by her side, not halfway round the world, looking for inspiration when you could get all the inspiration you need just by looking into her eyes!"

She defiantly lifted her chin and moved aside after letting him have it with both barrels. "What'll you have for breakfast this mornin'?"

Joachim laughed. He couldn't remain incensed with a woman whose heart was in the right place. She clearly liked him and Teddy. She thought she was giving him sound advice—which actually she was. If he thought it would be a wise decision, he'd be on the next plane to San Francisco. But how would it look? Teddy needed her space. And he needed to write the story that was beginning to unfold in his imagination. So even if Kathleen railed at him on a daily basis for the next three months, he was going nowhere near San Francisco until he completed the book.

Not even if he developed shin splits from the heavy-duty running he was going to have to do in order to dispel thoughts of Teddy's kisses.

"I'll have the usual, Kathleen: scrambled egg whites and toast," Joachim told her with a smile.

"It's worse than I thought!" Kathleen cried, stomping down the stairs. "Gone less than a day, and you're back to starvation rations."

Joachim went on into his bedroom for that much needed bath.

Eleven

Teddy was abruptly snatched from sleep's warm embrace by the violent shaking of her bed. At first she thought they were experiencing an earthquake, but after sitting up in bed, she spied her own little earthquake, his face lit up by a thousand-watt smile, jumping up and down at the foot of the bed.

Laughing, she threw the covers back and grabbed Alex around the waist, hauling him into her arms and kissing his cheek. "Now that's how I'm used to being awakened." She kissed his forehead.

Dressed in a pair of Woodstock pajamas, his hair matted from sleep, and clutching the stuffed leprechaun in his right hand, Alex smiled into his mother's eyes. "Missed you, Mommy."

Teddy rubbed her cheek against his. "I missed you, too, baby."

Placing him on the floor, she sent him off with a pat to the bottom. "Go on now, and keep your grandpa company in the kitchen while I get dressed." The aroma of Canadian bacon assailed her nostrils. She hoped her father was cooking his famous waffles to go with the bacon. She was famished.

Alex happily ran along, swinging the leprechaun at his side.

Teddy climbed out of bed and went to the bathroom to wash her face and brush her teeth.

Ten minutes later Alexander, standing in front of the stove, smiled at her. "What time did you get in this morning?"

Yawning, Teddy said, "Around four." She walked over to him and tiptoed to kiss his cheek. "How did everything go?"

Alexander put his spatula down to hug his daughter. "Just fine." He eyed the scar on her forehead. "Looks like it's healing well. Got a good scab going. So you weren't unconscious for long, huh?"

"Only a few minutes, I was told," Teddy replied, going to pick up a piece of bacon and nibble on it. Her eyes went to the electric griddle on the counter. It was closed and a thin stream of steam came up from it. "I might want a couple of those this morning."

Alex was at the table holding a conversation with the stuffed leprechaun while he ate his breakfast. Teddy smiled at the lovely picture he made: happy, carefree. She hoped she could always protect him from bad things. That's when her thoughts turned to Adrian.

Regarding her father with a slightly alarmed expression in her eyes, she asked, "Anything else from Adrian?"

Alexander told her about the man he'd seen, both at the mission and Carmel City Beach.

Being a photographer, Alexander had a keen eye for details, so Teddy didn't doubt he'd accurately identified the man from the two separate venues. "Think Adrian hired a private investigator to watch us?" she asked.

"Seems logical," Alexander said, lifting the lid on the waffle iron and removing four large waffles. He transferred them to a platter. "You won't talk to him. He needs to know what's going on in your life. He'll get that information any way he can."

Sighing wearily, Teddy went to the cabinet to get plates for her and her father, then returned and began filling them with waffles and slices of bacon. "I really don't know what he's thinking, Daddy. Why would he want to go back in time? Is it his screwy way of making amends? Is that it? Because if it is, I'd gladly lie and say I've forgiven him if that would satisfy him and keep him out of our lives."

They joined Alex at the table. A carafe of coffee, cups, and saucers were already on the table. After a moment of silent prayer, they dug in.

"You don't believe it's going to be that easy, do you?" Alexander asked, glancing at her over the rim of his coffee cup.

Teddy was busy wiping syrup off Alex's chin. "Just wishful thinking. No, I don't think it's going to be easy at all. For some reason Adrian believes he can correct his past mistakes with one fell swoop. All he needs is to get me to remarry him, he becomes the perfect father, we live happily ever after. He's totally delusional, Daddy."

Alexander laughed. "It's that ego of his," he began. "What you should do is let him get a taste of what being a real father is like. Don't fight him when he asks to take Alex for the afternoon. Once he has to go through an afternoon of trying to entertain an active two-year-old, he'll beg you retain sole custody."

Teddy grasped Alex, who'd jumped down from his chair, after consuming half his breakfast, by the arm. "No, you don't. Eat the rest of your breakfast, young man."

Alex poked his bottom lip out. "Mr. Green has to go potty, Mommy."

Teddy couldn't discern whether Alex was pretending, or referring to himself when speaking of his new toy, Mr. Green. "Okay, go on. But remind Mr. Green to put the toilet seat back down. And it isn't polite to swim in the toilet bowl, deal?"

Alex nodded in the affirmative and hurried from the room.

"See what I mean?" her father asked. "Adrian would have told the boy that stuffed toys don't use the toilet."

Teddy smiled and cut into another waffle with gusto. "These are delicious, Daddy."

"When are you going to tell me about Joachim West?"

"Well, there isn't much to tell. He was nice . . ." Teddy hedged.

"There's nice, and then there's *nice*. Which one was he?"

"The latter." She raised her eyes to his. She didn't need to say more.

Laughing, Alexander said, "How old is he?"

"Thirty-seven."

"I know he lost his wife several years ago. It made the news when it happened, his being a local celebrity and all." He paused to take a large swallow of his coffee. "I've read his books."

"I didn't know that!"

Her father gave her a silencing glance. "He writes about such dark subjects. A serial killer. A priest who has an affair with one of his parishioners. A renegade cop. It makes me wonder what kind of man he is. Oh . . . he's very talented. I just don't know if you should get involved with a man who writes so credibly about people who lack any redeeming qualities."

"The man I met was kind and thoughtful. He was a gentleman," she said quietly. "I've read only one of his books, *The God Gene,* and I thought it was brilliant. It was written with sensitivity and the kind of understanding I've come to expect from people of your generation, Daddy."

Alexander smiled knowingly. "Was that a nice way of telling me to keep my nose out of it?"

"No, that was my way of saying I've never known you to be judgmental. Why this sudden desire to protect me?"

"It isn't sudden, daughter. I've had that impulse since you were growing in your mother's womb, all safe and snug. I started worrying about you then. Now? Well, chalk it up to the sudden reappearance of Adrian Riley. He reminded me that when you met him, it was also your opinion that he was kind and thoughtful. The perfect gentleman."

"Why do you think I haven't dated anyone steadily since my divorce, Daddy? It's because I don't trust my instincts when it comes to men. But where will it end? With me alone, waving good-bye to Alex as he goes off to college?" Teddy cried. She momentarily closed her eyes. "I don't like envisioning that." Looking into her dad's eyes again, she went on. "Yesterday, I kissed Joachim good-bye and, I swear, by the time the train had pulled away, I'd convinced myself that was it. It was over. Even though we'd promised to keep in touch. Even though he'd assured me that when he got back, he intended to court me properly . . . those were his words." Teddy had never lied to her father. She'd been guilty of the sin of omission a time or two. But not that often. Therefore now she told him how she felt about Joachim. "He makes me believe in the possibilities."

"Such as?"

"That there really is someone out there for me. Someone I don't have to sleep with one eye open with. Even the fact that he was devoted to his wife and in some ways still is, endears him to me. It tells me something about his character. That he believes in fidelity. That he believes in till death do us part."

Alexander reached over and trailed a finger along her cheek.

Smiling at her, he said, "Daughter, there are two sides to that coin. When a man loses his wife, sometimes he can't move on. It's like he's in stasis, at a total standstill. In shock. He's afraid to love another woman, because somehow that would mean his love for his wife was a farce. The years glide by and before you know it, you're resigned to spending the rest of your life alone."

Teddy knew he was talking about himself. She was surprised, however, by the vehemence with which he spoke those words. Had she been remiss in never pushing him to get out and date more?

"Is that how you feel about your life, Daddy?"

For a split second embarrassment flooded Alexander's features, then he shrugged it off. "I'm too old to change my spots now."

"You're in your prime," Teddy disagreed. "You're in great shape. I don't see why you're not beating them off with a stick."

Alex ran back into the room and climbed onto his chair. He no longer had Mr. Green with him. He avoided eye contact with his mother. Teddy knew that was a sure sign he'd been up to something while he'd been away from the table.

Teddy pushed her chair back and got to her feet.

Looking down at Alex, she impatiently tapped her foot on the floor, waiting.

"Now Theodora, don't jump to conclusions," Alexander implored on Alex's behalf.

"It cost a hundred and twenty-five dollars the last time the plumber was out here," Teddy reminded her father.

Alexander quickly rose and left the room, heading for the bathroom. Teddy followed a bit slower. She had Alex, who was wriggling mightily, on her hip, held firmly under her right arm.

By the time she got in the hallway, Alexander was coming out of the bathroom with a sodden Mr. Green in his hand. "No harm done. He tried to flush it, but it wouldn't go down."

Teddy adeptly swung Alex up to a more comfortable position on her hip and glared at him. "Haven't I told you never to put anything in the toilet?"

Alex's eyes were downcast. He didn't respond to his mother's question. Teddy looked at her father. "Has he been acting-out recently?"

"No," Alexander replied. He'd turned away, holding the dripping toy at arm's length. He went to the laundry room adjacent to the kitchen to put it in the wash. Maybe it could be salvaged.

Teddy set Alex on the floor and squatted so that she would be eye level with him. "Why did you put Mr. Green in the toilet, Alex?"

"I didn't like him."

His reply concerned Teddy. Alex had always loved the things she brought back for him from her trips. He'd never purposely destroyed anything she'd given him.

"What is it about him you don't like?"

There was a long pause before Alex said anything else. Teddy understood. It hadn't been that long ago since he'd spoken his first words. But when he did speak, what he said threw her for a loop. "Who was that man in the black car, Mommy?"

A fully thought-out sentence. Not something said on the spur of the moment. Not for a two-year-old. He'd been turning that question over in his mind for days. Wondering.

He'd seen his grandfather react in anger to the stranger's presence. And perhaps the stranger had looked vaguely familiar to him. He had after all been shown his photograph on a fairly regular basis since he was old enough to comprehend differences in facial features. First by his mother. Then by his grandmother, who thought it was her sacred duty to make sure her grandson at least knew what his father looked like.

Teddy pulled Alex into her arms. "That was your daddy, baby."

"She did what?!" Adrian screeched into his cellular phone.

It was Friday night and he'd been having dinner alone at Pepper's Supper Club on Leonard Street in Tribeca when the phone rang. Smiling apologetically at the diners whose eyes were on him due to his outburst, he spoke more calmly into the receiver. "Who is this Joachim West?" He had heard of the writer before, but had not given him a second thought until now.

The woman on the other end gave him Joachim's literary résumé plus everything else she'd been able to glean from the files at *Contemporary Lives* and the Internet. "You don't have anything to worry about, Mr. Riley. I have it on good authority that nothing happened when she stayed with him."

"Who is your source?"

"I overheard her telling Joie Jackson that nothing happened between them," the woman said, trying to soothe him. Adrian detected something else in her voice, however. A hanging quality. As if she wasn't telling him everything. Maybe she was holding back some juicy morsel with which to entice him into giving her more money in the future.

"If I find out you're not telling me everything, I'll cut you off without a dime," he threatened.

"No, Mr. Riley. I promise, I'm telling you everything!" Her tone had become pathetically supplicating.

"All right," Adrian said, placated. "Later."

He hung up and returned to his meal.

Two extremely beautiful women were dining together at the table directly across from his. They'd been trying to get his attention all evening. He smiled at them now and indicated that they should join him with a cocky nod of his handsome head.

He was pleased with how quickly they abandoned their table for his. Both African American, one had long, straight hair. She was pecan tan with elegant features and a body that could have been achieved only through many hours in the gym. She sat closer to him. "Hi," she said in a throaty voice. "I'm Sherry."

"Yes, you are," he said. Her brown eyes were the color of the wine. But his gaze had gone to her friend who was more petite, with a lush figure. Her short, dark brown hair was a mass of soft waves. The way Teddy wore hers. She was lovely. Her eyes weren't as bold as her friend's. She had difficulty meeting his directly.

Shy, he thought. "And you are?"

"Teresa. But my friends call me Terry."

That cinched it. She had a deep, resonant voice, Sexy. If he closed his eyes, he could be convinced that it was Teddy who was sitting across from him.

"We have a winner," Adrian said, his eyes on her face.

The women looked at each other. The taller one humphed, then rose and quickly left the restaurant.

"We made a deal when we first saw you," Terry explained, her dark eyes bolder now. "Whichever of us you picked would pay for our meals. It seems I'm left holding the tab."

Adrian was thrilled by her audacity. A woman who knew what she wanted and exactly how to get it. Refreshing. He saw his waiter approaching and waved him over. "I'll be picking up the check for this young lady and her friend," he told him.

The waiter nodded, acknowledging the request. "Of course, Mr. Riley. Will you be having dessert tonight?"

Adrian was busy going into his wallet for his American Express card. Having located it, he handed it to the waiter. "No, thank you."

The waiter left. And Adrian regarded Terry with an appreciative smirk. "If I had met you two weeks ago, we would be horizontal by now. But I'm no longer that man. So thank you, Teresa, for proving that I still have it. Unfortunately for you, I'm reserving it for another woman."

Teresa pierced him with a malicious stare. "You're a pig!" she cried as she angrily rose. Her eyes flitted from side to side. She hoped no one who knew her had witnessed her degradation at the hands of this megalomaniac.

"Don't be angry, baby. You got a meal out of it," Adrian said reasonably.

Terry's eyes gleamed with unshed tears. She turned and willed her leaden legs to take her away from this nightmare as soon as possible.

Adrian watched her go. Leaning back in his chair, he felt virtuous for having resisted Teresa's many charms. He smiled. She was hurt now, but later when she thought about it, she'd understand that it wasn't safe picking up strange men. He'd done her a service.

Glancing at his watch, he realized he had just enough time to pick up his luggage at the apartment and get to LaGuardia. He was going to San Francisco this weekend.

"So have you heard from him since you got back?" Joie asked on a sunny Saturday morning as she and Teddy shared a bench in Golden Gate Park for cool-down calf stretches.

Teddy leaned languidly into her stretch, feeling catlike this morning after their three-mile run. "Yeah, he phoned me last night. I wasn't expecting it, so I know I sounded like a ninny when I screamed in his ear."

"You didn't!"

"I most certainly did." Teddy chuckled. "Oh but, girl, the sound of his voice," she sighed, "just brought back those two splendiferous—"

"Splendiferous?"

"Splendid, magnificent . . . there aren't enough words in my vocabulary to describe the two days we spent together."

Joie placed both Nike-clad feet on the ground and began doing some toe touches. They got the kinks out of her back. "What did you talk about?"

"What didn't we talk about? Everything. He told me about the book he's writing. Work's going well on that. He's at it day and night now that he has no distractions." She smiled, remembering how Joachim had called her a sweet distraction. "And he said he missed me."

Joie stood stock still, staring at Teddy. "He admitted that? So soon in the relationship? He actually used the words?" she asked incredulously.

"Actually he said, 'I long to hold you.' I interpreted it to mean he missed me."

"Mmm," Joie said, as if she'd just eaten something delicious. "Writers. I've gotta get me one."

Teddy laughed as she met Joie's gaze. "And what're you gonna do with that lawyer you have at home, miss? The one you married four years ago, and promised to have and to hold for the rest of your natural life?"

"He'd just better start saying something more romantic than 'I wanna get into your briefs, Joie,' that's all I've got to say on the subject," Joie replied with a humorous light in her large brown eyes.

In silent consensus they started walking back to where Teddy had left the Mustang. "Looking forward to having Adrian take Alex to his parents' tomorrow for Sunday dinner?"

Teddy's smile faded. "No, but I'm trying to do what's best for Alex. I feel so guilty for not recognizing the father-hunger in him, Joie. When he asked me who the man in the black car was that day, it nearly broke my heart." She almost teared up, but blinked, holding them at bay. "I should have been more observant. And the day Adrian showed up at my dad's place, I should have sat Alex down and said something to him then."

Joie wasn't about to allow her friend to beat up on herself. In her opinion Teddy had done a good job caring for Alex on her own. It was Adrian she wanted to string up by his privates and let him swing in the breeze. Teddy had been to Hades and back because of him. "You did what any other woman would have done in your position, Teddy: your best. Alex is a good kid, and that's entirely due to you."

"And you and Dad," Teddy was quick to add. "If I hadn't

had you two supporting me, especially when I was carrying Alex, I would have fallen to pieces."

"We supported each other," Joie corrected her. "Remember? I was carrying Bridgette at the time, too. We were a couple of whales."

A tall, good-looking black guy jogged past them. "Morning, ladies," he called, flashing them a winsome grin.

"Morning to you, too," Joie called back, rubbernecking.

Teddy playfully punched her on the arm. "Forgot you're married?"

"Hey, I'm married, not dead," Joie replied, eyeing the guy's well-shaped gluteal muscles. "Nice buns!"

"Joie, I can't take you anywhere," Teddy complained lightly.

The hunk, having heard Joie's comment, just waved and smiled as he continued running.

Margaret Elizabeth Riley looked over the dining room table with a critical eye. She wanted everything to be flawless today. The eight-foot-long antique oak table was covered in a white linen tablecloth and was set with her mother's china. They used the bone china only on special occasions. Margaret, a tall, full-bodied woman with warm brown skin and even warmer brown eyes, moved around the table, being certain each place setting held the appropriate items. Yes, Rose had done an excellent job. She hadn't forgotten the salad forks this time.

Margaret sighed contentedly and turned and strode through the swinging doors that led to the kitchen, the silken material of her ankle length dress swirling coolly around her long legs.

Rose, her housekeeper and friend after nearly twenty years, was peering in the oven, checking on the Virginia ham. She closed the oven door, straightening up. "A few more minutes."

Margaret walked over to the pantry near the back door and retrieved her apron, kept there on a peg, and put it on. "Good," she said of Rose's opinion that the ham was nearly done.

"Adrian and Alex will be here at four, and I'd like us to be able to sit down to dinner by five."

Rose, petite and stout, in her early fifties with caramel-colored skin, short natural hair which was brown but peppered with gray, smiled at Margaret. "You're really excited about Adrian bringing Alex to dinner for the first time, aren't you?"

Margaret pushed a tendril of long, curly silver hair behind her ear. "Yes, and you well know why."

Rose nodded. She knew. To Margaret, Adrian's behavior toward Teddy and Alex had set him apart among her children as her only failure. It didn't matter to Margaret if her children, three in number—Adrian, thirty-five; Chance, thirty-three; and Alia, twenty-seven—ever amassed millions or developed a cure for a major disease. No, what mattered to Margaret was whether they were decent human beings. Whether they showed kindness to others, gave back to the community. Because to Margaret, who had come from humble folks, unlike her husband, Winston, who was born with a silver spoon in his mouth—that hadn't prevented him from becoming a wonderful man—the measure of a man was determined by his ability to show compassion.

That Adrian would divorce Teddy because she refused to throw away their precious child—no one had told her, she'd surmised it; she hadn't lived fifty-five years for nothing—proved to Margaret that Adrian was sorely lacking in the compassion department. Selfish, willful. She didn't know where she'd gone wrong in his upbringing. Had she treated him differently, perhaps in some subtle way, than she'd treated Chance and Alia?

After much soul-searching, she'd decided she hadn't, and once she'd come to that conclusion, she placed the blame for his behavior squarely on the head of the one responsible: him. She'd laid into him good fashion, relentless, as only a mother could be.

When he'd phoned her last week and said he was bringing Alex to Sunday dinner, you could have knocked her over with a feather, she was so surprised. But then she thought, *Maybe some of what I've been telling him has finally sunk in.*

She would have to wait and see the final results.

Teddy held the dress shirt open for Alex to slip his arms into. He slowly complied and turned so she could button the shirt. This done, Teddy helped him into navy-blue trousers, zipped them, and buckled the belt around his waist.

"Sit on the bed, baby, so I can put your shoes and socks on."

Alex hopped onto his bed, looking down at her with solemn eyes.

"You go, Mommy?"

Teddy smiled up at him. "Honey, I've explained that this trip to your grandma Margaret's and grandpa Winston's is only for you and your daddy. Mommy will be here when you get back. You're a big boy, you can do this without your mommy."

Alex didn't look convinced as he sat and let her put his socks on his feet, then his highly polished oxfords.

As she was tying them, Teddy grinned at him. "So many things are changing, Alex. And I know you won't be able to understand why the adults around you are doing what they're doing. I'll try to explain things to you as they happen. But we love you, Alex, and we're doing this because we think it will make your life happier. Every little boy deserves a father. Your father has been away for a long time. Now he's back and he wants to make it up to you. So will you go to your grandparents' this afternoon and try to have a good time?"

A minuscule smile crossed his features.

Teddy pulled him off the bed and set him on the floor.

She reached for his hand. Alex placed it in hers and they left his bedroom, going into the living room. Teddy glanced at her watch. It was nearly two thirty, the time Adrian said he'd be by to pick Alex up.

She tried not to allow her reservations about the agreement to show, but she had misgivings. Trusting Alex alone with a man who knew nothing about children was one of them. But

Adrian would just have to learn swiftly. He'd made the mistake of disrupting their lives, showing up out of nowhere. Now he had to live with the consequences—which, she didn't believe he'd taken the time to turn over in his mind. Well, too bad. He'd appeared, aroused Alex's curiosity about him; now he'd better stick around long enough to satisfy it, or he'd have her to deal with!

Another reason she didn't feel positive about Adrian's desire to spend time with Alex was: what if playing Daddy didn't suit Adrian, and he once again abandoned his son? Then Alex would feel the full effects of his father's rejection of him. Formerly his father had been just an image. Someone the people around him talked about to him in order to assure him he did indeed have a father, albeit an absent one. If Adrian suddenly reneged on his fatherly duties, after spending time with him, garnering his love and trust, Alex would know what it felt like to be dumped by someone you love. Teddy never wanted her son to go through that.

The doorbell rang and Teddy sprang up from the sofa to go answer it. She left Alex, engrossed in a Nintendo video game, sitting on the carpet in front of the TV.

Adrian stood outside, a dozen red roses in tissue paper in his right hand and a wrapped gift in the left. "Hello, Teddy."

Teddy's eyes raked over his casual attire of a short-sleeved black T-shirt, his biceps straining against the material, and pleated slacks in camel. The buckle of the thin, brown leather belt lay flat against his rippled stomach. He stepped inside, the soles of his leather loafers not making a sound.

"Hello, Adrian."

He smiled, showing a glimpse of white teeth in his dark brown, clean-shaven face. "You look beautiful," he said, offering her the flowers.

Teddy turned. "I'd like a word with you in the kitchen, please."

Adrian had no choice but to follow her. He took in the spare, eclectic way Teddy had decorated the condo as he did so. Scandinavian furnishings on pine floors. Handwoven rugs in earth tones and a minimum of clutter. He liked it. But then

Teddy always had good taste. Not expensive enough. But good nonetheless. The place was small though. His son needed more space to run. He needed a yard to play in like the yard at the house in the Russian Hill area of the city. He still hadn't told Teddy about the house, it wasn't the right time. He'd gone ahead and purchased it in his name only. They could have her name added to the deed later, after they were remarried.

The kitchen was utilitarian, nothing remarkable about it. The kitchen in the Russian Hill house had every amenity imaginable: tons of space, a Mexican tile floor, double ovens, a restaurant-size side-by-side refrigerator. Everything at your fingertips.

His mind was brought back to the moment when his eyes fell on Teddy's hips, sensuously outlined by the form-fitting jeans she had on. A vision of her stepping from the shower unfolded in his mind. She used to step from the shower into a warm, fluffy bath towel, held up by him. He'd enfold her in the towel and pull her into his arms, then kiss the side of her neck, one of his favorite spots on her delectable body.

In that frame of mind, it was difficult to focus on what Teddy was telling him once they reached the privacy of the kitchen.

"Adrian?!"

"I'm sorry, you in those jeans . . . well, it got to me."

"That's what I wanted to talk about," Teddy told him, her gaze going to the roses, then back up to his face. "We're not dating, Adrian. Don't bring me flowers. And while I'm on the subject, you've got to stop sending me gifts, too. The FedEx people are beginning to give me irritated looks whenever I refuse delivery. So cut it out!"

Adrian had placed the flowers and the gift on the counter. He ran a hand over his hair now and regarded her with a warm expression. "You know I want you back, Teddy. I made that clear from the beginning . . ."

"And I made it clear that I don't want you back!"

"It's a woman's prerogative to change her mind," he told her with a crooked smile. He bridged the gap between them in a couple of steps. Teddy felt she should move away, but didn't. She wasn't going to let him think she was afraid of his nearness. He didn't do anything for her anymore, she told herself. She wasn't that gullible woman he'd married and dumped. That had to stay in the forefront of her mind: He'd dumped her.

His cologne wafted over her. She stood her ground. He was so close to her, she could feel his exhalations on her cheek. Looking up at him, Teddy said, "Three years of hating you has rendered me immune to you, Adrian."

He sighed and pulled her firmly against his hard body. "Well, it's only made me want you more."

Teddy reached behind her and pried his hands loose. "Your son is waiting to be taken to his grandparents' house for Sunday dinner, or have you forgotten?"

"Come with us, Teddy. My folks would love to have you."

Teddy laughed shortly. She'd felt his erection on her thigh, and for some reason when he'd said the words "have you," it had struck her as terribly funny. There he was, standing in her kitchen, trying to whip her into a sexual frenzy, and he was talking about his parents in the same breath.

She pushed against his chest with both hands. He held on to her. "We were good together, Teddy. You have to admit that."

"If you mean sex, then, yes, the sex was always good. It was good the night you left me, too. You were a veritable sex machine, Adrian. But I'm sure all your lovers before, during, and after our marriage have told you that."

Adrian pulled back, aghast. "I never cheated on you, Teddy."

He actually had the nerve to look hurt by her accusation. "I was always faithful to you, darling," he said softly, releasing her. The smile had disappeared. In its place was a dark, haunted aspect that confused Teddy more than his pulling her into his arms had. "I was selfish, my mind was only on getting ahead. I was many things, Teddy. But I never touched another woman while we were married. In fact, I didn't even look at another woman after I met you. You have to know that."

"Why? Why should that be plain to me? You tossed me

aside so quickly when you found out I was pregnant and averse to getting an abortion, that I naturally assumed you had someone waiting in the wings. Any woman would have thought the same thing."

"No, that wasn't it, Teddy. I was scared. I wasn't ready to be a father. I thought having children would prevent me from reaching my goals, our goals. You had a career that took you all over the world. Having a baby would change that."

"It has changed it," Teddy informed him stonily. She moved farther away from him, her eyes on his face. "But I expected my life to change, Adrian. It's changed for the better. That's what you didn't get. Having a child wouldn't detract from your life, it would add so many wonderful things to it: a sense of belonging. The knowledge that you can be responsible enough to care for another human being who is totally dependent upon you." She stopped. What was she doing, trying to get him to understand something only experience could teach? And his son was the best teacher.

Adrian watched her as she turned and began walking toward the exit. Her head held high, carriage erect, that hair, untidy and falling into her eyes. He had the impulse to go and push it out of her eyes. He wanted to comfort her. He needed to feel some emotion coming off her body aside from repulsion whenever he touched her.

He stopped her in her tracks with his next words.

"You're never going to forgive me, are you?"

Teddy slowly spun on her heels and faced him. Her eyes were dejected. "I loved you with my whole heart, Adrian. Not with some part of it that I picked and chose, that I could turn on or turn off at will. Forgive you? I have forgiven you. Because after all you're only human and prone to making mistakes. But I'll never forget what you did. And that's the reason I could never take you back. Somewhere in the back of my mind, there would always be a doubt, a nagging doubt, that you hadn't really changed at all. And that one day you'd rip my heart out again. There you have it," she said, her eyes challenging him to defy her. "Now leave me alone, Adrian. Be satisfied with being the father of a wonderful little boy, and forget about assuaging your guilt by re-creating our so-called happy marriage."

"Is that what you think I'm trying to do?" Adrian cried, his deep voice tinged with anger. Breathing hard, his chest expanding, he grabbed her by the arms, pulled her roughly against him and kissed her on the lips.

Teddy, taken off guard, was about to say something scathing. Her mistake, because as her lips parted, his were there, and then his tongue was in her mouth, the kiss deepened, and Teddy's knees weakened.

Adrian, accustomed to her body language, felt the tension siphoning from her and he relaxed his grip on her. His hands were then free to explore the achingly familiar feminine terrain of her form.

When he raised his head, it was to look deeply into her eyes. "Don't fool yourself, Teddy. You still have feelings for me. You once told me I was the only man you ever loved. Well, love covers a multitude of sins, Teddy, or so my mother always told me. I know you say you've forgiven me, but if that were true, you would also be able to have the faith in me that's needed in order to give me the benefit of the doubt. All I'm asking for is a chance. One chance to prove to you that I'm a changed man."

Teddy was so angry, she didn't trust herself to speak without shouting, and she didn't want to alarm Alex.

She calmly removed Adrian's hands from her body. Then she took a couple steps backward. "Like I've said, making a woman feel good has never been difficult for you. It's everything else you can't seem to manage: the day-to-day caring, the giving of yourself, the expressing of true emotions. I can get kisses and sexual release from anyone. But I don't want to spend the rest of my life with someone who has only that to offer."

Adrian licked his lips, then the corners of his eyes crinkled in a slow smile. "So this . . . Joachim West, he has the qualities you're looking for in a man?"

Teddy's eyes narrowed and her nostrils flared in anger. "It's true then. You're having me investigated."

Now that he saw he'd managed to set her on fire, Adrian was as cool as ice. "I'm covering all my bases, Teddy. You know what a thorough fellow I am. And, of course, I know what a hot-blooded woman you are. I can't fault you for seeking, what did you call it, 'sexual release,' in the arms of the writer. I haven't been celibate the last three years. I don't expect you to have been, either. I can forget about the writer, Teddy. It's in the past. This is the present. I want you back. I want us to be a family. So let's jettison all the nonsense and get back on track, shall we?"

Teddy's anger was replaced with horror once it dawned on her that he was deadly serious. He didn't care that she didn't want him back. It didn't faze him that she was emotionally involved with another man. All that mattered was his agenda. And unfortunately for her, she was at the top of the list. Numero uno. Her hands were balled into fists at her sides. She slowly raised her right hand, marshaling all her strength. Adrian was smiling smugly, as if he had her exactly where he wanted her. His square jaw looked like a good place to pound some sense into him . . .

"Mommy?"

Twelve

Kathleen appeared in the doorway of the library. She stood for a while, watching Joachim as he swiftly typed on the computer keyboard, his concentration so total, he hadn't noticed he was no longer alone. She sighed. If he always became this obsessed when he worked, no wonder Teddy didn't mind his going off somewhere to do it. He'd probably ignore his beautiful wife anyway. Kathleen had never known anyone so singlemindedly goal-oriented. He wrote from dawn till midnight, taking breaks only for small meals, running, and a few hours of sleep.

Clearing her throat, she said loudly, "William wants to know if you'd like to go fishing; bream are biting."

Joachim's fingers didn't pause. "No, Kathleen, I want to finish this chapter."

"And after that it'll be another chapter, and another," Kathleen complained, walking farther into the room. Her hands were in her apron. She kept them there because she'd be wringing them nervously otherwise. She had to buck up her courage to say what she had to say to him. "Mr. West . . ."

Joachim looked up. His square-chinned face now boasted a short beard. Kathleen thought he looked like a different man. He behaved like one, too. Even before Teddy's arrival, he'd been easygoing. And though she didn't know him well, she'd sensed he was on the whole a together person. Now he was intense, brooding. It was a little like watching Dr. Jekyll transform into Mr. Hyde.

"I was wondering if you'd heard from Teddy recently? How is she doing?"

Joachim frowned. Teddy. Why did she have to mention Teddy?

It was a challenge to keep the irritation out of his voice when he answered. He didn't need to be reminded of Teddy right now. Not when getting her e-mails was becoming so dear to him. Not when he missed her so much. Every day he eagerly sat down at the computer, anticipating those wonderful words: *You've got mail!* He felt foolish in his dependency upon seeing her AOL address come up when he clicked on that open mailbox.

However, seeing the expectant expression on Kathleen's face as she awaited his reply, he couldn't stay irritated. She liked Teddy. It was normal to ask after a friend. If he hadn't been so busy writing, it might have occurred to him to mention how Teddy was doing from time to time. Any normal husband would. And he hadn't told Kathleen the truth about him and Teddy yet.

"She's doing just fine, Kathleen. I heard from her this morning. She has a staff position at the magazine now, so she won't have to travel extensively anymore."

"That's good!" Kathleen said, her brown eyes animated. "Now once you return to San Francisco, there won't be so many separations." She paused, pressing her lips tightly together in indecision. Then she blurted, "So when are you going home, Mr. West?"

Shaking his head, Joachim laughed shortly. "Are you trying to get rid of me, Kathleen?"

"Yes!" Kathleen cried half indignantly. "Lord knows, you're breaking my back with all your demands. You eat like a horse, and you make an enormous mess." She almost laughed when she said that because Joachim had reverted to his bland diet after Teddy left, and if the man were any more compulsively neat, she'd wonder if he'd really been born a woman and had had a sex change operation. Her William was sorely lacking where picking up after himself was concerned. "No," she said, explaining. "The reason I asked is, Teddy's birthday is coming up and I assumed you would try to make it back home for that. Men! You never remember important occasions." She turned away, heading for the exit.

"Kathleen! How did you know Teddy's birthday was coming up?" Joachim asked, curious. Obviously Teddy and Kathleen had become quite chummy in the two days Teddy had been there.

Kathleen met his eyes. "When I found her bag at the O'Neils' I looked at her driver's license. She was born on June 24, 1969. The twenty-fourth is only days away."

Joachim rose, walked swiftly around the desk and embraced Kathleen. "Thank you. I have been a neglectful husband, Kathleen. You've saved my can. Teddy would've been upset if I'd missed her birthday."

He released her and Kathleen chuckled as she moved toward the door. "Upset? She would've skinned you alive. Never forget a woman's birthday or your anniversary. That's even more important." She squinted at him. "You haven't let that slip by, have you?" she asked suspiciously.

"No," Joachim said absently, his mind on Teddy. Ten days till June twenty-fourth. Teddy had been gone nearly two months. He looked back at the computer. He could have the first draft completed by then. The first draft was always the hardest because he wrote as if led by an unseen spirit: frenetically, with abandon, writing with emotional intensity. Then he went back over it, cleaned it up. Refined it. Put his indelible mark on it.

"I can see your mind is on your work," Kathleen said knowingly. "Well, I'm glad I mentioned Teddy's birthday . . ."

"Thank you, Kathleen," Joachim said sincerely, smiling at her.

"You can thank me by vacating the premises," Kathleen replied in her inimitable fashion. She left him alone then.

Teddy held the July issue of *Contemporary Lives* in her hand. Joachim's handsome visage graced the cover. She felt childishly elated, as if she wanted to kiss the lips of his photo and make a wish: *Please, God, bring him home soon.*

Joie caught her sitting at her desk, mooning over Joachim's photograph when she knocked and entered without waiting for permission. Teddy hastily opened her desk drawer and shoved the magazine inside.

"Too late, I already saw it," Joie joked, coming to sit on the corner of Teddy's desk. She gazed down at Teddy. "You've got it bad, girlfriend. No doubt about it. And I know just the cure for your malady. You, Melodie, and I are going out tomorrow night to paint the town crimson. When we're through with Frisco, it'll look like the second coming of Sherman," she boasted, referring to the Union general who'd led the army that had laid waste to Atlanta during the Civil War.

"I told you I wanted to spend my birthday in quiet reflection," Teddy said, only half serious. "Alex is spending the weekend with Adrian at his place, and I'm going to clean out my closets."

Joie reached over and placed her palm on Teddy's forehead. Withdrawing her hand, she said, "No fever. Look here, Teddy, you don't have a man to spend your birthday with. Your father is on assignment. Where did he go?"

"South Africa, to do a profile on President Mbeki."

"Yeah. Your father's out of town. Your son is with the spook for the next two days. You've got to let loose, girl. Have some fun." She smiled slowly. "If I could have, I would've had that fine Mr. West fly here and surprise you. Now that would've been a birthday present to top all others."

Teddy bent and opened the bottom drawer on her desk, retrieving her shoulder bag. Going into it, she extracted a folded piece of typing paper. "Read this," she told Joie, handing it to her.

On the paper was a haiku sent to her by Joachim:

> *Impetuous vamp*
> *Where passion and play converge*
> *Warrior-princess*

After reading it, Joie smiled broadly. "A man who can say what he wants to in a few words." She closed her eyes. "I need a moment here. I'm imagining Lee writing something romantic for me." The seconds stretched out to a minute and she still hadn't opened her eyes.

Teddy playfully shoved her.

"You should stop complaining about Lee. Paraphrase Chante Moore, girlfriend, and repeat after me, 'Joie Jackson gotta man.' "

"Joie Jackson gotta man!" Joie cried, getting to her feet as though she were about to shout hallelujah next.

Teddy laughed at her friend's antics. "I'm the one who should be complaining. All I have is the memory of two glorious days in Ireland with the man I've been waiting for, and wonderful messages from him on a nearly daily basis. But what I really want is to be in his arms."

Looking serious all of a sudden, Joie said, "I bet the next time he propositions you, you won't turn him down, now will you, sis? That sexual drought could have been at an end, but no . . ."

"Teddy!" It was Sylvie, sticking her head in the door. Then from behind her she produced a beautiful bouquet of pink roses. "For you," she announced, coming into the office and placing the flowers on Teddy's desk.

Hope sprang to life in Teddy. Could they be from Joachim?

"Thank you, Sylvie," she said, remembering her manners.

"You're welcome, enjoy," Sylvie called as she left.

Teddy rose and inhaled the sweet fragrance of the flowers.

"Read the card already!" Joie strongly suggested.

Teddy wanted to prolong the moment. Now she was in expectation of the flowers being from Joachim. When she read the card, however, she might find out they were from Adrian and the bubble would burst, leaving her deflated, dejected, and disgusted.

She smiled when she read the card. Meeting Joie's eyes, she revealed, "They're from Daddy. He says he's sorry he couldn't be here for my birthday, but that he loves me."

Now that she knew the flowers were from her father, she

felt slightly ashamed when she still felt disappointed because they weren't from Joachim. And why hadn't she heard from Joachim this morning? She usually had a message from him waiting for her when she logged on at home in the mornings before going to work. This morning, there hadn't been a message. She tried not to read too much into it. After all he was busy writing.

That night when Adrian arrived to pick up Alex for their weekend together, Teddy was ready for his usual assault on her senses. Ever since that Sunday afternoon when he took Alex to dinner at his parents', Adrian had made it his mission to entice Teddy in every way, shape, and form at his disposal.

He'd turned a deaf ear to her protests about the flowers. He brought her fresh flowers every time he came by for Alex. And he hadn't missed a Saturday outing in nearly two months. Teddy had to grudgingly respect that. But she told herself, he had more than two years of Saturday outings to make up for. So she cautioned herself about becoming too sympathetic toward him. That's what he wanted, she decided. He was going to wear her down bit by bit, and then the moment she showed the first sign of weakening, he'd pounce.

Tonight he showed up with a bouquet of spring flowers in a pastel palette of colors: pink, lavender, yellow. She'd stopped making a big deal out of the flowers.

Accepting them, she ushered him inside and closed the door.

Adrian smiled pleasantly, his dark brown eyes on her face. As she turned to head into the living room, he lowered his gaze to her figure, sexy in a short polo dress, the muscles in her shapely bronze legs and thighs flexing. He could see she still enjoyed running. The slowness of it seemed pointless to him. Too relaxing for his type-A personality. He worked out with weights; ran, fast, on the treadmill. Practiced karate. They were disciplines he could wrap his mind around.

"Alex is packing," Teddy told him as she strode back to the kitchen.

Adrian followed and watched her as she got a vase and put the flowers in water. Teddy had her hair pinned up. Adrian's attention was drawn to the gentle slope the back of her neck made. He recalled how much he used to love kissing her there.

"You let him pack his own things?"

"He knows what he likes," she answered. She hadn't smiled at him once, and he craved her smile.

"Your birthday's tomorrow. How're you going to celebrate?"

Teddy met his eyes. He was looking at her with laughter evident in his gaze. "We don't discuss our private lives, Adrian. You've got to get into this shared-custody thing. We are cordial to one another for the sake of the child. We are not friends."

"We could be, if you'd loosen up," he commented dryly.

"And pigs could fly, if they only had wings," Teddy said with a smile. "But neither of those things will happen anytime soon."

Adrian shrugged, smiling. "So, Teddy, how is your relationship going with the writer? Is he subjected to your caustic tongue on occasion, too, or is that reserved for me?"

Teddy chose to ignore that dig. She moved past him, going into the hallway. "I'll go see how Alex is coming along."

In the intervening weeks Adrian had hoped that Teddy's attitude toward him would begin to soften if his behavior was exemplary. If he proved that he was serious about being a part of Alex's life, which he had. He'd rearranged his schedule so he'd have all weekends off. He'd given up several promotional opportunities because of that. But those were the sacrifices, he was learning, a parent made in order to spend time with their children.

Frustrated by Teddy's coldness, he now cried, "I'm trying as hard as I can, Teddy!"

Teddy paused, turned and cut her eyes at him. "I'll let you know when you've tried hard enough."

She immediately regretted those words because it proved he could still get a rise out of her. That she was still capable of being touched emotionally by him.

A few seconds passed as they stood there in the hallway, their eyes locked in silent acrimony. Adrian was the first to move, going to grasp her by the arms and shake her roughly. "That's it, isn't it? You want to punish me for my sins. Make sure I've truly repented of my evil ways. You want to make me suffer as much as I've made you suffer." He laughed harshly as he bent his head, bringing his mouth only a fraction of an inch away from hers. "I can understand revenge, Teddy. I'm an old master at it. So don't play the game if you can't hang."

Adrian pulled her hard against him. "Feel that, Teddy? Even when I'm so angry with you, I want to throttle you, I still want you. Know this: If I didn't think I could eventually have you, I wouldn't bother. I'd just, as you've suggested, be content with having a wonderful son, and leave you alone. But I know you want me, too, Teddy. If you didn't, why would you even care about exacting revenge? If you have indeed gone on with your life, and the writer means so much to you, you wouldn't let my comments about your personal life affect you."

"You're wrong," Teddy told him in low angry tones. She jerked free of his hold. Backing away, her gaze slicing him, she said, "You're grasping at straws. What I'd like to know is why? You say your mother influenced the change in you. She must have done some powerful talking!"

Adrian shifted his weight and expressed air through his lips in an exasperated fashion. "A man has to grow up sometime. If I'm to leave anything worthwhile behind, I have to be willing to face the consequences of my actions. I love you, Teddy."

He saw the disbelief mirrored in her eyes.

"I know you don't believe that. But you're the only woman I've ever felt this deeply for. Before, and after you, I held myself, my emotions apart, not allowing anyone to touch me. You broke through that. *You* did. And I believe that's another reason I left you. In my mind you'd taken away part of the control I had over my own emotions. Then you got pregnant, and I saw even more of that slipping away. I know I'm not explaining this well, but that's how I felt."

Teddy sniffed derisively. "You're right, I don't believe you."

She continued down the hallway, with him behind her.

"You should come out to the house, check it out, make sure it's safe for Alex," Adrian said, changing the subject. Teddy had too much anger in her to be able to see his point of view.

Teddy, turning in the direction of Alex's bedroom, surprised him by saying, "All right, I'll follow you."

A more than two-hour layover in London set Joachim's time of arrival back in San Francisco at 8:15 P.M. on Saturday night. On the plane en route to the States now, he sat back on the plush seat in first class and tried to relax. *Maybe I should have told her I was coming,* he worried. *What if she's in Carmel at her father's?* No, she'd written a few days ago that her father would be in South Africa for a few weeks.

Adrian, she'd told him, in the attempt to prove himself a doting father, appeared every weekend to spend time with Alex.

She'd been open and honest with him by informing him that Adrian had set forth his intentions of winning her back. But she had assured him, she would never consider going back to him.

Joachim, who at this point knew without a doubt he wanted her in his life, felt he shouldn't put demands on her. She still had feelings for the father of her child. Whether they came in the form of deep-seated resentments, or dormant sexual urges, he was certain she still felt something for Adrian Riley. It was up to her whether or not she did anything about them.

However, Joachim would declare his feelings for her. She had continually been on his mind while he was in Ballycastle. He knew that he hadn't felt this way about a woman since Suzanne. What that meant, he had yet to define. He simply wanted to look into Teddy's cognac-colored eyes one more time. To feel that rush of emotion that overwhelmed initially, then spread a kind of spiritual calm over him.

"Mr. West?" An attractive flight attendant with mahogany

skin and hazel eyes had stopped next to his seat. She bent down close. "I'm sorry to bother you, but one of the passengers, an elderly woman . . ." She paused, her eyes shifting two rows behind her. Joachim followed her line of sight and saw a smart-looking black woman who appeared to be in her early seventies, smiling at him.

". . . wondered if you wouldn't mind autographing *The God Gene* for her." She promptly produced the book, along with a felt-tip pen.

Smiling, Joachim gladly signed the book and handed it back to her. "My pleasure."

When the woman saw the flight attendant returning with the book and that the mission had been a fait accompli, she mouthed, *Thank you* to Joachim. Joachim simply smiled. She reminded him of his grandma Eva.

Teddy might have been irritated when Adrian asked her what she was doing to celebrate her birthday last night, but she was a responsible mother and told him, in detail, where she, Joie, and Melodie were planning to go. She also left a message on her answering machine restating their itinerary, in case he forgot.

The limo—Melodie's idea and on her tab—pulled up in front of Teddy's place at seven thirty-eight. The three of them had agreed to wear something from their closets they had bought but hadn't had the nerve to wear in public. All women had that item of clothing that had looked good in the store, had graced the department store mannequin beautifully. But once they got it home, they had lost confidence that they'd ever look good in it, so it gathered dust in the back of the closet.

For Teddy it was a short, brown leather skirt, the hem of which fell a good four inches above her knees. It wasn't a crotch kisser, but it was the shortest skirt she had in her wardrobe. Hence the reason she'd never worn it.

Joie and Melodie spilled out of the white limo and Joie emitted a long wolf whistle when Teddy began coming down the steps from the condo. "Watch out! Girlfriend's on the prowl tonight."

Teddy threw her head back in laughter. "You're the one who looks like a jungle cat."

Joie was adorned in a tight stretch catsuit in a leopard print. Every curve of her five-foot-seven-inch body was revealed by the suit. "Lee took one look at it and didn't want me to leave the house," she boasted. "I believe I'm in for some good lovin' when I drag myself home in the wee hours."

Melodie, the tallest of the three women at five ten, laughed delightedly at Joie's remarks. She and Joie had met for the first time tonight when she'd arrived at Joie's address and gone upstairs at Joie's building and knocked on the door.

They'd taken an instant liking to each other.

Melodie was attired in a white body-hugging, sleeveless A-line dress whose hem came only two inches above her well-shaped knees. As a model her figure was flawless.

"And what's so daring about that?" Teddy asked, eyeing the dress.

Melodie turned around. The dress was backless, and it dipped so low that the crack of her butt was nearly visible.

"I want that dress when you tire of it," Joie said as the three of them climbed into the limousine.

Joie and Melodie sat facing Teddy, who was riding facing the back window.

Joie bent and opened the refrigerator, producing a bottle of champagne. She popped the cork and poured the sparkling champagne into plastic flutes held by Melodie. Melodie passed Teddy a glass as the driver pulled away from the curb.

Joie held the champagne bottle between her knees as she offered a toast. "To Teddy, and I quote: *'Impetuous vamp / Where passion and play converge / Warrior-princess.'* "

They touched glasses and drank deeply of the bubbly.

"So, Melodie," Teddy said, smiling, "what's going on between you and you-know-who?"

"Wait a minute," Joie cried, feeling left out. "There are no secrets between friends. Besides, you know I live vicariously through you . . . so spill!"

Melodie gave a dramatic pause, but her eyes were sparkling with mirth. "The Irish blues man." She smiled in Joie's direction. "He goes by the name of Frankie Ahern. Well, it seems Mr. Ahern has a penchant for salty song lyrics. My ears are still burning. As are other parts of my body."

"You like, then?" Teddy inquired, sure the answer would be positive.

"I like," Melodie confirmed, pulling the champagne bottle from between Joie's knees and refilling her glass. She offered more to Joie, who held her glass up. Teddy declined. "I want to be able to remember every detail of this evening."

"I like him so much, I invited him here for the fourth of July. I told him we were going to have a crab boil at your dad's place in Carmel, and that you'd extended the invitation to him."

"Testing the waters, huh?" Joie surmised.

"We've stayed up late, talking on the phone. Our e-mails are becoming erotic treatises. I have his photo. I want to get my hands on the genuine article."

"You can identify with that, can't you?" Joie asked Teddy teasingly. Teddy reached for the champagne. "A little more can't hurt." She held up her glass in a toast. "To three love-starved women out on the town. May we all find some good loving, and soon!"

They clicked glasses and drank every bit of the champagne from them. "Correction," Joie said with a grin. "Two love-starved women. Joie Jackson gotta man."

Melodie and Teddy began pelting her with salted peanuts from the snack bar.

Joachim checked into the Mark Hopkins Hotel. It was located on the southeast corner of Mason and California Streets in the Nob Hill area of the city. He didn't want to waste time taking a taxi all the way to North Beach, where his house was, showering and changing there, then having to come back into the city. Besides, Teddy's condo was in the Nob Hill area, too.

Once in his room he went straight to the phone sitting on
the nightstand, and dialed Teddy's number.

He was disappointed to hear she wasn't at home, and from
the sound of it wouldn't be for some time. However, he was
familiar with the restaurant and the club where she said she
would be. It shouldn't be that difficult to catch up with her.

Replacing the receiver, he began coming out of his
clothes.

It was nearly nine o'clock, Teddy and her friends were probably leaving the restaurant by now and heading to The Cypress, a trendy club in the Richmond district. He'd been there
a couple times himself. It was frequented by upwardly mobile
thirty-somethings who were interested in rhythm and blues,
and in meeting others of similar tastes.

After stripping down to his briefs, folding his clothing and
placing it on a nearby chair as he did so, Joachim went into
the bathroom and switched on the shower. He caught his reflection in the bathroom mirror. He ran his hand over the
beard. After the first two weeks, he'd wanted to shave it off,
it irritated him so. Razor bumps put in an appearance. It itched
constantly. But after a month the bumps cleared up, and now
the beard was soft, luxuriant, and he barely noticed it was
there until he looked into a mirror. Then he had to take a
second glance to assure himself he was the same man.

Coming out of his briefs, he stepped under the warm stream
of water, reaching for a washcloth and the liquid soap. With
each motion, his biceps moved up and down in his arms. His
thigh muscles flexed. The gluteal muscles formed deep in-
dentations on either side of his well-toned buttocks. All that
running had wrought a body he hoped Teddy wouldn't mind
touching. He wanted her to want him as much as he wanted
her.

His powerful hands moved sinuously along his hardened
body, and he couldn't help imagining Teddy there with him,
her small hands caressing him all over.

He reached down and switched off the hot water, leaving
on the cold. It was the only way he could banish thoughts of
Teddy.

* * *

"I've got it," Melodie and Joie both said, each of them reaching for the check the waiter held on a small tray.

Melodie snatched up the slip of paper and read it. "Let me get this one, Joie. You can pay the cover charge at the club," she suggested reasonably.

Melodie handed the waiter her Visa Gold card. He disappeared with it.

"Thanks to both of you," Teddy said, sitting back on her chair. "The cioppino was delicious."

Cioppino was a rich seafood stew, reminiscent of the French bouillabaisse. It was popular in many San Francisco restaurants. Being a lover of seafood, Teddy had the cioppino whenever she got the opportunity to go to a good restaurant, which wasn't often on her salary. So she'd truly enjoyed her meal tonight.

"I knew it was good to you when a whole loaf of sourdough bread disappeared as you were sopping it up," Joie joked.

Teddy stopped. Two white guys in business suits were staring at them. Or to be more specific, at Melodie. They were at the table facing Teddy. Melodie's back was to them, so she hadn't noticed their ogling.

"Uh-oh," Teddy said, her tone warning.

Melodie and Joie turned to look in the direction Teddy was gazing in.

The men were approaching their table with confident swaggers which, Teddy was willing to wager, were false. Just putting on macho airs in order to impress Melodie.

They were attractive. The taller of the two had dark brown hair and blue eyes. His friend was blond with brown eyes. Teddy thought that the stereotype of white males was the other way around: dark hair with brown eyes and light hair with blue. The two of them were tanned, and their suits, expensive. Young San Francisco attorneys, Teddy figured.

"Hi," the blond said, stopping between Melodie and Joie. He peered at Melodie. "Has anyone ever told you you look just like Melodie Morrison?"

Evidently, he'd decided that he couldn't possibly be fortunate enough to actually meet the real Melodie Morrison, so he'd assumed she was a look-alike.

"No kidding!" Melodie cried, going along. She smiled charmingly. Looking at Teddy, she asked, "Do you think I look like her?"

"I don't see it," Teddy said, sounding unconvinced. "You're much prettier than she is."

"And she's skinnier," Joie piped in. "Sister looks like she hasn't eaten all year."

"Oh, you are much prettier," the fellow with the dark hair heartily agreed. "And the eyes are different, too. Hers are not nearly as beautiful as yours are."

Melodie blushed. She sincerely felt bad for having deceived them. "All right," she told them. "Look guys, I really am Melodie Morrison, I was just pulling your leg."

The blond frowned. "No way!" he cried dismissively, frowning at her impertinence. With an insistent hand on his friend's shoulder, he said, "Jack, let's go before she tells us her friends here are Halle Berry and Angela Bassett."

Jack quickly retrieved his business card and gave it to Melodie. "I don't care who you are. I think you're gorgeous, and I hope you'll call me."

He then left with his buddy. Melodie read the card, "JACK STANDISH, ATTORNEY-AT-LAW."

"I knew it," Teddy exclaimed.

Melodie squinted at her companions. "You know, you two do look a little like Halle and Angela."

The Cypress was smoking, in the figurative sense. Smoking was not allowed inside the club. The band on the stage tonight played rhythm and blues with a salsa flavor. When the three women entered the room, male eyes drifted to Melodie, being the tallest of them, her long, straight auburn hair looking more red than brown in the flickering lights of the club.

They weren't seated at their table five minutes before a man approached them. He was in his twenties, dark-skinned, good looking—either Latino or a brother with fair skin. Teddy couldn't tell from her vantage point. "Hello, ladies, I'm Anthony," he said politely before focusing on Joie. "Would you please dance with me, pretty lady? I'd like to see what a leopard looks like in motion."

"Well, all right," Joie said cautiously as she got to her feet. "But watch yourself, because leopards have claws."

Anthony chuckled and reached for her hand as a slow song began.

In Joie's absence Melodie good-naturedly groused, "The only married one among us and she's already dancing. Am I losing it?"

Teddy, who was used to Joie drawing attention wherever they went, told Melodie, "Joie has an exuberance about her that men can spot a mile away. It's been that way ever since I've known her."

She and Melodie sat watching Joie gyrate to the music while keeping Anthony at a distance. He'd pull her closer, and Joie would push him away, never missing a beat.

"I think she'd better flash her wedding band under his nose a couple times to get his attention," Teddy said, laughing.

The band switched gears, playing an allegro number. Joie spun out of Anthony's arms in a salsa move, and walked off the dance floor, leaving her erstwhile partner gaping at her.

Laughing, she flopped onto her chair at their table. "Brother has a severe breast fetish. I had to give it up when he tried to remove this with his tongue." She held up a salted peanut. It had gotten lodged in her cleavage earlier, when Teddy and Melodie had thrown peanuts at her in the limousine.

"Another brave soul ventures forth," Melodie said, nodding her head in the direction of an approaching male.

Teddy and Joie turned their gazes on the tall, well-built black man. Only six feet away now, they admired the dynamic play of muscles in his taut body as he glided toward them, his stylish dark suit failing to disguise what a splendid specimen he was.

His dark slacks were pleated and draped his body so perfectly, they both sighed when their gazes drifted south, past his sinewy thighs. And his white shirt, open at the collar under his coat, was a sharp contrast to his dark skin.

"Forget Joachim West, Teddy, make *him* your birthday present tonight," Joie said reverently.

Teddy didn't say a word, but her face had broken into a wide grin as she quickly got out of her chair. Her friends watched, amazed, as she ran into the open arms of the stranger and kissed him. The girls' mouths fell open in shock. It wasn't a hello-how-are-you? kiss, but an I've-been-dying-to-touch-you-again, passionate clinch that left no doubt as to whether they'd met before.

"Whew!" Melodie expelled a breath. "I think Teddy's been holding out on us."

Joie, though, knew there was another explanation. And she suspected a rather nice one at that.

They had to wait a while for the explanation, however, for Teddy had totally forgotten they existed. All she saw was Joachim. Joachim, here, right before her hungry eyes. Joachim smiling gently at her. And that beard! She had to get her hands on it. When they parted, she asked breathlessly, "Is it really you?"

"Yes," he said, as he lowered his head and claimed her mouth again. The taste, the feel, the smell of him formed a triple treat for her senses. She fell into him.

When they parted this time, her eyes were misty. "Where are we?" Joachim kissed the tip of her nose. "We're in The Cypress, making a spectacle of ourselves."

That was when she remembered Joie and Melodie.

Finally Joie's suspicions were proved correct as Teddy, beaming now, led the handsome stranger back to their table. "Joachim," she said, peering lovingly up at him. "I want you to meet my two best girlfriends, Joie Jackson and Melodie Morrison."

Teddy and Joachim sat down.

"It's a pleasure, ladies," Joachim said, smiling warmly at them.

"Mmm," Joie moaned loudly, shaking her head in awe. Her eyes were on Teddy. "You didn't exaggerate one iota."

Teddy's cheeks grew hot with embarrassment, but Joachim just laughed. "Her description of you was pretty accurate, too."

Joie threw her head back in laughter. Her dark eyes sparkled. "Let me guess, she said I usually say whatever pops into my head first, right?" Her eyes were on Teddy. "That's why she loves me, she knows I'll give it to her straight."

"True enough," Teddy agreed.

"And you, Melodie . . ." Joachim said, his dark eyes on her, "you're the small-town girl whose talent and beauty propelled her to the top of her profession."

"I sound so boring compared to Joie," Melodie jokingly replied, crossing her long legs and regarding Joachim and Teddy with keen eyes. "So tell me, Joachim: Why you wanna go and surprise a girl like that? Teddy could have injured herself, the way she leapt out of her chair to fly into your arms."

Joachim was gazing deeply into Teddy's eyes as they sat close to one another, his arm about her waist, hers about his. "I wanted to be with her on her birthday."

A simple answer. But it meant the world to Teddy. "How did you know it was my birthday?" she asked softly.

"Kathleen told me," he said honestly. "And I'm glad she did." They had eyes only for each other.

Joie dramatically fanned her face with her hand. "Is it getting warm in here, or is it just me?"

She playfully nudged Melodie, inviting her to get in on the ribbing that was about to commence. "How long do you think they'll make small talk with us?" she asked, looking at Melodie.

"I suggest we let them off the hook," Melodie proposed.

"You heard her," Joie said to Teddy and Joachim. "Get out of here."

They didn't have to be told twice. Teddy rose first, her hand firmly in Joachim's. She bent and kissed Joie's cheek. "Don't

let that one get away," Joie whispered. Then she kissed
Melodie's. "Have fun," Melodie advised softly.

Outside the club Joachim wrapped her in his arms as they
waited under the awning for the doorman to hail a cab. Teddy
buried her nose in his chest, inhaling the wonderful male scent
of him, still not quite believing he was really there. She peered
up into his face. "I love the beard."

Joachim grinned. "I grew it for you."

"It's not bothersome . . ." she worried.

"Oh no, I'm quite used to it now," Joachim assured her. He
kissed her high on her right cheek. Then he raised a hand and
traced the scar on her forehead with a finger. "You can hardly
see it."

"I had that to remind me," Teddy said cryptically.

"To remind you?"

"That the two days we spent together really happened. It
was beginning to feel like a dream to me. A sweet dream that
I didn't want to wake up from."

Inwardly Joachim rejoiced at her heartfelt admission. He
was not alone in feeling that way. He'd almost convinced himself that Teddy was a figment of his overripe imagination.
Now, though, as he gazed into her face, her curly mop of hair
framing it so beautifully, he knew what it must feel like for
life in the desert to get rain after a drought. He was truly
grateful. It was then that he knew he loved her. Yes, he loved
her with his whole heart, and he'd do anything for her.

"Teddy, I got you something for your birthday." He paused
to reach into his coat pocket and bring out a tiny, blue velvet-
covered box.

Teddy accepted it, looking wonderingly at him. "What is
it?" Her heart picked up its pace.

"Open it," Joachim said with a warm smile.

She lifted the lid. Inside was a pear-shaped, ten-carat emerald ring in a twenty-four-carat gold setting.

"In honor of your stay on the Emerald Isle," he said, his
dark eyes glowing with a humorous inner light. "I had to guess
at your ring size. But Kathleen swore you were a size six."

"She got it right on the nose," Teddy told him. She couldn't stop looking into his dear face. What did this mean? It was too expensive for a friendship ring. But then she didn't know how wealthy Joachim was. Maybe the cost of the ring had been a drop in the bucket to him. However, no matter what he wanted the ring to represent, it was too soon in their relationship for him to be giving her such extravagant presents.

Regretfully, she closed the box. Meeting his gaze, she said, "It's beautiful. I love it . . . but I can't accept it, Joachim."

Joachim had been expecting her reaction. Teddy was an independent woman. Sensible, too. She wouldn't take that costly a gift from a man unless she was certain of how he felt about her—and of how she felt about him.

So he asked her the most logical question he could think of. "Tell me what your gut is saying right now." His eyes were intense. "Do you think you could ever love me, Teddy?"

Thirteen

Love him? Teddy stared at him for several seconds, without blinking. A warmth suffused her body, and her heart thudded against her rib cage. Love him. Her hand sought his, and that was when she felt the absence of his wedding band.

Teddy grasped his hand and he brought her hand up, placing it on his waist. Tenderly he kissed her forehead. "It was time, Teddy." He bent his head, peering into her eyes. "I'll always love her, but she's gone forever. I'm still here. I've known for a while now that I needed to do it. But you were the impetus. You, with your sweet, cocky, vulnerable self." He smiled. "I fell in love with the thought of you. Now, though, after seeing you again, I know I was fooling myself. I fell in love with you, the woman, not just the thought of you, but with you. So tell me now, do I stand a chance?"

Their cheeks had been touching as Joachim pleaded his case; now Teddy turned into him, her mouth brushing his. Their lips teased and tasted. Her lips parted, his tongue entered her mouth. Her core seemed to melt as their tongues danced back and forth, giving and taking, pleasure. She felt light-headed when they finally came up for air. "I would say the answer is a resounding yes!" she told him breathlessly.

The cab pulled up next to them. Joachim handed Teddy in and tipped the doorman.

"Where to?" Joachim asked her as they settled in the back-seat.

Teddy got comfortable in the crook of his arm. "My place is probably closer."

"I'm at the Mark Hopkins," Joachim murmured, nuzzling the side of her neck.

Teddy's body tingled down to her toes. "All right, the Mark Hopkins, it is."

"The Mark Hopkins," Joachim announced to the driver, who'd been patiently waiting for the lovers to decide where their assignation would take place.

He buried his nose in Teddy's hair, loving the flowery scent of it. "I finished the first draft. I was like a man possessed. Typing until my carpel tunnel syndrome kicked in. But I did it, and I have you to thank."

Teddy was so comfortable in his embrace, she'd closed her eyes as she fully appreciated the sensual experience this moment afforded. "Why? What did I do?"

Joachim shifted a bit on the seat. "When you told me your story, about you and Alex, and how Adrian abandoned you when he found out you were expecting Alex, it reminded me of my own situation with my mother. She was seventeen when she got pregnant with me. My father wasn't much older. Anyway she couldn't handle it. As soon as she had me, she handed me over to my grandma Eva. I only saw Earnestine once, maybe twice a year when I was growing up. And then it was at funerals, or on the occasions she was down on her luck and needed to borrow money from Gran."

"That must have been hard on you," Teddy said, turning to look up at him.

Joachim's eyes narrowed as he continued. "Hard on me? I don't think I missed anything. As a child I didn't know anything else except living with Gran. When I got to be a teen, I became a bit resentful of Earnestine. She was young, strong. I used to see her and ask myself why she didn't have the strength to care for me? Why pawn me off on an old lady? Well, I found out that that old lady had more strength in her little finger than Earnestine had in her whole body. As an adult I now realize that Earnestine did the right thing. There's no telling where I'd be if she had kept me. It seems she was never able to get her life on track. Going from one man to another. Anyone who showed her the least bit of affection . . . It was no life for a child. So in that way she displayed an uncommon strength."

"Is she still living, your mother?"

Joachim nodded thoughtfully. "Yeah, she's in Gainesville, Florida. Married for the fourth time. This guy seems all right. He works in construction. Earnestine works as a nurse's assistant at a hospital. I hear from her about once a year. I send her money every few months, not that she asks for it. I just don't want her to need something and not have enough to cover it, you know?"

Teddy smiled at him. "Yeah, I know. Your grandma Eva raised a fine man."

Joachim chuckled softly. "I don't know about all that. All I know is, Earnestine could've gotten rid of me, and she didn't so I figure I at least owe her something for that."

Teddy wasn't put off by the bitter edge to his voice. Somewhere deep inside, he still resented his mother for giving him away. Who wouldn't? The psychological cuts the experience had caused could take years to heal.

He sighed. "Anyway your situation led me to thinking of Earnestine. I started to sympathize with her. Then the character, Lottie, was born. Lottie who, when she was an innocent sixteen-year-old, was seduced by an older man and got pregnant, then was ostracized by her community in rural Mississippi of the late thirties. Can you imagine the recourse this girl had available to her?"

"Absolutely none," Teddy said emphatically.

"Exactly," Joachim said, continuing the story. "One weak moment, and her life's changed forever. She tries to be respectable, takes jobs in white folks' houses. But as an attractive single woman, white women don't want her working for them, believing she might try to seduce their husbands. Lottie meets this charming fellow who promises he'll take her to Biloxi. Biloxi is like New York City to Lottie. He does take her there but once there, he turns her out on the street."

There was a dramatic pause.

"Well, what happens?" Teddy cried, hooked.

"You can read it," Joachim simply said with a smile.

Teddy hugged him. "I can't wait!"

Joachim was warmed by her excitement. "If you hate it," he joked, "don't tell me, I'll be crushed."

"Tonight?" Teddy inquired, squirming in her seat.

Joachim laughed. "It sure doesn't take much to make you happy."

"Just you," Teddy told him, leaning over and gently kissing his mouth. "You make me happy."

"Teddy?" Joachim whispered against her mouth. He placed her hand over his heart. "Why did you agree to come back to the Mark Hopkins with me?"

Teddy instinctively knew what he was asking. Did she love him? He'd told her how he felt. Now he wanted the same reassurance.

She couldn't give it to him though. There were places in her heart that still needed opening. She knew it. Joachim spoke to her on several levels: She desired him, respected him as a writer and as a man with the capacity to be loyal to those he loved. And even to those he felt an obligation to, like his mother.

But how could she trust what she was feeling for him, when she'd made such a glaring mistake when choosing Adrian? She would require time to analyze the emotions he evoked within her. Time to make the right decision.

How would she explain that to him?

Joachim saw the war of indecision going on behind her eyes. And he loved her even more because of it. "It's too soon," he breathed. His lips caressed her soft cheek. "You don't have to answer. Just say you want me, Teddy."

"Oh I do," Teddy said, her eyes devouring him.

Joachim leaned forward, getting the cabdriver's attention. "A detour, my man."

A few minutes later Teddy sat in the cab while Joachim ran into a drugstore. He came back out, a small brown bag in his hand, and gave it to her. "I thought you grew out of being embarrassed to ask for these things when you became an adult. But no, I felt foolish when this little old lady, somebody's mother, handed me the package." Teddy snuggled close to

him, cooing, "Poor baby. Let me make it better." And she
kissed him hard on the lips. By the time they reached the Mark
Hopkins Hotel, Joachim was feeling no pain at all, Teddy had
worked him up into such a sexual frenzy.

The Mark Hopkins Inter-Continental was located at Number One Nob Hill. The elegant nineteen-story hotel was a
combination of French château and Spanish renaissance architecture accented by intricate terra-cotta ornament. Teddy
self-consciously smoothed her short skirt as she and Joachim
stepped under the wide forest-green awning over the entrance
and the uniformed doorman ushered them inside with, "Good
evening, sir, madam."

Hand in hand, she and Joachim went to the bank of elevators
just off the lobby and he pressed the Up button.

Teddy's insides were atremble. Here they were going upstairs with the express purpose of making love. She glanced
at Joachim, whose handsome face was a perfect example of
quiet contentment. No nervousness there. Did he know how
many times she'd envisioned this night? Tossing and turning
in her bed, wishing he was there beside her?

The elevator arrived, and they waited as several guests ex-
ited, then they stepped inside, alone. Joachim pressed the button for the fourteenth floor and clasped her hand in his again.
They had been silent for the last few minutes. Silent only with
their tongues—their eyes spoke volumes.

Joachim, a man who made his living because of his facility
with words, was afraid to say anything. He didn't want to
inadvertently say something which would spoil the mood. And
the tension between them was so sexually charged that he
didn't want to break that momentum. Anticipation was killing
him.

Two months ago when he'd boldly invited her to join him
in his bedroom, and she'd declined . . . Well, he'd understood.
That hadn't kept him from being disappointed. And in the
intervening weeks, his need for her had grown rapidly and
voraciously: He was at the boiling point. So she didn't love
him . . . yet. He loved her. He wasn't the type of man who
loved lightly. When he loved someone, it was forever.

Joachim unlocked the door and moved aside for Teddy to enter the spacious suite before him. Teddy's footsteps were muted by the thick, plush wheat-colored carpeting. The six-hundred-square-foot room's walls were painted in a creamy off-white. And the cherry-wood furnishings had the appearance of pieces that had the rich-patina wood acquired with age and careful polishing. There was the pleasant odor of jasmine in the air. Teddy walked into the sitting area and to the terrace door where she pulled open the glass door and stepped onto the glass-enclosed terrace. A breathtaking view of the city, the golden-hued lights of the buildings glittering like stars, lay before her.

Joachim smiled at the innocent picture she made. She took joy in the simple things life had to offer. He didn't join her right away. He went to the phone and placed an order with room service. It was nearly midnight, and they stopped taking orders after 1 A.M. So he ordered a bottle of sparkling cider, since neither of them were big drinkers, some fresh fruits, a platter of various cheeses, crackers, and a couple of warm grilled chicken breast sandwiches. That should hold them until morning.

Morning. Was he being too hopeful?

Teddy turned when she heard him behind her. Her hair bounced vibrantly about her head and her eyes danced. "Isn't this city beautiful at night?"

"Not half as appealing as you are watching it," he told her as he came close to her, reached up and brushed her hair back from her face. "How are Alex and your father, Teddy?"

Her skin looks like burnished copper in this light, he thought. His eyes rested on her lips, a bit swollen from kissing. They were the color of pomegranates, and just as sweet.

"They're both doing well. Alex is with his father this weekend. And Dad will be in Johannesburg for several more days. He should be home next Wednesday." She smiled mischievously. "So how did Kathleen know today's my birthday?"

"She took the liberty of looking at your driver's license when she found your bag at the O'Neils'. The woman has a memory like a steel trap. Too bad her mouth has never been that tightly closed."

Teddy tilted her head back, eyeing him suspiciously. "You like her, you know you do."

"She was harder on me than my own grandmother was when I was growing up. A day didn't go by that she didn't remind me that my place was here with you, my devoted wife. She was so relentless, I was almost tempted to tell her the truth just to see the shocked expression on her face."

Laughing, Teddy said, "Why didn't you? She's going to find out sooner or later anyway."

"Because I didn't want her thinking you'd deceived her. I didn't care what she thought of me, but she took an instant liking to you, and I didn't want your image tarnished in her eyes."

"Well, I like her, too," Teddy said. "But Kathleen's more worldly than you give her credit for. I think she would've understood. And our little ruse didn't hurt anybody."

"How're things going between you and Adrian?" Joachim asked, afraid he might succeed in throwing water on the fire that had ignited between them, but he had to know. Was she warming to Adrian since he'd demonstrated his willingness to be a father to Alex?

"He's obnoxiously sure that one day soon, I'll come back to him. So he brings flowers every time he picks Alex up. He insists that I'm resisting him only to pay him back for everything he's put me through."

"And?"

There was a hurt expression in Teddy's eyes. "God, Joachim . . . Don't you think I know my own mind? Sure I'd like to see him suffer for what he did to me and Alex. But as for withholding an undying love for him until I think he's been sufficiently punished . . . No! I don't love Adrian anymore."

"The dynamics of a relationship can be tricky. The familiarity of a partner, the very thing that drew you to a person initially, it can all work to form a bond that's very hard to break," Joachim warned gently. He held on to her hand. "I know what I'm talking about, Teddy. It took me four years to come to the point where I could give my heart to someone else, and my marriage ended with Suzanne's death. I knew there was no possibility of a reconciliation."

Teddy angrily wrenched her hand free. "You're just playing it safe, aren't you, Joachim?" She stomped back into the suite, leaving the terrace door open. Joachim followed. "You want to know if, somewhere down the road, you're going to have your heart trampled on by me, if I should suddenly realize I still love Adrian. Well . . ." She faced him. "You said you loved me, and you can't take it back. If you're going to be involved with me, you're going to have to take all the excess baggage along with the package. Adrian's my son's father. He's going to be in our lives for a long time. I've had to accept that." Tears sprang to her eyes. "Even though, God help me, I fought it."

Joachim was at her side in an instant. He pulled her roughly, because she resisted, into his arms. His embrace was intractable. She couldn't break out of it. "I'm not playing it safe, Teddy. I adore you. And I'm here for as long as you want me to be. But I had to know. Take it back?" He laughed shortly. "Baby, once the words *I love you* are out of my mouth, there is no taking it back. My love is like that little pink bunny, it just keeps going and going . . ."

Teddy relaxed in his arms. Joachim felt the tension evaporate, and he loosened his hold somewhat. Teddy tilted her head up, a smile on her lips. Joachim kissed her tear-streaked face repeatedly. She sighed. "I should be apologizing to you," she said softly.

"For what?"

"There I was, accusing you of playing it safe and I was guilty of the same thing. Earlier when you asked why I'd agreed to come here with you, you were really asking me if I loved you. And I couldn't answer you because I was afraid to, Joachim."

He instinctively wanted to comfort her, make her be quiet, get her composure. But he also felt she needed to get whatever she wanted to tell him out in the open. So he didn't interrupt her.

"How do I feel about you, Joachim?" She looked into his eyes. "As though there's a liquid fire inside me that can be put out only by your love. As if, like the Canticles say, 'Many waters themselves are not able to extinguish . . .' " She stopped, afraid she was beginning to sound foolish.

But Joachim was watching her with ardent adoration. "You like Song of Solomon?"

"The greatest love poem ever written," Teddy whispered. "Do I love you, Joachim? Yes, with everything that I am, or ever will be. But I'm so afraid . . ." Her voice broke.

Understanding her fear, Joachim simply held her against his broad chest, letting her give him her pain. *She loved him.* All right, they were cooking with gas now.

Teddy pressed closer to him, calmer now and relieved to have told him how she really felt. The warmth of his body, the aroma of the male scent of him mixed with Obsession for Men, wreaked havoc on her senses. She felt a quick, heated urgency begin to grow deep in her female center. Her nipples felt almost painful as they hardened and pressed upon the silken material of her bra.

Joachim bent his head and kissed the side of her fragrant neck. He removed his arms from around her and immediately put his hands to work by removing her cocoa-colored jacket. He folded it and placed it on the beige barrel-shaped chair in the seating group nearest to the bed. Then he shrugged out of his jacket and put it on top of Teddy's. "Let's get comfortable, shall we?"

He took Teddy's hand and led her over to the couch, not the bed, she impatiently noted. But they had all night. So she tried to slow down her racing libido.

She sat down—however, Joachim crouched on one knee before her. When she saw him reaching for her foot, she nearly had a spontaneous orgasm right then and there. He met her eyes, his deep brown ones caressing her face. Then he slowly removed her pumps, sat them under the edge of the couch and then he sat on the carpet, took her stocking-clad foot in his strong hands and gently massaged it. Sighing, Teddy sank into the soft folds of the couch and closed her eyes. After Joachim had worked his magic on her left foot, he started in on the right one.

This done, he got on both knees in front of her, pulled her close and began unbuttoning her dark brown silk blouse. When he was halfway down, he reached inside and cupped her breasts through the bra. Bending his head, he kissed the tender skin of her cleavage, his warm lips lingering there a moment. Teddy held his head, loving the feel of his soft natural hair against her splayed fingers.

Joachim finished unbuttoning the blouse, and Teddy allowed it to fall from her shoulders. The blouse stayed on the back of the couch because Joachim's attention was intently focused on the bra, which was the type that fastened in the front. He gave a silent prayer of thanks for the person who'd invented them. The hooks and eyes were dispensed with in a matter of seconds and Teddy's full, dark brown–tipped breasts burst free from their constraints and spilled into his hands.

Joachim slowly lowered the straps one by one, leaning over to kiss Teddy's shoulders after dispensing with each strap. He trailed kisses from her clavicle to the tip of one breast, his tongue flicking out to leisurely work the bud until Teddy moaned with pleasure.

Teddy scooted to the edge of the couch and reached for him, arching her back as she grasped his loose-fitting shirt by the collar. "Take it off," she demanded huskily.

Joachim was thoroughly enjoying the feel, the taste of her, but what the lady wanted, the lady got. He reluctantly withdrew and allowed Teddy to unbutton his shirt. It fell to the floor. Teddy ran her hands over his bare chest. He rose, pulling her up with him. Teddy went into his arms. Now they were both naked from the waist up.

Her golden-brown skin was the perfect complement to his rich, darker nutbrown shade. Teddy couldn't get enough of touching him. Her hands traveled over his back as he held her. Then to the backs of his arms. The muscles there were rock-hard—she felt them flex and it sent a thrill of excitement through her.

Joachim was having trouble with the button on the back of

the leather skirt. "You're going to have to turn around," he
said. Teddy did, and he deftly undid the button and pulled the
zipper down. Teddy wiggled her hips and the weight of the
leather, along with gravity, did the rest. The skirt fell to the
floor with a soft plop and she turned to face Joachim, clad
only in a pair of satiny bikini panties in apricot.

Teddy was self-conscious all of a sudden. Her right hand
went to her stomach. She had stretch marks there, courtesy
of her pregnancy. Would they turn Joachim off?

Joachim knelt before her and his fingers were on the waist-
band of her panties. Teddy reached down and stayed his hand.
Joachim gazed lovingly up at her. "I want to make love to all
of you, Teddy."

Shivering slightly, Teddy allowed her hand to fall. Joachim
kissed her flat belly before continuing. Teddy tensed. When
the panties were at her feet, Joachim reached down, Teddy
stepped out of them, and Joachim pulled her firmly toward
him. His tongue made circles around her belly button, then
he moved downward and Teddy tensed again. He tasted the
inside of her right thigh. Teddy was weak with expectation.
As he worked his way to the triangle that was the center of
her womanhood, she could take it no longer. "Now, Joachim.
I want you now!"

"Not yet, baby," Joachim whispered.

There was a knock at the door.

Teddy nearly jumped out of her skin.

Rising, Joachim smiled at her. "It's just room service.
While you were enjoying the view, I ordered a few things."

Teddy looked around her—there she was, standing stark-
naked in the middle of the room. She hastily began picking
up her clothing. "I'll wait in the bathroom," she said. She
threw the pieces of clothing she had in her hand onto the couch
and fled.

Joachim laughed softly and went to answer the door.

The uniformed hotel employee, a young black male with
a baby moustache, rolled the laden cart into the room.

"Just leave it," Joachim told him, going into his pants
pocket for a gratuity.

"Should I come back later for it?" the young man inquired, referring to the cart. His palm closed around the cash. His eyes went to the discarded clothing on the couch. "You can leave it outside the door if you wish."

"I'll do that," Joachim said, abruptly showing the young man to the door. "Thank you very much."

With the door securely closed and locked, he strode across the room toward the bathroom. "Coast's clear!" he called. Teddy came out of the bathroom attired in one of the white, fluffy bathrobes the hotel provided for its guests.

Joachim laughed. "No more interruptions, I promise."

Teddy's eyes held a mischievous expression.

Joachim opened his arms, inviting her to come to him.

"What did you order?" Teddy asked, walking around him and into the suite.

Joachim smiled. So she wanted to play, did she?

While Teddy investigated the foodstuffs on the cart, Joachim unbuckled the belt at his waist and unzipped his pants.

Teddy lifted a silver cover and reached in to get a grape from the fruit bowl. There were strawberries, white grapes, red grapes, yellow apples, red apples, Bartlett pears. With her back to Joachim, she popped a red grape into her mouth.

"Teddy?"

She turned, and nearly swallowed the grape whole. Joachim was completely nude. She bit into the grape, the juice was tart yet sweet. Her smile faded. The playful punishment she'd intended to mete out for the interruption was instantly forgotten. He was exquisite. The sinewy muscles of his body moved fluidly, sensuously, as he came toward her. The air caught in her throat. She lowered her eyes to his semierect manhood. Then back to his eyes. With a gulp she swallowed the remains of the grape.

"I don't know if I'm ready for you," she said breathlessly.

Joachim came up behind her and pulled her against him. She closed her eyes and leaned into him. He untied the sash on her robe and pulled it off her shoulders, pausing to kiss the hollow of her back. The robe fell in a heap around her feet. Joachim cupped her breasts from behind, then ran his hands along both sides of her, outlining her figure. Finally his hands rested on her voluptuous hips. He didn't have to press against her for Teddy to know he was fully engorged now.

Teddy was so aroused, her pleasure points: nipples, her female center, throbbed.

Joachim turned her around to face him. His dark eyes were drunk with passion. She could see the excited rise and fall of his chest. "I love you, Teddy."

He didn't wait for a reply—he scooped her up into his arms as if she weighed next to nothing, and carried her to the king-size bed. Once there he sat on the side of the bed, looking down at her. "Shall we finish what we started?"

He then gently pushed her back on the bed and once Teddy was prone, he spread her legs and bent his head to kiss her sweet inner thigh. He followed the triangle where her thighs met with his firm, wet tongue. Teddy moaned deeply, and her muscles seemed to turn to jelly at his touch.

"Don't stop," she cried.

And he didn't, not until she was trembling and thrashing on the bed with multiple orgasms.

After her second orgasm Joachim rose and put on a condom. Lying on her side, Teddy watched him. She was nearly spent, but the sight of his body sent ripples of anticipation through her. What would he feel like when he was fully inside of her?

Joachim returned to the bed and Teddy pulled him down for a deep kiss. Then she pushed him onto his back and straddled him. Joachim smiled. He loved the strong self-assurance she'd gained once they'd started making love. She had been shy at first, probably because of those tiny stretch marks on her stomach. Did she believe they would cool his ardor? He thought every inch of her was beautiful. He shivered when she took him in her hands for the first time. Her determined eyes met his, and she rose, positioning herself over him. He was at the mouth now and she pushed. She felt tight around him. He throbbed as he slid fully inside of her and Teddy threw her head back in a guttural sigh. "Oh yeah!"

Joachim squeezed her hips, heightening the sensation for Teddy. She continued to moan with each thrust. Joachim felt her body quiver. She gave a sharp intake of breath and blew it out. Their fingers were threaded together as the rhythm of their bodies climbed to a crescendo. Teddy leaned close to his face, her own glistening with perspiration. Joachim's brow was beaded with sweat.

Teddy felt Joachim's grip tighten, and she knew he was at the edge. She was almost there, too. She rose up, he almost came out of her, and at that moment Joachim groaned, and Teddy knew he was in the throes of an orgasm as his body bucked against hers. Her body was rocked by an orgasm at nearly the exact moment and she fell on top of him, exhausted. Thinking she was too heavy on him, Teddy went to roll off him, but Joachim held her there. "No, don't move yet."

Teddy sighed and stretched contentedly.

Joachim chuckled. "You sound like a cat with its belly full of cream."

Teddy kissed his chin; his beard tickled her mouth. "You wore me out, boy." Rubbing her hand over his beard, she added, "I loved the feel of this all over my body."

She noticed his eyes closing. "Give me a minute or two, baby, and we'll start all over . . ."

Teddy shook him. "You're not going to sleep!"

"Well, I did just fly in from London tonight," Joachim murmured in a nearly unintelligible voice.

"Why didn't you tell me?"

"It never came up."

Teddy untangled herself from his arms and rose. Joachim was too sleepy to stop her. She kissed his lips softly and pulled the covers up around him. She stood for a moment, watching him. Then she went in search of something to quench her thirst.

Going over to the cart a few feet away, she got the bottle of sparkling cider and removed the cork. There was a slight pop, but not loud enough to disturb Joachim. She poured about four inches in one of the crystal wineglasses on the cart and drank as her eyes surveyed her surroundings. Clothes were

strewn all over the place. Her clutch? Where had she dropped
it upon entrance into this pleasure palace? Ah yes, there it was
on a chair near the door.

Walking to where she'd left her robe nearly two hours ago,
she bent, picked it up and slipped into it. Tying the sash, she
looked around her, wondering where Joachim had stashed his
manuscript. He'd come straight here from the airport, so it
had to be somewhere in the suite. The closet was the logical
place, so she went in there first.

Joachim's bags were on the floor of the closet, lined up
according to size. He'd taken the time to hang up a few pieces
of dress clothing, probably the ones he'd chosen from when
he'd been preparing to dress and go surprise her. As she was
moving the clothes around on the rack, peripherally she
caught sight of a brown leather pouch behind the largest suit-
case. She squatted, and with a little effort, pulled it free.

Once it was in her hands, she had second thoughts. Sure
Joachim had told her she could read it, but he hadn't given
her permission to go riffling through his belongings to find
it. Curiosity won over propriety, however. She took it back
out to the suite, found a chair next to a lamp, sat down and
unzipped the pouch.

She was hooked from the first paragraph:

> *For all the evil done them at the hands of men, it's*
> *a wonder some woman hasn't risen up and led her*
> *sisters in a bloody revolt—something along the lines*
> *of Nat Turner's infamous Southhampton Insurrection.*
> *It may still be in the works; so men . . . sleep with*
> *one eye open, get rid of all the butcher knives in your*
> *house, and for God's sake learn to put the toilet seat*
> *down. Lastly if you should meet a looker on the street*
> *who goes by the name Lottie Washington, pick up your*
> *pace, brother.*

Teddy smiled as she got comfortable in the armchair. A
woman-scorned story written with humor. A nice change of

pace from all the men-are-dogs, I-finally-woke-up-hear-me-roar relationship literature saturating the market.

The room was quiet except for the sound of Joachim's breathing and of her placing each page, as she read it, underneath the thick stack as she progressed. She admired Lottie. Pregnant at sixteen, she'd struggled to find her place in life. Had survived in a society where women were seen as harlots when they conceived out of wedlock. Teddy cheered for her when Lottie, confronted by Joshua, who'd fathered her child years ago, stood her ground when he asked her if it were true that the boy, Caleb, now a fine teenager, was his. Joshua, a wealthy widower by then, had been in a loveless marriage. His wife—so he said—hadn't been able to give him a child. Lottie sensed being a father was supremely important to Joshua. Besides, she'd grown to detest him over the years; even though when she'd lain with him, she'd truly loved him. It was the treatment he'd shown her afterward that had turned her against him. When she'd told her parents who the father of her child was, he'd denied everything. He owned the only black funeral parlor in town. A prosperous business, since clients were steady and there was nowhere else blacks could turn in their time of need.

So when he'd wanted to know if Caleb was his, Lottie had told him, "Marry me and he'll be yours."

No amount of threats, cajoling, or money would make Lottie disclose the truth of Caleb's birth until Joshua consented. To rub salt in the wound, Lottie insisted on a big public wedding, inviting all the hincty blacks who'd formerly looked down their noses at her. Some didn't show, but most did, out of curiosity as to how brazen Lottie would behave on her wedding day.

Lottie looked and acted like a queen. She was beautiful in her white organza gown, a bouquet of fresh orange blossoms in her hands, her son Caleb at her side in place of her father, who adamantly refused to attend. Her mother was there though, having defied her husband to see her only child get married to the richest man in town.

Teddy was interrupted by a deep chuckle.

"I see you found it."

Grinning like an idiot, Teddy placed the manuscript on the table next to her chair and rose. Joachim stood about five feet away, dressed in the other robe that had been hanging behind the bathroom door.

Teddy walked into his arms and he squeezed her tightly.

"It's magical," she told him, peering up into his eyes, her own misty.

"It's funny and warm and heartbreaking." She turned to look back at the spot where she'd left the manuscript. "And I've got to know how it ends."

Joachim had other ideas. "I was thinking about a shower," he said, kissing the skin over her clavicle. "And after that something to eat, and after that something even better to—"

Teddy had placed her hand over his mouth. He kissed the palm of the hand she'd silenced him with. Then he grasped it and pulled her toward the bathroom. "Come on, sweet girl, I'll tell you how it ends while I'm washing your back."

Teddy giggled as she happily went along with him. "You wouldn't dare!"

"You know, Teddy, those words aren't written in stone. It's only the first draft. I could change everything about the book before it's done," Joachim warned, his tone playful.

"You mean you'd kill Lottie off, or something like that? Oh no, you don't, buster. Not if you don't want me to turn into that demented character in *Misery* and hunt you down!"

"You haven't finished it, how do you know Lottie doesn't die?" Joachim teased mercilessly.

Teddy paused in her steps, her mouth open in shock. The expression in them was stern as she looked at him. "Did you kill her?"

Joachim laughed. "You really do like her, don't you? No, baby, Lottie doesn't meet the grim reaper."

Teddy breathed a sigh of relief. Eyes narrowed, she confidently told him, "I knew you wouldn't kill her."

As they stood facing one another in the spacious bathroom, Joachim turned to untie her sash and help her out of her robe. She did the same for him.

He then turned the water on in the shower. "Warm or nearly hot?"

"Warm," Teddy answered, pulling two washcloths from the towel rack and handing him one. In the shower stall they took turns standing under the spray. And lathering each other's bodies.

Teddy noticed a scar low on his back, it was around an inch long and due to his skin being keloid, was puffy looking, although it had probably healed years ago. "How did you get this?"

"Some guy I got into a fight with in our dormitory's recreation room, when I was a sophomore at Alabama A&M."

"Over what?"

"A cutie who, he thought, was his," he replied, facing her.

Teddy grabbed his buns and pressed closer to him. "A cutie, huh? Was she southern, too? Extremely pretty? And did that coward who stabbed you in the back eventually marry her and live to rue the day?"

"I see you've heard this story before."

"Or one like it. Details, darling."

Joachim smiled at the mention of the endearment. "Say that again."

"Darling."

He kissed her, savoring the moment. He was someone's darling.

"We have a crab boil every Fourth of July at my dad's place in Carmel. Of course, who can get full on crabs? So Dad also barbecues and we have a blast listening to his old forty-five's while he explains the difference between his music and the mishmash, his words, that we listen to today. Would you be my date, and save me from being the only adult there without a date three years in row? Last year even Dad brought someone: a tourist he met at the mission. Unfortunately she met another dude when she went back home, and married him the following spring," she said wistfully. "I think Dad really liked her."

They were sitting across from one another, in matching robes, after devouring the chicken sandwiches and half of the bottle of sparkling cider that Joachim had ordered from room service.

Joachim gave her an enigmatic smile.

"What?" Teddy asked, puzzled by his expression.

He reached across the table and clasped her hand in his, then his gaze lowered to their hands. "I just enjoy sitting here, listening to you talk." He did. It was a genuine pleasure, listening to the woman you loved talk about the people she cared for. Hearing the warm cadence in her voice. Seeing the light that came into her eyes when she was especially excited. Heaven.

Teddy smiled as she ran her other hand through her damp hair. She sought his eyes. She knew he was introspective, whereas she was extroverted, given to prattling on about any bit of trivia. Opposites really. But she loved everything she knew about him. There was so much more about him she didn't know. But she didn't want to rush things. Theirs was a love that would grow with time, season into a rich bouquet whose potency would last them the rest of their lives. She knew this with every fiber of her being.

Joachim brought her hand to his lips and kissed each finger. His dark brown eyes held a glimmer of profound sadness. Teddy's smile faded. He slowly parted his lips to speak, and Teddy winced inwardly. What could be the matter?

Joachim released her hand, and abruptly stood.

"Race you to the bed!"

Teddy's chair nearly toppled as she pushed it back with her legs in her haste to win the bet. Joachim, having longer legs, was around her in no time. Seeing her chance, Teddy leapt onto his back. Laughing, they fell onto the bed in a heated clinch. "I hit the bed first," Teddy claimed. "What do I win?" Joachim removed the emerald from his robe pocket and put it on her finger.

Fourteen

Sunday afternoon Adrian brought Alex home over two hours late. By the time he put in an appearance, Teddy, who'd been on pins and needles because he wasn't answering his phone, was spoiling for a fight. At the door Adrian walked past her with Alex in front of him. Teddy closed the door and bent to hug Alex. He fidgeted in her arms. She scrutinized him. His large eyes were not as animated as they normally were, and they were slightly bloodshot. Teddy saw red. What had Adrian done, let Alex stay up to watch late-night TV?

She tenderly kissed Alex's cheek. "Honey, why don't you go play in your room? Mommy needs to talk with your daddy about something."

"Okay, Mommy," Alex said softly. His eyes went to his father, then back to his mother's face. Teddy set him on the floor, and after a couple of backward glances he left the room.

Teddy walked within three feet of Adrian, and said in low tones, "What did you do, let him stay up all night?"

Adrian, looking well rested himself and impeccably dressed as always gave her a disdainful look. "We rented the new Tarzan video and he had to watch it four times. He wouldn't settle down. It was either the video, or he'd just sit there like he was catatonic. If he wasn't pretending to be dead, he'd scream for you, looking at me as if I were a stranger who'd snatched him off the street! Don't give me attitude today, Teddy. Because I'm worn out."

Teddy scrutinized his face. His looks could be deceiving. Maybe Alex had put him through the wringer last night.

"We're late," he continued, "because I fell asleep after attempting to give him lunch. Why is he so finicky? He wouldn't eat the ham sandwich I made for him. Turkey? That stuff wasn't going to get past his lips. Finally he deigned to eat a hot dog."

"I told you he liked hot dogs. But I don't give them to him too often, because they're not good for him. He's a smart kid—what he can't get from Mommy, he'll get from Daddy. What else has he been getting away with these past few weeks?"

Adrian rolled his eyes. "I've been a little slack on the bedtime rules."

Arms akimbo, Teddy asked, "How late has he been staying up?"

"Eleven. Last night, it was after midnight when he finally fell asleep."

Exasperated, Teddy blew air between full lips. She met his gaze. "You can't let him get away with breaking rules, Adrian. He'll run all over you—which apparently he has been." Her eyes narrowed. "Stop allowing your guilty feelings to make you a soft touch. Kids from broken-marriage households know how to play the game to their advantage. Sure Alex is only two and a half, but he's already an old pro at it. We have to set rules and abide by them . . . for his sake."

The tension in the air had dissipated. Now they were just two parents trying to figure out how best to raise their son.

Adrian smiled down at her. "Teddy, I admire you. Anyone who can take care of that bundle of energy seven days a week has earned my respect."

Teddy laughed. Shaking her head in amazement, she said, "Just keep coming around, you'll earn your stripes, too."

Adrian chuckled. He'd always loved the way her eyes crinkled at the corners when she laughed. Suddenly he realized how lonely he'd been for her smile. A fierce sadness descended upon him.

Teddy noticed the change in his demeanor.

Unable to discern the reason behind it, she didn't want to risk an inquiry, because he might read more into her concern than was intended. So she continuing smiling, hoping the moment would pass.

Adrian wouldn't allow it to.

Moving closer to her, he grasped her by the forearm. "Teddy, what can I do to prove that I've really seen the light, and that I love you and Alex, and I want us to be a family? Anything! Just tell me what you want," he pleaded. They stood gazing into each other's eyes, Adrian's imploring, Teddy's bewildered.

If he had asked her that a month ago, she would have probably laughed in his face. Because then she was of a mind to be cruel to him. She wanted to pay him back for every grievance he'd visited upon her the last three years. Spite was the order of the day.

Now, however, she had Joachim. He loved her. She loved him. She was willing to let her anger go. Loving Joachim had taught her that. How could she love him with a pure heart, when some corner of it was full of bile? No, that was no way to begin a new life. And that's what she wanted with Joachim. A new life. One they would create together.

So she had to put her bitterness toward Adrian aside.

He was her son's father. For the sake of all concerned, she would have to learn to get along with him. This recent incident with Alex's staying up too late had brought that home for her. In order to be good parents to Alex, they needed to cooperate with each other.

In keeping with her new attitude, she smiled up at Adrian and said, "You're off the hook, Adrian. All right? I forgive you."

Adrian pulled her into his arms in one quick movement. "Oh baby, I never thought this day would come!" He squeezed her so tightly, Teddy could barely breathe.

She squirmed. "Uh, Adrian? Let up a little, will you?"

Adrian loosened his grip. "Sorry," he whispered in her ear. He rocked her in his arms. "You don't know how happy you've made me, Teddy. Finally we can be a family. We—"

"Wait a minute," Teddy cried, glaring at him. "That's not what I meant!"

Adrian held her by the shoulders as he returned her glare. "But you said—"

"I said I forgive you. I didn't say I'd marry you."

Adrian looked relieved. Then he started formulating plans in his mind. He smiled warmly. "Not right away. We should spend some time getting to know each other again. You and Alex should come to New York, Teddy. You can work anywhere. You can probably walk into the offices of any major magazine in the city and get on the staff," he said excitedly.

Teddy wrenched free of his hold. She stared at him as if he'd gone off the deep end and she was witnessing his descent. "Calm down. Let me explain what I meant." She spoke slowly and clearly, hoping he wouldn't misinterpret her words this time. "You and I have to be able to agree on how we want to raise Alex, Adrian. That's why I said I'd forgiven you, so there wouldn't be that barrier between us that would prevent us from doing our very best to give Alex a safe, secure childhood. There is no us, Adrian. I'm involved with Joachim now. I love him and—"

"You love him?" Adrian asked, his voice low and tightly controlled. He smiled, and his smile was more frightening to Teddy than any grimace she'd ever seen. His eyes were cold, the smile not affecting them in the least. It was only a mask, Teddy realized. The smile was meant to throw her off. The eyes, however, betrayed his true emotions.

He grabbed her roughly by the arms so suddenly, Teddy didn't have time to react. "You can't love him. You haven't known him long enough!" He shook her violently. Her head snapped back. "I should shake some sense into you, you silly, trusting fool! Love him?"

Teddy hauled off and kicked him in the shin.

Adrian immediately let go of her as the pain shot through his left leg. Teddy got safely out of range. She wasn't going to get caught off guard again. She smiled as he bent to rub his leg. She was wearing leather clogs that had wooden soles. She hoped he was in agony. How dare he touch her! She felt like going over and kicking him in his good leg.

She gingerly rubbed her neck. She'd probably be sore tomorrow. And her arms, where his fingers had dug into her flesh, would be black and blue. She'd never taken abuse off of any man, and she wasn't about to start now.

"Get out," she ordered him sternly as she walked rapidly to the front door and held it open.

Adrian hobbled to the door. He wasn't finished with her yet though. "You'll pay for this, you ungrateful little sl—"

"Watch your mouth!" Teddy said sharply. "That's no way to talk to the woman who's the mother of your child. Now limp on out of here before I—"

"Some mother," Adrian said, straightening up. He couldn't bear to put any weight on his left leg. "You spent the night at the Mark Hopkins with that writer, probably doing everything that came into his filthy mind. You're so easily led, Teddy. An innocent compared to most women your age. I was your first lover . . ."

"A minute ago you were about to call me a smutty name," Teddy pointed out. "Make up your mind."

"No, Teddy, you make up your mind," Adrian countered. "It's either your writer or your son. When I came here today, I was willing to overlook your night with him . . ."

"His name is Joachim West."

"I know his name, Teddy. I know everything about him. Did you know he came from dirt-poor Alabama sharecroppers? Sharecroppers, in the twentieth century! Now that's a nothing existence. And you know what they say: Nothing from nothing leaves nothing. And that's what he's going to leave you with, Teddy: nothing. Because when I'm done with you, you will have nothing, and no one."

"I bless Joachim's sharecropping family for sending him to me. It doesn't matter where a man comes from, only where he's going."

She then slammed the door.

Adrian had to scurry out of the way or risk getting his fingers pulverized. Luckily he got away unscathed, but the amount of wind cooling his face told him she'd given it all she had. He smiled. That was the Teddy he knew and loved.

He paused in the hallway to rub his throbbing leg. He'd better make a doctor's appointment and have that looked at.

Teddy stood on the other side of the door seething with anger. She should have known he was still having her watched. Even after she'd made a point of accusing him of it. When he'd admitted to hiring a private detective to collect information on her, she had thought he'd have the decency to quit after being caught red-handed. But no, not Adrian. He hadn't changed a bit. Still trying to manipulate those he claimed to love. Restructuring the world according to his own personal blueprints.

Alex looked up when she entered his bedroom. "Mommy, is Daddy gone?"

Daddy? Teddy thought, a spark of jealousy igniting in her. That was the first time Alex had called Adrian Daddy. Formerly when referring to him, he'd simply said *he* or *him.* Or in some cases, *the man in the black car.*

Teddy went to sit next to him on the carpet. She ran her hand over his curly baby-fine hair. "Yes, he's gone. Did you have a good time this weekend?"

Alex surprised her by climbing into her arms. Teddy smiled down at him. He'd missed her. He grinned, showing perfect tiny white teeth in his brown face. "Daddy let me swim in the pool, Mommy. We had fun!"

"That's good, baby. You remember what I told you about the water, don't you? Never go near the water unless you have an adult with you. Remember?"

"Yes, Mommy."

"So when you're at your daddy's house, and he isn't around, but you really want to go in the pool, what do you do?"

"Get Daddy."

"That's right, baby." She hugged him tightly.

"Can't breathe, Mommy," he mumbled.

Kissing his sweet cheek, Teddy let go of him. "Alex, I want to tell you about a good friend of mine whom I'd like you to meet real soon."

* * *

"Do you have any idea what happened to him?" Teddy asked Gail Fisher, whom she was interviewing for a human-interest story.

Gail, forty-two, had recently been released from prison after spending twenty years behind bars for possession of cocaine. When she was twenty-one, she'd been in love with a man who, she later learned—but by then the knowledge was of no use to her—was one of the major dealers of cocaine in the Bay Area.

When she went to prison, Gail had been the mother of a one-year-old daughter. Her daughter had been reared by Gail's mother. Now Gail sat across from Teddy in her mother's modest living room, smiling at the reporter. She was trim, attractive, and quite intelligent. She'd earned her bachelor's degree in English while incarcerated. She seemed to be mulling over Teddy's question. Her hand nervously went to her short black natural as she crinkled a pert nose in a medium brown face. "He wrote me nearly every month, asking for my forgiveness," she said, her voice stronger than Teddy imagined it would be when she finally got around to answering the question—if she chose to answer. "He admitted to lying in order to keep from going to jail himself. I showed the letters to my lawyer. He was able to get a hearing. But the judge ruled that it was inadmissible evidence, evidence after the fact. The fact was they'd found two pounds of pure cocaine hidden in my car seat. I knew nothing about it. But it was in a vehicle that I owned."

"You learned a hard lesson," Teddy sympathized.

Gail raised her gaze to Teddy's. "In answer to your question—no, I don't know where he is. I don't care to know. All I'm concerned with now is my family—"

"You just found out you're a grandmother," Teddy coaxed.

Earlier she'd been introduced to Gail's mother, her daughter, twenty-one, the same age her mother had been when she'd gone to prison, and her daughter's two-year-old daughter. Four generations of women.

Now Teddy and Gail were alone in the living room.

"Yes!" Gail said, smiling happily. "Kiana. She looks just

like her mother did at that age." She frowned, remembering all the years of growing up she'd missed with her daughter. "It's a blessing that they've been able to forgive me."

"Forgive you?" Teddy inquired mildly. "Gail, you didn't do anything wrong."

"Oh but I did," Gail disagreed. "I let a man come between me and my child. I'll never forgive myself for that."

"But your daughter doesn't hold you responsible for what happened; she told me that herself."

"My mother did a good job raising Andrea."

"Mrs. Mosley says she took Andrea to visit you as often as possible. Don't you think you had a hand in rearing your daughter, too?"

"Yeah, I was the perfect example of what not to be like," Gail joked. Teddy had detected a sad note to her voice, and guessed that even if Gail did believe she'd been a positive influence on Andrea, she wouldn't admit to it. She was still in the midst of self-flagellation.

"The state of California has agreed to pay you nearly a quarter of a million dollars for what they're calling 'lost wages.' Do you believe it's the state's way of saying you were falsely imprisoned for something your ex-boyfriend had done?"

"I believe it is, but they'd never put it in writing," Gail stated bluntly.

Teddy nodded in agreement. If they put it in writing, that would give Gail's lawyer something to sink his teeth into. Then the state would be out of one heck of a lot more money than a measly quarter-million.

Teddy rose and shook Gail's hand. "Thank you for a very moving interview, Gail. I wish you the best."

Gail stood also. She was a couple inches shorter than Teddy's five six. "Do you think this article will help other women out there who might be in the position I was in?"

"I'm sure it'll be an inspiration to everyone who reads it, Gail, not just to women who may be going through what you did," Teddy told her truthfully. Then she spontaneously hugged Gail Fisher.

Gail, not used to the physical display of emotions, after years of going without, was stiff at first. But then she hugged the reporter back and smiled warmly when they parted. "Thank you, Teddy."

"It was my pleasure, Gail."

A few hours later Teddy was sitting at her desk fine-tuning the article when the phone rang. She placed the receiver on her shoulder, holding it with a little neck action. "Hey, Teddy here."

"Hey, yourself," Joachim said, his voice laced with laughter.

"Sweetie . . ." Teddy purred.

"I miss you."

"Miss you, too."

"Is Adrian taking Alex for the weekend again? After what happened between you, I thought plans might have changed."

"No . . . he's no longer pretending he's in love with me, thank God, but he says he'll be here to pick Alex up Saturday morning. Why do you ask?"

"Well, Conal and Erin are dying to meet you. They were wondering if you could come to dinner Saturday night. The Seteras will be there, too. You remember I told you about them."

"Yes! Nicolas and Alana. He's an inspector with the San Francisco Police Department and she owns a catering firm. Sound like nice folks." She sighed. "Meeting your friends for the first time. I'm nervous, sweetie."

"You don't have a thing to be nervous about. They're as down to earth as you are. Conal takes some getting used to. But if you can stomach rough language and coarse manners, you'll stay around him long enough to discover he's really an old softie."

"Okay. I'm looking forward to it."

"No, you're not, I can tell by your voice," Joachim contradicted, laughing softly.

Teddy laughed, too. "All right, I'm still nervous. But they're your friends, and I'm sure I'll like them. I just hope they like me. Fourth of July's coming up—haven't you been a little anxious about meeting Daddy?"

"I'll win him over just like I won Alex over."

"You can't bring him *Star Wars* action figures."

"How does your father feel about exotic dancers?"

"You know exotic dancers?"

"Not my taste . . ."

"I should hope not!"

". . . but a pal of mine goes for them," he finished with a chuckle. On a more serious note, he added, "I'm not nervous about meeting your dad because I love you. Even if he hates me on sight, that isn't going to change how I feel about his daughter."

"He isn't going to hate you. He's just wary of anyone I date. My marriage to Adrian made him that way. He's concerned I'm going to make the same mistake twice, you know?"

"Of course I understand. He loves you and he wants you to be happy. I want you to be happy . . . with me. So if your father asks me to jump through hoops on the Fourth of July, baby, I'll do it."

"Even if he sets them on fire?" Teddy asked sweetly.

"I must have a pair of fireproof drawers around here somewhere," Joachim joked.

The Ryanses' home sat on a gentle hill in the Marina District. It was a two-story villa-style home designed to resemble Italian baroque architecture. The natural stone color was in perfect balance with its surroundings. As Teddy and Joachim stepped onto the front portico, there was a light breeze, the air felt cool on their skin and the faint, sweet scent of oleander, native to the area, was in the air.

Joachim had advised Teddy to dress casually. "You never know what the evening will dissolve into when you go to Conal and Erin's home," he'd told her. He explained that although Conal and Erin had been married only a little over two months, they'd been living together for nearly five years. "They were an old married couple long before they had the ceremony."

Teddy smoothed the top of her sleeveless, mandarin Chinese-inspired emerald-colored silk pantsuit. The outline of a white lotus flower was emblazoned across the chest. She had on a pair of delicate leather sandals, also in emerald, the straps of which tied around her ankles. Her curly hair was brushed away from her face. Joachim was simply dressed in a pair of black slacks, a loose-fitting white cotton shirt with a mandarin collar and a pair of black leather oxfords. Teddy's eyes raked over him. He always looked good, but you could tell he hadn't spent much time deciding what to put on. He'd probably gone to his closet and absently pulled pieces of clothing off hangers and put them on. But then he wasn't meeting her friends for the first time.

He reached over to press the button to the doorbell and Teddy placed her hand over his, stopping him. "Are you sure this outfit is all right?" she asked, glancing down at her outfit.

"You look beautiful, baby."

"You'd say that even if I were wearing a croaker sack."

Joachim laughed.

"What do you know about croaker sacks?"

"Daddy says they were burlap sacks that people used to carry things in when he was growing up in Mississippi. A croaker is a type of fish, and when they'd catch them, they'd store them in the burlap bags and take them home."

"I know what a croaker sack is, I just never imagined you'd know."

The door suddenly swung open and a big man with curly light brown, almost blond, hair stood laughing at them, his blue-gray eyes alight with humor. "Hey, stop arguing on my front porch—you'll make it seem as if we're unsuitable neighbors," he said in a distinct Irish accent. He yelled into the night, "We don't know these people, they're just trying to sell something!" Standing between Teddy and Joachim, he placed a hand on each of their backs and shoved them into the foyer. "Get in here!"

Once inside he shut the door and hugged Joachim, patting him roughly on the back. "I see Ireland did you a world of good!"

As Teddy watched the two friends embrace, a petite woman with short black hair, fair skin, and dark blue eyes strode into the room. "Conal," she cried. "Were you screaming at the neighbors again? They're going to think you're a madman."

She'd been speaking to her husband, but her keen eyes were on Teddy. She went to Teddy and smiled warmly, offering her hand. "Hello, my dear, I'm Erin Donagal . . ."

"Ryan!" her husband corrected her as he released Joachim and went to stand next to his pretty wife. He placed his arm about her shoulders. She smiled up at him. "It's been Donagal much longer than it's been Ryan," she told him.

Husband and wife were both attired in blue jeans and shirts. His shirt was denim, long-sleeved, Western, with wooden buttons. Erin's was short-sleeved, royal blue in color and silk.

"Yes, but it's Ryan now, so get used to it," Conal bantered playfully.

"If you'll both be quiet a moment, I'd like to introduce you to the woman I love," Joachim interrupted, his dark eyes caressing Teddy's face, which had grown hot with embarrassment. He should have warned her he was going to say that. *The woman I love.* Why couldn't he have said *my date?* Or *my good friend?* Announcing her as *the woman I love* put his friends on notice. Here she is. I've chosen her. I don't care what your opinion of her is. We're together, and that's that!

Teddy expected reprisals. A cool look perhaps. A nose turned in the air as if to say, "You might have chosen her, but you chose badly, old friend. She isn't good enough for you."

Instead Conal let out a whoop and hugged Joachim again, and Erin, a complete stranger, threw her arms around Teddy's neck and cried, "I'm so happy!"

"Thank you," Teddy replied softly, incredulously.

Conal pulled the two women apart and claimed Teddy, wrapping her in his beefy arms. "Welcome, Teddy. Welcome to the family." He set her away from him, his eyes misty. He then turned them on Joachim's smiling face. "Well, you weren't lying when you said she was lovely. Now let's go see how many pieces of my baby back ribs she can put away in one sitting."

He placed a hand on the small of Teddy's back, directing her toward the rear of the house.

Teddy glanced back at Joachim, as if to say, "Help!"

Before they made it down the hallway, heading for the kitchen or the dining room, Teddy assumed, they were met by an attractive African-African woman waddling down the aisle. She had on a cream-colored, short-sleeved pantsuit with a scoop neck. Behind her was a tall, good-looking black man with a strong, square chin. He was looking after the very pregnant woman with concern mirrored in his dark, downward-sloping eyes.

"Lana, I didn't mean it; you're gorgeous. *Te quiero,* Lana. *¡Por siempre!*"

Lana paused to say something in Spanish, which Teddy, fairly fluent in Spanish, interpreted as meaning, "You can kiss my behind, fool!"

"Nothing would give me more pleasure!" the man cajoled lovingly.

They all stopped in the hallway, as it was clogged anyway. Erin made the introductions.

"Teddy Riley," she said, "please meet Alana and Nico Setera."

Alana smiled warmly at Teddy. "Hello, Teddy. It's a real pleasure to meet you."

Alana Setera had flawless café-au-lait skin, wavy, coal-black shoulder-length hair, large, wide-spaced brown eyes with golden flecks in them. Her nose was short, well shaped, and underneath it was a full mouth with sensual contours. She placed her hand on her huge belly as she turned back around, obviously having changed her mind about leaving the room in which she and her husband had just argued. She noticeably ignored Nico as she passed him, with Teddy at her side.

Joachim shook Nico's hand. "Hey, buddy."

They let the Ryanses, Teddy, and Alana get ahead of them.

"What's the matter?" Joachim inquired, referring to the scene between Nico and Alana.

"I told her she was bigger than she'd been when she was carrying Nicky, and she bit my head off."

Joachim chuckled.

"Are you nuts? Of course she's bigger, she's carrying twins. And don't you know you should never comment on a pregnant woman's size? Even if she asks you if she's getting bigger, your only reply should be: Baby, you've never looked more beautiful to me.' "

"She *is* beautiful to me," Nico lamented. "But for this I'll be in the dog house all evening."

"Well, *dog*," Joachim said sympathetically, "at least you've learned a valuable lesson. Now go make nice with your beautiful wife."

Whereas the Ryanses' home in Ballycastle was decorated in country contemporary, their San Francisco home was done in ultramodern. With the help of a Feng Shui expert, Teddy noted. Feng Shui is the ancient Chinese art of promoting balance and harmony in one's environment. The words mean wind, and water, and refer to the perpetual flow of energy in the natural world, which the Chinese believe humans have to be in harmony with in order to be completely healthy.

Teddy knew of the burgeoning practice whereby so-called experts in Feng Shui came to a person's home or workplace to "balance" the flow of energy, or chi, because nearly a year ago, she'd interviewed a young actress who swore by it.

As they were all seated in the living room having coffee and dessert, Teddy mentioned to Erin that she'd observed that their home was laid out according to the Feng Shui principles.

"You're a practitioner?" Erin asked excitedly.

"Oh God," Conal cried, "don't get her started on that nonsense. She'll be giving a lecture before it's over with."

Erin pursed her lips and rolled her eyes at her husband.

"Here's a man who swears he's seen a real fairy . . ."

"I was stoned out of my head at the time!"

". . . and he refuses to believe there's a right way and a wrong way to position the possessions in your living space."

"Listen to this," Conal said, looking into the faces of all his guests. "The staircase in your house should not face the door because they believe all good things will flow out of the door and onto the street. Now if that isn't total bunk, I don't know what is."

"If you're so vehemently opposed to the practice, why did you allow me to use it in our home?" Erin asked, thinking she had him there.

"Because I love you and I want you to be happy. I'm a heathen. I don't care about artful surroundings. All I care is that you're there beside me when I close my eyes at night."

Erin got up, strode across the room and fell into her husband's lap. Looking at their guests with a happy expression on her face, she said, "You can't argue with that!"

Nico glanced longingly at Alana whose attitude toward him had been icy all evening. She allowed a small smile to escape, and his handsome face broke into a huge grin.

He'd been sitting on the couch beside Joachim, but he got up and went to sit next to her on the love seat. He whispered something in her ear and she giggled softly, her large brown eyes sparkling.

Teddy, on Joachim's right, reached for his hand.

"You were right—I love them," she said for his ears only.

Joachim gazed down into her eyes. John Coltrane's *A Love Supreme* was playing softly in the background. "I think the feeling's mutual. But I believe it's time to call it a night, my love, because I'd like some private time with you."

He rose, pulling her up with him.

"Everyone this evening has been a most welcome respite from the everyday cares and the harrowing vicissitudes of life—but it is my opinion that the evening has fizzled and it's time to seek refreshment elsewhere."

"Is that as bad as you can do?" Conal challenged, rising.

Joachim had informed Teddy earlier that he and Conal always ended the evening with as horrible an example of bad

writing as they could come up with. She had to admit,
Joachim's parting words had been pretty bad.

Conal cleared his throat, preparing to offer his version.

"Ladies and gentlemen, madames et messieurs—it is with
profound regret that I have to say adieu. And in parting from
you now let me express my humble thanks for your gracious
hospitality of which, I'm certain, kings and queens have not
availed themselves of any better!"

The assemblage groaned in unison.

Frowning, Erin went and gave her husband a pity hug.
"Honey, you win hands down."

As Teddy hugged Alana good-bye, Alana said, "Teddy, I
hear you have a little boy. Our son is nearly three. How old is
yours?"

"Two and a half . . ."

"Perfect. Call me. Let's set a play date for them. They
should get to know each other. And it'd give us time to chat,
too."

"All right, I will," Teddy promised, pleased Alana had
asked.

On the drive across town to Teddy's condo, a comfortable
silence settled between them. Joachim was paying close attention to his driving. Saturday night brought out a whole
different class of nuts. Kids trying to impress each other by
racing from stoplight to stoplight. A slew of celebrants who'd
had too much to drink. Teddy's mind was on Adrian. What
exactly was he up to anyway? After their last fight, she'd been
prepared for him to go straight to his attorneys and ask them
to begin building a case against her. Of course, he could have
done just that. He simply hadn't told her. She made a mental
note to phone Billie Roman Monday morning and tell her
how Adrian had threatened her, saying that when he was done
with her, she would have nothing.

Had they been empty threats, made in the heat of the moment?

She didn't know. Adrian had phoned her the next day and

calmly assured her that in spite of the nasty words they'd thrown at one another, they had to work together and make Alex's life as carefree as possible. That meant he would be there on Saturday morning, as planned, to pick Alex up for their outing and sleepover. Teddy didn't protest, but she'd reminded him that he was seeing Alex because, out of her desire to see Alex happy, she was allowing it.

She didn't tell him, but she'd allowed things to remain as they were only because she'd seen the change in Alex toward his father. Not just the fact that Alex was now referring to Adrian as Daddy. That wasn't the half of it. It was the hero worship she saw in Alex's eyes whenever Adrian walked into a room. That got to her. Alex was learning to love his father. It was all so unexpected. Teddy hadn't counted on Adrian coming back into their lives and in her mind's eye, she'd imagined herself, years from now, being a single mother. Going to all of Alex's Little League games solo. Alex having only one of his parents at his high school and college graduation ceremonies. Now there was the possibility that Alex would not have to be without a father any longer. And Teddy wasn't about to do anything to mess that up, even if it meant swallowing her pride.

"You're awfully quiet," Joachim said just as he turned onto Lombard Street, where Teddy's building was located.

"I was just sitting here trying to figure out what Adrian's game is," she told him, turning sideways to look at him. "I wish he'd just go ahead and sue me for custody and get it over with. The suspense is killing me. I know he's going to eventually get around to it, the question is when."

Joachim pulled into the parking lot at Teddy's building, chose a spot not far from her door, put the car in park and switched off the ignition. He met her eyes. Their faces were illuminated by the amber light spilling into the car's interior from the streetlamp a few feet away. They unbuckled their seat belts.

"You're worrying about something that may never happen. Suppose he chooses not to sue you for sole custody but instead goes to court to have the judge grant him joint custody? How would you feel about that?"

Teddy laughed shortly. "You're thinking like Joachim West, not Adrian Riley. You might do something that reasonable, but it hasn't been my experience that Adrian reacts with logic. He figured his career would benefit if he didn't have me, like an anvil I suppose, around his neck." She sniffed. "Hey, that appears to have worked. He's at the top of his field. What is there to stop him from also reasoning that Alex would be better off with him a hundred percent of the time?" A lump formed in her throat, and she had to clear it before continuing. "It's conceivable that he could win, you know. In recent years the courts have been very sympathetic toward fathers. Mothers aren't always the usual victors in child-custody battles anymore. Especially if the father can prove the mother has been negligent."

"He'd never be able to prove that, Teddy. You're a wonderful mother."

"Up until two months ago, I traveled a great deal. There weren't many nights I missed putting Alex to bed, but still . . ."

Joachim pulled her into his arms. He couldn't bear to hear the anguish in her voice. Teddy allowed her shawl to fall from her shoulders as she closed her eyes and snuggled close to him.

"Baby, no matter what happens, I'll stay by your side. We'll fight him together. And I want you to talk to me—don't hold anything in. I need to know how you're thinking, because I don't want you doing anything desperate."

Teddy raised her eyes to his. She smiled. "Don't worry, I'm not going to shoot him."

Joachim returned her smile. "That's not what I meant. When a case is ruled in favor of one parent over another, the loser has been known to flee with the child." He gently tweaked her cheek between his thumb and forefinger. "If it comes to that, baby, we go together."

Teddy sighed, feeling as if a ton of bricks had suddenly been lifted off of her. What had she ever done to deserve a man like this? Her eyes gleamed mischievously as she regarded him. "Hey, we could live in Ballycastle. We'd integrate the neighborhood. Be the first black family ever to be permanent residents. Demand that they start teaching black history in the schools."

"Celebrate Martin Luther King Day," Joachim said.

"Start the Ballycastle Blues Festival."

"Or," Joachim suggested as he bent his head to kiss Teddy's mouth, "we could live in Bali and wear next to nothing on the beach every day."

"That has my vote," Teddy whispered against his mouth. Their lips touched, drew back. She tilted her head to the side, to avoid a nose crash, breathed out, and Joachim fully claimed her mouth. His right hand was in her hair, at the back of her head, pressing her closer to his hungry mouth. The kiss deepened, and Teddy's hands found their way to the front of Joachim's shirt where they automatically began unbuttoning it so she could get to his hairy chest. She turned her head to the side, severing the connection. "Shall we move this inside? I wouldn't put it past Adrian to have someone watching my place, just waiting to snap suggestive photos of us."

Joachim reluctantly released her and got out, walked around to Teddy's side, opened her door and offered her his hand.

Teddy climbed from the Ford Expedition and they sedately strolled up her walk, to her door, where she unlocked the door and they went inside.

Once inside, though, all decorum was abandoned as they began coming out of their clothes in the foyer, laughing uproariously as they tried to beat each other's time.

Teddy removed her top and threw it in his face, thereby slowing his progress. At that moment Joachim was coming out of his slacks, hopping on one foot. He caught Teddy's top and placed it on the tall brass hall tree standing next to the door. "Don't treat your clothes that way, young lady," he said with mock sternness.

Teddy's hands were on the clasps of her bra. She saw him watching her, and she paused, her large eyes meeting his. Then she smiled playfully and took off in the direction of her bedroom.

"I can't seem to reach the clasps," she called over her shoulder as she ran. Laughing, Joachim finished pulling off his slacks and threw them onto the floor, forgetting his neatness fetish, and was in hot pursuit. "I think I can help you with that."

Fifteen

"Alex, go play in your room while Daddy's on the phone," Adrian said irritably. "Excuse me for a moment, Rita." He placed the cellular phone on the kitchen countertop. He'd been making Alex a peanut butter and jelly sandwich when his agent, Rita Harris, had phoned with good news: The network had picked up his hour-long news magazine program for next year. Now they were in the process of negotiating his salary and, if the ratings continued to be as good as they were now, the amount of money he'd earn in bonuses.

He just needed a solid ten minutes to talk with Rita uninterrupted. That meant he had to get Alex to either quiet down, which wasn't going to happen, or leave the room for a while.

Alex was on his knees in front of the sliding glass door that led to the pool area. A toy helicopter was in his right hand and he was making the sound effects. Adrian went and knelt beside him and clutched his chin between strong fingers. "Hey, Alex. Do your dad a favor, huh? Take the helicopter to your room, will you? I'll make your sandwich and bring it to you in there."

Alex was so engrossed in his make-believe battle scene that the action continued even while his father was speaking. But he nodded his acquiescence, indicating that he'd heard his father. Rising, he ran in the direction of his bedroom.

Adrian sighed and walked back over to the counter to pick up the phone. "I'm back . . ."

More than twenty minutes later, he hung up the phone and realized the house was silent. When Alex had gone to his room, Adrian could still hear him making the helicopter sounds, albeit at a greatly reduced volume, coming from down the hall.

He couldn't recall when he'd stopped hearing Alex. He smiled. Maybe the kid had worn himself out and lain on the floor and taken a nap. It wasn't the first time Alex had done that. Just last week he'd gone to sleep in front of the TV in the middle of a Tarzan marathon. If Adrian never saw the apeman again, he'd be happy.

Entering the bedroom quietly, in case Alex was sleeping, he paused in the doorway, his eyes scanning the room. Alex wasn't on the thick navy-blue carpeting. The helicopter was though, lying on its side a few feet into the room. He went and picked it up, dropping it into the big toy box in the corner, shaped like a red fire engine.

Alex loved hide-and-seek, that's probably what he was up to at this very moment, hidden somewhere in this room.

"I wonder where Alex is," Adrian said aloud. Sometimes when he made comments when looking for Alex, Alex couldn't suppress a giggle, thereby giving himself away.

This time, however, there was only silence.

He went to have a peek in the closet anyway, just in case Alex had fallen asleep in there amid several oversize plush toys.

He completely pulled the wooden sliding-door back, making sure he looked into every darkened crevice. No Alex. "Ah well, I suppose Alex isn't in here. I'll have to go look in the den next."

He didn't go look in the den. He went over to the twin bed, got on his knees, pulled up the skirt and was prepared to cry, "Gotcha!" But Alex wasn't underneath the bed, either.

The kid was getting good at hide-and-seek.

Getting a bit impatient now—after all he'd told Alex to go to his room and wait until he brought his lunch in, and he'd disobeyed him—Adrian hurried down the hallway, through the kitchen, then to the den. The den was Alex's favorite room in the house because that's where the entertainment system was located. Nintendo mesmerized him. A DVD player and a big-screen TV with Surround Sound enchanted him. Adrian felt a bit guilty, allowing gadgets to entertain his son, but honestly Alex had too much energy for him and he welcomed any distraction that would give him a moment's respite.

He surveyed every inch of the seven-hundred-foot-square room. His son was not there. His jaw set in an irritated expression, he went to search the rest of the house.

Alex crouched behind a lounge chair, believing the kitty couldn't possibly see him through the translucent plastic strips and flowery cushion. If he could sneak up on him, he'd have a better chance of catching him. And if he caught him, maybe Daddy would let him keep him. Kitties were nice to pet. His grandma Margaret had a big, fluffy white one with purple eyes. Her name was Tomasina. Tomasina liked it when you gently ran your hand over her back. She'd arch her back and purr. You could feel the purr all the way up your arm when she did that. But for some reason, Tomasina didn't like it when you pulled her tail—she'd turn and try to scratch you, or spit at you. He'd tried that only once.

This kitty was smaller than Tomasina, and was grey with spots and white socks. Its meow sounded pitiful and scared. Alex wanted to go and scoop it up in his arms and hug him, hold him tight, so he'd be safe.

In the distance Alex could hear his daddy calling his name. He wanted to answer. Knew he should. But if he did, the kitty would get scared and run away. He'd explain to Daddy why he hadn't answered him after he caught the kitty.

The calico cat, only six months old, wandered closer to the child. He'd smelled the child when he'd entered the yard. He liked the smell of children because children were often kinder than adults. They would pet him, and sometimes give him bits of food. Then the adults would come and tell the children to leave the cat alone, they didn't know where he'd been. He could have some kind of disease. And the children would mind their parents and chase him away. His footpads were sore from walking, and he hadn't had anything nourishing in a long time.

Maybe this child, who smelled like milk, would give him something to eat.

Alex watched the kitty as it lowered its nose to the pool tile, sniffing. He's hungry, Alex decided, and concern for the cat made him reveal himself. He slowly rose to a standing position.

"Hello, kitty," he said in a soft voice. "I won't hurt you."

The calico cat trembled slightly, but didn't run away.

Alex took a step around the lounge chair. He didn't see the large metal screw lying there, left over from when the workmen had delivered the pool furniture last week and had had to screw the umbrella top to the glass table. When his tennis shoe-clad foot came down on the screw, the sudden feel of something foreign on the bottom of his foot surprised him, causing him to lose his balance. He fell over the lounge chair, and since the chair was only a foot from the edge of the pool, he bounced on the chair and rolled headfirst into the water.

Alex's small body was jolted by the cold water, but he tried not to panic as he kicked and broke the water's surface, his nose above water now. He tried to remember what his mommy had taught him. Tilt your head up. Look at the sky. Relax. Get on your back. Imagine yourself as light as a feather. Don't struggle, Alex. Now, float . . .

Hearing his mommy's voice in his head helped him for a while, but then he thought about his daddy. What if his daddy was still on the phone, and he wouldn't come look for him for a long time? He tried to grab the edge of the pool, where the concrete was rough to the touch, not slippery. In order to do that he had to slowly roll onto his side, and remember to kick his legs, like his mommy had taught him. Kick, so you won't sink, baby. That's a good boy! He kicked with all his might, but he was still sinking. And he was too far away from the edge. His arms weren't long enough to reach it. He opened his mouth to yell for his daddy and swallowed water. He spat it out and turned his head to the side, his little legs kicking, kicking. *Daddy!* he screamed in his mind. *Help me, Daddy!*

Adrian had come back into the kitchen, hoping to find Alex sitting at the table, making his own peanut butter and jelly sandwich. Sometimes when Adrian was making it for him, Alex would confidently pull the spreading knife from his daddy's hand and do it himself. "Mommy makes it with more jelly, Daddy," he'd inform him with an angelic grin.

And your mommy wouldn't misplace you, either, Adrian thought grimly. Where *was* that boy? He walked past the work island, toward the counter where he'd left the cellular phone. His eyes looked in the direction of the sliding-glass door. That's when he saw it standing open a good six inches. He never left the door ajar. He knew he'd checked the lock last night before retiring . . .

There was only one explanation. Alex had gone out that way. Adrian was out the door in a split second, his eyes searching the pool area . . . an overturned lounge chair near the edge of the pool . . .

Panic gripped him. He ran toward the chair. A scrawny cat dashed across his path, almost tripping him. The cat screeched and kept running. He uttered an expletive and ran faster.

His heart was beating fast. Pumping hard. He could feel it contracting—the sound was thunderous in his ears. Then he looked down, and saw Alex's small body, just beneath the surface of the shallow end. He ran and stepped down into the water and grabbed Alex under both his arms. He hurried over to the pool steps which were only three feet away. No distance for him, but a million miles away for a small child. Alex lay limp and unresponsive in his arms.

Adrian couldn't think straight. Tears clouded his vision. He had one logical thought in his mind: something he remembered from a news story he'd done on children and safety in the water several summers ago. CPR. He recalled that in the case of a drowning victim, the body should be positioned so that the lungs could drain of water while being resuscitated. He quickly sat down on a chair and placed Alex on his lap, with his head tilted back, almost dangling off his lap. He placed his face close to Alex's face, hoping to feel his breath on his cheek. Nothing. "Oh God, help me!" Alex was so small, he was able to place his mouth over both his nose and his mouth. He gently blew his breath into Alex's lungs, saw Alex's

chest rise slightly. Then he did the two-finger compression of
Alex's chest. Two fingers only on small children, he recalled.
Help me do this right, Lord. "Alex!" He felt like shaking him.
One good shake and he'd come around. But he knew that was
only wishful thinking. Follow the procedure. Another breath
into Alex's lungs. Compression. Breath. Compression. How
many minutes did he have before brain damage? He couldn't
remember that part. And how long had Alex been in the water?
His mind was racing.

How had Alex gotten by him in the first place? When had
he gone out the sliding-glass door? He'd been so involved
with discussing his salary with Rita. Pursuing the almighty
dollar, oblivious to everything else, including his son. Then a
horrifying thought came to him. He hadn't wanted Alex. Had
demanded that Teddy abort him. This precious child, who had
only wanted to live and be happy. Now fate, facetious as ever,
was giving him what he'd wished for—when he no longer
wanted it. All he wanted now was for Alex to open his big
brown eyes and call him Daddy again. *Daddy,* the most wonderful word in the English language. Tears rolled down his
face. But he didn't quit breathing into Alex's lungs. He would
not quit . . . ever!

Suddenly Alex jerked on his lap, his eyes opened, a panicked expression in them. He coughed violently and vomited
pool water from his burning lungs. He wheezed. Adrian
abruptly turned Alex onto his side so that the water could
drain from his lungs better. Alex began to cry, and it was the
best sound Adrian had ever heard in his life. Cradling Alex
in his arms, he ran into the house through the sliding glass
door, and went to pick up the cellular phone. His fingers, as
if of their own accord, dialed 911.

While he waited for the dispatcher, he could feel every
inhalation and exhalation Alex made, he was so sensitive to
his movements. Alex was crying softly now, still wheezing.
But even the wheezing sounded less congested. Adrian rocked
Alex in his arms. "You're gonna be okay, baby." His tears
mingled with the water on his face. "I'm so sorry, Alex.

Daddy's sorry he didn't reach you sooner. So sorry, baby. I love you, Alex. I love you so much . . ."

At the breakfast table Joachim reached over and playfully twirled the emerald on Teddy's finger. He looked into her eyes. "Why don't we make this an engagement ring?"

Teddy swallowed hard and stared at him. This morning her curly hair was in disarray. The bathrobe she was wearing, although clean, had seen better days. And she'd taken the time to wash only her face and brush her teeth. Barefaced and just plain bare underneath the robe, his question had caught her off guard.

But that was Joachim. Nothing had been typical with him. No pretenses, no games. He told you how he felt. He told you what he was prepared to do about those feelings. And he expected no less of you.

Therefore she voiced her fears. "I love you, Joachim, and my gut tells me to say yes. But don't you think we should slow down a bit? We've known one another only a little over two months . . ."

"Slow down for what, for whom?" Joachim asked as he threw his napkin onto the tabletop and pushed his chair back, rising. He was dressed in the same clothes he'd worn last night. They were a bit rumpled, but still looked good on him. Turning his back to her, he ran a hand over his wavy cap of hair, a frustrated gesture Teddy was familiar with. Looking back at her, he said, "When are you going to stop being Adrian Riley's victim, let your fears go, and start making decisions based on your feelings and not your reservations?"

Teddy could never take an accusation sitting down. She came out of her chair, walked over to him, and tilted her head up defiantly. "I am *not* Adrian Riley's victim," she cried. "I'm nobody's victim!"

Shaking his head, Joachim smiled slowly as his eyes solemnly regarded her. "As long as his treatment of you dictates how you react to every other man who comes into your life, you're his victim. Just as I for years had convinced myself

that there was no one else out there for me after Suzanne, you
have convinced yourself that you ultimately can't trust another
man because one of them treated you badly."

"That's not it," Teddy denied, her voice lacking conviction.
That most certainly was part of it, she silently admitted. Did
she distrust her feelings for Joachim? No . . . She went to him
and placed a hand on his cheek, and lovingly gazed up at him.
"There are so many things we don't know about each other
yet: What's your favorite book of all time? Your favorite dish?
Your favorite movie?"

"All trivial," Joachim said as his eyes caressed her face.
"Invisible Man" by Ralph Ellison. My grandmother's chicken
and rice. *The Great White Hope,* starring James Earl Jones."

Teddy went into his arms and pressed her ear against his
chest. True, he was moving way too fast for her. But who was
to say tomorrow was promised to them? Only God knew how
many years they'd have together. He'd thought he would have
Suzanne forever, too. She'd been certain she and Adrian would
be that sweet old couple holding hands while strolling along
the pier. Life offered no promises, no guarantees. And, let's
face it, when you were on your death bed and gasping for one
more breath, you wouldn't care how many material possessions you'd acquired during your too-short life. No, you'd
want one more glimpse into the faces of those you'd loved,
and who'd loved you. That's all that mattered.

"Joachim . . ."

The phone rang.

He tightened his grip on her. *Let it ring,* was his silent plea.

"It could be important," Teddy said quietly.

He released her. "You're right. Better get it."

He watched her as she hurried to the counter and picked
up the receiver of the cordless phone and brought it to her ear.

"Hello, Teddy here."

Joachim moved toward her. He saw her frown, and then the
expression in her warm brown eyes went from complacent to
horrified.

"Stop it! I can't understand you! Pull yourself together.
Where are you? What hospital? Adrian, talk to me!"

He was standing next to her now, waiting. She glanced up at him, confusion written all over her face. "Okay, San Francisco General. We're on our way."

She hung up the phone and was already walking toward the hallway. Running, actually. "Alex fell into the pool." Her voice quavered. "I don't know how he's doing. Adrian was crying so hard, I couldn't get much out of him."

She was in her closet now, looking for something to jump into quickly. She pulled off her robe, standing naked. Then it occurred to her: underwear. In the bureau in the bedroom. She hurried out of the closet, crossed the master bedroom, quickly pulled open the top bureau drawer, chose a pair of panties. Opened the second drawer from the top and chose a bra.

"I'll go get the car and pull right out front," Joachim told her, turning away. "You can just run out of the door and into the car."

"Hurry, please!" Teddy cried desperately.

Joachim left.

She ran back into the closet and pulled a pair of jeans and a denim shirt from hangers. It didn't matter if they matched or not. She couldn't see colors or textures at that moment anyway. Just Alex's face in her mind's eye. Alex, whom she'd blithely allowed to go off with that totally irresponsible, self-centered rat, Adrian. Where was he when her son had been wandering around outside? *Outside,* where she'd given Adrian firm instructions, Alex was never to go alone.

She'd gone to Adrian's new house only to make certain it was safe for Alex to stay there. She knew Adrian's invitation to her that day had been designed to impress her and make her realize the depth of his devotion to her and Alex: "Look, Teddy, I bought you a house in a neighborhood where you always wanted to live. Look at the yard, big enough for Alex to run and play in. Big enough to have a dog if he wants one. Two dogs! And Mexican tile, Teddy. You always loved Mexican tile."

She'd gone from room to room with him, putting up with his riding commentary. "Of course, if you don't like the color, you can always change it." She hadn't said a thing, one way

or the other. They'd already had one argument that day, she
didn't want to get into another, especially with Alex right there
with them.

When they'd come to the pool, she'd asked him when he
was going to have the safety fence installed. "With small children in the house, you'll need a fence with a gate that locks.
Something kids can't open. They're drawn to water."

Dressed now, she paused in the foyer long enough to grab
her purse from the hat tree, then she was sprinting down the
steps, and Joachim, as promised, was waiting out front, the
motor running in the Expedition, her door already flung open
for her.

The soles of Adrian's wet shoes squeaked on the waiting
room floor outside the intensive care unit. Alex was awake
and breathing on his own. But he'd gotten water in his lungs
and the doctors were determining if they'd sustained any damage. Adrian had been so emotional—wanting to know if each
procedure would cause Alex any pain, becoming belligerent
when one of the nurses produced a needle large enough to
inoculate an elephant with, and said they were going to draw
the water off Alex's lungs with it—that the head doctor had
ordered Adrian to leave the room. He was only obstructing
the competent care of his son.

It had been twenty minutes or so since he'd phoned Teddy.
At least he wasn't weeping anymore. He'd cried like a baby
when he'd phoned his parents with the news, too. Margaret
had dropped the phone and run out of the kitchen where she'd
been preparing Sunday dinner along with Rose. Rose picked
up the receiver and told Adrian, "I think it's safe to say your
mother is on her way." Then she talked to him in her calm,
reassuring manner until he'd brought himself under control.
He'd never noticed what a wonderful person Rose was—but
she'd refused to hang up until he, she'd said, sounded more
like himself.

Now Adrian wondered what he normally sounded like to
Rose. Had he always remembered to be polite to Rose all the

years she'd taken care of them? He'd been a teenager when Rose had been hired by his mother. An arrogant little know-it-all. On top of that, he'd been a slob. Leaving his bedroom a mess every morning. It would be miraculously picked up when he returned in the afternoon. He'd never once thanked Rose for that. Even though his parents had made it his responsibility to clean his own room.

He squinted at the double swinging doors that served as the entrance to the intensive care unit, willing someone to come through them and tell him something positive about Alex. He was still staring at the doors when Teddy and Joachim came up behind him. "Adrian."

Teddy almost didn't recognize the bedraggled man coming toward her, his eyes glassy with unshed tears, his clothing, wet, sticking to his body. And were those his shoes making those noises? The anger she'd been saving up ever since he'd phoned, relishing the thought of venting it on him, fizzled.

She tried to step to the side when he threw himself on her, but was too slow in reacting. He hugged her, and he felt like a wet dishrag. Smelled like chlorine and perspiration. Not exactly a pleasant combination.

"Oh, Teddy, I'm so glad you're here." He hugged her tightly. "He's awake, but water got in his lungs and they're removing it. Someone's supposed to come out here and tell us something as soon as it's done."

Joachim stood to the side, a silent observer.

This wreck of a man didn't look like the Adrian Teddy had described. He looked shell-shocked, like one of the Vietnam veterans he'd interviewed some years ago for a book he was writing about the Vietnam War. Haunted eyes. The eyes of a man who'd seen too much. Something earth-shattering had happened to Adrian Riley today. Almost losing Alex had profoundly affected him.

Teddy gently but firmly pushed Adrian away, looking him in the eyes. "I'm going to go back there and see what I can find out. I can't bear to wait any longer."

Adrian nodded. He appeared as if he was about to say something, then clamped his mouth shut, biting his bottom lip.

With a glance in Joachim's direction, Teddy turned and left the waiting room, going through the swinging doors.

Joachim approached Adrian. "I saw a coffee machine back there. How about a cup?"

Frowning, Adrian met Joachim's gaze. How could he accept a kindness from the man who'd ruined all his plans of winning Teddy back, and reclaiming his family?

"Look," Joachim said, his voice low and steady. "I know we're at odds, but for Alex's sake, can't we get along, just for today?"

Adrian was emotionally drained. He didn't have the energy required for a confrontation with West. And what good would it do, anyway? Teddy had made her choice. Alex needed him calm and together when he went back there to see him.

So he gave a nod in Joachim's direction. "All right, thanks. Coffee sounds good."

Joachim left the waiting room.

On his way out, he passed a handsome African-American couple in their late fifties. They both had silver hair, and looked as if they'd recently returned from church services. He was in an expensive navy pinstripe suit and she was in an elegant pearl-gray dress whose silken fabric swished around her long legs.

Adrian was so relieved to see his parents, he felt like crying again. He managed to hold the tears in check though. He'd never cried in front of his father. His mother, only once. When he'd been overlooked for a first-string position on the football team when he was in ninth grade. He'd come home from school and sobbed on his mother's bosom. She'd comforted him for a few minutes, then told him to try out for another sport—football wasn't everything. He took her advice and ended up becoming captain of the varsity basketball team by the time he was in twelfth grade.

Margaret rushed forward and hugged her son in spite of his wet garments. "Where is he? Can we see him?"

Adrian told them what he'd told Teddy less than ten minutes ago. "Teddy's back there with him now."

His father regarded him with a questioning appraisal. "Why aren't you back there, son?"

Feeling inept and embarrassed, Adrian reluctantly told them how his behavior had gotten him banned from the examining room.

When Teddy walked through the double swinging doors, she'd gone straight to the desk at the nurses' station. A trim, redheaded male nurse, whose name tag read J. STEIN, R.N., was busy typing on a computer keyboard. He glanced up when he heard her clear her throat, a look of annoyance in his brown eyes.

Teddy smiled nervously. "My son was brought in here a few minutes ago. I'd like to see him, please."

"Your son's name?" he asked with brisk efficiency.

"Alex Riley . . ."

"Yes, of course." He walked from behind the desk and crooked a thin finger in her direction, then he began walking swiftly down the corridor, confident that she was right behind him, as he didn't look back once to be certain of it.

He stopped at a closed door, knocked twice and opened the door. After peering in to make certain it was all right for a civilian to enter, he opened the door a bit farther and allowed her to precede him. Then he walked around her, into the room where Alex was sitting on a bed with three adults surrounding him.

When Teddy saw him, she pushed past J. Stein, R.N., and went straight to him. Alex looked up and smiled at her. "Mommy!" he whispered, his voice hoarse.

From years of experience, the hospital staff knew it was best not to get in the path of a mother trying to get to her child. They fanned out, giving Teddy plenty of space.

Alex had on a hospital gown, the back closed with Velcro. It was much too large for him, and he looked like a waif to Teddy, his eyes big and sorrowful. But he felt warm and solid. Alive! He clung to her like a baby chimpanzee would to his mother, his arms and legs wrapped tightly around her neck and waist. She rocked him in her arms as tears of relief flowed down her cheeks. "Everything's all right now, baby. Mommy's not going to leave you."

"I fell in, Mommy. And I couldn't get out."

Teddy continued to rock him as she cooed, "I know, baby. I know it was an accident. Don't talk now. Let the kind doctors and nurses finish taking care of you. Then you can tell me all about it later."

"Tell Daddy to feed the kitty, Mommy," Alex said, and yawned.

"We gave him something to relax him," a young man in a white coat, obviously a doctor, explained. "It'll make him drowsy. But the effects will wear off in a couple of hours."

Teddy regarded all three of them in turn. J. Stein, R.N., had slipped from the room, since he'd done his duty and was no longer needed.

The two males and one female, she could see their name tags now and realized one was a resident, one a nurse and one a respiratory therapist, approached the bed again after Teddy placed Alex on it and told him to lie still.

"He doesn't appear to have any damage to his lungs," the doctor told her as he raised the front of Alex's gown, placed the stethoscope against Alex's bare chest, and listened. He was silent a moment or two. He glanced up at Teddy. "Sounds better." He turned his gaze on Alex. "Alex, how would you like to go to a room filled with toys and lie in bed all day eating ice cream?"

Alex looked to his mother for permission.

Teddy smiled and nodded yes.

"Yes, thank you," Alex politely answered the doctor.

Teddy came back through the double swinging doors and four pairs of eyes intently stared at her. Seeing Winston and Margaret there made Teddy realize she hadn't phoned her father yet.

"They're taking him to the children's ward. He's breathing

fine now, but they want to keep him overnight for observation."

Margaret enfolded her in her arms. Winston came to plant a fatherly kiss on her forehead. Adrian rocked back on his heels, he was so pleased to see her with a smile on her face. That meant Alex truly was doing better. Joachim simply smiled warmly when Teddy's eyes met his. She smiled back, her love for him shining in her eyes.

Margaret recognized that look for what it was, after setting Teddy away from her and regarding her with sympathy. "So our boy is doing better. I'm relieved to hear it." She sighed. "Lord, I think I aged ten years on the drive over here." She laughed. "This calls for a celebration!" She looked at Winston. "Come on, darling. I know there must be a gift shop on the premises. Let's go buy Alex some of those colorful balloons he loves so much." Winston smiled at his wife of thirty-seven years.

"Whatever you say, sweetheart."

They walked away arm-in-arm.

Teddy approached Adrian.

Joachim, guessing that she'd like a bit of privacy, walked out into the corridor adjacent to the waiting room.

Thankfully it was a slow day in the pediatric wing, so Teddy and Adrian were now alone in the waiting room.

On the drive there, she'd imagined all the biting words she'd say to him. Accuse him of negligence. Threaten to never allow him within a hundred feet of Alex from now on. Vilify him in every way she could think of. But if there was one thing she'd learned since having Alex, it was that all parents make mistakes. Parenting was a trial-and-error proposition. The same thing could have happened when she was watching Alex. And then she would be the one standing here, looking pitiful, dejected, as if she were about to face a firing squad.

She broke the silence between them with, "Alex wants to see you."

Adrian let out an agonized breath, looked into Teddy's eyes a moment longer, then turned to go to his son.

Teddy joined Joachim in the corridor. She gratefully

walked into his open arms and closed her eyes as her body shuddered with formerly unexpressed relief. "That was too close for comfort."

Then she remembered she'd left him and Adrian in the room together while she'd gone to check up on Alex. Her eyes sought his. "Adrian didn't attack you, did he?" she asked, concerned.

Joachim chuckled as he tenderly rubbed her back. "No, baby. We behaved ourselves."

"Sweetie, your eyes are watering," Teddy said as she cocked her head to the side and smiled at Joachim.

"They're good if your eyes water," Joachim said, sniffing as he bit into a crab leg. The hot peppers Alexander used in seasoning the soft-shelled crabs were burning all of their tongues, but that only made them eat more, because the sweet meat of the seafood was as habit-forming as popping peanuts at a baseball game or eating popcorn in a darkened movie theater. One was never enough.

"Well, these are definitely good then," Frankie Ahern said, his eyes watering also. He smiled at Melodie, who was gulping a diet soda. "Good God," she said, after placing the can on the tabletop. "Nothing extinguishes this fire."

"Oh you're a bunch of wusses," Joie said, standing to grab another crab from the pile of steaming crabs in the middle of the newspaper-topped table. She pulled the legs off and consumed the meat in them one at a time, biting the shells with skilled precision and sucking the meat out. Then she opened the body of the crab up with her thumbnail and slurped the juices within. "Now that hits the spot."

Her husband Lee, a tall, strapping two-hundred-pound guy who could bench press three hundred pounds, looked at her in awe.

"Baby, you've got skills."

"And don't you forget it," Joie told him, throwing a seductive glance his way.

Alex squirmed on Teddy's lap. "Wanna play now, Mommy."

"All right," Teddy said, allowing him to jump down. She knew the enticement of Bridgette would be too much for him to resist. Bridgette sat between her parents at the long table in Alexander's backyard. She'd been quietly observing Alex all afternoon. Her mommy had told her about Alex's accident and she wondered if Alex would feel like playing with her today. So she'd patiently waited until he gave her the signal that all was well, then she'd scooted under the table and crawled around the sea of adult legs, peeped her head out from underneath the table and growled at Alex like a dog. Alex laughed delightedly, and took off running. Bridgette scampered to her feet and gave chase.

Teddy got up to go check the lock on the gate they'd recently installed that separated her father's goldfish pond from the rest of the backyard. Everything was in order. She went back and sat down.

Alexander and his date, Yvonne, an enrollment specialist at a nearby university, came through the back door carrying platters of barbecued chicken and barbecued ribs.

"Okay, who's ready for some real food?" Alexander asked.

Teddy sighed contentedly. Her father was in his element. To have friends and loved ones surrounding him while he fed them with good food, and a generous helping of laughter, until their sides split made him a happy man.

And now there was Yvonne, who with her warmth and bountiful spirit seemed to illuminate all the dark places in him. Teddy was thrilled to learn of their chance meeting—in Johannesburg, South Africa of all places—when Yvonne's flight had been delayed and Alexander was her seatmate on the trip back to the States. They had chatted amiably the whole trip, and by the time the plane landed, Alexander had the petite, pretty woman's phone number and the promise of a dinner date and dancing afterward.

"Eat it while it's hot," Alexander admonished as he and Yvonne placed the heavy platters in the middle of the table. He pulled out a chair for Yvonne and they sat down, too.

Alexander's gaze settled on his daughter, who at that moment was looking at Joachim with such affection that his father's protective instincts kicked in.

He liked the writer. Joachim West was down-to-earth and he had a quiet intensity that Alexander admired. He was at ease with everyone. Plus, Alexander noted, Adrian had never looked at Teddy in quite the way Joachim did: as if she were the most enchanting creature ever to grace the planet. That's how he used to look at Michelin. But the most compelling piece of evidence that had been in Joachim's favor was the fact that Alex loved him. Earlier that day Alexander had peered out his kitchen window and seen Joachim, on his hands and knees in the garden, searching for lizards alongside an excited Alex. And when Joachim had managed to catch one, he picked it up and held it between his fingers while Alex ran his hand along the trembling reptile's scaly body. Then they'd released it, and Joachim had picked Alex up, placed him on his broad shoulders and taken him for a ride, Alex's laughter reverberating throughout the lush green garden.

Teddy tore her eyes away from Joachim long enough to rise and offer a toast. Everyone picked up their drink of choice and raised it. "To my father, Alexander Tate, who knows how to throw a party."

"Here, here!" Frankie heartily exclaimed.

"I know that's right!" Joie agreed.

"Way to go, Mr. Alexander," Lee piped in.

"My sinuses are clear for the first time in months," Melodie said, to which there were good-natured guffaws.

Yvonne added her silent congratulations by placing her small hand atop Alexander's, a gesture he fully appreciated as his broad smile indicated.

"To good friends," Teddy continued. She looked at Joie and Lee. "Old and new." Her gaze shifted to Melodie and Frankie, after which she smiled warmly at Yvonne. "And to our precious children, who fill our lives with joy, and sometimes agonizing pain, but that comes with the territory."

Alex and Bridgette were making a racket in the background

as they played tag: running, squealing, making joyful pirou-
ettes that made the grown-ups' hearts glad to watch.

When Teddy sat back down, those around the table thought
she was finished, but she wasn't. She reached for Joachim's
hand and to the amazement of those looking on, she kissed
the palm. "And last, but never least in my heart, to the man I
love . . ."

Everyone, especially Joachim, waited impatiently for her
next words.

". . . Joachim. A few days ago you asked me if I'd marry
you. Well, before I could answer, we were thrust into a crisis.
So I'm answering you now. Yes, if you're certain you want to
spend the rest of your life with a woman who cries at the drop
of a hat . . ."

"Owns about a hundred of them," Joie put in, picking up
on the hat theme.

"Looks darn good in a hat," was Melodie's contribution.

Laughing, Alexander ordered, "Knock it off, you two. This
is serious business here."

Teddy and Joachim hadn't heard a word of the exchange
because they were lost in each other's eyes. "Marry me?"
Teddy whispered, her lips inches from his.

"In a split second," Joachim replied as his mouth pressed
firmly against hers.

General bedlam ensued as the folks around the table offered
congratulations in the form of shouting, laughter, and, in Joie's
case, a couple of shrill screams.

Teddy and Joachim parted. In his eyes she saw their future.
And it looked *good*.

Dear Reader:

I live in Florida. Every year, I hear of small children drowning in pools because of lack of supervision. Please, if your little ones have access to a pool, be sure you're right there watching them, and that you also employ safety tactics such as using a gate that locks.

If you'd like to drop me a line, you may do so by using these addresses:

Janice Sims
P.O. Box 811
Mascotte, FL 34753-0811

e-mail: jani569432@aol.com

web site: http://janicesims.jumpbooks.com

And check out Romantic Tales, a marvelous site for a peek into what's new in romance: http://www.romantictales.com/

BOOK YOUR PLACE ON OUR WEBSITE AND MAKE THE ARABESQUE ROMANCE CONNECTION!

We've created a customized website just for our very special Arabesque readers, where you can get the inside scoop on everything that's going on with Arabesque romance novels.

When you come online, you'll have the exciting opportunity to:

- View covers of upcoming books

- Learn about our future publishing schedule (listed by publication month and author)

- Find out when your favorite authors will be visiting a city near you

- Search for and order backlist books

- Check out author bios and background information

- Send e-mail to your favorite authors

- Join us in weekly chats with authors, readers and other guests

- Get writing guidelines

- AND MUCH MORE!

Visit our website at
http://www.arabesquebooks.com

Coming in April from Arabesque Books . . .

__SWEPT AWAY by Gwynne Forster
1-58314-098-0   **$5.99US/$7.99CAN**

As the head of a child placement agency, Veronica Overton never expected to be crucified in the press by fiery advocate Schyler Henderson. With her reputation shattered, Veronica searches to rebuild her life and unexpectedly discovers a sizzling attraction to Schyler that she is determined to resist . . .

__STAR CROSSED by Francine Craft
1-58314-099-9   **$5.99US/$7.99CAN**

Jaded Fairen Wilder is unsure if she can ever risk caring for anyone again. But now the one man who helped her survive her pain, Lance Carrington, is back, still a suspect in his wife's murder. The couple must face down a vicious enemy together . . . and learn to trust in their growing love.

__DESTINY by Shelby Lewis
1-58314-100-6   **$5.99US/$7.99CAN**

Recluse Josephine Brennon is shocked when the ruggedly handsome drifter Hannibal Ray is able to open her heart to love. But these two loners must fight the town's most influential citizens and open up to each other completely . . . if they are to claim the love that is their destiny.

__ALL THAT MATTERS by Courtni Wright
1-58314-101-4   **$5.99US/$7.99CAN**

Honey Tate has returned to New Orleans to restore her family's home and discover the truth about her father. Although her search puts her at odds with lawyer Stephen Turner, passions soon flare between the two and they must find their way through pain and secrets if they are to find true love.

Call toll free **1-888-345-BOOK** to order by phone or use this coupon to order by mail. *ALL BOOKS AVAILABLE APRIL 1, 2000.*

Name _____

Address _____

City _____ State _____ Zip _____

Please send me the books I have checked above.

I am enclosing $_____

Plus postage and handling* $_____

Sales tax (in NY, TN, and DC) $_____

Total amount enclosed $_____

*Add $2.50 for the first book and $.50 for each additional book.

Send check or money order (no cash or CODs) to: **Arabesque Books, Dept. C.O., 850 Third Avenue, 16th Floor, New York, NY 10022**

Prices and numbers subject to change without notice.

All orders subject to availability.

Visit out our web site at **www.arabesquebooks.com.**

THESE ARABESQUE ROMANCES
ARE NOW MOVIES FROM BET!